NEW YORK REVIEW BOOKS
CLASSICS

ON THE YARD

MALCOLM BRALY (1925–1980) was born in Portland,
Oregon. Abandoned by his parents, Braly lived between foster
homes and institutions for delinquent children, and by the
time he was forty had spent nearly seventeen years in prison
for burglary, serving time at Nevada State Prison, San Quentin,
and Folsom State Prison. He wrote three novels behind bars,
Felony Tank (1961), *Shake Him Till He Rattles* (1963), and
It's Cold Out There (1966), and upon his release in 1965
began to work on *On the Yard*. When prison authorities
learned of the book they threatened to revoke his parole, and
he was forced to complete it in secret. Published in 1967, after
Braly's parole had expired, *On the Yard* received wide acclaim.
It was followed by his autobiography, *False Starts: A Memoir
of San Quentin and Other Prisons* (1976), and a final work of
fiction, *The Protector* (1979). Malcolm Braly enjoyed fifteen
years of freedom before his death in a car accident at age fifty-
four.

JONATHAN LETHEM is the author of nine novels, including
Girl in Landscape and *Dissident Gardens*, and five collec-
tions of stories and essays, including *The Ecstasy of Influence*.
For NYRB Classics he has written the introduction to *A
Meaningful Life* by L.J. Davis and, with Alex Abramovich,
edited *The Store of the Worlds*, a selection of stories by Robert
Sheckley. He teaches at Pomona College and lives in Los
Angeles and Maine.

ON THE YARD

MALCOLM BRALY

Introduction by
JONATHAN LETHEM

NEW YORK REVIEW BOOKS

New York

This is a New York Review Book
Published by The New York Review of Books
435 Hudson Street, New York, NY 10014
www.nyrb.com

Library of Congress Cataloging-in-Publication Data
Braly, Malcolm, 1925–
  On the yard / Malcolm Braly ; introduction by Jonathan Lethem.
     p. cm.
  ISBN 0-940322-96-X (pbk. : alk. paper)
  1. Prisoners—Fiction. 2. Prisons—Fiction. I. Title.
  PS3552.R28 O5 2002
  813'.54—dc21

                                          2001006227

ISBN 978-0-940322-96-7

Book design by Lizzie Scott
Printed in the United States of America on acid-free paper.
10 9 8 7 6 5 4

TO KNOX BURGER

INTRODUCTION

THE MIND flinches from the fact of prisons—their preva-
lence, squatting in the midst of towns and cities, their role in
so many lives, and in the history and everyday life of our
country. And when the mind does find its way there, it wants
the whole subject covered in hysteria and overstatement.
Let prisons be one simple thing—either horrific zoos for the
irretrievably demented and corrupt, or inhumane machines
which grind down innocent men. Let them stand apart as
raw cartoons of black-and-white morality, having nothing to
do with the rest of us—we who live in the modulated, ambivalent, civilized world "the novel" was born to depict. We
might secretly feel prison doesn't *need* a novel, that it instead
needs a miniseries or the Op-Ed page.

Malcolm Braly's *On the Yard*, temperate and unhysterical
as its title, is the novel prison needs. It's also a book any lover
of novels ought to know, for its compression, surprise, and
wry humor, for its deceptively casual architecture, and for
characters and scenes which are unforgettable. Of course,
readers may be compelled to read realistic novels set in war
or plague or prison by uneasy cravings to know particulars of
lives they hope never to encounter more directly. And Braly
surely has knowledge we don't, tons of it. During a miserable,
nearly fatherless childhood, Braly began acting out his griev-
ances through a series of petty and eventually not-so-petty
burglaries, until, in the company of some reckless partners
in crime, he found himself in an interstate chase which

climaxed in a gun battle with police, then capture and imprisonment. Upon his first release he slipped back into a desultory pattern of minor crime; eventually managing to spend a majority of his first forty years of life behind prison walls without having murdered or raped, without having even stolen anything of much value.

Apart from knowledge, Braly possesses an insouciant tone of confidence which causes us never to doubt him, and which is more persuasive than any fact: if these things can be taken as givens, taken almost lightly, then truly the prison is another world as real as our own. But beyond reportage, or tourism, *On the Yard* succeeds because through its particulars it becomes universal, a model for understanding aspects of our self-wardened lives. Inside and outside prison walls human beings negotiate, stall, bluff, and occasionally explode in their attempts to balance ecstasy against ennui, to do more than merely eke out their narrowing days on earth. But Braly skirts allegory: his book is much too lean and local to bother with that. The reader supplies the allegory.

The novel could be said to center on the plateau and fall (we never witness his rise) of Chilly Willy, a prison racketeer who deftly controls a small empire of cigarettes, pharmaceutical narcotics, and petty bureaucratic favors, orchestrated by a routine of minimal violence and, as his name suggests, maximum cool. Despite his name, and the outlines of his career, he's a deeply real and human character, even a sympathetic one. We watch as Chilly manipulates the razor's-edge power dynamics of the prison until a single miscalculation causes him to lash out. It is then that the prison administration undertakes Chilly's destruction, by the simple act of placing a receptively homosexual cellmate in his previously solitary cell. The new cellmate serves as Chilly's mirror—not for a repressed homosexuality, but for the fact that his manipulations had always had concealed within them a grain of solicitude, perhaps even disguised family feeling. The men Chilly commands are under his care, however apparently dispassionate a form this care has taken. Sex becomes the means of Chilly's self-destruction—but then nearly every character in the book is shown in a second act of self-destruction inside the prison, which recapitulates and confirms an initial act outside.

The novel *could* be said to center on Chilly's fall, except it barely centers anywhere, moving by its own cool strategy through the minds and moments of dozens of characters, some recurrently, some only for a sole brief visitation which nearly always proves definitive. Three or four of these are into the minds of the prison's keepers, including that of the morose, long-enduring Warden. The rest are a broad array of prisoners, some "hardened" repeaters, some newly arrived at San Quentin, some floating in between and trying to measure the rightness and permanence of their placement inside those walls. All but the craziest and most loathsome—like the shoe-sniffing, anal-compulsive Sanitary Slim—are presented at least briefly as potential audience and author surrogates. All of them are rejected, either gently or rudely, by the end.

This is Braly's brilliantly successful game—he's a master at exploiting the reader's urge to identify with his characters. The results are estranging, in the best sense: both funny and profound. Each character undergoes a sort of audition. The first pair of candidates is offered in Chapter One: Nunn, a repeat offender shuffling his way back inside and trying to come to terms with his propensity for self-defeat, his missed opportunities during his brief stint outside, and Manning, a sensitive and observant first-timer who has overturned his innocuous life with a sudden and incomprehensible crime of sexual perversion. The reader begins to squirm in a way which will become familiar—ordinary guilt and innocence will not be our map here. Braly is enormously conscious of the effect of withholding the criminal histories of certain of his characters, while blurting others. His writerly pleasure in this game is tipped in comic miniatures like this one: "He lit his cigarette, then held the match for Zekekowski, noting again how finely formed Zekekowski's hands were, actually beautiful, the hands of a . . . of an arsonist, as it happened."

If the men glimpsed in Braly's San Quentin break into roughly two groups, Manning and Nunn are typical of each: those who are career criminals, and those who have committed single crimes of impulse—the molesters and wife-killers. Braly leads us gently to the irony that the former commit relatively harmless crimes and yet are compulsively recurrent, whereas the latter are morally abhorrent yet less likely to return to the prison after their release. The impulsives are frequently bookish and bourgeois, unlike the careerists in outlook or temperament, and with a tendency to look down on them as lessers. At the extreme we meet Watson, a priggish impulsive: "Watson stood with culture, the Republic, and Motherhood. . . . He had killed his two small sons, attempted to kill his wife, . . . all because his wife had refused a reconciliation with the remark, 'John, the truth is you bore me.' " Watson defends himself in a therapy session, claiming, "I see no point in further imprisonment, further therapy, no point whatsoever since there's absolutely no possibility I'll do the same thing again." And he's immediately teased by the raffish, Popeye-like career criminal Society Red, who says, "That's right. . . . He's run out of kids."

More sympathetic is Lorin, a fragile jailhouse poet who cringes inside fantasies of Kim Novak and notebook jottings like "Yet I am free—free as any to test the limits of my angry nerves and press the inner pains of my nature against the bruise of time." Braly doesn't hold such sensitivity up for either mockery or admiration: like other responses to the condition known as San Quentin, it is simply presented as one possibility among many. Nearer to the author's own sympathies—or so a reader may suspect—is Paul Juleson, Lorin's sometime mentor and protector. Juleson at first glance seems

the most resourceful and best equipped of the prison intellec-
tuals, and therefore both a likely survivor and a good bet
for author's proxy. In a flashback we learn that he killed his
wife; the hell of his short marriage is portrayed with dev-
astating economy and insight, and the violence of his crime
doesn't impede our inclining toward Juleson's sympathies.
Richard Rhodes, in *The New York Times*'s original review of
On the Yard, came out and said it: "Juleson is probably
Mr. Braly's alter ego." Yet I don't think it's so simple as that—
and certainly Braly denies us the usual satisfactions of root-
ing for this character when, despite all his wiles and wisdom,
Juleson puts himself in the path of Chilly Willy's contempt
by a dumb play for a few packs of cigarettes.

From that point Chilly and Juleson catalyze one another's
destruction. It is as though each man has been fated to expose
the weakness in the other. So if Braly has an alter ego in the
book, it is split, in an act of symbolic self-loathing, between
these two men. Rhodes, in his otherwise admiring review,
went on to call the book "curiously ambivalent, as though
the author had not yet sorted out his own attitudes when he
wrote it." I think this ambivalence, far from unintentional, is
in fact the essence of Braly's art. The criminal professionals
are not so different from the middle-class murderers after
all—they are united in self-destruction. San Quentin exists,
at some level, because these men need a place to solve the
puzzle of their lives by nullification. It also exists because of
our society's need to accommodate that nullification, giving
it four square walls, a pair of coveralls, and a number, as well
as a few perfunctory hours of group therapy a week.

In other words, if it's difficult to discern with whom Malcolm Braly identifies, this is likely because Malcolm Braly
doesn't identify with himself. Not exactly. This becomes
plain in Braly's *False Starts*, his extraordinary memoir of his
childhood, and of his pathetic criminal and prison careers.
In this second masterpiece, published ten years after *On the*

Yard, Braly marvels extensively at his own tropism for the prison, at those miraculous self-sabotages which led him again and again to the miserable comforts of incarceration. We learn that during one break-in he actually managed to accidentally leave behind a slip of paper bearing his full name and address, as though desperate to devise a path back inside.

Standing outside *On the Yard*'s character scheme is the lanky teenage sociopath, Stick. Leader of a mostly imaginary gang of fascist hoodlums called The Vampires, Stick is a cipher of human chaos, and he eventually brings down an unlikely destruction on the prison. Stick's uncanny near-escape is by hot-air balloon, one painstakingly constructed by his cellmate and stolen by Stick at the last moment. This reveals a vein of dreamy masturbatory fantasy, a childishness, which our fear of criminals and prisoners usually conceals from us, but which Braly doesn't want concealed. The balloon is an unusually direct symbol for any novel, but especially Braly's. Nonetheless, it bears evidence of that ambivalence which marks all the characters and their strivings: when examiners consider the crashed balloon they find it scored by excessively reworked sewing, which has weakened the fabric: "[the stitches] suggested an analogy to hesitation marks in a suicide." Stick also, it seems to me, reveals *On the Yard* as being a 1960s California book, and San Quentin in the Sixties as being oddly subject to the same propensity for utopianism and social experiment as the Bay Area within which the prison darkly huddles. In an eastern prison Stick might more likely have been drawn into some preexisting gang or mafia: thirty years later he'd be a Crip or Blood. Here he's free to self-invent, and so becomes a prognostication of Charles Manson or Jim Jones.

Malcolm Braly's life was sad, triumphant, and sad again. He lived mostly inside for twenty years, until his writing, together with the will and generosity of Gold Medal Books editor Knox Burger, provided a rescue. He died in a car accident at fifty-four, leaving behind a wife and infant daughter—Knox Burger has said he was "fat and happy." His peak as a writer came in the two complementary books, the novel and the memoir, and in the memoir he says about the novel, "I was writing over my head." A reader needn't explore the earlier books to confirm this, for Braly is working over his head in *On the Yard* in the sense that any novelist is when he has moved beyond his tools, or through them, to experience a kind of transubstantiation with his characters. At those moments a writer always knows more than he ever could have expected to, and he can only regard the results with a kind of honest awe. The book is no longer his own, but a vehicle by which anyone can see himself both exculpated and accused, can find himself alternately imprisoned and freed. Braly's novel is something like Stick's borrowed balloon, in the end, a beautiful, unlikely oddment rising from the yard of San Quentin, motley with the scars of its making and no less perfect for showing those "hesitation marks." It rises above the prison walls in a brief, glorious flight, before gravity makes its ordinary claim.

—JONATHAN LETHEM

ON THE YARD

As a general rule, people, even the wicked,
are much more naïve and simple-hearted
than we suppose.

—FYODOR DOSTOYEVSKY
The Brothers Karamazov

Born in this jailhouse
Raised doing time
Yes born in this jailhouse
Near the end of the line

SOCIETY RED was the first man on the yard that morning. He sidled out of the south cellblock, turning up the collar of his faded denim jacket as he squinted resentfully at the cold gray sky. A sudden gust of wind caused him to hunch his shoulders and duck his head while he began to pound the heel of one Santa Rosa hightop against the other, three times; then he shifted to bang the second shoe against the first—tamp, tamp, tamp—and he continued this monotonous and joyless dance as he peered uneasily around the prison's big yard, seeing it as he had seldom seen it: quiet, empty, an acre of bare blacktop enclosed within the high concrete walls of the cellblocks. A huge pen.

Society Red found the silent emptiness disturbing even though he knew that within the hour over five thousand inmates would stream from the mess hall, coiling into the yard, a restless spawn, an immense aggregate creature, the life of the big yard, that also *was* the big yard, as the residents are actually a town.

Other inmates were drifting out behind him now, but Red was still depressed. He thrust his hands into his hip pockets, palms flat to his lean backside, and continued punishing one Santa Rosa against its mate while he venomously cursed the cold. High on the north block wall he glimpsed a gun bull, symbolic as a scarecrow, and watched a seagull drifting down to hit the blacktop with an awkward waddle, where it scavenged a scrap of orange peel floating in the gutter.

3

Red was slightly over six feet, bone-thin, and awkwardly made. His face was so densely freckled it appeared rusty and gave his sharp features a raw, humorous aspect. His eyes were yellow as a goat's, but the vivid orange hair that had prompted some forgotten humorist to call him Society Red had long since faded and thinned away to a clown's half-bald ruff. He had been jailing for thirty of his forty-five years and was now a five-time loser. Still he didn't consider himself a failure, simply because it had never occurred to him he could be confined in any such square john term.

The photo on the ID card he carried in his shirt pocket showed him the face of a man already harshly worn by age, dim, defeated, a caricature convict impossible to imagine except above his big number, drenched in the pitiless light of a mug shot. But even the first of his numerous mugs, taken at only sixteen, had shown him the face of a born wrongdoer, one the law had quickly recognized as its own, and his subsequent ID's, taken at various times, on several occasions had even recorded changes Red was pleased to consider improvements. That original mug shot, now fixed to the first page of his cumulative case summary, still preserved the images of his formerly legendary ears, jutting from his head like the handles of a loving cup (he'd heard the wheeze a thousand times), and his huge front teeth had still pushed from his mouth like the tusks of a beaver. Between the bat ears and the buckteeth he had been a comic gargoyle whose first fever- ish pursuit of several half-grown neighbor girls had moved them only to fits of giggling.

Much later, it was his disfiguring ears that were altered first. One of the pioneer prison psychologists developed a theory that inmates who suffered such comic deformities formed com- pensatory mechanisms, of which their various felonies were merely symptoms, and their rehabilitation needn't be sweated out in the stone quarry, making little ones out of big ones, when it could be found under the knife of a cosmetic surgeon.

Society Red was scheduled, with a dozen others, for plastic surgery, which it was hoped would leave him free to be as honest as anyone else. Surely too modest a goal to tax more than lightly the magical skills of a plastic surgeon, but then his time was donated, and he had apparently tried some technique he didn't care to risk on a cash customer, because when the bandages were removed Red's ears were greatly altered, but it was difficult to characterize the difference as an improvement. One ear pinched to his skull as if stapled there, and the other still flew at approximately half-mast, but he figured if they'd sliced his ears clean off it would still be a small price to pay to be rid of something so full of meanness and trickeration as that compensatory mechanism which had forced him to steal, not for wheels, women or money, but only as some sorry-assed symptom.

When he next made parole, he quickly discovered that his cosmetic ears cut no ice. The bitches, as he put it, still wouldn't let him score on their drawers, but continued to deal way around him as if they sensed some violent far-out freakishness thrashing around in his hectic yellow eyes.

He decided he couldn't make it without wheels so he hotwired a new Buick convertible, and finally managed to pick up a girl in the Greyhound Bus depot. She'd just arrived nonstop from Macon, Georgia, with one change of clothes in a paper bag.

"This your machine?" she asked, smoothing the Buick's leather seat.

"Sure. You like it?"

"It's most elegant."

She was so mortally homely Red figured she'd come near scaring a dog off a gut wagon, and she was built like a sack of flour, heavy, shapeless, and white, so he drove straight up into the hills, parked and reached for her. She was already slipping down the leather seat.

"You got something in mind, California?"

Red experienced a momentary uncertainty, staring down at the girl's shadowed face. She was stretched flat now, her legs slewed off to the side and her scuffed black shoes rested on the floorboards.

"Maybe," he said.

"Some of them old things back home would be halfway to Kingdom Come already."

He brushed up her cotton dress, and clambered awkwardly over her as she adjusted her underwear, and began to push uncertainly at her general softness until she shifted skillfully beneath him, and he plunged wildly, pounding his head against the car door.

"Jesus, Savior . . ." she murmured.

In moments Red found himself wildly contorted on the car seat, the homely shapeless girl pinned beneath him, and he pulled back to look down at her face.

"You're some peehole pirate," she said pleasantly.

Red grinned. "What happened to your tits?"

She shrugged, shifting her heavy shoulders. "They wouldn't make a pair of doorbells."

Red drove back to his hotel and slipped the girl up to his room, where she immediately washed the clothes in the paper bag and hung them over the radiator to dry. Then she kicked out of her shoes, pulled her dress over her head and wandered around the room wearing only her drawers and a pair of red anklets. Her pale blue eyes were aimless.

"First ho-tel I was ever in," she said.

"It's a fleabag," Red said from where he had sprawled on the bed.

She inspected the tiny desk, the letterhead notepaper and a clotted straight pen propped in a dry inkwell. "Real high-tone," she said. Then she turned to Red. "I'm called Mavis."

"Mavis how many?"

"Just Mavis. I bet they call you Red?"

"*Right!* Give that lady the fur-lined pisspot."

Mavis laughed. "Ain't you the one."

"You know you're making me horny again parading around pract'ly bare-assed."

"Let's turn the light out and get in your bed."

"Okay, if you want."

Red stripped, palmed the wall switch, and turned to the pale island of bed. With the light off, a scarlet glow outside the windows, reflected from a large neon sign, became apparent. The sheet was tinted; Mavis appeared to be blushing. It occurred to Red this would be the first time he'd ever had a girl in a real bed, one who would sleep beside him.

In the morning, she said she'd turn a few tricks, and Red figured she might as well, since she looked better bending over anyway. They were busted a few days later by the hotel detail, who told Red the girl was fourteen and a runaway, and he had his issue of big-time trouble. For years he told the story, always ending, "Shit, I thought she was twenty."

That was the jolt when he blew his pickets. The cell lieutenant, exercising his gift for confusion, moved Society Red in with a weight lifter, called (always behind his back) Pithead. Pithead suffered from a smoldering case of acne, a festering and angry rash spreading over his cheeks, jawline, neck, and shoulders. He blamed his affliction on dirt, and he was a tireless clean freak who liked the cell spotless. But Red didn't figure to bother himself with excessive cleaning, and he was never in any particular hurry to take a shower. He observed that water caused iron to rust, and frequent showering increased your chances of catching cold. His socks fermented.

Pithead sullenly tormented his pimples while Red explained why it was senseless for him to degenerate into a neat freak behind his acne, since it couldn't be caused by dirt, because, as Red admitted in a nice display of candor, he was considerably dirtier than Pithead, and he didn't have one pimple. Probably Pithead had bad blood.

Pithead ground his teeth, his eyes blinking with furious revulsion. He knew what caused his acne. It was sin, and dirt was sin made visible. He sent by mail order for various medicated soaps and took nightly sponge baths, which caused Red to chuckle with amused tolerance. "Pithead's queer for soap," he told his buddies on the yard. "He sleeps with a bar under his pillow and sniffs it while he lopes his mule."

But then one day when Red made afternoon lockup, he crawled into his bunk already half asleep, and accidentally stepped on Pithead's pillow, depositing a crescent of dust and grease. When Pithead came in later, the first thing he saw was Red's footprint. He stared down as astounded as if it were the hoofprint of the Fiend, and it did appear to smolder with sin.

"Hey, man," he told Red. "You stepped on my pillow."

Red yawned hugely. "No shit, did I?"

Pithead changed his pillowcase and stretched out in his bunk, his arms folded behind his head. He stared steadily up at the outline of Red's body pressed into the webbing of his springs. Finally, he said, "That was cold, man." Red was asleep.

The next morning, when Red stumbled groggily from his bunk, seconds before unlock, he had to brush by Pithead to get to the toilet. But nothing warned him, as Pithead pivoted sideways and, winding up like Whitey Ford, copped a Sunday, smashing Red flush on the mouth. Red sprawled against the wall, his mouth filling with blood. "What the fuck?" he demanded. But just then the unlock bell sounded, the bar freed, and Pithead was out of the cell. He paused on the tier to yell back, "Step on my pillow, will you, you filthy son of a bitch!"

When Red tried to wash his face he discovered one of his front teeth was barely hanging, and the other was loose. He passed on breakfast and caught the head of the dental line. The dentist smiled but didn't ask questions. He told Red he could probably save the tooth, but he hesitated to blow the life back into anything so singularly unlovely. He suggested they pull both front teeth and fit Red with a partial. But of course if Red wanted to keep his own teeth—

"Yank the bastards, Doc," he said. "Those snags have whipped me for a lot of action."

The yard was growing crowded. Hundreds of men were now walking steadily from one end to the other, pounding the blacktop, and a great many more were gathered under the rain shed in small groups, exchanging the idle topics of a thousand mornings. All wore blue denims, but the condition of their uniforms varied greatly, the tidy, the slovenly, and the politicians in their pressed pants—starched overalls, Red thought mockingly—their polished free-world shoes, and expensive wristwatches.

Red was waiting for his hustling partner, but he rapped to anyone who passed by. He liked to bullshit, play the dozens, and when some clown stopped to call him "old tops and bottoms" he quickly said, "Your mammy gives up tops and bottoms."

"I heard yours was freakish for billy goats."

"She used to sport a light mule habit," Red returned, his yellow eyes beginning to light with pleasure. "But she wrote and told me she was trying to quit."

The clown smiled. "Red, you think you'll ever amount to anything?"

"Next time out I figure to file my pimp hand."

"Next time? You've already beat this yard long enough to wear out two murder beefs and a bag of robberies."

Red shrugged. "Off and on, I've been around awhile."

"The big yard's a cold place to fuck off your life."

Red's eyes began to grow vague as he lost interest in the conversation. Cons busted into jail, then spent half their time crying. And all the sniveling didn't make anyone's time any easier to do, any more than it shortened the length of a year. You did it the easiest way you could and hard-assed the difference. The big yard was an undercover world if you knew how to check the action, and something was always coming down. You could make a life on this yard, and you could die on it.

"What's to it, Society?" someone else asked.

"Not much. You want to grease armpits and wrestle?"

A man walked by carrying a cardboard box and sporting parole shoes. Red knew he had made his date and was heading out. By ten he'd be free, on his way to the city, and before the day was over some fish would be coming in to replace him. This happened every day. The gradual turnover was constant. Only lifers and a few other longtimers stood outside this process.

For a moment Red thought about the men waiting somewhere in some county jail, still unaware they'd be hitting the big yard before the day was out. Then he saw the bookmaker he worked for, and walked over to take his station beside him.

1

Two HUNDRED miles to the south in the Delano County jail, Jim Nunn was the first prisoner on the court chain down from the felony tank. He was keeping his cool. He'd been through it all before, several times in different counties, and nothing in the routine of jail, trial, conviction, or sentence could any longer surprise him. Today's chain was running for sentencing, and when the deputy unlocked his cuffs, Nunn gestured into the bullpen at the hidden courtroom beyond and asked, "This where they give out the free board and room?"

The deputy smiled mechanically. "This is it," he said and began to uncuff the next man. Nunn stepped into the bullpen. They're all the same, he thought bitterly. They all look the same, smell the same. He sat down on one of the two benches that faced each other in this narrow, featureless room.

Henry Jackson, a tall, very dark Negro, stepped in. He smiled at Nunn and said softly, "Well, sport, here we is."

Nunn smiled back. "You come to get your rent paid too?"

Jackson winced humorously. "Mos' likely that be what happen."

"They told me if I couldn't do the time, I shouldn't mess with crime."

"That's the troof." Jackson shrugged and sat down beside Nunn. "Well, they won't be gettin them no cherry." He looked up as another prisoner, released from the chain, entered, and asked Nunn, "How many of these dudes you think we take with us?"

"Enough," Nunn said. "They keep that prison full."

"They do that."

Nunn watched the other prisoners enter the bullpen. He thought of them in terms of their crime. Two Checks, a Manslaughter, a Burglary, the Baby Raper, and three kids, one a stone nut, with a four-dollar robbery to divide between them. Nunn rubbed the back of his neck and tried to remember his last good fix. The memory brought no ease. He started as the metal door leading back to the county jail slammed shut; he heard the solid thrust of the bolt. In an hour or so, whenever the judge got ready, they would be led out for sentencing. Nunn felt but slight suspense. He knew he was going back to prison. He would be sentenced and delivered by midafternoon.

He turned to ask Henry Jackson, "What's for chow on the main line tonight?"

"Friday? Tha's fish, ain't it?"

"That's right, fish."

"And cornbread. Apple pie."

"Yes, and all the water you can drink."

"Tha's right, go heavy as you like on water."

Nunn shook his head in mock sorrow. "Jackson, I think we have fucked up."

"You bes' tell it like it is."

"The judge'll tell it."

"Well, he the *man* today."

"That's right, and tonight he won't even remember what we looked like."

Was that what bothered him? Nunn wondered. Did he wish he'd had the brains and the balls for some spectacular offense, some legendary crime, rather than be, as he knew he was, just one more small gray malcontent? Yes, he wished he was someone else. His eyes searched the faces in the bullpen and in the saddest, the weariest, he saw some furtive hope. Even the Baby Raper appeared to believe he could be forgiven. Baby raping didn't necessarily make him a bad fellow. He just forgot to ask for ID. It could happen to anyone.

"Hey, Manning," Nunn called.

The Baby Raper looked up. "Yes," he said.

"What're you looking for out there?"

"In court?"

"Yes, what do you expect?"

"I don't know."

"You think you'll get the joint?"

"I don't know."

Henry Jackson leaned over to whisper to Nunn, "Iffen he don't get the joint the ducks in Mississippi wear rubber boots."

"Yeah, and there ain't a cow in Texas."

Both men smiled at Manning, the Baby Raper, without a trace of friendliness.

Will Manning sensed their mockery and distaste. Could he blame them? How might he have once felt, before he had made his incredible discovery? After more than half a life-time, during which he had considered himself—what comfortable shorthand would he have used? Honest? Honorable? Decent? No, he would never have claimed so much. Halfway decent is precisely how he would have classed himself. And after better than half a lifetime of halfway decency he had suddenly discovered, in a few vivid moments, that he was a filthy degenerate. The phrase was not his own. His wife had supplied it.

He took the display handkerchief from his breast pocket and wiped his forehead. The bullpen was too crowded. They shouldn't herd men together like livestock. Too much body heat. The air was hot and stale, depressed somehow with a profound fatigue. A naked two-hundred-watt bulb burned through a haze of cigarette smoke.

Manning folded his arms across his chest, trying to compress himself to avoid touching the men seated on either side of him, but the less room he managed to take, the more they took. They seemed to swell and flow around him as if their clothes were full of some warm, corrupt, half-fluid gelatin. The rhythm of their breathing seemed as intimate as his own.

He stared down over his folded arms, past the points of his neat black shoes, and tried to think only of the stains on the metal floor. One, a ragged oval, seemed briefly like an island, a tobacco-colored island in a flat green sea. He moved his foot to cover it. Island population destroyed in senseless accident. Would senseless accident imply there could be a sensible accident? It would be better if he didn't have to think.

He took a comb from his inside coat pocket, awkwardly, trying not to jostle the men crowded against him, and began to comb his hair. Automatically he shaped the pushed-up wave he still affected over his narrow forehead. Year by year, since his last year in high school, this crest had grown steadily smaller, a visible record of the hidden shrinkages taking place somewhere within his spirit, and now, suddenly, he felt a strong wave of disgust. The tattered plume of an aging stud, who never had the occupation, only the ornament. He raked his comb straight back to destroy his modest crest and accidentally dug his elbow into the ribs of the man on his right.

This individual, wrapped in a filthy tan overcoat many sizes too large, jerked around and fixed Manning with sick, accusing eyes. "Take it easy."

"I'm sorry," Manning said automatically.

"Buddy, sorry's a word I'm tired of."

Manning turned sharply away to avoid the odor of decaying teeth, and, as if a signal had been given, everyone stirred. The prisoner on the other side of Manning, a heavy man in suntans, wearing a maroon sport shirt with six small black buttons at each cuff, lifted his head from his hands. His cheeks were mottled from the pressure of his fingers and his eyes were miserable.

"What're they doing out there?" he asked of no one in particular.

From the opposite bench Nunn leaned over to inquire in a parody of polite interest, "You pressed for time?"

The other prisoners laughed, and Henry Jackson joined in. "You jus' hold yore cool," he told the man in the maroon sport shirt. "They got an assload a time out in that cou'troom —alls you got to do is back up and get it."

"That's right," Nunn agreed. "We're all about to get screwed, and without the benefit of intercourse."

"No Vaseline neither," Henry Jackson added.

The prisoners laughed again. "What's funny?" asked the sick-eyed man Manning had jostled. "What's supposed to be so damn funny?" he asked again with forceless bitterness.

"It'll come to you," Nunn said.

"That it do," Henry Jackson added.

"Like, when rape's inevitable," Nunn continued slyly, "relax and enjoy it."

Manning felt the blood burning in his face as he stared at the metal wall above the heads of the prisoners seated on the opposite bench. He wouldn't look at them for fear they were all smiling at him. Instead he found himself studying a crude drawing of a man and a woman making love. The genitals were grossly exaggerated, and in the balloon above the woman's head she was saying: *Moan! Oh, do it to me, Big Daddy!* While Big Daddy had been made to say: *Shake that thing, Bitch!*

Manning shuddered. The obscenity was as intolerable as the feel of slime. He closed his eyes, but the grotesque caricature immediately came to life in his mind, and the figures began to move in a slow grind of animal pleasure. The image seemed to tip as somehow his viewpoint altered and he became involved and once again saw Debbie's soft young face turned aside on her pillow, her profile in places almost indistinguishable from the white cloth and in others chalked vividly against the black tangle of her long hair. He saw her eyelids flutter and once again felt the first subtle shift of her hips

15

beneath his own, and again, as he had that night, he gasped. After years of dullness a wave of fierce and masculine energy had trapped him like a rabbit in a snare and exposed him as an object of disgust and derision. He opened his eyes. No one was paying him any attention. Nunn was rolling a cigarette, his motions precise to the point of fussiness, and Henry Jackson was watching as if he were trying to memorize how it was done. Manning looked away and found himself staring at a tall, very thin boy who was drawing still another picture on the wall.

Sheldon Wilson, sometimes called Stick because he was over six-foot-three and under one hundred and sixty pounds, was drawing the Vampire. The Vampire had the Devil's hairline and nostrils round and dark as pennies. The fangs, drinking teeth soon to be set to the world's soft throat, were blunt and functional as soda straws.

Stick's two followers, both with the title of General, watched their leader work. One was seventeen, the other eighteen. The younger had the round dull eyes and slack mouth of a borderline defective, while the older seemed only slightly brighter. Stick, in sharp contrast to his Generals, had an air of sullen keenness. A dark, mean look. His narrow face was shaped like a trowel, and his eyes, small and set close together, were the rivets that fixed the blade to the handle. He was nineteen, and before he was sixteen he had been expelled from several high schools. Twice for hitting teachers, both women, and a third time for breaking into the school at night to paint Fascist slogans in the hallways. He had also invaded the girls' lavatory, broken open the sanitary pad dispenser, and scattered the pads. Following this incident a school psychologist characterized him as "seriously disturbed" and recommended treatment in an institutional setting, which Stick knew in plain words meant he should be stashed in some nut house, and, in his own phrase, he cooled it. He became quiet, withdrawn, and normal enough if one ignored the large swastikas on the cover of his binder. And he wasn't the first boy to have found a kind of negative magic in this discredited symbol; in a way its banality was almost reassuring. Then the swastikas were replaced by the Vampire.

The three of them, the Generals and Stick, comprised the total membership of the Vampires, an organization dedicated to world domination. They stood convicted of robbery, an attempt to levy tax for their treasury, which at the time of their arrest totaled three dollars and ten cents. The money was first held for evidence, then returned to the man they had robbed. They had spent ninety cents on cigarettes, candy bars, and a bottle of Royal Crown Cola.

A key sounded, and Stick looked up from his drawing to watch a mild-looking deputy standing in the open courtroom door. The hands holding a clipboard were slender and well kept. Stick's eyes narrowed scornfully. He stared at the black gloss of the deputy's boots.

"Henry Jackson?" the deputy called from a typewritten list.

"Yessir, tha's me."

"You're first at bat, Henry. Take off your cap and come along."

Jackson snatched off his paint-stained golfer's cap and stuck it in his back pocket. *"Yessir,"* he said again, this time with a hint of derisive broadness. He winked a yellowish eye and grinned over his shoulder at the men behind him. "Here we goes," he said.

"Play it Tom," Nunn advised.

"Oh, yes, I plays it Tom."

When the door closed behind the deputy and Henry Jackson, Stick turned back to his drawing and began to trace a hairline mustache on the Vampire like the one he wore himself, although his own was as much burnt match as it was whisker.

The youngest General leaned over to whisper, "What you think they're gunna do to us?" He looked at the door. "Out there?"

"I told you not to worry about that."

"Yeah, I know, but I keep wondering—"

Stick regarded his Generals calmly. "Does it matter?" he asked softly, his ear appreciatively tuned to the coolness of his voice. "Does it matter what they do?"

"No, but I can't help—"

"That's right," Stick broke in. "It doesn't matter. They get their licks in now. We get ours later." He nodded with confident emphasis, and hooked his thumb at the door leading to the courtroom. "And these crud, and all the crud like them, will get scraped up in the street and shoved into the sewers."

The Generals nodded in hopeful agreement. For a moment they appeared as pleased as children who have been promised a favorite treat.

Again the door opened. Henry Jackson stepped through, still smiling, though now his smile seemed numb.

"What'd you get?" Nunn asked.

"Well, I got enough," Henry Jackson said, pulling a crushed and broken cigarette butt from his shirt pocket. He looked at the butt, saw it couldn't be lit, and dropped it to the floor. "But not so much I cain't hack it," he continued. "Iffen the man figures he's got it coming I guess I can do it."

"I guess you *will* do it," Nunn said.

"Ain't no guessin to that, is there, pops? When the man sticks time to your ass you better be able to do it."

"You can hack it. You've worn out beefs before."

"That's the troof."

Again the key sounded, and this time Stick heard the deputy calling their names. He stood up briskly and motioned the Generals into line behind him. They marched into the courtroom, but the martial and menacing effect Stick had planned failed when the youngest General was unable to keep in step. They lined up beneath the bench at attention, largely ignoring their parents seated in the first row beyond the rail. The lawyer hired by their parents made a brief speech, but Stick didn't listen. He concentrated on the judge's eyes. He wanted this judge to remember him as he intended to remember the judge. He knew his own eyes were charged with power, a cold power, and he drilled his icy strength into the judge's brain until he could send his thoughts like commands . . .

—Let the Vampire go, he willed the judge to say.

Then he heard the judge sentencing them to the state prison. His head jerked back as if the judge had hit him, and the youngest General was crying openly. Stick heard his mother calling his name in that same tearful whine he hated so much, and he ignored her now as he had so often before.

Then the deputy was leading them back towards the bullpen and they followed him like stunned children, but when the door closed behind them, Stick pulled himself up tight, and told his troops to snap to. "Stop sniveling," he told the youngest General. "So they send us up there—does that mean we have to stay?"

And in Stick's mind at this moment was born a curious hybrid, bred in part from his simplified re-creation of Napoleon's triumphant return from St. Helena, mated with his recollections of the late-late show where Humphrey Bogart crouched in the shadows of a prison wall while the searchlights lashed around him like the tentacles of an enraged squid.

Manning watched the other prisoners take their turn in the courtroom. A few won probation or short terms in the county jail, but most returned sentenced to state prison. He heard Nunn whistle softly and say, "That judge is savage. He's killing people left and right."

"His woman holdin out on him," Henry Jackson said. "No cock can sure make a man red-eyed."

"That's right," Nunn said. "He figures if he can't get none, ain't nobody going to get any."

Manning's turn came, and he walked out into the bright sterile atmosphere of the courtroom with the sense of a diver returning to the surface after many hours in the dark and murderous bottoms of the ocean. He scanned the seats and immediately saw his wife in the back row. He had neither seen her nor heard from her since the morning of the day she had reported him to the police. No visits or letters, nothing to indicate that she had realized her act had been as destructive as his own. Then he was close enough to see the set of her face. She had come for revenge.

Manning's lawyer joined him before the bench and began an unemotional plea for probation. Manning heard himself described as a "good citizen" with an "impressive service record." Look at the judge, Manning told himself, but his gaze drifted away. His lawyer was continuing: ". . . crime of passion in the truest sense . . . not his natural child."

The judge had removed his glasses and folded his hands. Manning, finally able to meet his eyes, saw they were narrowed in distaste.

"Probation denied. In the opinion of this court the law doesn't provide an adequate punishment for one who violates his own home and fouls his young like an animal. You should be altered by surgery."

Manning bowed his head, scalded with shame. The judge was rapidly repeating the legal formula sentencing him to prison. His lawyer was patting him on the shoulder, saying, "Sorry, Will, I thought we might squeak by."

"How long? How long is that?"

"I'd have to check, but I think it's one to fifty years."

"Fifty years!"

"Don't let the fifty scare you. You could be out in a year."

He turned to see the back of Pat's tan coat as she passed through the swinging doors. Then the bailiff was motioning him back towards the bullpen. As he left the courtroom he found himself wondering if he would have to cancel his insurance.

2

TRANSPORTING convicted prisoners, now literally convicts, to the state prison is the responsibility of the sheriff, and the county had converted an old school bus into a prison van. Welded bars over the windows enclosed the driver in a separate cab, and the original orange-and-black had been repainted gray. Manning had occasionally noticed this van. It had seemed to move in a cloud, not of disgrace, or danger, but enveloped by a separate atmosphere. A stout gray bird of passage coming from one alien land, bound for another.

Prisoners were transported in white coveralls, but it wasn't until Manning stepped into the embarkation cage in the basement of the county jail and saw the stacks of coveralls that he remembered the men visible through the bus windows, all in white, orderly as Trappists. When he saw the piles of handcuffs and leg-irons he understood why they had been orderly.

They were stripped, searched, and told to tag their civilian clothes. After they changed into the coveralls, the leg-irons were fastened to their ankles, and they were led out to the bus, which sat parked in an alley. The seats were filled from the rear and Manning found himself next to a window, sharing a seat with Jim Nunn. Henry Jackson was just in front of them.

Manning looked out the window, but there was little to see. The bare brick side of the building that had held him for six weeks, and the even bright humps of parked cars. At the end of the block a woman crossed the mouth of the alley.

"Goodbye, Mama," Henry Jackson said.

Two deputies worked down the aisle rapidly fastening the handcuffs, and when they finished they locked the door of the driver's compartment behind them. The motor came to life.

When it became apparent they were going to pass through the center of town, Manning hid his face in his hands. He didn't want to be seen. But neither did he want to see. Still, in his mind he watched the familiar buildings, one by one, fall away behind.

"Well, that's it," Nunn said, and Manning lifted his face from his hands to look at his seatmate.

For the first time he realized how ill Nunn appeared. His bitter face was grayish, and took a clownish cast from his wide red mouth, but there was nothing of the clown in his eyes. He lifted his hands to look at the handcuffs, studying them with distaste. He made a wry noise and said to Manning in normal tones, "We haven't left ourselves much, have we?"

"No, I guess not."

"You get used to it."

"What's it like?"

"Dull," Nunn replied without emphasis. "And that's about it. If you're not uncomfortable, you're bored. No kicks. No broads. No dope. And no hope. Besides that the food's bad."

"Can you study there? Take up something?"

"You probably couldn't find a better place. They have schools. You can take up a hobby." Nunn smiled. "Like my hobby was smuggling dope."

"You're not serious?"

"Of course, I'm not serious." Nunn leaned forward to Henry Jackson in the seat in front. "How'd you like a bag of that good smack?"

Jackson turned, grinning. "Do rabbits like tender young peas? But to tell the troof, sport, I been messin with that charlotte. That stuff do burn your arm up. Make you look like vampires got aholt a you."

"That shit scares me. I keep thinking I'm going to go into some kind of madman act."

"You mos' likely thinkin right. Your cap get pretty loose sometimes. Well, we ain't gunna have no such worry for a while anyway."

"That's a lock."

As the two men had been talking the bus had reached open country, and now they were passing a stretch of fenced pasture where a small herd of black-and-white cows were grazing. One looked up to watch the bus with a round and empty eye.

Music began to come from a loudspeaker in the back corner. The song was one Manning had often heard Debbie playing in her bedroom.

Stick and the Generals were singing along with the record. They seemed in a good mood and Manning supposed a kid could convince himself this was something of an adventure. He settled back and found himself listening to Henry Jackson describing his arrest for something he called "carpet game."

"See," Henry was saying, "I knew I should of never played in my own neighborhood. I knew that. But I seen this chump and he looking fat, fat, and I knew I could play on him, so I shoots. Ask him did he want to juge a colored girl. Yeah, that's what he wants. So I take him to the shitter at the Mae-and-Ida rooms, and tell him the girls get twenny.

"Twenny! he says. He want to dick a little. Says he jus' want to use it awhile, not buy it outright. I say, twenny the reg'lar price for high-class girls like these, and if you want to fuck get twenny outa your hide. Tight as he is I don't think I get any backs at all, but he comes up with a twenny, and I go stand in the hall for a few minutes. Then I drives back on him and say, Now you bes' to give up your hide till you gets done with the girl. I takes care of it for you. We been having trouble you johns getting robbed while you in the rooms. Given the house a bad name. So I bes' take care of it for you until you finish.

"Girl waitin, he ask? I say, oh, yeah, she waitin. She real fine. So he hands over his hide, better'n a hundred in it, and I tell him some door to go knock on and splits.

"Well, that fool holler kidnap. Picks me out of the mug file. And they busts me right offen my own corner. Po-lice go to talkin kidnap, and I say, Stop right there, since when you callin carpet game kidnap. They say, Jackson, you got too much class to be no Murphy man, but you got real high kidnap potential. They made me sweat some, but I finally gets them to break it down to grand theft. I tole em I couldn't build no kidnap time less'n they promised me I could live forever."

Manning noticed that Nunn was smiling, so he leaned over to ask, "What's a hide?"

"A billfold."

"I had something like that happen to me when I was in the Army. Only I was with the girl and the man came in an shook me down. Held a knife on me."

"That's badger," Nunn said. "Any fool with a broad can work that. The carpet game takes a schooled hustler. He makes everything up as he goes along. It's an art. He's got nothing but a place to stand, a hand to reach with, and a mouth to say 'Gimme.'"

"It's interesting," Manning said, hoping his tone didn't suggest patronage. He sensed that it wouldn't be wise to have yourself considered a snob. Particularly since he had already formed the definite impression that most of these men would consider themselves superior to him simply because of the nature of his crime. He had been surprised to find Nunn so cordial, but then Nunn's present mood was as somber as he had known him to be during all the weeks in jail. Everyone was quiet. The radio had moved on to an older and softer tune. The boys were no longer singing.

Stick was on a private trip. His eyes were closed, but he was awake and on the infinite screen of his inner eyes another reality had formed in which the bus was rolling through wilderness country. It had been miles since they had passed a building of any sort, and the only thing, other than the road, recalling civilization was the telephone line, a single black thread scalloped from pole to pole.

Stick followed the wire where it shimmered against the intense blue of the sky, and when he noted the pattern broken up ahead, the cut line dangling impotently against the pole, he permitted himself a slight smile. Around the next turn the road was blocked by a large black tank. The bus braked and swerved, stopping inches from the massive treads. The bleak muzzle of the 20-mm turret cannon swiveled to cover the driver of the prison van. A soldier, black-uniformed, jumped from the hatch carrying a Sten gun. He wore the Vampire shoulder patch. Vampire insignia were painted on the side of the tank.

The soldier ran to the bus door, attached a shaped thermite charge to the lock, shielded his eyes at the brief flash of intense blue light, and was as quickly moving through the door, his gun at ready.

—We intend to free our leader, the soldier announced to the deputies. Are you permitted to surrender or must I shoot you?

—I've got a family, the gun bull said.

—My mother, the driver added.

The soldier caught sight of Stick. Instantly he shifted his gun to make a Roman salute.

—You're delivered, Vampire.

The other prisoners were looking around anxiously to see who it was the soldier had addressed, and Stick, with a sense of timing he had never managed in real life, paused for three beats before he stood up and casually returned the salute.

—Well done, he said crisply.

He strode down the aisle, his irons and cuffs magically vanished, his coverall transformed into a uniform tailored entirely from black leather trimmed with silver. He gestured at the driver and the gun bull both hunched in entreaty.

—Kill these defectives, he ordered, and watched impassively as the Sten gun coughed rhythmically. He turned to stand at the head of the aisle, legs spread, arms akimbo.

—I'm freeing you, he told the other prisoners, and offering you this chance to join our movement. Because you were with me during these my darkest times, it is my intention to form you into an Elite Corps, to be known as the Death's Head Corps, and you shall henceforth act as Standard Bearers for all ceremonies attendant upon my own person, in addition to serving as my private bodyguard. This honor to continue in your lines. This honor to continue in your lines. This honor . . .

The dream faltered. Reality rushed on Stick like a wave of thick white dust, sifting into his mouth, into his eyes. The illusion of dust was so strong he leaned over to clear his mouth and spit on the floor. Both Generals were asleep, the youngest with his mouth open. Stick realized on reflection that it would be a mistake to escape from the bus in transit. Such an escape would be routine, but to escape from the prison itself would be a legendary act. Stick closed his eyes again and began to stage this new myth.

"They couldn't prove I'd stolen the suit," Nunn was saying, "but they could prove I had it and that I knew it was stolen, which is all they need for Receiving Stolen Property. The Narcos set me up. First they send the guy to sell me the suit. I give him a lightweight fix for a two-hundred-dollar set of skins, and he tells me I'm doing him a favor, then when they bust me he takes the stand and hangs me. But it was the fuzz's action from the door. They wanted me gone."

"But why?" Manning asked. "I mean what did they have against you?"

"They thought I was a major connection. Hell, I had to hustle like a one-armed paperhanger to keep myself straightened, but the fuzz sometimes get sold on their own fantasies. For some reason they gave me star billing on their hit parade. I got jacked up and shook down so many times it seemed like my pockets were always inside out and my sleeves at half-mast, and the more I came up clean the surer they were I was dirty in some big way. Then some little junior flip bitch oh-deed, and—"

"What?"

"She overdosed and died in a car at one of the drive-ins, and that fired up the dope-in-the-playpen hysteria, even though the girl had quit school a year before and for six months had been making it with Spades. Jesus, I don't know anyone who has stuff to waste on high-school cunt. That's probably another of their fantasies. Like the sex-crazed dope fiend, which is about like a sex-crazed vegetable. The average dope fiend is nothing but a poor, sick, sad cocksucker, who wants nothing except to be left alone and on the nod. No chance. There's no material there for a big pop fantasy, produced and directed by J. Edgar Hoover."

Nunn paused and shrugged, smiling wryly. "Anyway, that's my sad story." He began to roll a cigarette with the deftness of long practice. The handcuffs didn't seem to hamper him. "You want one of these?" he offered.

"I couldn't get it together," Manning said.

"I'll build you one."

Manning hesitated as he recalled Nunn's thin bluish tongue darting out to wet the seam. "No thanks, I'm trying to quit."

"More power. You'll be better off if you can. Half the joint is usually trying to figure some way to keep smoking, and a few packs of cigarettes will buy things you wouldn't imagine.

I've a good buddy who loans cigarettes and collects interest just like a bank—"

Nunn broke off to lean across Manning as he read a mileage sign posted at the side of the highway. "They're making fair time," he said. "We'll eat mainline tonight."

Manning nodded mechanically. He sensed the threat of the prison swelling ahead, and it seemed to him he was being swiftly carried into a savage and violent past, to which his own savagery justly condemned him. Briefly he saw Debbie spread on the ground, gasping with pain and terror, no blood, not even any pain. His shame yielded to a numbing sense of loss, and the knowledge of how cruelly he had been cheated.

He raised his hands to rub his eyes, glancing at his seatmate to see if Nunn had observed his distress, but Nunn was resting with his eyes closed, his head swaying slightly with the motion of the bus.

Manning turned to look out the window. They were passing through open country. There were only occasional meandering rows of fence posts, sometimes broken by the X of a distant gate. They passed a wooden barn painted *Mail Pouch Chewing Tobacco*. Half a mile farther on a small billboard, lettered in bright red, blue, and yellow, said *Jesus Died for You*. Along the horizon a range of indigo mountains rose as if generated from the mists of distance, and the highest peaks were flecked with white.

Manning felt a warning twinge of hunger. He had never been a sentimental outdoorsman, had seldom left the city, but now he stared out at the passing landscape with a sharp sense of imminent loss. Then they were coming into the outskirts of a town, the air brakes hissing as the bus slowed. They halted for a red light, and Manning stared down at the women crossing the street. Already they seemed remote.

"Hey, Big Mama," Henry Jackson called softly to a fat woman in shorts, pushing a market basket. "Bet I make you shake and holler." He turned to inform his seatmate, "Them big old fat things'll fool you."

"Jackson," Nunn said without opening his eyes, "is it true your old lady wrestles main events?"

"Rassles main events with me, that's what she do."

"Jackson," Nunn said dryly, "you're full of petrified apple butter."

Jackson laughed and stretched. Manning was dozing. He drifted back and forth between waking and sleeping as the bus covered the remaining miles to San Francisco. He was asleep crossing the Golden Gate Bridge or he might have seen the prison first from a distance.

"There it is," Nunn said. "The asshole of creation."

The bus had followed the edge of the bay along a stretch of tidal flats, black mud rank with oil, and turned beneath the shoulder of a barren hill, deeply scarred by an open-pit quarry, and suddenly faced the massive concrete walls. A wide blacktop driveway led straight up towards a large steel gate. They passed a post office, a lunch stand, a curio shop, then entered a stretch like any residential district, houses half hidden in a wealth of shrubbery, while on the wide lawns several men in blue denims leaned against the handles of lawn mowers, staring up at the bus. A small boy in a red windbreaker and a little-league ball cap delivered papers on his bicycle.

The actual prison bore little resemblance to Manning's fearful preconception, a blurred projection formed in his mind from the hundred transparencies of fiction and legend which had somehow combined to form the illusion of substance. All the components of the motion picture prison were evident —armed guards, high walls, the cyclopean gaze of waiting searchlights—but they seemed diminished, without harmful vitality, sapped by the fresh green lawns, the numerous beds of bright flowers, even by the walls themselves, which were painted a pastel green trimmed in dusky pink.

"All out for Disneyland," someone in front cracked.

"You'll think Disneyland," Nunn said quietly.

The bus was parked on the blacktop beside the large arched gates, and the county officers began to remove the restraining gear. Unchained, the prisoners filed from the bus and passed through a sally port in the gate while both a deputy and a prison officer made a head count.

Manning followed Nunn into a narrow concrete room, where wooden benches, painted forest green, stretched along the side walls. The far end was walled by a massive iron door, also provided with a smaller sally port at which a guard with a single large brass key stood on duty.

"This is called between gates," Nunn said. "One more and you're in."

Manning recognized that the area served as a traffic control point. A dozen inmates sat scattered along the benches. They stared openly. One was a gaunt man with a raw humorous face and yellow, grinning eyes.

"And there's another sissy breaking back into jail," he suddenly announced loudly.

Nunn, glancing in his direction, exclaimed, "*Red!* Society Red! You still blowing smoke? No one yells 'sissy' faster'n an undercover fruiter."

Red clapped Nunn on the arm. "Buddy, what're you doing back?"

"Winter's coming. It gets cold under those bridges."

"So you couldn't hold your mud?"

Nunn shrugged. "I had a nice ride."

"You look like you kicked an ass wiper."

"An oil burner."

"You get any good ass?"

Nunn grinned. "You horny old fart. How's Chilly?"

"Cold as ever. Slipp'n, slid'n, easy rid'n. You know Chilly."

"Has he still got the book?"

"Sure, he picked the series again."

"He's good."

Red nodded. "He's sharp, that's all. While these other rump-kins are standing around picking their noses, Chilly's thinking. What'd you bring back anyway?"

"Receiving. One to five."

"Well, that'll hold you. Might as well settle down and walk it off."

"I'll have to make up some new lies."

Red grinned. "Make em about young skunks you scored on. Maybe you can ease from under the freak jacket you've been carrying."

"Oh, I don't know," Nunn said elaborately. "A freak jacket doesn't seem to bother you much."

"Your mammy's freak jacket don't bother me."

"Only because your own mammy wore jockey shorts and kept her dildo on the mantel."

Red grinned delightedly, remembering this game with Nunn, and he almost shouted, "She kept it on the mantel when she wasn't cramming it in your mammy's prune."

An enormous guard with small metal sergeant's chevrons attached to his collar stepped through a metal door in time to catch Red's last cap. He smiled, showing small, very white teeth beneath a glossy black mustache.

"Red," he asked in a surprisingly light tenor voice, "how many rounds was it your mother went with Archie Moore?"

Red turned quickly. "Sarge, you know I don't play no dozens."

"I should hope not. A nice boy like you. Now, get the hell out of here and give me a chance at these fish."

Red said quickly to Nunn, "I'll tell Chilly you just drove up."

"Okay. See you on the yard."

The sergeant studied them impassively for a moment, then

he said, "We've a little processing to get through, but if you keep it moving it shouldn't take long." He pointed at the door he'd stepped from and Manning noticed it was lettered *Receiving and Release*. "Right in there," the sergeant invited pleasantly.

They entered a second room where five rows of wooden benches faced what seemed to be a booking counter. In a back corner an old view camera pointed into a raw plywood booth, bleached with floodlights. An inmate in neatly pressed blues was making some adjustment to the camera and he looked up briefly to examine them with remote green eyes. Automatically they took seats on the benches. The sergeant went behind the booking counter where he had a swivel chair padded with pillows. Before he sat down he explained that they were going to take mug shots, and anyone who needed a shave would find a razor and blades in the washroom. He studied them briefly to see if they understood, then lowered himself into the chair and swung his feet onto the counter.

The inmate photographer had already started work, spinning a piano stool to lower it for Henry Jackson. In his turn, Manning stared soberly into the light, his head tilted in obedience to a sign which ordered *Look HERE*. The sign was stapled to the belly of a nude whose right breast had been inked into a target, so her rosette and nipple formed the bull's-eye.

When they had all been photographed, the sergeant ordered them to strip down and throw their coveralls into a canvas laundry basket, and their shoes, socks, and underwear into a cardboard box next to it. "You take nothing—nothing—inside the walls. Any personal valuables, rings, watches, pens, lighters, will be stored here and returned to you at the time of your release. Throw your smokes away. Now come up here one at a time for a skin shake."

The sergeant stepped in front of the counter and began to instruct the first of the now naked men. "Lift your arms." He looked at the armpits. "Run your fingers through your hair.

33

All right, open your mouth. Wider. Okay, skin it back. Lift your balls. Turn around and bend over. Spread your cheeks. Okay, lift your feet. The right. Now the left. Okay, get a blue coverall over there, and put on a pair of those cloth slippers."

One by one they fumbled awkwardly through the humiliating examination, except for a few, like Nunn, who ran the routine briskly as if it were an exercise they had performed often, and took a sort of pride in knowing well. Numbly, Manning took his turn, and gratefully slipped into a worn coverall, patched at both knees. He sat down and watched the Wilson boy, who had waited until last. His extreme thinness made him appear frail in spite of his height, and his skin was very pale. He stepped in front of the sergeant and stood with his eyes half closed, breathing through his mouth. His face seemed lumpy. He lifted his arms when he was told to, but he hesitated before opening his mouth, and then only parted his lips.

"Much wider," the sergeant said. "Show some tonsil."

Stick thrust his head forward and jerked his mouth open inches from the sergeant's face, who swayed back and looked at Stick thoughtfully.

"All right, lift your nuts."

Stick thrust his pelvis forward and exposed his scrotum.

The sergeant's eyes flickered. He spread his legs, and his hands, the backs nested in the fat swelling above his wide belt, closed into fists. "All right, son," he said softly, "let's have a look at your ass."

Stick stood rigid.

"Don't you hear well?"

Still Stick didn't move.

"Don't be modest. I see a lot of assholes. They all look the same."

"Fuck you," Stick said.

The sergeant nodded with the appearance of satisfaction, and pressed a button set in the base of his phone. "This is a place," he told Stick, "where you can buy a great deal of trouble very cheaply." He lit a cigarette. In less than a minute the door flew open and three guards entered on the double.

"The goon squad," Nunn whispered to Manning. "The tall one is called the Farmer." Manning saw a man close to six and a half feet tall, with a brown face, weathered as old leather, and steady tobacco-colored eyes. His wrists were large and red.

"The fat one's the Indian."

Only a few inches shorter than the Farmer, the Indian carried three hundred pounds of dense flesh. His head, the size and shape of a basketball, rested on a triple chin. His eyes were small, bright, and good-humored.

The third member of the goon squad was a small Negro, five-six, almost dainty, with a smooth, shapely otter's head. He moved with conspicuous grace, and his lips were creased in a dreaming smile.

"And the Spook," Nunn continued. "He's smart and very bad news."

The sergeant nodded at Stick, who hadn't moved, and told the Spook he had refused to bend over. The Spook's smile deepened. The Farmer and the Indian closed on Stick like fingers of the same hand as they armlocked him from either side. They raised him straining to his tiptoes. The Spook looked up at him. "You see, you've aroused our curiosity."

The Indian and the Farmer bent Stick as easily as they would break a shotgun. The Spook pried open his clamped rump. Stick jerked wildly and made a hissing noise. "My, my," the Spoke murmured, "not a feather on him. Some jocker's due to score." He looked up at the sergeant. "You think he might have something keister-stashed? We can X-ray."

"No," the sergeant said. "He's just some kind of nut."

The Spook studied Stick knowingly. "Yes, he's some kind of nut."

"The psych doctors can classify him, that's what they're paid for."

"Yes," the Spook said softly, "they tell everyone what kind of nut they are, which helps a great deal."

The sergeant smiled and nodded.

"The shelf?" the Spook asked, indicating Stick.

"Yes, put him in a holding cell. I'll think up some charge before I go off duty."

Stick was toe-walked, still naked, from the room, but the Spook stopped to pick up one of the denim coveralls before he followed. He paused in the doorway to make a brief inspection of the other new arrivals. He smiled faintly when he recognized Nunn. "Your boss know you're back?" he asked.

"Probably."

"Take care," the Spook said, and left.

"What will they do to him?" Manning asked Nunn.

Nunn smiled. "Nothing. A few days isolation. They get nutty kids like that all the time. They make them feel foolish, and they quiet down."

"I think that boy's sick."

"He's subject to be considerably sicker before he gets out."

The skin shake continued without further incident, and when the last of the new arrivals had been passed, they were taken through the final gate into the actual prison. Manning was surprised to step out into a garden, similar to the block-square parks in downtown areas, crisscrossed with walks and dominated by a central fountain. The fountain appeared to be dry. Manning turned to find Nunn smiling at him.

"They call it the Garden Beautiful."

They were conducted to a building designated "distribution," where they were outfitted with cell supplies: two sheets of unbleached muslin, a pillowcase, three woolen army blankets stenciled *State of California*, a set of earphones, a small metal mirror, a teaspoon, a comb, a paper sack of unflavored tooth powder, a toothbrush, a bar of soap in a plain white wrapper, a razor, a package of razor blades, and a book of rules and regulations. Next they were outfitted in blue denim uniforms, underwear and heavy brown shoes. Then they were led across the big yard towards the south block. The big yard, the true center of the prison, was a blacktop enclosure the size of a football field, bounded on three sides by the inner walls of the cellblocks, and on the fourth by the mess hall and kitchens. These structures formed walls forty feet high, painted the same pastel green, and made of the sky a long narrow rectangle. A sea smell was in the air, mixed with the stronger odor of the tidal flats and the hundreds of pounds of fish frying in the kitchens. Manning was reminded of an amusement park. The impression was bizarre, but it was there in the sun-softened asphalt, the roar of thousands of men gathered in a small space, the smells of salt, decay, and fried fish. Triple loudspeakers mounted high in each corner of the yard blasted rock and roll.

As the fish were led in through three-post they were greeted with a gale of whistling and catcalls, and as they were walked down the edge of the yard a number of inmates ran alongside them yelling, "You and me, baby. You and me." Or, "Put that pretty thing in my cell." The comments were broad, the invitations facetious, but the real content was hostility, as if the whistles and calls were fists and bricks. Manning sensed the hatred even though he couldn't as quickly determine the motive, but the thought that disturbed him was that he might be changed as these men must have been changed, shaped and molded to fit the habits and passions of this thousand-legged animal that was greeting them with such savage and contemptuous mockery.

"Don't let it bug you," Nunn said. "This is sort of a tradition."

It seemed to Manning that every prisoner in the big yard had joined in the shivaree, just as it seemed to him they were all identical—jeering mouths wrenched open under the round stiff-billed hats. Actually less than a third of the yard was engaged in active hazing. Many stood and stared for no better reason than that it was something different to look at, and almost everyone searched the new faces for a friend, a buddy fresh from the streets. Still others noted hopefully the large number of fish, because they saw the prison as if it were a giant bin, and if busload after busload of fish were stuffed into the bottom of the bin it only stood to reason that the pressure of the growing population would shove them out the top a few months earlier. It was true, facilities throughout the state were dangerously overcrowded, but the cynics maintained they would be housed three to a cell before a single man was released a day early.

Now they were moving along a row of wooden tables, constructed like picnic benches and painted the same forest green, where a dozen domino games were in progress. Each table was the center of a crowd, players and their audience, and the games were being conducted with great animation and a running scrimmage of loud talk, insults, depreciation, and repeated invitations to "get fucked." Scattered through the domino crowd like tortoises somehow abandoned in the monkey house were a few chess players. They hunched over their boards in fierce concentration, and seemed oblivious to the bedlam around them.

"Chilly," Nunn was shouting. "Hey, Chilly."

Manning followed the direction of Nunn's eyes and noticed Society Red playing dominos with three other men. He was partnered with a slender young man who was bent forward studying the pattern of the game, and when he made his own play he didn't just place the domino on the table—he swung his hand over so hard and fast centrifugal force fixed the tile to his fingers until it slapped against the table, and was then deftly flicked into play. The whole action was performed with the vigor and style of a tennis smash.

"Five-four, hit the door," he chanted, then turned to look at Nunn. His eyes were bleak.

"Goddam, Chilly," Nunn said.

"Sucker, just what the hell are you doing back?"

"The wheels came off."

"They always do, don't they. On the first hard bump. All right, you're back. We'll rap tomorrow after breakfast."

"Same office?"

"Now what do you think."

As they were moving away, Chilly took a partial pack of cigarettes from his pocket and threw them to Nunn. He shook his head, and turned back to the game.

"If Chilly wasn't doing the big bitch," Nunn told Manning, "he'd own half this state."

"The big bitch?"

"Forty to life and that's as hard as they come."

"But he seems so young."

"Chilly's twenty-five, maybe twenty-six, but he was born old. They've got him made, that's why they tied him down with so much time. He'll walk someday, but it's going to be awhile."

They were entering the rotunda of the south block—skid row, Nunn called it—where all new men were automatically celled. A block officer read their cell assignments from an onionskin flimsy. Manning drew A-3-64.

"Where's that?" he asked Nunn.

"Third tier, A-section, cell sixty-four. Come on, I'll take you halfway."

A case of wide metal stairs led up through the center of the block, and through the open metal door on each landing Manning received an impression of shadowed space and somehow dampness. On each landing they also passed a utility tunnel, crowded with pipes and wiring, and they seemed to stretch for a mile before they terminated in small rectangles of light. They were closed by barred doors and behind one of these doors an inmate, wearing a leather belt clustered with tools, stood waiting to be released.

"Just drive up?" he asked.

"Yeah," Nunn answered.

"Where'd you come in from?"

"Delano."

The floors were concrete and had once been painted a deep maroon that had now worn away to a pale tint, except in the corners where the original paint was still clinging in shrinking islands. All light was fluorescent, the fixtures clung to the wall like phosphorescent fungus, and did little to brighten the natural light that filtered through the paint, dust, and bird droppings that coated the outside windows.

Nunn paused on the third landing and pointed out a door with a large A painted on it. "Right through there—and take it slow. Keep dummied up until you learn your way around."

Manning started down the tier. The cells were numbered from one. He could see more of the building now, and the outer shell was similar to an enormous hangar, while the actual block of cells occupied the center as if it were a separate and smaller structure stored in the larger one. There was a steady and undifferentiated drone, a thousand conversations muffled in the concrete walls, broken by an occasional shout, and through this was threaded an intimation of music that seemed to be coming from everywhere at once as if it were a property of the air. Later Manning was to realize that this impression was created by the earphones, two in every cell, no one audible in itself, but together they created a subliminal murmur. It was *Tales from the Vienna Woods* he heard as he walked along the third tier for the first time.

The cells reminded him vaguely of exhibits, their uniform size—yes, they were like the window displays in the museum of natural history, where stuffed animals had stood each in a static splinter of its particular habitat. The cells in similar fashion reflected the men who lived in them, though the variation was naturally limited. Some were elaborately decorated with curtained shelves, set solid with family photos and

Christmas, Easter, and birthday cards grouped like shrines. Other cells were filthy—a shambles of peeling paint, floors furred with dust, the space under the bunk packed with old newspapers and magazines. Some displayed the Virgin, others were decorated with the calendars distributed by various religious organizations. Manning saw models of hot-rods, original oil paintings, hand-tooled copper plaques.

As he passed each cell he was aware of heads swiveling to stare at him, heads as meaningless as flesh-colored balloons with features painted on them.

"Hey, pop, where'd you fall from?"

"Did you just come in from Bakersfield? Did a stud called Jingles come in with you?"

"Hey, mac . . ."

"Hey, buddy . . ."

"Hey, man . . ."

". . . what's happening out in that free world?"

Manning hurried on, his face half hidden in his blanket roll. When he reached the cell assigned him he was shocked to find another man already inside. He had been hungering for solitude. Now he had to step into this tiny room and share it with a stranger.

The inmate was sitting in the top bunk, his back against one wall and his feet propped on the other. The cell was so narrow his knees were still as high as his head. He was reading. He glanced sideways, saw Manning, and closed the book on his finger. He took in the pillowcase of cell supplies and the blanket roll and for a moment his face betrayed disappointment—then he smiled.

Manning received an impression of dense black hair, a white eroded complexion, and light blue eyes sunken under heavy brows. Then a guard far down the tier was manipulating the automatic controls, causing a sound like muffled but rapidly approaching gunfire as the stops in the lever box were tried and discarded one by one until the door of cell 63 jerked and rolled open. Manning stepped in, holding his gear in front of him, and the door slammed at his back.

"Just come in?"

"Yes, an hour or so ago."

"Just an hour ago . . . oh, my name's Juleson. Paul Juleson." He held out his hand.

"Will Manning."

They shook hands solemnly.

"I'm afraid," Juleson said pleasantly, "that you're stuck with the bottom bunk. Not that there's any big difference. The light's a little better up here."

Now that he was inside, Manning realized that the cell was much too small to hold two men. It was no more than four by ten feet in floor space, and around eight feet high. The double bunk filled half the cell, the sink and toilet bowl protruded into what was left. Above the sink two warped wooden shelves teetered on L-braces. One shelf was stacked with books, the other was empty.

"That's your shelf," Juleson said, having followed Manning's brief inspection. "For your toilet gear and anything like letters you want to keep. Have you been here before?"

"No, this is my first time."

"I thought it might be. These cells were originally designed for one man. It's a hardship, but you get used to it."

"It was the same in the county jail. Always crowded. Men sleeping on the floor."

Juleson smiled and his somber eyes flickered. "The jail business is picking up. When they built this place they had no idea how popular it was going to become."

Manning walked to the rear of the cell and looked at the toilet. It had not been designed for comfort and below the waterline the bowl was deeply stained. "You hear about these places all your life," he said quietly, "but you never quite realize they exist in the same world you live in."

"I'm not sure they do. If there is an underworld, this is it. I've talked to men who have pulled time all over the country and they say it's the same everywhere. Here, I'll help you make up your bunk."

The routine task was grotesquely complicated by the confines of the cell, but Juleson showed Manning the method by which countless convicts had assisted each other to make their beds over the years. When the bunk was square Juleson jumped back into the upper and picked up his book.

"This is my fix," he said. "I lead other people's lives."

Manning slipped into the lower, and lay face up staring at the metal webbing bellied down in the rough contours of Juleson's body. Every time Juleson shifted to turn a page the entire bunk swayed. The subtle feeling that he wasn't well began to come on Manning again, and, even as he thought about it, his lips seemed to be swelling, growing thick and hypersensitive. A stitch ran down his side.

"What would happen if you took sick while you were locked up like this?" he asked.

"We'd rattle the bars until someone came to see what was wrong." Juleson's face appeared, upside down, over the edge of his bunk. "What's the matter? Don't you feel well?"

"I feel all right—I just wondered."

"The medical attention isn't bad. Sometimes you might get a fast shuffle on the sick line, but you have to remember that every shuck in the prison's in that line trying to play on the doctors for a cell pass, or a few days in the hospital. But if they see you're really sick, you probably get better attention here than you would on the streets. A lot of high-class specialists donate their time over here."

Manning wanted to continue the conversation, but he couldn't think of anything to say. He nodded to signify his thanks and Juleson went back to his book. Manning rolled over on his side, and his breath came with the tension of the awareness that he was breathing at all. His throat was thickening again.

"Shine em up!" someone said sharply outside the cell. Manning rose up to find himself staring into a pair of violently bitter eyes—green as he would imagine the deepest shades in the heart of an iceberg.

"Take off, Slim," Juleson said from the upper bunk.

"Ain't talking to you. I'm asking this new fellow if he'd like to get his shoes shined."

"I'm telling you to get out of here," Juleson said with greater force. "Now move on, you unclassifiable degenerate."

"Talk smart, don't you."

"Get!"

The man slipped away, his eyes lingering over Manning's feet as he left.

"Who was that?" Manning asked.

"Sanitary Slim. He's some kind of machinery. He always comes around and hits on the fish to shine their shoes. It's an obsession with him—he's got it like cancer."

Bells began to ring and minutes later the men from the yard were beginning to file in. More bells, and they stood up at the bars to be counted. Still another bell, and they were released, tier by tier, for dinner. Manning followed after Juleson and they entered what appeared to be an enormous cafeteria. They waited near the end of a long line that was passing in front of the steam table. Somehow Manning had expected silence, but the air was heavy with the shuffling blur of private conversation multiplied many times over and punctuated with the sharp clicking of metal on metal, speeded by repetition until it seemed like the whirring of a cloud of aluminum crickets, and added to this was the deeper racket caused by the beating of dippers against the trays as they were passed along the steam table. Manning closed his eyes.

"Hey," Juleson said quietly.

"I'll be all right."

"Believe me, you get used to all this—and maybe that's the worst thing that happens to you."

The food was better than the food he had been eating in the county jail, but he had no appetite for it. He picked at the edge of his fish, and drank half a cup of black coffee.

"Aren't you going to eat?" Juleson asked tentatively.

"No, I'm not hungry."

"May I have your fish? And the pie if you don't want it?"

"Certainly, help yourself."

Juleson hesitated, then drew Manning's tray next to his own. "I'm always hungry," he said in an apologetic tone.

Another bell sounded to send them filing from the mess hall, back to the cells. Again Juleson settled down with his book and Manning lay beneath him listening to the dry *flick, flick* as he turned the pages. Manning's mind began to move relentlessly towards the inventory he knew he had to take, and had been putting off ever since he heard the judge intoning ". . . as the law prescribes." And with those words killed Manning right there in front of his bench, executed his past and all the meaningful continuity of his life, destroyed Willard Manning and left an unknown in his place, a man whose nature and future he was afraid to guess at.

He was forty-four and it was apparent. He was soft and his wind was going. He had an incipient hernia, and definite hemorrhoids and there was no way to guess what illness and disabilities might be waiting in the gradual deterioration of his health. His upper teeth were false, and one dentist had already advised him to have the lowers extracted as well.

He didn't know how old he would be when they handed him back the right to wage economic war. But he might well be fifty. How would he survive? Who was going to hire a middle-aged, unbonded accountant with no record of previous employment? Who was going to hire a morals offender even with his excellent employment record? Yes, they would reason, but who knows what ideas he may have picked up in prison, what friends he might have made, schemes entered into. Why risk it? He's fifty anyway. They say you can never cure a sex offender.

What would he do? It seemed hopeless—at best the rest of his years would shiver in the shadow of his former life. But it never occurred to Manning to give up.

As he was falling asleep, he tried to remember the date. It seemed important he know what day it was, but he wasn't surprised when this simple fact eluded him. It was only by going back to the day of his arrest, when all normal time had ceased, and working forward week by week, that he was finally able to tell himself that it was November the 16th.

3

 $P_{\text{AUL JULESON}}$ read for an hour and forty-five minutes. Then he put his book aside, sat up tailor fashion, and started to roll a cigarette. He used the state-issue tobacco—it was free, but not exactly a bargain. There were two types available— a fine powdery rolling tobacco, called "dust"—and a pipe cut which wasn't quite inferior enough to warrant a derisive nickname. Originally the state tobacco was thought of as an important step forward in the advance of penal reforms because just previous to the first free issue two men had been killed for debt—between them they had owed four bags of Bull Durham. If the prison were to process tobacco and make it available to everyone, no one need die because he had borrowed a sack of Bull Durham he couldn't repay. But they had reckoned without the universal contempt for welfare of any kind, and the specifically convict resentment of anything provided by the state. The only inmates who smoked the tobacco were those who had absolutely nothing else and no way of getting anything and were still so lacking in pride they could acknowledge this publicly. It was widely held, though Juleson did not agree, that the state tobacco was deliberately spoiled, held to the lowest quality, so no one could possibly prefer it to the tailor-mades and pipe tobaccos sold on the inmate canteen at retail prices and, presumably, retail profits.

Juleson smoked the pipe cut, after first picking out the twigs and gravel and straining it through a piece of window screen. Sometimes he even washed it in an effort to eliminate the ancient musty taste that was its indelible hallmark. After that it wasn't too bad. But hard to roll. The smoke he was now finishing up bulged ominously in the middle. He frowned, studying his product—the paper was weakened with his saliva and if he tried to smooth out the hump he would probably tear the roll in two. He shrugged and lit up. He couldn't get the damn things rolled right. He'd been fooling with them for three years, five months, and some days, and he still couldn't roll a decent smoke.

Don't ask me, he said to the silent companion in the back of his head, I don't know why I don't quit. The flame started to trace up the seam as it will on a loosely rolled cigarette, but by holding it carefully in two fingers he managed to smoke some of it before it fell apart scattering coals and tobacco over his pants. He brushed the fire onto the floor. He still wanted a smoke.

Why didn't he find some comfortable way to earn a few packs a week? He thought, as he so often had, of the various methods available, but they were all such desperate shifts— little more than outright begging—selling your desserts, washing another man's socks and underwear. If you wanted to take the risk you could stand point for one of the poker or dice games, or run for one of the big yard books. You could make home brew and sell it. And at the bottom of the pile— or the top, Juleson acknowledged, depending upon your point of view—you could hire out for beatings, knifings, and other collection or revenge work.

As he knew from many previous reviews, he didn't want to do any of these things, or rather he didn't want the cigarettes badly enough to lower himself a little deeper into the greasy sump he conceived of as the institution's aggregate spirit —there were acids there which could dissolve the identity.

He had returned to his book before he remembered his birthday. He would be thirty next week. Not difficult to understand how he had forgotten it. Turning thirty in jail was many times more disturbing than turning twenty or twenty-five, just as the older prisoners always seemed more pathetic than the younger. It was the degree to which a significant part of an inmate's life was committed to the prison, and this degree had nothing to do with the amount of time he had been imprisoned, but was determined by the time he had left in life in which he could hope to be free of it. In passing thirty Juleson felt he had left behind, necessarily forever, the possibility that he would be freed as a young man. And he could resent this and regret it at the same time as he harbored the conviction that he did not deserve to ever be released. But the birthday check . . .

An aunt, who made her home in the state of Washington, always sent him a five-dollar money order for his birthday. Over the years the amount had never varied—he received the first the year he had turned ten and five dollars glittered like all possible fortune. And now twenty years later it would only buy two cartons of cigarettes, and yet that seemed no less a fortune. It wouldn't be necessary for the check to come, he could borrow a carton tomorrow at 3 for 2, the standard rate of interest. Chilly Willy, the biggest of the lenders, had stuff stashed all over the institution. A carton to him was no more than a wet butt.

Juleson picked up his book, but he couldn't get back into it. When he had first come to prison he had been able to loan himself to the most obvious fiction, timeworn devices held him enthralled simply because no matter how impoverished they were, or lacking in freshness, they were more interesting than the life around him. But over the years he was losing the capacity to respond. He sometimes spent his entire lunch hour prowling the shelves in the library without finding a single book he could read with pleasure. With many the tone and content of the first page was sufficient to cause him to return them to the shelf, and even with those books he checked out there were still a number he later discovered he couldn't read. He sometimes withdrew as many as twenty-five books a week, and when he found one he could enjoy it was an event in his life. He had long since read the world's classics, and current novels by first-rate writers were in great demand, and it was only rarely he was able to find one of them on the open shelves. Still he continued to read constantly. There was nothing else to do.

His new cell partner appeared to be asleep. He was fortunate to have drawn this apparently decent man. He wondered how Manning would fit into the prison zoo. Would he hop around and grunt and apologize continually because he wasn't covered with fur, or would he adopt Juleson's own strategy and hide out in a corner watching the animals from a distance and taking every precaution necessary to keep free of them in all essential ways?

It was too early to expect to fall asleep, but he undressed and got under the covers. He stared up at the mottled ceiling and automatically the defenses he had raised against his memories moved in to protect him. He refused to remember even after three and a half years, but his sense of loss still retained its power to punish him. In his unguarded moments he missed small things—the sound of high heels on a pavement, sweet smells, and the pleasure he had found riding home on the bus after a day's work. He missed dogs and children.

He drifted into one of his favorite fantasies in which he had the power of teleportation and could move anything anywhere just by thinking it was where he wanted it. He flew out over the prison above the solid square heart of interlocking cellblocks, over the cream stucco and red tile of the education building, where in another incarnation he had once worked, he passed along the length of the old industrial building and around the walls that closed in the lower yard, noting the laundry, the foundry, the power plant, and pausing to float high above the sally port he caused its double gates to be deposited in the Sahara. Then he drifted over the athletic field and dispatched the metal goalposts to the Gobi. Turning back to the old industrial building he removed all the fire escapes that clung to it like blackened ivy and lodged them on a glacier north of Mount Doonerak. He stripped the gun rail from the north block and watched it vanish into the Brazilian rain forest. The all-clear light followed. The chair from the gas chamber, an apple green with sturdy straps, he deposited in the governor's mansion, drawn up to the table ready for the governor's breakfast.

As a last gesture, he hoisted the roof from the rain shed, a thousand square feet of galvanized iron, and wedged it into a rocky pass near the top of the Canadian Rockies.

He did not intend to be destructive, he thought, still drifting through the cool night; he only wanted to disrupt their air of grim seriousness and point out that they were all involved in the same cosmic joke.

The fun would come in the morning when his quixotic subtractions were discovered. He decided to wait. His revenge was Puck's revenge, a mockery, still he needed to see it, but he saw no reason to wait alone and he began to leaf through the slender album of his experience for a companion. He considered a slender violet-eyed girl named Janice Lee. He had never done more than kiss her and her untasted charms had thus proved more durable. He placed her sitting on the edge of his bunk, and had her turn slowly, her violet eyes opening like soft flowers, to discover him waiting for her.

—Why, Paul—how nice.

—Hello, Janice Lee. Are you still whacky for khaki?

—Oh, you remember that? I married a Navy man. Didn't I write you once and tell you?

—I think you did.

—I told you how unhappy I was.

—Yes, I remember.

He reached out to take her arm. He could recall the right qualities of softness and warmth as if he were actually feeling them. He began to concentrate in an effort to bring back every detail, not only of Janice Lee, but of all that was essentially female. He kissed her deeply and her breast formed beneath his hand.

—Why didn't you answer my letter? she asked.

Before he could catch himself he had answered, Because by that time I was married myself. And Anna Marie, his wife, entered his mind with the force of a scream, and the whole juvenile masturbation collapsed in an instant.

At 10 P.M. the light went out, controlled from a panel in the block office, and Juleson turned to the wall. He pressed his forehead against the painted cement for the coolness. His pillow seemed to grow hot as soon as he put his cheek against it, and he turned it repeatedly, shifting the cooler undersurface to the top. He would not sleep until he could forget how badly he wanted to be unconscious. He was aware of Manning shifting restlessly beneath him. Finally, the other man got up and used the toilet. His breath seemed labored in the silence of the cell. He was standing and he seemed to remain, half leaning against the wall for several minutes.

"Don't you feel well?" Juleson asked in a whisper.

Manning's voice shook. "I'm afraid I'm sick."

4

THE PRISON is never at rest. The incident rate slows at night, but it doesn't ever cease. It slows because with the exception of a few trusted to watch over the vitals of light and heat, the entire inmate body is confined in cells from 10 P.M. to 7 A.M. It doesn't cease, because they are locked two to a cell. They gamble, fight, build fires, practice various perversions, and sometimes kill one another.

At night the guard staff is reduced by two-thirds and the ratio then runs at approximately one guard to a hundred and seventy-five convicts. The night bulls would find themselves in a desperate minority if the cons ever broke loose, but they never have, and first watch is considered an easy turn reserved for young and inexperienced officers, or old screws pushing retirement, or the cowards afraid to beat the yard shoulder to shoulder with the enemy in the blue uniform.

These first-watch officers walk the gun rails, their flashlights lingering over the barred gloom of the lightless cells, tier on tier, five tiers high, one hundred cells long. From the gun rail the block looks like a metal honeycomb, or perhaps more accurately like a huge multiple trap, sprung now on its unimaginable quarry while the will-o'-the-wisp of the trapper's flash moves from snare to snare in quiet approval. Other night bulls sit out in the towers above the floodlit walls and blocks. They sip black coffee, read girlie magazines, or watch the moonlight slowly shifting on the empty concrete seventy-five feet below them. The prison seems like a walled city, smothered under a rigid curfew, governed by an alien army.

The gun rail guards are required to wear crepe-soled shoes, and they try to move silently, not, as any con is quick to say, out of consideration for inmate sleep, but to cause those who might plot at night to think of the gun bull as drifting like a shadow—a phantom who in as many imaginations could silently keep all the thousand cells under simultaneous surveillance. In dull fact their approach is betrayed to those who have reason to listen by the creaking of the leather harness that supports the guns, both rifle and pistol, they are required to carry.

Terrence Preston was embarrassed by these deadly tools. Two seemed excessive. He even wondered if he really needed a weapon at all since the most he usually saw of an inmate was an occasional blurred smudge of white tee shirt moving in a lightless cell. He had been warned—first by the training officer, then by his watch lieutenant—of the times when cell bars had been secretly sawed, and inmates had suddenly appeared, incredible aliens, in guard country. Guards *were* killed, his superiors had impressed on him. Still Preston couldn't imagine an inmate on the gun rail. He tried to picture one swinging over on an umbilical of knotted sheets, a handmade knife in his teeth, desperation in his heart . . . Preston smiled. He couldn't see it.

He paused to push a scrap of orange peel from the rail and listen to the soft *pat* as it hit the concrete below him. Inmates were always throwing garbage onto the gun rail and Preston felt the practice represented an expression of hostility. It was a point worth making in his psych class tomorrow. The garbage would traditionally relate to feces. He smiled again. The infant inmate throwing feces at the father guard. But couldn't it as easily be a gift? An offering of something precious? Even a gift of love? He paused. There was a suspicious neatness, a jigsaw puzzle banality to the smooth interlocks of his speculation. He paced off another leg of his round and stopped to rest on the uncloseted toilet provided against an emergency. For a moment he had had an uneasy feeling, now he nodded firmly answering some invisible authority— it was a good point. Preston frequently made such points, based, he told his fellow students, on his observation of the inmates. Actually he had never spoken to an inmate. His "points" served to light his single distinction. He was working his way through college as a prison guard. He liked answering the questions he was always being asked. He had decided to take his degree in psychology and continue to work in the prison as psychologist. He believed he could help these men.

"Preston!"

He heard his name in a hissing whisper and looked down to discover the floor officer directly beneath him. The upturned face in the extreme foreshortening appeared to be sprouting shoes from immediately under the chin.

"Yo," he whispered back.

"Come over to A-section and cover me. I've got a sick one."

"Right."

He followed along above the floor officer, watching the circle of his hat below, until they reached A-section, then he took up a position close to the center of the section and held his rifle at port. A door crashed, hurled by mechanical hands, and a sighing murmur ran through the block as if the men had collectively groaned and turned in their sleep.

"Radio," some man called irritably.

"Radio yourself, punk," someone else called.

Then Preston heard a sound he dreaded. In one of the cells just across from him an inmate hidden in the darkness was pushing his breath through his teeth to make a noise like air leaking from a punctured inner tube, bubbling through the spit. Preston knew what to expect.

"See the sweet little bull?" an anonymous voice asked in a tone that combined both amusement and obscenity.

Preston jerked his eyes away. He felt his face growing hot. Pay no attention to them, his watch lieutenant had told him; if they see they're getting to you they'll never let you up.

"Pussy on the gun rail," another voice called.

"Hey, sucker, don't rank my action," the first voice continued with mock seriousness. "I saw her first. Didn't I, baby? Slip over here on the tier and I'll give it to you through the bars."

Preston lifted his hand suddenly, then didn't know why he had lifted it. In confusion he tugged at the brim of his hat and adjusted the temple bar of his heavy-rimmed glasses. He made himself stare sternly at the open cell. In a moment a half-dressed man appeared, his arms wrapped tightly around his chest, and even from the rail ten feet away his shivering was obvious.

"Go right down to the office," Preston told him.

"Let me come down to the office," his hidden tormentor began again. "I'll make it good to you."

"Knock it off, men," Preston ordered, unconsciously dropping his voice a half-octave below its normal pitch, and he heard his tone, hollow and absurdly faked like that of a boy of ten picked to play Daniel Webster in a school pageant. He cringed even before the delighted laughter started.

The sick one was shuffling down the tier and Preston quickly turned to shadow him. He pretended not to hear the chorus of whistles.

The sick man was taken up to the massive double doors that opened to the prison hospital, and there he had to wait for fifteen minutes until an officer showed up with the key.

The clinic filled the front section of the hospital block. At night a Medical Technical Assistant, universally shortened to MTA, a free man, was on duty there, and he, in turn, was assisted by two inmate orderlies. This night the MTA was playing chess with one of the orderlies, the board set up on the treatment table in minor surgery, while they leaned over it propped on their elbows. The second orderly sat on the instrument stand watching without much interest, swirling two inches of lukewarm instant coffee in the bottom of a jam jar. The clinic had the lunar appearance of all large white rooms lit with fluorescent light and the faces over the chessmen were blue-tinged as putty.

When the key sounded in the lock, the MTA looked up to watch the ponderous door swing slowly out, exposing a widening section of the south block rotunda, its riffraff drabness in vivid contrast to the bright arctic order of the clinic. The sick man slipped in, still hugging himself, and a guard followed. The MTA blew his breath out through slack lips in a weariness colored with theater. He turned back to the game and with his index finger gently nudged his rook a single square right, opening a discovery check by a patient bishop that had stood waiting on the same square since the third move of the game.

"That's got you," he said.

"Maybe," the orderly mumbled, "and maybe not."

The MTA snorted and started over towards the sick man, rubbing his densely furred arms and yawning. "What's your number?" he asked.

"I don't remember."

"Come on."

"I just came in today."

"I see. Well, we wouldn't have a card on you anyway. What's the trouble?"

But before the sick man could begin to tell him, the MTA had his ears plugged with a stethoscope. He checked him over rapidly, told him flatly that the most serious thing wrong with him was a bad case of dandruff, gave him an ounce of diluted bromide, and ordered him back to his cell.

"They can't sleep," he told the guard, "so they might as well come on down and see what's going on in the hospital. They figure the doctor might invite them to share a jug."

He knew it was more than that. There came a night, the first night or the hundredth night, when they had to ask someone, anyone, to care about them. They had to prove that help and comfort could still be summoned, that they wouldn't be left alone to die in the dark.

The orderly was still studying the board.

"Come on, Ghost, concede, and we'll play another," the MTA said.

"Concede shit," Ghost said tightly. "There's an out somewhere."

"You could tip the board over."

"There's an out."

"Well, while you're looking for it, Joey and I'll go up and shoot that cancer."

Joey drank the last of his coffee and reached over to put the jar in the surgery sink. He slid loosely from the instrument table and opened his fly to resettle his shirt. Then he smoothed and straightened the creases in his hospital whites. His hair was carefully combed. His eyes were quick.

They stopped first at the hospital safe in the pharmacy where the MTA logged out an ampul of morphine. Joey was required to stand clear while the combination was being worked, but once the safe was open he joined the MTA and selected a syringe which he took to the sink to test for cloggage. The needle was clear and the water spurted in a thin sturdy thread. He passed the syringe to the MTA.

The cancer was in a single room on the third floor. He was terminal, his pain beyond control, but massive doses of morphine eased him and permitted him some sleep. He was awake when Joey and the MTA entered and his eyes turned to them in the slow devoted reflex of an old dog. He tried to smile, but pain tore the intention before it could form on his mouth—he grimaced instead.

The MTA loaded the syringe and handed it to Joey to administer.

Joey smiled, his eyes oblique. "We should mainline him. Give him some final kicks."

The MTA frowned and shook his head. "Knock that off. This isn't funny."

Joey shrugged and lifted the cancer's wasted arm. Under the watchful eye of the MTA he placed the needle against the loose flesh. The MTA saw the needle slide in but what he didn't see was that Joey had positioned it so low on the arm —and the cancer's arm was so thin—that when he pressed it home the needle went clear through the patient's slack muscle into the soft flesh at the base of Joey's own thumb. He pushed the plunger and felt immediate warmth etch the veins of his forearm. A moment later a sensation he always thought of as a big soft pumpkin hit the back of his head.

On the way back to the clinic the MTA said, "That stuff doesn't seem to help him much."

"They get that far gone, nothing helps much."

"How do you suppose he feels dying in a prison hospital?"

Joey shrugged and looked away. "It's like dying anywhere else, I guess."

When they reached the clinic the phone was ringing, a call to condemned row, and they left again with Ghost still frozen in the bishop's ambush.

Condemned row, almost always called death row except in official documents, is buried deep in the center of the north block, guarded there by the mass around it like a fragile organ. The MTA and Joey had to pass three manned and locked doors, besides a remote-controlled and telescanned elevator, before they entered the bland white-tiled corridor, lined with cells which were painted in three alternating pastel shades: primrose, dusty pink, and nile green. It was drenched with light, the tile blazed and the eyes of the officer on duty were weary and red-rimmed. The death row sergeant, his feet crossed on a gray metal desk, sat at the head of the corridor.

The MTA asked, "Anything serious?"

"I doubt it," the sergeant said. "It's Wagner. He's got a gut ache."

He took a leather pouch of large keys from his desk and called to the officer on the door, "Back me up. They're going to take a look at Wagner."

"Isn't he the kid that shot a cop in Oakland?" the MTA asked.

"That's him. Eighteen when he pulled the trigger. I doubt he sees nineteen."

"No hope of commutation?"

"Not a ghost," the sergeant told him, whispering now because they were outside Wagner's door.

Wagner's cell was painted primrose, a little larger than a mainline cell. A bunk, a stool, a metal table all were bolted to the floor, and his light bulb was barred away in a little cage of its own as if its offense were even greater than Wagner's.

The MTA knelt by the side of the bunk. "What's the trouble, kid?"

"My gut. I ate that greasy hamburger."

"Better let me take a look," the MTA said, pulling the gray blankets away from Wagner's chin. It disturbed him to discover Wagner was small, maybe a hundred and twenty pounds, no more than five-five. He probed the flat white abdomen for rigidity and finding none he dosed Wagner for indigestion.

He smiled. "Okay, kid, that'll take care of you." He stood up and nodded at the sergeant.

"Doc," Wagner said. "Look, Doc, how about a goofball?"

The MTA frowned. So that was it. And why not? Movie broads gobbled up yellow jackets like they were jelly beans, surely this dead kid ought to rate one.

He gave Wagner a Nembutal, drew him a cup of water, and waited until he had made sure the boy had swallowed it—a routine death row precaution like the plastic spoon Wagner was given to eat with and the locked razor he shaved with.

As they left, Joey said, "Take it slow, man."
And Wagner sat up to answer, "I take it very slow."

He remained sitting to watch the door close, folding into darkness, a darkness where the judas window hung like a square, gray, and stationary star, the only light now except for its own faint reflection from the white metal toilet top hanging in the corner, unconnected, like a ghostly zero.

It was his own fault he couldn't sleep. He took too many naps during the day. He warned himself against it, thinking of the slow night hours to wear away without any possible distraction except his own disabled thoughts. But the temptation to sleep, to forget, was too strong. Through the months he had spent on death row, that part of each day which he could hope to lose in sleep had grown shorter and shorter. He tried exercise, hundreds of push-ups, deep knee bends; he paced his cell. Nothing helped. It didn't occur to him that if to be unconscious was better than waking, then to be unconscious forever might be best of all.

Instead he dreamed of miracles. The miracles of the future: commutation to life imprisonment, abolishment of the death penalty, wild, impossible escapes, and the outbreak of the total atomic war. And the miracles of the past. In his mind he started out again and again the night of the robbery, but he left his gun unloaded. Or he dreamed he had shot to the side, the floor, the ceiling, anyplace but into the cop, whose death was going to cause his own.

He got up and, wrapping a blanket around his shoulders, sat on the toilet. Sometimes if he sat up awhile he would begin to feel sleepy. The hard toilet made the bunk seem comfortable. He rolled a cigarette and smoked it, flicking the ash between his legs.

The few times he was able to think about the night he had killed the policeman with the hard precision of true recall, he realized that there had been no intention on his part which he might have deflected or reversed. Again he would see the cop flash in front of him, and instantly he felt his hand jump as if pulled by the gun. As if the gun had been set to make its own murder.

There was nothing he could have turned back—except not to have robbed the store, not to have had the gun, not to have been in reform school where he had learned to want the gun, and, ultimately, not to have been himself.

Gratefully he felt the first sweet drift of smoke as the Nembutal began to work in his bloodstream.

In the condemned cell next to Wagner's, Oscar Raymond Johnson, convicted of the rape-murders of two women, both in their sixties, caressed his crotch as he thought: They goin fry my ass like a egg, but, man, man, man, them grannies was good.

Directly behind Wagner's cell, across a narrow utility tunnel clogged with the thick black bowels of the sewage system, was another cell, a twin, a Siamese twin since they were wired from the same outlet and a single valve released water to both toilets. But while they were identical physically, spiritually it was as if one twin had been assured he would die within the month, while the second had found no reason to doubt he would continue to live forever.

Stick was confined in the second cell—a holding cell in the isolation unit known as the shelf. The goon squad had hustled him into the cell and he had been ignored since, except for his evening meal served from a portable steam table. He had flushed the food down the toilet.

He had been drawn up tight. For a long time he had walked up and down and occasionally he slapped the side of his face smartly as if a gnat had just landed on his cheek. His eyelids had seemed to be twitching and his armpits were cold. Every few minutes he had pressed against the door trying to see through the hairline crack at its edge, but he could make out only a formless green blur which he knew to be the far wall of the corridor. Then he moved to the back of the cell and jabbed the round button above the sink to watch the water pour into the basin. In time he realized he was thirsty and he bent to gulp at the stream as if he were biting it. The excess water spilled down the side of his chin and wet the collar of the blue denim coverall they had given him to replace the one he had worn from Delano.

When fatigue had worn the harshest edge from his tension, he began to look around for something to draw with and discovered a pencil stub hidden under the mattress. The lead was worn down smooth with the wood, but he managed to sharpen it with his teeth, biting the wood away until enough graphite was exposed to mark the wall. He drew the Vampire.

Then he lay down to stare up at the bare ceiling. After a while his immediate awareness began to blur and he felt better. He sensed he was growing stronger and stronger and the indication of his increasing strength was the poised glow of well-being in the pit of his stomach. He didn't need his arms to read the message of his power, he felt it in his gut at its source.

He stood up and, moving with a polished coolness suggestive of the floating grace of an athlete caught on slow-motion film, he broke the metal door from its frame, crumbling it as if it were cardboard, and stepped into the corridor. A bull came running towards him, clearly running from pure reflex. The stunned amazement in his eyes was delicious. Deftly Stick swooped and seizing the officer by the ankle he spun around in a half-circle and pitched him the length of the corridor. His scream printed itself in Stick's mind as EEEEEEEEEEEEEEEE—the first E an enormous yellow capital which funneled off, smaller and smaller, until the final E vanished in a tiny star at the point of impact. A second officer sat at a metal desk. He was swooning with terror.

Stick tore open the door to the elevator, but discovered the car was at the bottom of the shaft. Rather than wait for it to rise, he slid down the cables, and plunged through the side of the shaft to land lightly in the north block rotunda. They were waiting as he had known they would be—ranks of uniformed men with square white teeth and tiny black eyes. Their heads were covered with scarlet bristle. They closed on him behind the jagged flare of small arms fire. He arched his chest and the bullets glanced off harmlessly, bouncing back to kill his attackers. He grew steadily stronger. He looked up to see the convicts watching him, tiers of them pressed against the bars of their cells.

—Free us, Vampire, they called. Free us and we're your men.

They shook the metal doors in their frames until the block thundered. With great clarity he saw his Generals, both in the same cell. They stood at attention as he had taught them, pounding their chests in the Roman salute, their faces firm with pride.

—Free us, Lord.

He wrenched the door from their cell and they fell in behind him as he moved down the tier tearing off each door as he came to it. His army formed behind him. His army formed behind him and began to sing, and their voices combined into a single voice . . .

Someone shouted and the singer fell silent. It was a moment before Stick realized he had shouted. He turned over and pressed his face against the hard pillow. He tried to guess the time. If he knew what time it was he would know how many hours he had been alone. No one even bothered to open the small metal window to look in on him. Were they that confident there was nothing he could do?

He stripped the top blanket from his bed and stuffed it into the toilet. He began to press the button. The toilet was a Standard Instanto and without a reservoir to refill it flushed constantly. Soon water was flowing across the floor and beginning to drain through the crack at the base of the door.

The water was around Stick's ankles before the door flew open and it was free to rush into the corridor. The officer looked at his wet shoes, then looked at Stick.

"You miserable punk," he said.

Still they didn't beat him. They stripped off his coveralls and locked him in a different cell, and he found himself naked in an absolutely bare room. The monotony of cement was broken only by a three-inch hole in the middle of the floor, and directly above the hole, higher than he could reach, a light burned behind a frosted pane. When he stretched out to put his ear to the hole, he heard running water. He caught the faint scent of urine and sat up quickly, his mouth working with revulsion. This is the end of the line, a voice in his head said quietly. You made it in record time. The cement was cold against his bare skin, and he stood up to begin pacing. He began to slap his cheek. He paused and ran his thumbnail down the concrete wall. The surface was hard and smooth and his nail turned under. He couldn't even draw the Vampire. You've got to play it keen, he whispered to himself. Keen. He crooned the word, seeking comfort in the thought of its power.

The MTA returned to find that Ghost had conceded the game in his absence, but had managed to sour the concession with his usual soreheadedness. Ghost had simply cleared the board, boxed the men, and retreated into the clinic can to practice on his guitar. He was trying to learn "Your Cheatin' Heart." This was the song he intended to sing to his wife when he became a big-time country and western singer. She was a dirty, cheating, loose-legged slut, and he intended to make it plain for the whole world to see. He didn't picture it too clearly but usually he seemed to be wearing a white hat and a white leather jacket with fringe and he was sitting up on the back seat of a white convertible, big as a goddam iceberg, his eyes real cool and careless, and he'd be loving up some cute little ol' gal sitting beside him—some way he'd make that bitch regret the day she started shacking with that fool and cut off his smoke money.

The MTA heard Ghost's guitar, muffled by two doors, but he didn't go in to ask about the game because he knew from experience that Ghost would claim he had found a way to avoid the mate, but had just got tired of waiting around, and it was only an old game anyway.

The MTA was busy again in twenty minutes. A Mexican boy called Baby de Flats had slashed up the face of another Mexican boy known as Conejo with a ragged sliver of glass from a broken Pico Pico Hot Sauce bottle. Baby had heard indirectly that Conejo, his cellmate for six months, had been a narcotics snitch on the streets.

The MTA worried about the effect of hot sauce in open wounds, got the O.D. out of bed to come in and take a look. The inmate photographer, immediately summoned from his cell, arrived to take a series of photographs, front, left profile, right profile, of Conejo's face recording the cuts in the event Baby was tried for assault. As he was kneeling for the full-face, Conejo's eyes cleared for a moment. He looked at the blood on his hands.

"I ain't no snitch," he said.

The watch lieutenant preserved the sliver of Pico Pico Hot Sauce bottle in a manila envelope, which he locked in the hot room. He called the hospital to learn that the O.D. had Conejo half mended and that complications were not anticipated. Then he phoned the warden's residence to report the incident.

Charlie Wong, the warden's inmate houseboy, answered the phone.

"Let me talk to the old man, will you, Charlie."

"Ver' solly, Loot, Missy Sheeley he no here."

"Well, where is he?"

"He say, he go eat with some klind animal."

"What?"

"Animal. Some klind animal. Missy Sheeley he say—"

"Go screw yourself, you slant-eyed bastard," the lieutenant said and hung up. He took a pad from his desk and began to write his report.

The animals Charlie had the warden eating dinner with were Moose. The Loyal Order of Moose, seventy-five strong, and just now listening to their own chairman introducing the guest speaker.

Warden Michael L. Sheeley listened to his own introduction with an expression so utterly neutral that each individual Moose, once the open secret was out, could read there his own conception of an ideal prison warden. His thoughts, however, were far from neutral. He looked down, seemingly in modest avoidance of the chairman's enthusiasm, to check the fatty rim of Virginia baked ham left on his plate. He hoped he had managed to eat enough of it to avoid offending any of the brothers. Sheeley enjoyed addressing civic organizations and fraternal orders, he was able to describe and win some support for his various reforms, and he recognized enough of the player in himself to enjoy his turn, but the edge was lost to the relentlessly unvaried dinners: small stony peas, frozen mashed potatoes, and a thin oily slice of ham. Charlie, his houseboy and cook, had explained to him that ham offered the minimum expense and trouble to a caterer and that unless some alternate was specifically requested ham was inevitable. This served to add resentment to an already well-established distaste. He was once again wondering if he could successfully fake an ulcer when he heard polite applause and turned to find the chairman flourishing his palm. Sheeley rose smiling.

For the Moose he gave one of his set talks. "Prisons Are Not for Punishment" elaborated on the text that the bare fact of confinement was a heavy punishment, a sufficient punishment, and that this time should be spent by an inmate as comfortably and constructively as reasonably possible.

The applause at his conclusion was mild. He bowed into it acknowledging his disappointment that what he felt it important to say was not what they hoped to hear from a prison warden. They expected theater—stories, pictures of grotesques and human curios, and details of various executions. Some of these questions came later as the dinner was breaking up. Four or five businessmen and a possible reporter detained Sheeley as he was preparing to leave. One, a pinkfaced fat man who wore a pearl ring on his little finger, asked, "In confidence don't you think our prisoners are being coddled?"

"No, I don't think they are."

The possible reporter—Sheeley was basing his guess on nothing more concrete than that the man wore a sport coat and needed a haircut—took it up. "Warden, I remember reading somewhere that over fifty per cent of your parolees are returned on violations. It wouldn't seem that your prison frightened them much. Perhaps it beats working?"

"They're required to work in the institution. Some work hard—"

"And some don't."

"That's true," Sheeley admitted. "We're badly overcrowded, there aren't enough jobs for everyone. We need larger facilities."

"Ever larger?" the possible reporter asked meaningfully, but before the warden could answer the man with the pearl ring had interrupted.

"What about sex," he wanted to know. "What do they do about sex?"

"The same thing most boys do."

"Surely, you have some problems along those lines, Warden?"

"Yes, some. There is bound to be a certain number of inverts and degenerates in any group of people, and naturally in a prison population the percentage is apt to run higher."

"How do you control these people, or do you let them run wild?"

"No, we segregate them when we discover them, but many develop a complete cover personality and are nearly impossible to detect unless the officers catch them right in the act."

The possible reporter asked, "Do you see many of the executions, Warden?"

"I'm required by law to witness them all."

"And how do you feel about them, are you—"

"They make me sick," Sheeley snapped. "Now if you gentlemen will please excuse me I have to return to the institution."

He drove to the prison by himself, using the car the state furnished him. When he turned onto the access road above the institution he slowed to watch the lights moving over the walls like golden fans. He traced the perimeter to check the green all-clear glowing secure at the tip of each tower. What an incongruously beautiful scene it made, the prison like a dense and massive castle, elfin with Christmas light, and all repeated, if magically reversed, in faithful detail on the still dark water of the bay.

He found Wong nodding in front of the TV. "You didn't have to wait up, Charlie."

Wong smiled shyly. "I think maybe you be hungry, boss. That ham not do much for you, all right?"

"Just a sandwich then. And a glass of milk."

While he waited he sat at his desk and read some of the

memos he hadn't found time for during the day. There was one marked Confidential, from the captain of the guard, stating that his informants were still reporting large quantities of contraband nasal inhalers within the institution, but he couldn't trace the source. Also there were rumors of marijuana which could mean a new route had been opened up.

The warden removed his glasses and rubbed his eyes. Their tireless ingenuity! He recalled the time he had ordered the locks changed in the prison commissary, and two days later an inmate had been apprehended with a complete set of keys to the new locks. If only there were some way to reach into their minds and switch such intelligence and energy into constructive channels, but if this were possible the prison would never have been built.

He replaced his glasses and noted *Keep watching, they'll slip* on the margin of the captain's memo. It was true. Sheeley had worked up through the ranks and he was quite familiar with the inmate weakness they called showboating. The prisoner who held the power to regulate the traffic in inhalers would have to talk about it, floor show, and let it be known that he was Big Dad to all cotton freaks, and he would be subtly pressured into this dangerous admission because there was so little in the prison routine that could make a man feel important, or in any way special, or, for that matter, even simply feel like a man. The need for recognition grew like hunger. In time he would showboat and the captain would hear about it.

Wong brought a turkey sandwich and a glass of milk on a tray.

"You better go on inside, Charlie. Thanks for waiting up."

"Okay. What time you get up?"

"The usual."

"You be plenny tired, boss, better to sleep in."

"No, I've a lot coming up tomorrow. Good night, Charlie."

"Okay. Night, boss."

Wong left by the front door, but turned quickly and ducked into the garage where he loosened the right front hubcap on the warden's car. In the space behind it he found a kilo of pot and—he grinned happily in the dark—a small cake of yen-shee where they had been hidden for him by Sammy Low, Charlie's cousin and fellow member of Hop Sing, while the warden was addressing the Moose.

Charlie made no effort to hide his loot. He dropped it into his jacket pocket, replaced the hubcap and started towards the front gate. He passed through the double doors, grinning, nodding, and wearing the invisibility that shrouded him as a joint character, who could move with no more notice than "that crazy Chinaman" into the most closely controlled areas of the prison.

Once inside he took a deep breath and started through the Garden Beautiful towards the brightly lit trap known as four-box. Four-box was the main custodial nerve center within the walls, and all traffic from one part of the prison to another passed in front of its large curious windows. At night Old Tom sat in this web's center like a huge, benign, and drowsing spider. Old Tom was regular, a good bull, which meant he didn't like going through all the red tape involved in reporting a beef, but neither could Old Tom be taken for granted. About one night a month he was prodded into wakefulness by an intense and smoldering irritation and on such nights he would literally beef you because he didn't like your looks. This peculiar and curiously regular trait was popularly attributed to menstrual snappishness, an attribution as mean as it was unlikely, for Old Tom, whether male or female, was thirty years free of the moon, and his appearance was so gross as to make Dog Breath, an awesomely homely Negro fruiter, appear a vision of feminine loveliness.

Charlie, still playing it bold, walked by four-box with no more than an airy wave for Old Tom, who appeared half asleep, sprawled so deep in his swivel chair his hooded eyes were just visible behind the khaki mountain of his belly. Charlie made another twenty feet.

"Hey, Wong," Tom said, ominously out of his chair, standing in the four-box door motioning him back. "What would I find if I was to shake you down?"

Charlie stopped five feet away and grinned delightedly. "Plenny, you find plenny. Much mari-ha-ha, maybe a little yen pox—and a flied egg sandwich. You keep sandwich, okay, boss?"

Old Tom smiled sourly and waved him on with a hand that looked like a softball mitt left out all winter and chewed by anything hungry enough to waste time on it.

"That Chinaman's a goddam nut," he said to Angelo. Angelo didn't answer and Tom hadn't expected him to.

Angelo, between his rounds as night fire watchman, sat behind Old Tom on an apple box, padded by the simple device of nailing a pillow across it. Angelo was seventy-nine and serving his fifty-sixth consecutive year in prison. He was twenty-three the last time he had kissed a woman, and that woman was his wife the week before he cut off her head. Legend had it that he took the severed head, hidden in a paper bag, to the bar where he did his drinking. He ordered whiskey, and when the drink was placed before him he pulled the head from the bag, sat it up on the bar and told it, "Now nag, you sonabitch."

This is just a story, and Angelo had been in so long, longer than any other prisoner, because he refused to leave and return to a world he remembered only as something he might have dreamed. When, on his rounds, he passed one of those points in the institution from which the lights of San Francisco are visible the sight had no real meaning to him. Once in a while he stopped to stare at the glistening and mysterious hills across the bay with the same sense of awe and apprehension with which early men viewed the stars.

His rounds were made hourly throughout the night. First he checked the education building, shuffling down the main aisle, shifting the watered beam of his old flash along the upper walls because he felt himself severely regarded by the painted eyes of Ralph Waldo Emerson, Thomas Alva Edison, Theodore Roosevelt, Justice Holmes, and the other heroes of the republic hung here for the beneficial aura of their moral charisma. His light respectfully touched each portrait, surprising the watching face in the shadow of its frame, and to Angelo this was a ritual as solemn as the Stations of the Cross because he believed these men to be former wardens, dead now, arranged in regal succession, and he thought he remembered Emerson as that sonabitch Pennypacker, who built a brick kiln with public funds and made a fortune selling labor-free brick, watered with convict sweat and baked with convict hate. Angelo had worked the kiln in the first years of his imprisonment when he still had a chest like a barrel, curved mustaches as bold as scimitars and a man's capacity for hating.

After the ed building, he checked the chapels, the dental department and the hobby shop. Then he turned down the steep and lightless hill that led to the industrial alley. Here the cats met him.

There might have been anywhere from five to twenty cats rubbing joyously around Angelo's legs depending upon how long it had been since custody had last sacked up the excess and tossed them into the bay. This routine reduction of the cat population was clearly necessary, otherwise the institution would have been quickly overrun by them, but few inmates accepted this ecological justification and it was understood by the majority that bulls were natural bastards and if nothing else to kill was handy, they'd kill cats.

Two cats had risen above this law, because for cats the law could still spare by regal whim, and both hero and fool, those mythic twins, had claimed their traditional immunity.

The fool was called Puchuco. He was tailless, cross-eyed, castrated, and all of one ear and half of the other had been chewed off. His head was flattened and lopsided like a rain-softened ball, and his right hind leg was drawn up until the paw rested an inch above the ground. When he howled at night it was painful to hear.

Sometimes the evening classes in the ed building looked down into the moonlit well of the industrial alley to see Puchuco playing there. Dancing a grotesque and halting ballet with a crumpled newspaper or a wad of cotton waste, he stalked this phantom prey with a parody of feral urgency like an overgrown and mutilated kitten. Those watching usually laughed, but a few grew angry and said, "Someone ought to pity that poor fucking cat enough to kill it."

The hero was a giant black tom with yellow eyes, a witch's cat, seamed with honorable scars, whose expression was so steady and still it seemed a look of utter certainty. The other toms were terrified of him and wouldn't come within a dozen yards when he was eating or courting. The inmates hailed him as Joe the Grinder, giving him the same wry name they gave to the man who made it into their wife's bed while they were locked, hopeless and despairing, in jail. Joe the Grinder wore their suits, wrecked their car, dug up their stash, played with their old lady's tits as she wrote: "Dear John, I miss you so much . . ." And, sooner or later, knocked the bitch up, at which point he split. The tom operated with equal ease. He was Joe the Grinder in his heart, as who might not wish to be, and the cons spun his nightly exploits into sagas of envy.

For a few moments each night here at the head of the industrial alley Angelo was the God of cats. Then the meat he had scavenged for them from the abandoned trays in the mess hall had been divided among them, and Angelo moved on into the shadows of the alley until his torch caught the unmatched and zany luminescence of Puchuco's eyes peering down from one of the metal steps of the fire escape that climbed the side of the industrial building like a rusty Z.

"Here, ol' fellow," Angelo crooned softly.

Puchuco made a noise deep in his throat and his eyes disappeared for a moment to reappear a step lower.

"Come, ol' cat. You come eat."

Angelo sat down on the bottom step and pulled the last of the meat from his pocket to spread it on the step above him.

"I ever hurt you?" he asked Puchuco.

As the cat began to eat, Angelo rubbed the knobs of torn flesh around his mutilated ears.

Angelo ended his round with the old industrial building, a huge boxlike, and half-empty structure that had been condemned for ten years. The gym was on the third floor, the second floor was used for storage and sometimes football chalktalks and play rehearsals. The ground floor still housed working shops, and Angelo paced slowly between the stands of bulky machinery, not always certain any more just what it was he was looking for.

At one-thirty-five an officer with a prisoner in chains was admitted through the front gate. Tom didn't recognize the officer.

"Higgins," the officer said, offering his hand. "I'm from Camp Fourteen. Up in Del Norte?"

"You come a ways."

"Yes, it's a piece," Higgins admitted.

"How's the weather up there?"

"Winter's set in. We're already up to our ass in snow." He took off his uniform cap and looked at the lining. Apparently satisfied with the way it was holding up, he put it back on his head.

"This here boy, now," he said, nodding towards the prisoner standing quietly in handcuffs and restraining gear. "He took off on us. Gave us quite a chase until we got the dogs after him. They turned him up fast enough, shivering so hard it's a wonder he didn't shake his goddam teeth loose. Cold, weren't you, boy?" Higgins invited the prisoner to confirm it.

The prisoner shrugged, causing his chain to clink musically. "I was doing all right until you put dogs in the game. Them lousy bastards would starve before they'd track for food, but give them a chance to hunt a man and they can't start fast enough."

"You might as well get that iron off him," Tom told Higgins. "He ain't going to do no successful running from here."

"Didn't do no successful running from camp neither," Higgins said.

"What's his name? I'll phone control and get him a cell."

"Sarich."

Higgins removed the restraining gear with practiced efficiency. "You got smokes?" he asked.

"You know I ain't," Sarich said.

"Here." Higgins handed him a partial pack and Sarich sneered at them before he put them in his shirt pocket.

"I forgot you smoked them fruiter cigarettes."

"They're better for you," Higgins said mildly.

"Sure, they give you mentholated cancer."

"Frank, why did you rabbit? I can't figure it out. Was someone in camp putting pressure on you?"

Sarich scowled. "There ain't a swingin dick in camp that could do me harm and you know it."

"Well, what the hell did you run for then?"

"I felt like it."

"But you only had a few weeks left."

"I felt like it," Sarich said harshly. "What's so hard to understand about that?"

Old Tom finished on the phone and swiveled around to face them. "Take him over to the south block," he told Higgins. "They'll be waiting for him. Then you can be on your way back."

Sarich jammed his hands into his pockets. For a moment his eyes looked raw and his sneer seemed almost painful.

In the south block rotunda he said so long to Higgins and went to wait by the office window. An inmate keyman loitered there, a nut Sarich remembered from before. They called him Jo-Jo and no one added "the dog-faced boy" because Jo-Jo was too big and his expression too strange. This night he wore the top to a suit of Navy surplus wool underwear, jeans held up by the heavy belt that also supported his pouch of large brass keys, and slippers knitted out of string. His head shaven, his eyes depthless, his hands enormous, he was slowly chewing a wad of paper he had torn earlier from a magazine cover.

"Where'd you come in from?" he asked.

"Camp."

"Beefed in?"

"That's right. Where they going to cell me?"

"Up on the fifth."

"You know who I'm going in with?"

Jo-Jo chewed slowly. If he was thinking, it wasn't possible to see any evidence of the process. Finally he said, "I don't pay no attention."

The officer came and they took Sarich up on the fifth tier, and while Preston, the gun rail officer, stood by, they locked him in the dark cell. The other man was only a heavily breathing mound of shadowed blankets.

Back in the rotunda Jo-Jo settled down on the wide metal steps and pulled the magazine from his hip pocket. He couldn't read and he had already looked at the photographs many times so he was able to turn directly to his favorites. One was a young fair-haired girl, nude and showing herself except for the just sufficiently cocked leg that obscured her final mystery in shadow. Her eyes were lowered but the delicate pink nipples of her small breasts stared triumphantly at the lens.

His other favorite picture was very different. The people, a man and a woman, were dressed: the man in a dinner jacket, the woman in a cocktail dress. They sat at a small table and held glasses half full of some red liquid, and the people seated at the surrounding tables were watching them with polite admiration. The girl was beautiful, but when Jo-Jo imagined himself to be the man in the dinner jacket seated across from her, he never went on with the dream and imagined himself taking this girl home. He just sat and looked at her and sipped the red liquid and didn't have any trouble finding something to say that wouldn't sound like he was dumb or crazy. That was all, but he found it even more satisfying, in a different way, than the things he imagined with the girl whose breasts were bolder than her eyes.

He studied these pictures off and on through the night. Then at 4 A.M. he went up and unlocked the cells on the mess hall and kitchen bars, and at four-forty the officer pulled the bars releasing the white-uniformed cooks, waiters, and kitchen utility men to straggle down, bitching monotonously and without real bitterness, to prepare a breakfast certain to please only the head steward who wouldn't, of course, eat it.

At five Jo-Jo started unlocking the entire block. He walked rapidly along the tiers, his steps exactly metered so it was three steps, key in, turn and out, three steps, key in, turn and out. He never broke stride, never missed the keyhole or bound the key turning it, and the men waking up in the cells would hear a metronomic series of clicks, gradually rising or falling in pitch, depending upon whether Jo-Jo was moving towards or away from them, and after listening awhile to see if the rhythm would falter, they thought when it didn't, "That nut Jo-Jo's on the key."

Terrence Preston followed Jo-Jo's progress from the gun rail, watching with fascination as he had every morning since he had been assigned the post, still waiting for Jo-Jo to miss while hoping he wouldn't.

Only a moron, Preston had concluded, could be capable of

such single-minded concentration. Anyone with even the most rudimentary spark of intelligence would think something—that would at times throw him off his rhythm, but Jo-Jo moved on, robotic and inexorable and, Preston imagined, mindless as the broom enchanted by the Sorcerer's Apprentice.

Actually, in a small crystal globe deep in his slow brain, Jo-Jo was still smoothing the satin lapels of his dinner jacket and telling the girl something nice about her hair, and the hypnotic click of the key entering lock after lock was as remote as the street noises outside the imaginary restaurant.

5

"THINK OF all them fools out there bustin their asses so them bitches can sit under those hair dryers," Chilly Willy said idly.

It was six-thirty by his watch. He knew the sun was probably shining already out there in the free world, but it hadn't yet crested the high walls of the big yard. Chilly was cold but he was trying not to show it. He had read somewhere that if you relaxed when you were cold, rather than hunching and shivering, it was easier to bear. It seemed to be true. He wasn't comfortable, but neither was he giving anyone the satisfaction of appearing uncomfortable.

"Sure," Society Red was saying, "but look at all the bedtime action those fools are getting." Red jumped up, spun around and shouted "Hot cock!" like a street vendor.

"That's a trick's notion," Chilly Willy said, amused scorn playing in his eyes. "I don't know, Red, I'm trying to educate the fool out of you, but sometimes I wonder if it isn't buried too deep."

"I ain't real swift," Red acknowledged slyly. "If I was I wouldn't be beating this yard morning after morning."

Chilly smiled at the shaft. Red was the type of stud that just when you were sure he was a fool and a clown came up with something half sharp.

The two men were watching the other inmates straggling from the mess hall. It was a hungry morning. There were three such mornings and today's was French toast, an offering so distorted in mass production that it was often referred to as fried linoleum. Another hungry morning featured a stack of thick and sodden hot cakes cooked hours before. The third and most dreaded was a notorious concoction known as the square egg, prepared from powdered eggs and fatback, baked into rubbery sheets, which were cut into square servings. The square egg was universally regarded as inedible.

Hungry mornings meant little to Chilly Willy. He seldom ate mainline chow. At the moment he was looking for someone who owed him, who could be pressured into standing in the canteen line for rolls and coffee, sometimes an hour's wait, and a job so humble he wouldn't even ask Red to do it unless it were important.

"And here he comes," Red said, "just like he never left."

Chilly turned to watch Nunn walking towards them through the clusters of shivering cons sheltered under the rain shed. He moved as if he were seriously ill and there was nothing in his drained and leaden face to contradict this impression except the brittle light of his flat gray eyes.

"You come back to die?" Chilly asked.

"No, to build myself up. Those streets tear up your health." The two men shook hands.

"Well, what'd you bring this time?" Chilly asked.

"Nothing much. A one to five for Receiving."

"Receiving?" Chilly was incredulous.

"They set me up, Chilly. They flat set me up. In court they claimed I'd turned out Jimmy Brown—you remember him?"

"The freak they used to call Frosty?"

"That's the one. They claimed I put him to boosting for his fixes."

"Did you?"

"More or less."

"That's you then, isn't it?"

"One stinking suit. That's what they nailed me on."

"It was good enough, wasn't it?"

"I guess it was. We're not holding this conversation in the lobby of the St. Francis."

"And how many times have you stood right here and said no one but a fool would steal anything but money?"

"Okay, Chilly."

"I hope you looked real clean in that hot suit."

"It didn't fit."

Red started laughing and Nunn turned to ask, "You still putting out them withered backs of yours?"

"I ain't puttin out nothing 'cept'n old people's eyeballs."

"Well." Chilly ignored the byplay. "You had your vacation. How long? Seven months?"

"Closer to six."

"That's no record, but you're whipping around pretty fast. Well, it's only a nickel, even if they stick it all to you, you can still see the end of it."

"Chilly, you going to score?" Red wanted to know.

"Just hang tough until I find a horse to put in the line."

Nunn slapped his hollow stomach. "Good. Long as I've been looking at that slop, I still can't eat it. You'd think I'd get used to it."

"It's not really food," Chilly said in the solemn mocking tone he thought of as his educational voice. "It's more like fuel. Like Presto logs. It'll keep you moving around if you don't want to move too fast, and they're not keen to have you move too fast anyway."

"This time I'd like to make some of those variety shows they put on for the free people. They scoff them good steaks."

"What're you going to do on the variety show," Red wanted to know. "Perform on the meat whistle?"

"Hit it, punk," Nunn said. "I wouldn't move in on your specialty."

"Your mammy's specialty," Red countered.

But Nunn had turned back to Chilly. "How about it, Chilly, couldn't you get us on the show as stagehands, or some other lightweight shuck. We could lay up and eyeball them fine broads, then fix on free-world food."

"Maybe," Chilly said.

"You want to get in some righteous eyeballing?" Red asked, beginning to clamor for attention. "Make it to church. Some of them Christer broads are all right."

"All right for your mammy," Nunn said. "Adenoidal, pinch-breasted, dry-crotched, nowhere bunch of hymn-singing pigs."

"Your mammy's a pig."

Chilly Willy sighed. "Sometimes I wonder why I stand out here year after year listening to you two swapping mammies."

"Because you got nothing better to do and nowhere else to do it," Nunn said in a much different tone from the one he used for banter with Red.

Chilly smiled an acknowledgment, but made no answer. He had continued to monitor the men who were still filtering from the mess hall, and now he stepped forward to call, "*Larson!*" Then he hooked his thumbs in his back pockets while he waited for Larson to come to him. Chilly Willy wasn't corny. He created an impression of taut, finely drawn, but elastic strength, and with it there was a contrary suggestion of denseness as if he would be difficult to move from any spot where he had chosen to stand. His eyes were habitually mocking, elaborately insincere, but they also conveyed a sense of still, cold bottoms.

"You owe me?" Chilly asked when Larson was shuffling unhappily in front of him. Larson nodded. "And you've been owing me for some time?"

Nunn and Society Red watched, but without any pose of menace. Menace wasn't their game. Each of them in his own way was interested in the discomfort Larson was so obviously experiencing. Society Red inserted his left index finger in his right nostril and his eyes grew somber as he mined this lode. He removed something, examined it, then wiped it on his pants leg.

Chilly was nodding thoughtfully. "I may have to sell your debt to Gasolino for collection. You've heard of Gasolino?"

Larson had. Everyone had. Nunn and Society Red were smiling now watching the dismay on Larson's face. They were Gasolino's buddies and this was their share of his power. Nunn had come up in the same four-square blocks with Gasolino, the lapland between a poor white neighborhood and an even poorer Mexican neighborhood, and they had smoked their first pot together, tea they had called it then or gage, and banged their first bitches and gone on heavy together. Now they all knew Gasolino had flipped—the evidence was clear in his round mad eyes. For years he had been sniffing the carbon tet from the joint fire extinguishers. The Mexican boys had named him Gasolino because he drank gasoline mixed with milk.

He was an excellent collector of bad debts not because he was the most dangerous man in the prison, though he was dangerous enough, but because he didn't seem to be afraid of anything. He was always laughing even when he was sticking shoe leather to someone's head.

"I'll get it up, Chilly," Larson was saying. "Everything's been going sour on me, but I got stuff coming. You'll get paid."

"I better. And for now, suppose you jump in that canteen line and get me a package of rolls and three jars of coffee."

"Sure, Chilly," Larson said already moving. "Glad to."

Nunn watched Larson take his place at the end of the line. "Fear's an awful thing to see," he said lightly.

"Yeah," Chilly agreed. "We'll brood about it while we scoff them rolls."

The big yard was beginning to clear. The last men had moved reluctantly from the warmth of the mess hall and now the sluggish traffic was shifting through the big gate at the head of the yard. The guards stood with their hands in their pockets, neither looking nor not looking. Occasionally they said "move along" to no one in particular. Assigned men were supposed to be going to work, but since out of the five thousand there were over fifteen hundred unassigned it was impossible in most instances to know who was supposed to be heading towards their jobs and who didn't have to—or didn't get to, depending upon their individual attitude. The guards watched the blue figures moving along with denim collars turned up and long-billed caps pulled down and they quickly became a shuffling blur. "The bastards all look the same," the guards said. They were like cowboys riding the edge of a vast herd—and only the exceptional or troublesome animal ever became fixed in their minds as an individual.

By seven-thirty Chilly's horse was fifty men from the head of the canteen line, and the sun they still couldn't see was beginning to glow on the breasts of the seagulls drifting restlessly from wall to wall. The domino games were starting, and a quartet of Negroes were loud-talking each other, their voices clearly audible a hundred feet away.

"Sucker, you bes' be keerful. I stick big-six to yore ass."

"Now, you jus' signifying, fool. I got big-six myself."

"Maybe you eat it too."

"Get on! You can't play no dominos, you jus' play mouf."

They slammed the dominos at the wooden table with furious energy.

The yard crew, all outpatient psych cases, came sweeping down with street brooms. They moved in a line like beaters attempting to flush a tiger. They flushed orange peels, apple cores, and empty cigarette packs.

Chilly was beginning to take a few bets. He was currently booking football. In the winter he booked basketball and in the spring and summer baseball. When the tracks were running he booked horses. He was prepared to make some bet on any fight, national or local, or any other sports event except marble tournaments and frog jumping contests. He felt he did well.

By convict standards he was a millionaire. In various places throughout the institution he had approximately three hundred cartons of cigarettes. Several men who had reputations for holding big stuff were little more than the managers of one of Chilly's warehouses. He never exposed their floor shows. They took heat off him and when occasionally they were busted and the cigarettes lost to confiscation, Chilly accepted it as a business reverse. If he cornered every butt in the joint and a year of futures he still wouldn't have anything, but the slower and more difficult accumulation of soft money could some day mean something. In the hollow handle of the broom leaning carelessly in the corner of his cell he had a roll of bills totaling close to a thousand dollars. If the Classification Committee became careless he might get a chance to use it.

This was money he had made handling nasal inhalers. The economics of this trade were fierce and the profits, by anyone's standards, enormous.

Chilly had hit the big yard broke at twenty-three. He had borrowed enough to subscribe to a national sports sheet, and by consistently following the picks of the experts, rather than betting by signs, hunches and hometown prejudice, he had won far more than he had lost. A steady flow of cigarettes had moved into his hands, but they had proved an inconvenience and he had decided to put them to work. He needed an important horse, a free man horse, and he had finally settled on a clerk in the mail office, a small man with meager eyes and a sad fringe of soft hair. His name was Harmon and he was partially crippled. Chilly had made friends with Harmon and had spent hours telling Harmon how different kinds of girls were, thinking with some bitterness that he probably knew even less from actual experience than the small brown man who listened to him so avidly. On Harmon's birthday Chilly had given him a hand-tooled wallet he had taken in lieu of a debt from an inmate hobby worker. In the secret compartment he had placed a twenty-dollar bill. Harmon hadn't returned the bill to Chilly, and he hadn't reported it to custody either. He's ready, Chilly had decided.

But it had been another month before Harmon would start packing. He had been scared, but he had been greedy, too, and he had wavered, and once had almost cried. But Chilly had continued to press him until Harmon agreed to smuggle the nasal inhalers in his lunch. Then, of course, he hadn't been able to stop. Chilly paid him well.

These inhalers of various brands were packed with an average of three hundred milligrams of amphetamine sulphate or some similar drug with the same properties, and retailed in any drugstore for approximately seventy-five cents. Harmon was paid two dollars for each tube he smuggled in, and Chilly, without ever touching them, turned them over to his front man in the gym.

At this point the inhalers were cracked open and the cottons in which the active drug was suspended were removed. It was tacitly understood that if a tube were cut into thirds, the thirds were sold for halves, and if it were cut into fourths, the fourths were sold for thirds, on down to tenths which were actually fifteenths. Such a fifteenth, wrapped in wax paper, was sold for either three dollars soft money or a carton of cigarettes. The profit was approximately thirty-five dollars on a single inhaler.

The wads of charged cotton were known as leapers because of the energy and optimism they released in the men who choked them down, but except for those just below Chilly no mainline user ever managed to secure enough of the drug to do more than mildly stimulate himself, and having already paid high for this, he promptly paid a second time with a sleepless night where he lay up listening to the faint jingle and creak of the guards moving through the darkness, and continued to pay through the memories of the women he had once known, more vivid now and swelling until they seemed almost tangible in the feel of his hot crumpled pillow and the lonely dream of his hand. And pay finally watching the bars emerge against the dawn of another prison day.

"No more," they said. It was better to build time as a vegetable than to suffer as a man. But a week would pass and this powerful antidote for monotony would begin to seem attractive again, and they would find themselves thinking, "If I could just score enough to really get on." And they would start scheming on the money that would further enrich Chilly Willy.

The money came in over the visiting table. Their women brought it—the mothers, daughters, girl friends, aunts, grandmothers, sisters, and wives. Custody was aware of this, and procedures had been established to prevent it, but there was a major flaw in their routine. It had long been observed that officers conducting shakedowns were skittish around the crotch. They slapped vigorously and thoroughly up the legs until instinct warned them that their next upward reach would encounter the mechanism hanging there and they stopped suddenly and shifted their attention to another part of the body. Some inmates had small pockets sewn in the crotches of their shorts, others carried a piece of adhesive tape to fix the bill to their scrotum.

Money flowed in steadily, saved out of the women's small salaries, saved out of their pension and welfare checks, not only as a further gift of life to their fathers, sons, husbands, and brothers, but because the women almost always hated the system of bars, locks, and badges more than their men.

The edge of the sun was beginning to show over the east block before the rolls and coffee were delivered to Chilly. The yard began to warm, the sky was clear. They unbuttoned their jackets. During the fall and winter, any day it didn't rain was a good day.

Chilly opened the rolls and squeezed one of them. He

smiled wryly. These rolls sat in a supermarket until it came time to rotate them, then they were sold without reduction in price on the inmate canteen. That this practice differed in no essential from selling a third of a tube for a half was an irony that wasn't lost on Chilly Willy.

"Want some of this hardtack?" he asked Nunn.

"Try me," Society Red said, already reaching for a roll.

"I would," Chilly said, "if only you weren't so godawful ugly."

"Put him face to the wall," Nunn suggested.

"It don't help. His backs are like a bramble patch."

"I got your bramble patch hanging," Red countered.

"Don't trip over it."

Red scowled in confusion. He was obviously trying to come up with something sharp.

"And don't start in on my mammy," Chilly said quietly.

"I wouldn't do that, Chilly."

"Just don't. Sometime I'd like to see one morning go by without dragging our mothers into it."

Society Red nodded respectfully while Nunn watched with a faint smile. They squatted down on their heels like Yaquis, the open package of rolls in the center. There were eight rolls, two apiece and two left over. This arithmetic was of vital interest to Red. He wasn't able to enjoy the roll he was eating because he was afraid he was going to have to settle for two rolls while the others ate three apiece. It wasn't just his hunger, and he was hungry, but each time he was sloughed off with the short end of the goodies his place in the group was clearly defined for that moment—a mascot, or a pet. Under this pressure he remembered an entertainment he had planned, and he took a coverless magazine from his pocket. The edge was frayed and soiled. Opening it to a photograph he passed the magazine to Chilly.

"How'd you like to stick this fine freak bitch?"

Chilly glanced at a woman posed in a brief costume of

feathers and rhinestones. He was automatically suspicious of any leading question and in addition there was something odd about the woman, something indefinable; it was sufficient to cause him to flip back to the masthead of the magazine. It was titled *Gay*. He handed the magazine back to Red.

"You were right about the freak part."

Red looked put down. "How'd you figure it was a freak, Chilly?"

"A man in trick pants is still a man."

Nunn said, "I've seen them when you couldn't tell them from broads. Real freaks."

"If I couldn't tell a sissy from a broad, I'd begin to worry about myself," Chilly said.

Red replaced the magazine in his back pocket. "As far as I'm concerned there ain't no difference. Action's action."

Nunn rocked on his heels, sipping his coffee. He held out his hand to watch his fingers tremble. "I'm whipped," he said. "I had an oil burner going. The nut was a bill a day."

"I told you," Chilly said.

"That's easy to do."

"I still told you."

"What do you want? A medal or some kind of a certificate?"

"I want you to stay in shape to take care of business—now that playtime's over."

"Shit, I might just jump up and file my nut hand."

"You already did that when you went out there and strapped that habit on your ass."

"Ahhh, I don't know, Chilly, sometimes it was like part of me was dead, and it was worth anything to be able to forget it for a while."

"By hiding?"

"Why not?"

"Well, there's nothing to hide in here. The joint's clean of heavy."

Nunn shrugged. Talk faltered and they sat in silence. Red was starting on his second roll.

"*¡Ese!*"

They all looked up to see Gasolino standing over them. Short, massive, heavy-headed, his hair chopped off short and smoothed down over his forehead with a thick pomade. His eyes seemed mostly iris and they held no true focus. He might be looking straight at you, and he might not. No one could tell, and few wanted to ask.

"What's happening, *maníaco?*" Nunn asked.

Gasolino stared at him. "Hey, what you doing back?"

"I didn't go out. I was in the hospital."

"*¡Verdad?*"

"Righteous. How you making it?"

"I'm straight," Gasolino boasted. His eyes glittered and his hand sketched a slow dreamy oval in the air.

"What're you straight on?" Chilly asked. "Lighter fluid?"

"No, man, good stuff."

"Glue from the furniture factory," Nunn said.

Chilly kicked the package of rolls. There were two left. "Eat these damn things," he told Gasolino.

Gasolino squatted down between Nunn and Society Red, and pulled the package towards him with one hand, scooping the remaining cellophane free with a bearish swipe of his other hand. He took half a roll in one bite, and chewing, unable to talk, he motioned for Red's coffee. Red handed it over and quickly folded his arms. He turned to find Nunn smiling at him.

"What's funny, you tuberculosis-looking mother fucker?"

"Red, you're a side show."

Society Red started to say *Your mammy's a side show*, but he remembered Chilly's warning and kept silent.

Gasolino cleared his mouth and leaned towards Chilly. "You got any action for me?"

"Nothing right now."

"I get restless. Then these bulls start looking easy to me." Gasolino grinned. "Maybe I fire on one of them."

"That's a good way to get your ass gang-stomped," Red said. "They work on you in shifts."

"It's a form of group insurance they've devised," Nunn added.

But Gasolino only stared at them, grinning his contempt for anything bulls might find to do.

A young guard walked up to them. His face was stern, probably because he was afraid no one was going to take him seriously. "If any of you men are assigned, you'd better move out."

They didn't move or answer.

"Oberholster, I know you've got a job."

Chilly stood up slowly. It was closely timed. Twice the young guard opened his mouth to say something, then hesitated, uncertain. Then Gasolino started hissing through his teeth.

"Knock that off!"

"¿Qué?" Gasolino asked blandly, his eyes opaque and dim.

The guard made a shooing motion like a farmwife hustling chickens. "All right, break it up. Move along. Oberholster, you better get to work."

Chilly moved off, Red at his side. After a few steps he started whistling "When They Ring Out Those Golden Bells," a hymn he had heard his mother singing many times. He didn't remember the words or even that it was a hymn, but he whistled forcefully down the scale where his mother had once sung: "A glor-ee hal-a-lu-ya ju-ba-lee!"

"I'll think I'll hit the gym," Red said.

"Okay, I'll see you up there."

As they were passing the long stucco building that housed the education department, someone hailed Chilly, and he turned to find a man he knew as Juleson coming towards him. Juleson was a notorious state man. He had a yellow pencil behind his ear, and a bunch of keys hooked to his belt.

"Oberholster, can I borrow a box at three-for-two?"

"Maybe. Which draw will you pay on?"

"The second draw in December. That's about a month."

"That's right. Did you learn lightning calculation in there?" Chilly indicated the ed building.

Juleson smiled. "How about it?"

"Sure, three-for-two's my game. What kind you want?"

"Camels."

"Come on up to the gym, I'll get them for you."

The gym was reached by crossing a narrow footbridge that spanned the industrial alley and then climbing three flights of metal stairs that zigzagged up the outside of the building. On the stairs, Chilly touched the keys at Juleson's belt. "You must be a wheel," he said.

"Half of them don't open anything."

"Then you might say they were decorative?"

"They were on the ring when they gave it to me. They don't give me a feeling of mastery, if that's what you're getting at."

Chilly smiled. "Curiosity's my vice, and you're a stud who provokes curiosity."

They were entering the gym with its stench of sweat and liniment. "Not intentionally," Juleson said. Their shoes rang hollowly on the splintered planks.

"That makes a difference."

He went up to the wire cage from which the athletic equipment was issued, and asked the inmate on duty, "Caterpillar around?"

"Caterpillar!"

The stuttering rhythm of a speed bag was audible from the boxing section, and from the opposite side in the weight-lifting section came the thump and ring of iron. A young blond man, over two hundred pounds, stepped through a door in back of the equipment cage.

"What's happening, Chilly?"

"Give this stud a box of Camels."

"Three-for-two?"

"Yeah, but—" He turned to Juleson. "You pay me. That'll put it on a more personal basis."

Juleson appeared vaguely uneasy, but he accepted the carton of cigarettes Caterpillar brought from the back room, and told Chilly, "Thanks."

Chilly watched Juleson walk away and start back down the steps. He turned to Red. "That's one box I hope I get beat for."

"You're jiving."

"What's a box?" Chilly asked.

"It's the idea of it—no one burns you."

"That's right."

Chilly started off, then turned back. Red was already headed for the boxing section. "Hey, Red, let me look at that freak book."

Lieutenant Olson, the officer in charge of household and the cellblocks, was cocked back behind his desk when Chilly entered the office. A jaunty fifty, he wore his uniform cap on the side of his head and affected a large soft knot in his tie His expression was lively, shrewd, and cynical. He was known as a good bull.

Now he made an elaborate pantomime looking at his watch. "Where you been, hotshot?"

"At my office," Chilly said as he riffled quickly through the papers that had accumulated on his desk. "That is until one of your baby screws ran me off." He turned to smile at the loot. "I wonder how he knew who I was?"

"We point out our natural monuments. And just incidentally, the heat's coming down on gambling. They might close you up."

Chilly plugged in the coffee pot. "I'll just open up again."

"Why not? As long as we've got you around, we always know who to watch."

"Well, I'll be around," Chilly said agreeably.

"Oh, they might make a mistake and cut you loose one of these days."

"Lighten up, Loot, I've still got nine years to the board and they'll automatically deny me three more before they even start talking parole. You're looking at the only man in this state who ever got hit with the big bitch before he was twenty-three years old."

Lieutenant Olson shook his head slowly. He was hooking paper clips into a chain. "I still don't see how you managed that."

"I lucked it."

"Well, you'll make it out one of these days. You'll still be a young man."

"Sure."

Chilly said "sure" without bitterness, it was just an agreeable noise, but the lieutenant sat up abruptly, balled his paper clip chain, and tossed it into the desk drawer. "No system's perfect," he said. "Anyway, what the hell, if they'd let you out last year, you'd be back by now with a new number."

"Most likely."

"Look how you operate in here. I couldn't begin to list the shit you're in or have a piece of and I have people telling me stories every day. Just for openers, how many cons have you put that crazy Mexican on?"

Chilly shrugged. "You people let him run the yard."

Olson was silent a moment, then he asked, "You going to make coffee, or just boil the piss out of that water?"

Chilly stood up to fix the coffee.

"I don't understand why you don't straighten your hand. Sooner or later the word's going to come down on you, and we're going to *have* to bust you—one way or another."

"Loot, this isn't Sunday."

"Okay, okay, it's your life."

Chilly smiled. "In a manner of speaking."

And Lieutenant Olson smiled back. "Okay, Chilly, pour the coffee. I don't pretend to understand you, and if I did I'd hire on as a psych—they're making better money than correctional lieutenants."

Chilly placed the loot's coffee at his elbow. He returned to his own seat, stretched out, and propped his feet on the carriage of his typewriter. "Well, then," he said, automatically assuming his educational voice, "strictly to facilitate the continuation of your meteoric rise through the department, and because we're such tight buddies, you can't expect a man to straighten up his hand if you don't give him any room to hope in. Now, that's me. You show me where I can make an A on that great report card in the sky, and I'll listen. I won't like it because it's not my game, but I'll listen, and if you can make sense maybe I'll play. But you can't do that. I don't see any light and there aren't any windows you can open for me. But I'm not crying, so why should you care how I amuse myself?"

"I'm told it hurts our image."

Chilly stared for a moment, then burst out laughing. "I pass. I can't top that."

"Seriously, Chilly—" Lieutenant Olson began.

"I know you're serious, Loot. So am I."

When he finished his coffee, Chilly started typing out the distribution sheets for the day's supplies. He worked at this until Lieutenant Olson left to make a round of the blocks. When he heard the door close behind him he kicked his typing table hard enough to send it speeding across the room to slam against the far wall.

"Who does he thing he's shucking?" he asked out loud. Why didn't he go over to the hospital and tell some amputee, Grow legs, it embarrasses me to look at you?

Chilly walked over to look out one of the narrow barred windows that vented the back wall. He could see a corner of the football field, and beyond that a guard tower where a gun bull stood smoking a pipe, his rifle held at port, and beyond that there were several smooth crowns of green. Hills in back of the prison. A roan pony stood on one of them. In the moment that Chilly saw it, it tossed its head, galloped over the crest and was gone.

Chilly turned away. He walked to the door and called the porter. Then he sat down at Lieutenant Olson's desk. The porter came in, an old, white-haired Negro. He nodded and smiled. "Yessir."

Chilly tossed the paper clip chain on the desk. "Take that apart," he instructed, "and put the clips back in the box."

The porter nodded again, no longer smiling. "Yessir," he said, beginning to fumble the paper clips through his blunt fingers.

6

JULESON wasn't enjoying the first cigarette as much as he had expected to. He sat at his desk in the education building smoking as deliberately as if it were a task he had been assigned, and the cigarette seemed dry and hot, without flavor. It occurred to him the carton might be stale. The cigarettes used to pay gambling debts were often passed from hand to hand until the pack was crushed before anyone actually smoked them. If half the things whispered about Oberholster were true, he was still holding cigarettes taken in a year ago. He imagined Caterpillar's thought: This stud ain't a regular. A regular, a tribesman, wearing his regularity like a bone in his nose or a caste mark on his forehead.

At this unexpected hint of bitterness, Juleson brushed aside his suspicions, and crushed the first cigarette in his ashtray. His expectations usually exceeded the accomplished reality. It was time, time and past time, that he accepted this and learned to question his eagerness. Now it occurred to him he could have made better use of his birthday gift. He could have used it to buy a toothbrush and some toothpaste. He hated the chalky taste of the state tooth powder and the brushes they furnished were worn limp in a week. He could have also bought peanut butter. It had been years since he had tasted peanut butter. Or shaving cream—his beard was too heavy for face soap. Other things available on the inmate canteen came to mind. If his aunt were going to send fifty dollars instead of five dollars he could find ways to spend it all. Still, there would be a dollar something left after he paid Chilly Willy, he would have to make better use of it.

He lit another cigarette and studied the inmates waiting to see his boss, Mr. Cleman, the supervisor of vocational instruction. Most waited patiently, but a few squirmed on the straight-back chairs as if they were locked in pillories. Mr. Cleman was still in records searching their central files to determine if they met the criteria established for the different trade training programs.

Juleson was not impatient at the delay. When Mr. Cleman returned all he would have to do was see that the men reported for their interviews in the proper order. Like most phases of his job this required only a quarter of his attention and a fraction of his energy. The only troublesome feature of the interview line was that the inmates persisted in imagining he had some influence over Mr. Cleman's decisions, and sometimes he was subjected to pressure from the applicants for special treatment. A few threatened, occasionally someone tried to buy, but most begged. Juleson winced each time he heard the ingratiating "Hey, man ..." He told himself they were trying to accomplish something, and in most cases something constructive—trade training was almost the only sensible way for a prisoner to occupy himself—but their methods, their clumsy attempts to con him were deeply embarrassing in much the same way as it depressed him to watch a chimp mimicking a man. Further, it bothered him to have to refuse them; not only would he have liked to help, but he knew they didn't believe him when he said he couldn't. He knew they put him down as a prick, or, in their contemptuous phrase, a state man.

He rocked around in his swivel chair and stared up at the portrait of Henry David Thoreau. Behind him Thomas Jefferson was hung, and in the glass partition that closed off Mr. Cleman's private office he could make out his own shadowy image. Down the length of the building his fellow inmates were working in wooden pens. Most were sitting idle, but a few, the teachers' clerks, were busy correcting papers.

Restlessly, Juleson stood up and snubbed out his cigarette. He walked to the end of the aisle, nodding at the officer in the custody office, and drank from the water cooler. Above the hum of the cooler's motor he heard the murmur of the classrooms located on the lower floors. Returning, he stopped on impulse at Lorin's desk to ask, "You got any coffee?"

Lorin looked up, shaking his head. "I'm sorry." He was a fresh-faced boy of twenty-two, whose blond hair even cropped down to a few inches in length still formed a wavy froth. His eyes were clear and intense, open so wide they appeared to be strained. He seemed to give off an odor, both sour and musty, as if he seldom changed his underwear.

"My mother hasn't written in three months," Lorin continued. "I'm out of everything. Have you asked Hudson?"

"It's all right. I don't really want it."

He offered Lorin a cigarette and lit another himself. He riffled the stack of student papers on Lorin's desk. "Uncovering any hidden mathematical genius?"

"If there's any here, it's too well hidden." Lorin picked up one of the papers he had finished. It was red with check marks and corrections in Lorin's minute and perfectly formed script. "Fractions," he said scornfully. "You'd think they were attempting group theory."

"For them it is group theory, whatever that is. It's as difficult and they don't see the point of it. Those colored boys and Mexican boys in the elementary classes don't give a damn about fractions except when it comes to cutting up an ounce of stuff. The only reason they enroll at all is because the parole board tells them to get their asses in school and at least learn to read and write. Even if they should learn something by accident they're still not going to read anything except movie marquees, street signs, and speedometers."

"It's depressing," Lorin said with an air of rigidity, his eyes widening still further with indignation until the white was visible all around the iris. "It's depressing to be ordered to involve myself in this kind of waste. I have my own work to do."

"No one can say the effort's wasted, though I have to agree it looks as if it were—" Juleson started smiling. "Have you ever heard the story they tell about Tannenbaum?"

Lorin shook his head.

"Tannenbaum came in about the time they started the first school. He was here for stealing a cow and he couldn't even write his own name. So they decided they'd make a pilot case out of Tannenbaum and educate him so he would never again have to resort to cow theft. They say he struggled up to the sixth grade before they paroled him. Anyway he was back in three months with a new beef, but not cow theft—he came back for forgery."

Lorin smiled faintly. His attention had drifted while Juleson was telling the story. Now he asked, "Do you know anything about a tier tender in the south block they call Sanitary Slim?"

"Just what everyone else knows—he's a nut."

"Is he dangerous?"

"I don't know. I wouldn't think so. Is he trying to shine your shoes?"

Lorin blushed and nodded.

"Ignore him."

"That's like telling me to ignore a dinosaur outside my cell."

"That's not true, Lorin," Juleson said kindly. "He's not a dinosaur, he's a sick old man. If you ignore him, how can he bother you?"

Lorin answered with difficulty. "But why should he have picked me? The implications are—" He broke off and stared at his desk top. Then began again in a lower voice, "The implications are disturbing."

"He hasn't picked you. He has a route. He's all over the block like a bad odor. You're a nice-looking boy, Lorin."

"You mean girlish-looking?"

"No, I don't mean that at all. Look, you're not going to spend your life in here, don't start buying the critical judgments of this swamp. You have a good future ahead of you."

"If they ever let me out."

"They'll let you out."

Lorin smiled uneasily. "They don't appear to be in any hurry."

"Your number'll come up."

Juleson reached over and picked up a piece of blue-lined binder paper where Lorin was writing out a list of words. He read the first few: Crystalline, Gelid, Nascent, Alluvial, Fracto-nimbus . . .

"What's this?" he asked.

"I'm conducting an experiment to determine if poetry can be constructed on mathematical principles." He indicated a thesaurus sitting at the back of his desk. "I'm taking the words from Roget. He understood categories."

"Is he your new hero?"

"I admire him."

"And Hegel's out?"

Lorin frowned. "There were certain inconsistencies."

"I'm not sure, but I don't think that's news."

"You know I don't accept authorities or counter-authorities. The old breed—" He smiled apologetically at Juleson, since Juleson at close to thirty was categorically a specimen of the old breed. "The old breed were frequently motivated by considerations no more serious than their own vanities. The intrinsic value of their work was of secondary importance to them. They advanced theories and refuted them like quarreling children. But a conception doesn't belong to the man to whom it occurs. It doesn't belong to anyone. A slender handful— Archimedes, Newton—understood this."

"But there'll be more?" Juleson asked lightly, both to deflect the tide of Lorin's seriousness, and because he too was anxious not to embarrass his friend and he was willing to appear to be going along with Lorin's fantasy.

"There are more now. A new species hidden throughout the world. Still too young, still without access to the levers of power..."

Lorin went on describing the benevolent and dispassionate revolution he envisioned, and again Juleson found himself trying to remember the title of the science fiction novel where he had first encountered this particular plot. If he could remember the name he might be able to locate it in the library, and, through the inmate numbers on the withdrawal slip, he could discover whether Lorin had read it. Lorin had the highest IQ in the institution, and while it would be considered outstanding anywhere, it was phenomenal only in comparison with the prison average. Unfortunately this distinction, like his good looks, had not worked to Lorin's advantage.

Lorin continued, the excitement rising in his voice, and Juleson beginning to shift restlessly saw Mr. Cleman coming through the front door, walking with his jerky, eager stride, his arms loaded with folders, his pockets stuffed with notes to himself. "Excuse me," Juleson said to Lorin and went to join Mr. Cleman.

"Good morning, Paul. Are we ready to go?"

"Yes sir, they're all waiting."

"Good, good. There's some fine prospects in this bunch."

Mr. Cleman was always optimistic. The smallest advance, the slightest hopefulness was enough to engage the warm tide of his good nature. Juleson could not always agree, but he felt fortunate to be working for such a man rather than some dreary time server, or one of the pompous blanks or vicious little opportunists who infested the administrative staff. He called the first man and sent him into Mr. Cleman's office and watched as Mr. Cleman shook his hand and offered him a chair. He smiled faintly at the puzzled expression on the inmate's face. Mr. Cleman had a stock of a dozen well-worn stories which he used to illustrate any point that might come up. Sometimes the connection was too remote to trace, obscured in the warm haze of Mr. Cleman's mind, but the inmates always listened hopefully, unless they were hostile, certain they were never going to get a fair shake and anxious to prove that no one was fooling them, then Mr. Cleman could be surprisingly short. "Cry somewhere else, kid, I'm looking for men who want to learn."

Juleson sat down at his own desk and lit another cigarette. When I consider how my time is spent . . . The line was one that formed and reformed in his mind until it blurred into the meaningless rhythms of a charm, a charm against, if nothing more, his self-pity. He didn't like to think about the small gray days that were accumulating into years. His merry-go-round, not of zebras and unicorns, but blind mice. Six days a week he spent at this desk, and Sundays he stayed in his cell to read. Sometimes he saw one of the weekend movies. One Fourth of July he had watched the boxing matches, once he had attended a Christmas show featuring night club acts that were currently appearing in San Francisco. The men seated around him had screamed themselves hoarse. He had envied their easy enthusiasm, but had been unable to shake the unhappy feeling he was an outcast staring through a window to watch a celebration he could never hope to attend.

The interview line finished before noon, and Mr. Cleman went out to the shops. Juleson, as he usually did, used his lunch break to go to the library. When he returned Lorin was deep in the thesaurus adding to his lists. He walked on to his own desk and started one of his books. He read until ten after one, when he suddenly remembered it was his therapy day and he was already late. He checked out of the education building, and crossed the yard towards the hospital.

He found his group already gathered, sitting in the usual symbolic circle. The therapist, a Dr. Erlenmeyer, occupied what was intended as just one more chair, but the group automatically polarized wherever he seated himself. He was dressed entirely in shades of brown, and his shirt was darker than his coat. His glasses were tinted a pale tan, and his full head of hair seemed soft and dusty.

"You're late, Paul," he said, in a tone that didn't admit the obvious quality of his remark. His voice was opaque.

"I lost track of the day," Juleson said.

This hung in the air for a moment like a palpable lie, then settled into the heavy silence. The group had nothing going. No one, as they said, was coming out with anything. Juleson settled around in his chair, careful not to look at Erlenmeyer, who might try to make him feel responsible for this wasteful silence. Once Erlenmeyer had stressed how therapy was working on them even while they sat dumb, as sometimes happened, for the entire hour. But he didn't like their silences.

Next to Juleson, Zekekowski was cleaning his fingernails. Bernard stared fixedly at the coal of his cigar. Watson looked at Dr. Erlenmeyer, waiting for Erlenmeyer to recognize his superior qualities. Navarette was slumped low in his chair, arms folded across his chest, and he appeared to be examining the ceiling. Society Red jiggled his feet and whistled soundlessly. Miller, Redburn, and Zubiate slouched apathetically.

Five minutes passed. Erlenmeyer felt through his coat pockets and brought out a tobacco pouch and a curved pipe with a yellow stem. He packed the pipe carefully, lit it, and drew on it once or twice before he let it go out. Juleson couldn't remember seeing him smoke a pipe before.

Finally, Erlenmeyer cleared his throat to ask, "Why do you suppose Paul is late so often?"

They looked at each other to see if anyone were going to attempt an answer. Bernard only shrugged; he didn't care.

After a moment, Zekekowski said quietly, "He's got better sense than the rest of us."

"What's that, Zeke?" Erlenmeyer asked.

"I said, he's got better sense than the rest of us," Zekekowski repeated, his alert and vulnerable brown eyes partially sheltered beneath his lowered lids and thick lashes. His voice was marred by a faint stammer of nervous excitement.

"Do you believe that?"

"No, Paul's running on dim lights."

"Then you said it to be hostile?"

Zekekowski spread his arms. "I couldn't be hostile. They've got me on chlorpromazine. I'm packed in cotton batting."

Erlenmeyer frowned. "Who prescribed chlorpromazine?"

"Dr. Smith."

Erlenmeyer turned away, and again the group fell silent, a silence modified only by the faint creaking of the wooden chairs as they shifted their weight, and the gradually increasing drone of a floor buffer somewhere out in the hall. Juleson folded his arms, unfolded them, then folded them again. He crossed his legs. Several times he thought he could make out the tune Society Red was whistling. Erlenmeyer relit his pipe. The silence lasted five or six minutes.

Then Zekekowski asked, "You don't think I should get the chlorpromazine?"

"I prefer to restrict it to ward patients," Erlenmeyer said carefully.

"I was jumping out of my skin."

"Anxiety has its uses."

Zekekowski shifted nervously, his eyes glowing behind the shelter of his lashes. "I'm never going to be able to dance. I'm disqualified. You know that."

Erlenmeyer said mildly, "I don't know anything of the sort."

"The all-purpose schnook," Zekekowski continued. "So I shouldn't be able to sleep either. Why not? Why should Zekekowski be able to sleep when he can lay awake and consider what a mess he is."

"You weren't sleeping well?" Erlenmeyer asked.

"I wasn't sleeping, period."

"I see. Paul, do you think Zeke's a mess?"

Juleson answered reluctantly. "No, of course not."

"And he's a qualified mess inspector," Zekekowski said in quick dismissal.

"What do you think of this kind of outburst?" Erlenmeyer continued to force still another comment from Juleson.

"He's using the hour," Juleson said. Noticing that Society Red had closed his eyes in the shadow of his cap brim, he continued, "As long as he doesn't disturb Red's sleep."

And Red said quietly, "Just leave me out of it, sucker."

"Is that all you have to say, Lester?" Erlenmeyer asked.

"That's about it." Red pushed his cap up with one finger. "Unless you can tell me if I'm going to get my stuff when I go to the board?"

"I don't know any more than you do."

"What're you going to write down on me?" Red persisted.

"That sometimes you manage to stay awake in class and contribute to the confusion."

"That's cool. You could say I was the most outstanding example of complete and total rehabilitation you ever laid eye to."

"Why don't you tell them?" Erlenmeyer suggested.

"Shit, they know I lie. I've used every shuck there is, and some I made up myself." Red grinned, his yellow eyes flickering. "I even got religion once. I steady schemed on that church. Got saved every Sunday, and squeezed that Bible till I near wore it to tatters. Domino, they gave me a parole behind it. I was supposed to join some missionary outfit, but I got sidetracked somehow in Frisco. Another time I went in heavy for Alcoholics Anonymous, not that I ever did much drinking, but I couldn't remember my name. Then I volunteered for some medical experiment where they shot us full of bugs, then tried to cure us. They said I made the bugs sick. So now I figure I got just one shuck left, but it's the biggest shuck there is ..." Red paused smiling.

"Yes?" Erlenmeyer said.

"No shuck at all. They won't know what to think."

Zekekowski spoke up. "If you're reduced to telling the truth, you're in serious trouble."

Red nodded, "I'd say that was as plain as the balls on a tall dog."

"You better tell them you love the Pilgrim fathers, Nathan Hale, the Unknown Soldier, Donald Duck, and every other lump of humanity down to the last shivering bushman, that's what you better do, and—"

"Really, Dr. Erlenmeyer, must we listen to this primitive cynicism every week?"

Watson had finally spoken. Formerly a mild-mannered and mother-smothered high school teacher, he had killed his two small sons, attempted to kill his wife, cut his own throat, then poisoned himself, all because his wife had refused a reconciliation with the remark, "John, the truth is you bore me."

Watson stood with culture, the Republic, and Motherhood, and at least once each meeting he made a point of reaffirming his position before launching into his chronic criticism of the manner in which his own case had been, was, and would be handled. "... and I've been confined almost two years now, and I see no point in further imprisonment, further therapy, no point whatsoever since there's absolutely no possibility I'll do the same thing again ..."

"That's right," Red said softly. "He's run out of kids."

And Zeke whispered, "I just wish he'd taken the poison *before* he cut his throat."

Watson ignored the whispering, if he heard it at all, and went on, clearly speaking only to Erlenmeyer. "Surely, Doctor, as a college man yourself you must realize that the opportunities for a meaningful cultural exchange are sorely limited in an institution of this nature. Of course, I attend the General Semantics Club and I'm taking the course Oral McKeon is giving in Oriental religions, but these are such tiny oases in this desert of sweatsuits and domino games, and I can't understand why everyone is just thrown together without reference to their backgrounds, or the nature of their offense. Thieves, dope addicts, even sex maniacs—"

Zeke threw his hands up in mock alarm. "Where'd you see a sex maniac?"

"I don't think it cause for facetiousness," Watson said coldly. "Just yesterday I found occasion to step into the toilet off the big yard and one of the sweepers was standing there masturbating into the urinal."

"That's horrible," Zeke said. "What'd you do?"

"I left, of course."

"Naturally. It violates the basic ideals of Scouting."

"That's just Bubbles," Red said. "He's in there all the time. But he ain't hardly taking his hank, cause he ain't got no nuts. Cut em off himself with a razor blade." Red smiled as he watched Watson turn pale.

"I don't believe that," Watson said.

"Ask Bubbles if you can take a look. He'll show you."

Watson shifted in his chair so he wouldn't have to look at Red, and Red figured he was shut up for another week.

"Does anyone remember what we were on when the hour ended last week?" Erlenmeyer asked.

Juleson sensed his face growing bland as he avoided the therapist's eyes. No one answered his question.

"Wasn't Paul about to tell us why he fought with his wife?" Erlenmeyer leaned forward to look into Juleson's face. "Do you want to go on?"

The class turned to watch Juleson. For months Erlenmeyer had been prodding him to discuss something he didn't even want to think about, and their subtle conflict had created a certain small suspense. They were curious as to what Juleson would say, what they might hear him admit to if he ever did open up.

"You did fight?" Erlenmeyer asked.

"Yes, we fought."

"What over?"

"Anything. Pick something. We could find some way to fight about it."

"Did you fight often?"

"After the first year."

"What was the underlying cause?"

"If I'd known that," Juleson said, a stain of bitterness in his voice, "she'd be alive today."

"What do you think now?"

"We weren't much alike. Maybe we were at first, but we were just passing each other, moving in different directions. The longer we were together the worse it got. Like strangers in the same house. Neither of us had anything the other wanted any more, and we both pretended it wasn't like that, but neither of us fooled the other, or even ourselves. It was bad. Very bad."

"Then why didn't you leave her?" Erlenmeyer asked gently.

"I didn't want to. No, I couldn't. I don't know why, but I couldn't."

"I think that's a question you should learn to answer."

"It's hard to see how the answer could help much any more. She's going to stay dead."

"It could help you. Your life isn't over."

But Juleson couldn't quite believe his life wasn't over, that his life hadn't ended with Anna Marie's, kicked out of him by his own feet as hers had been. He reached for a cigarette, and then automatically offered the pack to Zekekowski. He looked up to find Society Red smiling at him with sly speculation and he experienced a twinge of uneasiness as he recalled the cool mockery with which Oberholster had questioned his keys.

For that matter, why hadn't he removed the useless keys? Another question to answer.

Erlenmeyer was still watching him from the round tan ambush of his glasses. No more, Juleson begged silently. No more. He lit his cigarette, then held the match for Zekekowski, noting again how finely formed Zekekowski's hands were, actually beautiful, the hands of a . . . of an arsonist, as it happened.

Then Bernard, who had sat through hour after hour without ever having made a comment, unless the quality of his silence might itself be taken for a single, sustained shout of resentment, finally spoke up to ask in a strong country voice if they could force a man on parole to live with his wife.

"You don't want to go home to her?"

"I guess I don't."

"Why is that?"

"I heard some stuff. One of my homeboys come in last week, he told me."

"What did he tell you?"

"Told me she's been putting out," Bernard said, staring at the floor. "To my buddies."

"They don't sound like the kind of buddies a man needs."

"Ain't their fault. If it's pushed up to them, they're going to take it, wouldn't matter if it was the President's old lady, but you tell me how I'm supposed to go out there and look them in the eye, knowing all the time I was laying up in this jailhouse they was sticking my old lady?"

Erlenmeyer didn't try to answer this question. Instead he got Bernard to admit that if his wife were in the hospital for a long time, Bernard would probably be unfaithful to her, and while he was quick enough to spring Erlenmeyer's trap, he was equally quick to maintain that this was different.

"It's different with a man. Any man figures to get something strange ever' once in a while. That's nature."

"Exactly how is it different?"

"Christalmighty, if you don't know, how the hell am I s'posed to tell you? It's different, that's all. A woman's s'posed to stay to home, not go flashing round no honkytonks by herself, taking up with the first stud who'll buy her a beer. Now, what the hell kind of woman is that? You want a woman like that?"

"But your wife wasn't like that when you were home with her, was she?"

"I guess she wasn't."

"So, when you're home again why wouldn't it be the same?"

"Not goddam likely. She's got a taste for cheating by now, much dick as she's been getting put to her. Prob'ly has to cross her legs to keep her guts from falling out. I don't want it. I wouldn't piss on her. Not after she shamed me with my buddies. Not if she was the last woman on earth."

Erlenmeyer was looking at his watch. "Well, I'm sure the parole authorities will let you live by yourself if this is still what you want to do when the time comes. And that's it for now. I'll see you all next week."

Juleson finished the day at his desk, and at the four o'clock whistle gathered his books and joined the crowd heading for the blocks. He found his cell partner, dressed in new blues now, already waiting for the bar to be thrown.

"How did it seem today?" Juleson asked.

Manning smiled, apparently glad to see him. "Better," he said, "but—I guess the word I want is 'alien.'"

"When it no longer seems alien, you'll know you've heard too many bells."

"Too many bells?"

"Just an expression—another way of saying you've done too much time."

The block bell rang, as if on cue to aid Juleson's illustration, and the bars were thrown. They entered the cell. "Go ahead and wash up, I'll wait until you're through," Juleson said, still unconsciously acting as a host. While he was waiting he continued reading. He read steadily, except for the time it took to go to the mess hall and eat, until seven, when he lowered his book to his chest and went to sleep.

He had one of his rare dreams of mastery in which he was engaged to a popular young television star—a girl so young their relationship would have seemed grotesque in the waking world. His entree to her had been his musical talent, and when at one point he sat down to a piano he was surprised to discover he could play it, but, even in the dream, he was embarrassed to find himself playing "The Flight of the Bumblebee." He played it *bravura*, watching his hands reaching for chords his mind could not foresee. He expected at any moment that his hands would betray him, that the Bumblebee would disintegrate into musical gibberish, but he finished firmly and sat listening to the applause.

Then without transition, he was kissing the girl, apparently for the first time because she drew back to tell him, "Don't move your head so." And she mimicked his style of kissing with cruel precision. He kissed her again, pressing his open mouth hard into hers. The moment widened without effort, both of them motionless, and when they parted he was unmoved, but she looked up at him with soft eyes.

—With the lights off, she said.

Someone came up at this point to ask him to play the piano again, and he started to go with them, but the girl pouted.

—I want Paul to kiss me with the lights off. He never has.

He woke up. As the mood of the dream slipped away he recognized it as adolescent in its coloring, and he felt a nostalgic longing for that lost country whose heightened values had poisoned his adult life by exposing its drabness.

He climbed from his bunk to get a drink of water, and noticed Manning lying on his back staring up at the springs. "How do you feel tonight?"

"I'm not sick," Manning said.

"If you start to get sick, raise a holler, I'll start banging on the bars again."

"I'm not going to get sick. I'll be all right."

"Good."

As Juleson was drinking, he noticed Sanitary Slim pass by on the tier, his eyes restlessly invading each cell, and he thought briefly of Lorin. And then of Zeke. For a moment his original hatred of the prison pressed against the layers of his studied indifference.

7

LORIN WAS celled alone by order of the psych department, and in his three years of confinement this was the only time the meddling of the psych department had pleased him. Now he no longer needed to practice the tedious maneuvers necessary to quiet and evade a cell partner's curiosity as to the nature of "all them funny marks" he filled his notebooks with. His photo albums were secure from prying and insensitive eyes. His poems unread, undefiled.

He sat writing, his paper supported on an unfinished piece of plywood. He wrote: *This box is in a box, which is in another —infinite to the nausea of great space.*

He paused and began to chew the end of his pencil. It was a new pencil and flecks of yellow paint stuck to his lips. That evening in the dining room he had overheard someone make the comment that he looked like Kim Novak. The recollection slipped from the back of his mind, and again he blushed painfully.

He began to write again: *Yet I am free—free as any to test the limits of my angry nerves and press the inner pains of my nature against the bruise of time.*

The pencil found its way back to his mouth—having recorded one thought it needed to be charged with another. Again someone whispered: Kim Novak. And another added: Ain't she looking good. Consciously he pictured his brain as a large oyster coating this irritation with the luster of a pearl. But his thoughts were lifeless, pale beside the vigor of his shame. He sighed and removed the pencil from his mouth.

The aftertaste of cedar reminded him to wipe his lips. Then he dated his entry.

He heard the noise of the lower tiers showering and the scene came to him like a tableau from Dante. He saw two hundred men trying to shower in facilities that wouldn't have been adequate for twenty, a writhing tangle of soapy bodies struggling for a place under the shower heads like piglets fighting for access to one of their mother's tits. Lorin erased the image as too wholesome. He saw a knot of worms pulled from a bait can.

He replaced his notebook on the shelf and paced for a while beside his bed. The paint had worn away to the bare concrete under his feet just as night after night he had worn the edge from his nerves. The paint did not replace itself. Once he stopped and studied himself in the mirror.

Lorin was sentenced for Grand Theft Auto. He had stolen the car because his own had broken down and it was imperative that he have a car not only to live in, but to drive from the park where he spent the nights to the library where he spent the days. When he had tried to explain the importance of his work to the arresting officers they had grown thoughtful and noncommittal. During the entire arrest and court procedures no one had listened to him without evident sympathy, still he had had the impression he was caught in the works of a mindless machine which could find no way within its programming to release him. Now he missed the nights in the park, sleeping with his knees drawn up on the front seat of his car, the early mornings playing chess with vagrant perverts before it was time to drive to the library, and there his orderly numbers formationing on the clean white paper, neat and intricate as ants.

Sentenced to prison for his first offense, he had promptly committed another when he scored too high on the battery of tests they administered to every new arrival. Much too high. His IQ pulsed ominously in the minds of the parole board.

They condemned him with a cliché as worn as "criminal genius," and Lorin, whose sense of humor sometimes supported him, saw reflected in their attitude the burning eyes of Dr. Fu Manchu.

He stopped pacing and began to look through a stack of coverless, grimy, and fragmenting movie magazines he had acquired in trade for a week's desserts. His eyes brightened with anticipation, and in a moment his breath caught. Diana! She was photographed at a typical Hollywood party and the camera had arrested her in the act of turning towards her date, her face vivid with animation. Lorin took the blade from his razor and cut Diana free of her escort. Now he could imagine her smile was for him.

He took his notebook from the shelf and, looking at the photo, started another poem:

> O Lady
> To see you
> In your lovely
> Lovely
> Lovely
> White and lovely
> Is to love thee
> Is to love thee
> In the radiant chalice
> Of the night

"Lovely, lovely, lovely, white and lovely," Lorin reread softly.

He took his photo album from its hiding place beneath his mattress and began to look for the proper position in which to place the new picture. Lorin was arranging the pictures in groups he thought of as fugal. Diana in a hundred poses invited, provoked, and challenged. She was a starlet who had entered Hollywood as Miss Dairy Products of Wisconsin, and

117

Lorin was in love with her. He had idealized her into a nymph of delicacy and a Héloïse of faithfulness and wisdom. He saw them holding hands as they listened to Purcell, Monteverdi, and Mozart, or discussed symbolic logic and group theory.

He placed the photo and copied the new poem beneath it. Some day he would give Diana this book. He dreamed how that would be. How her eyes would shine with instant comprehension of his every nuance. How she would give him her hand to hold and how he would tell her about his Theory of Identity, his discovery which was going to revolutionize thought and speed man forward so swiftly he would look back on his former self as he now looked back on a Neanderthal. How he had invented seventy-two new mathematical symbols and filled over three hundred pages with equations . . .

Sometimes he had her interrupt at this point to say, That's not necessary, Lorin. And he would explain that he only wanted her to be proud of him.

—But I am. You've reworked my heart in your own image. I feel cleaner, purer.

—Did you ever . . . he sometimes tried to ask.

—Ever what?

—You know. With boys?

—Well, Hollywood. My career was terribly important to me before I met you . . .

—You don't have to talk about it. Just promise me it's over.

—Of course, Lorin, unless you . . .

—I'll never soil you by thought, word, or deed. This is the promise Lorin imagines he will make to her. And then they seem to dissolve in a warm and scented silver mist until they no longer have bodies, but are released as pure spirits to the sweet cohabitations of the mind.

"Lovely, lovely, lovely, white and lovely," he whispered again.

As he put away his photo album and got out the notebooks

dealing with his Theory of Identity, he noticed Sanitary Slim sweeping outside his cell.

Sanitary Slim paused in his work, leaned on the handle of his broom, and stared into Lorin's cell with an eye as bright as a snake's. The boy was a punk. Old Sanitary knew, he could always tell. Never came down to take a shower, crapped after the lights went out, wouldn't look a man in the eye.

"Hey, boy," Slim called. "When you going to let me shine them shoes."

Lorin made several careful and deliberate marks before he turned to say. "No, thank you."

A punk! Sanitary Slim could always spot them. He stared hotly at Lorin for a moment, then made a disagreeable noise with his lips, and continued on down the tier, sweeping with great care. A tall dried old man with a nose as sharp and red as a beak, whose lips were locked in a vice of chronic disgust. His shirt collar and sleeves were buttoned tight, winter and summer, and he wore a faded denim cap, pulled straight down over his eyebrows, and in the shadow of the bill his eyes blazed with a hectic and feverish vitality.

He considered turning Lorin in. Sanitary Slim was violently revolted by every form of erotic expression and he considered it his duty to tell the captain of the guards the names of all the punks his instincts uncovered, as well as those who didn't keep their eyes to themselves in the shower, or hung around the urinals, or walked and whispered together as couples. He was equal death on dirt and disorder and he made no firm distinction between the two forms of contagion. Sparkling toilets and a rigid anus were equally wholesome. Touching, rubbing, stroking, sucking were all the same as filth—shades of the same horror.

He was a marvelous janitor. Even the most obscure corners were dust-free; floors gleamed, windows sparkled. His specialty was shoes. He made them glitter. What few staff members even suspected, though a number of inmates had guessed, was that Sanitary Slim had been left a single exception through which the steaming drive of his own sex escaped. He got his shining shoes. Each stroke of the brush increased his excitement until he rocked and moaned on his stool crooning to the shoes like a lover. And some shoes, like women, were better than others and Sanitary Slim yearned after Lorin's with a smoldering passion.

Punk! he snarled again. Ain't tooken a shower in weeks.

That night Sanitary Slim dreamed he was an enormous white slug rolling in the warmth and pleasure of his own slime. He woke to nausea and a violent headache. It was the middle of the night, but he rose and scrubbed out his sink and toilet for the second time in twenty-four hours. Then he went back to sleep and had the same dream again.

Lorin rarely dreamed and he woke the next morning from a smooth darkness with a question already formed in his mind: Why not let him shine your shoes? Whatever his obsession is, how can he involve you if he only wants to shine your shoes? But he knew he couldn't allow it. The unconscious resistance he felt in his own mind warned him that the compromise would be a costly one even if the exact price remained obscure to him.

He got up and tried to take a sponge bath in the few ounces of hot water allowed him for shaving. There was enough to wash his armpits. He was sure he was beginning to stink. Yesterday in the lunch line someone had deliberately moved away from him. He shaved in cold water and though his beard was slight the razor pulled.

He spent the day at his desk in the education building. He finished early with the papers he was required to correct and returned them to the teacher. He wanted to talk to his friend Juleson, but Juleson seemed disturbed over a letter he had been expecting and had so far failed to receive. Lorin reminded him of how their mail was frequently delayed for several days in the censor's office, and Juleson agreed absently, and of course it had already occurred to him. None of them were quite sane on the subject of mail.

He added a number of new words to his list—rodomontade, callipygian, corybantic—and lost himself in the cool delight of Roget's categories. The work of identification had always been pursued by the few, the elite. Above him on the wall Albert Einstein appeared friendly and a little dull.

When he returned to his cell that night he had his mind made up that he was going to take a shower. His crotch was beginning to chafe, and his feet and ankles were black. But when the shower bell rang and he stepped out on the tier, naked except for a towel knotted about his waist and his shoes, he found Sanitary Slim leaning on his broom watching him. Lorin wouldn't have been more frightened if Slim had been a crocodile that had somehow learned to walk erect and use a broom. A strange wild animal, urged by unknown hungers. Lorin retreated into his cell. He went to bed and turned his face to the wall.

He listened to the sound of the showers until the water was ringing on the empty concrete as the fortunate few, the block workers, took their showers alone. Then silence.

"Hey, boy. You, boy! You let me shine up your shoes, I'll give you five packs of smokes. Spit polish and all."

Lorin rolled over to stare up at Sanitary Slim's face—bisected by one of the bars, a raw green eye stared from either half. The split mouth was riven with tension.

"You're psychotic," Lorin said.

"What's that you said?"

"You're crazy."

"Don't you go talking like that. That ain't no way to talk to a friend. You talk nice to old Slim and he'll do up your shoes till they sparkle like new money."

"No, not now. Not ever. Now you leave me alone."

"You ain't being nice," Sanitary Slim accused.

Lorin was silent.

"How come you don't never take a shower?" Slim asked.

"I shower at work."

"Ain't no shower in the ed building," Slim said triumphantly. "Now what you want to lie for?" Slim's face grew severe. "Maybe you showering somewhere with your jocker? What you letting him do to you, boy?"

"I fail to see where my personal habits, whatever they might be, are any of your concern."

"Punk!" Slim hissed. "Smart-talking little punk. You take keer, boy, you hear me? You just take keer."

That night Sanitary Slim dreamed he was being cut up by huge knives that hissed all around him. The light flashed from the blades as they beat like the wings of metal birds. His blood boiled out. Corrupt and warm it rose around him until he awoke choking on his own saliva. Lying there in the dark he conceived the first of his plans to get Lorin's shoes.

8

MANNING spent his first days in prison submitting himself to various measurements. He had deliberately constructed a mood of passivity with which he endured this. In a room still titled Bertillon they had recorded his height, weight, body build, coloring, distinguishing scars or tattoos (he had none) and taken six sets of fingerprints. The next day he was given a thorough physical examination, pronounced fit, and certified for "light to medium heavy work." The following day he was given a battery of tests—AGCT, Kuder Preference, MMPI, and many others. Finally he was interviewed by a psychologist.

The psychologist kept Manning waiting for an hour and fifteen minutes. He sat on a narrow white bench in the hospital corridor watching the doctor through the glass windows of his office. He appeared to be deeply involved in another interview. From where he was sitting Manning could see only the inmate's back, but he saw the doctor clearly enough to make out the thin black hair sketched on his white skull, as even as ruled lines, and the foreshortened ellipses of his glasses. The name on the door was A. R. Smith.

A few feet further down the corridor an old man was lying in an oxygen tent. The gently pulsing mask covered the lower part of his face, and his eyes were closed. One bone-thin arm hung over the edge of the bed, the hand stirred slowly. A very tall blond nurse came to take his pulse. When she looked up her eyes were cool, inward, and her face seemed as small as a child's. She left and in a moment was back with two orderlies who wheeled the old man away. As they passed

Manning, the patient's eyes opened, but his expression didn't change in any way.

The coming interview made Manning nervous. He counseled himself against hope, but Juleson had told him the psychiatric department's recommendation would weigh heavily in his case and he was shading his acceptance of imprisonment by hoping it might still somehow be dissolved. More than he was caught in concrete and steel, he was caught in words and paper, and someone might nullify these legal charms, someone who could look into him and recognize his essential guiltlessness. Perhaps A. R. Smith. Manning combed his hair, and wiped his hands on a handkerchief. Once he looked up to find the psychologist's eyes on him.

When the inmate already being interviewed rose to leave the office, Manning was surprised to discover it was the boy called Stick. He hadn't seen Stick at all since they had led him from Receiving and Release. Now he was smiling at the doctor, talking with considerable animation. But a moment later when he passed Manning on his way out of the hospital, Stick's face had gone dead. He walked swiftly, affecting a sort of glide Manning had noted in some of the younger inmates, and as he continued down the corridor he flipped up his shirt collar. If he had noticed Manning at all he had decided to ignore him.

When he was finally called himself, Manning found his hand so sweaty he had difficulty turning the doorknob. He entered the office wiping his palms on his pants.

"Willard Manning?"

"Yes, sir."

"Sit down, Mr. Manning."

The small office was decorated with reproductions of paintings, clipped from some magazine like *Life*, mounted on sheets of colored paper. Otherwise it was featureless. A desk and two chairs. From A. R. Smith, Manning received an impression of neatness and very little else. Many another small, balding man might have worn a mustache and heavyrimmed glasses, but Smith was clean-shaven and his glasses were as functional as a tool. A manila folder was open on the desk in front of him and Manning was able to see that the contents were charts and duplicated reports, but he was unable to read any of it. His own last name was neatly lettered on the tab, followed by the number they had assigned him.

"Are you familiar with the term pedophile?" Smith asked without looking up.

"No, sir."

"This is a term we use to describe a person who finds his love objects among immature children—"

Manning winced, and Smith, who looked up just at that moment to catch the involuntary spasm, continued evenly, "Would you say such a term described you?"

"No. Not at all."

"The probation report describes your stepdaughter as appearing younger than her true age."

Manning remained silent. Smith had not quite turned his statement into a question. Now he persisted. "Is that an accurate description."

"She's a delicate girl—small."

"Small in what way?"

"Just small. She's a little girl, but very active, healthy."

"Small for her age?"

"Yes."

"What is her age?"

"Fifteen."

"A small, delicate girl who looks younger than her fifteen years," Smith stated as if he were making an entry in a ledger —his voice was free of challenge or judgment.

Manning heard the door open behind him and he turned to see a civilian, holding several memos.

"Excuse me," he said to Smith, "I didn't realize you were busy."

"One moment, Dr. Erlenmeyer, I have something here . . ."

Smith opened his desk drawer and removed a folder identical to Manning's, except it was lettered *Wilson*. He handed the folder to Erlenmeyer and asked, "Have you encountered this young man? The one they call Stick?"

"Briefly. When he was testing."

"Would you spend an hour with him? There is something about him—" Smith glanced at Manning. "Something disturbing. He's too cooperative in light of the probationary report."

Erlenmeyer looked up from the folder with an expression of interest. "He apparently has bright-normal intelligence and I would have guessed dull-normal."

"Yes, yes, he's alert. You will see him?"

"Of course, if you think it advisable."

Erlenmeyer withdrew quietly, and Smith shifted back to Manning, his expression preoccupied for a moment. Then his attention returned. "Now, Mr. Manning, would you tell me how you feel about the crime for which the state has imprisoned you?"

"I don't know."

"You feel something, though?"

"Yes, yes—of course."

"Why do you say, 'of course'?"

Nothing came to Manning's mind. It was as if his brain were disabled. He sat silent, sensing the color rising in his face for Smith to note and interpret. Something had to be said.

"It was an impulse."

"An impulse?"

"That night, what I did. It was an impulse."

Smith rolled back in his swivel chair, and Manning noticed the dark hair growing deep in his nostrils. "An impulse," Smith repeated, and Manning became aware of how keen this man's eyes were, a pale blue that now flashed with a cool light as if just turned on. "Suppose you try to tell me just what happened and how you felt about it at the time?"

Again Manning was unable to make any immediate answer and he sensed his silence stretching like a fissure in the earth between them. He found himself trying to remember why it had been necessary to use the upstairs bathroom. He hadn't intended to climb the stairs or he would have put on his slippers. But at the door of the downstairs toilet he remembered that the water flushing in the bowl sometimes woke Pat up.

"I got up to go to the bathroom—sometime after midnight, I guess—and on the way back I looked in on Debbie. I wasn't thinking anything. I don't remember thinking anything at all . . ."

The wedge of amber light from the small bulb at the head of the hall had spread like a path across the carpet exposing one saddle oxford with a white sock crumpled in it, and climbed the edge of the bed to discover her face and shoulder. Her blankets had slipped to the side. She stirred.

—Debbie, he called softly. Are you all right?

When she didn't answer he thought perhaps he should cover her shoulders. The house had grown cold.

"I touched her," he told Smith, "and then I couldn't let go."

"You don't mean that literally?"

"That was the feeling I had."

"Did she wake up?"

"I don't know."

"She didn't say anything? Make any outcry? Ask you to stop?"

"No. I thought she might be asleep, even though that didn't seem possible, and then—"

"Then what?"

"She responded," Manning said defiantly. "At the end she responded."

Smith nodded. "I see."

And Manning felt like a sick animal, its teeth bared in this last shred of corrupt male vanity. Still it was true. He had been both shocked and delighted at the vigor of her response.

"How had she acted around you previous to this?" Smith asked.

"How do you mean?"

"Was she affectionate?"

"Yes, she was always an affectionate girl, very affectionate. Even after she began to . . . to mature."

"And how old was the girl when you married her mother?"

"She turned eleven the week after we were married."

"Did you think of her as your own daughter?"

"No, nothing like that."

"Nothing like what?"

"As if she were my own daughter. Nothing like that. I knew I was attracted to her. She used to come to breakfast in her robe, and I wouldn't mean to look, I'd tell myself not to, and then I would be looking. I suppose I have a poor character. Her mother would tell her to put some clothes on and they'd start arguing, and Pat would say, Your father this, or your father that, and Debbie would say, But Will's not my father. Then Pat would really blow up when she called me Will and Debbie would start crying, which I hated to see. It was beginning to be bad. Other times when I was passing her room, the door would be half open and I'd see her in her slip or less. She was so beautiful, so young, and sometimes it would come to me that in a few years at most she'd be gone, and Pat and I would be alone, alone and growing older."

Manning paused and Smith asked, "Were your relations with your wife normal?"

"I suppose so."

"You're not sure?"

"How would I know? She wasn't very interested, but I was never much of a man with women. I didn't get married until I was forty. Before that, well, I had a girl now and then. A few times I paid for it—particularly in the service. I think Pat wanted a home, and she was no young woman herself. She wanted to get married and I thought if I was ever going to marry I'd better do it soon. At first she was warm to me, but she cooled off and then it was one thing or another. I stopped asking her because I didn't like to hear her excuses."

"It was your wife who reported you to the police, wasn't it?"

"Yes, she did that. I told her myself. It wasn't Debbie. I told her. I'm not sure just why."

"Were you afraid the girl would tell her?"

"No, Debbie would never have told her. I told her a few nights later when we were in bed. I'd touched her and she'd turned away, and I found myself telling her. I couldn't see her face, but she didn't seem too upset. She said that she'd rather talk about it in the morning, but the next morning neither of us mentioned it, and then that afternoon they came to the firm and arrested me."

"Were you surprised when the police came for you?"

"Not really. It was almost as if I had been expecting them. They told me I'd have to come with them, and I said, All right."

"All right? Did you mean that all had been put right?"

Manning frowned, "I don't know . . ."

Smith opened his desk drawer and took out a cigarette. He looked up to find Manning watching him. "Would you care for a cigarette?"

"Yes, please."

Smith removed another cigarette. Manning couldn't tell whether they were in a pack or loose in the drawer. They lit up and Smith took several drags like a thirsty man drinking, the cigarette held between the tips of his thumb and forefinger. He smoked awkwardly like a boy.

"You were saying earlier that you acted on impulse," he continued. "Do you still believe this?"

"Yes, sir."

"You hadn't thought of your stepdaughter in this way?"

"No, not quite like that. I'd kept it out of my mind. Sometimes the thought would come to me, but I'd be disgusted with myself and push it aside."

"Now, the girl, what do you think she felt?"

"I don't know."

"Did you think about going to her room again?"

Manning looked away to answer, "Yes, I thought about it."

"Would she have received you again?"

"I had that feeling."

"That she would have been willing to take her mother's place in your life?"

"At the risk of offending you, Doctor, she seemed to get a great deal more out of it than her mother ever did."

"That doesn't offend me. The situation is a common one, it only becomes uncommon when it becomes an accomplished fact and also a criminal matter. How do you feel about having been sent here?"

Manning shrugged, "I don't know . . ."

"This is a real thing," Smith observed mildly, watching his pencil doodle a frame for the game of tic-tac-toe. "You must feel something about it?"

"It isn't that—well, naturally, I'm upset."

"Why do you say 'naturally'? We have men here, many more than you might think, who aren't upset at all. They—" Smith penciled a fat zero in the center of the tic-tac-toe frame. "They like it here."

Manning looked doubtful. "I've heard some kidding. The same as in the service when we used to say someone had found a home in the Army, but this is different."

"How is it different?"

"The whole feeling's different."

"You're talking about your own feelings of guilt, but suppose you didn't feel guilt, then how would it be different?"

"You still have more freedom in the Army. We had passes, furloughs."

"The professional inmate takes his paroles as furloughs. Perhaps he doesn't always realize this, but he leaves with some money and a fresh charge of energy, and when his money is gone in a month or two he does some desperate or foolish thing and finds his way back ... to his outfit. But that is not you. Mr. Manning, how do you plan to spend your time here?"

"I'll study. Try to equip myself to make a new life whenever I'm freed."

"You don't sound too hopeful."

"I'm not too hopeful, but I don't know anything else to do."

"I'd like you to think about entering one of our therapy groups. It may not help you, but it can't do you any harm."

Manning began to shake his head, but Smith cut him off, "I'm afraid it's not voluntary. I sometimes give that impression because I feel participation should be voluntary if it is to have the best chance of proving effective, but men with offenses such as yours are required to attend by the parole board, and any parole consideration is contingent on such therapy, though not necessarily on the recommendations of your therapist. There are several groups functioning at the moment. One that I share with Dr. Erlenmeyer and others conducted by Mr. Hamblin and Mr. O'Malley. Offhand, I should think you'll be assigned to the group conducted by Dr. Erlenmeyer and myself since it is currently the smallest."

Smith closed the folder. He smiled faintly and said, "I hope things go well for you—as well as they can at this point."

Manning returned his smile gratefully. "Thank you."

That afternoon in the cell Manning told Juleson something of the interview while Juleson sat cross-legged on his own bunk, his book closed on the finger that was marking his place. Even as he was speaking Manning found time to note that his cell partner, he already thought of Juleson as his friend, wasn't looking well. He was always pale, his eyes weary from steady reading, but now his skin seemed worn, and his expression betrayed anxiety.

When Manning finished, Juleson said, "Smith's a good man. In my opinion anyway."

"He took after me, hammer and tongs, like a district attorney."

"Yes, on an initial interview. He hasn't much time to find out all he needs to know. There are some dangerous and violent men coming into this prison and it's his job to earmark them if he can. Where a psychiatric hospital might allow weeks before attempting a diagnosis, he has to make out on a few tests and an hour's interview. If he runs into someone way out, he'll follow up, but otherwise that's all the psych department most cons ever see."

"I have to attend therapy."

"Which group?"

"He said probably his, his and some other doctor."

"Erlenmeyer. That's my group. Smith and Erlenmeyer are supposed to share it, but these days it's mostly Erlenmeyer."

"What's he like?"

"I don't know. I think he would have made a good dentist, or maybe a pediatrician." Juleson leaned over the end of the bunk to look out the bars. He could see only a few feet in either direction.

"Did the mail go by?"

"Yes, a few minutes ago."

"Jesus," Juleson said softly. He settled back on his bunk, opened his book, and then closed it again.

"It'll come tomorrow," Manning said.

"I hope so. If it doesn't come pretty soon I've got my dumb ass in a sling."

"Is it a serious matter?"

"It could be. I don't know. If it doesn't cost me anything else, it will at least cost me some embarrassment." He looked over at his shelf where only three packs remained of the carton. "I had to jump in and involve myself."

"I could write Pat for money, but I'm not sure she'd even answer. Still I could try?"

"No, that's not necessary, Will. If you haven't even written for yourself, and I know there are things you'd like to have, how could I let you write for me? I got into this mess by myself and I'll find some way out of it."

"It'll come tomorrow," Manning said.

But it didn't. Juleson checked at the mail room at noon and there was nothing for him. By this time he was certain there wouldn't be—the situation was beginning to assume the classic outlines of the other traps he had set for himself in the past. You fool, you fool, he told himself, and he could think of nothing more damning to say. His aunt was an old lady, any number of things could have happened to her during the year. But you couldn't wait, could you?

Nothing had ever come to him as quickly as he had expected and he had always grabbed.

He returned to his desk in the ed building and tried to consider what he should do. He should immediately tell Oberholster that his money hadn't fell in, that he would need an extension, but he knew himself well enough to know he would put this disagreeable errand off as long as he could. And there it was—that was him.

He put his head in his hands and thought of the men he might have been. He became aware of someone close to him and looked up to see Lorin.

"Don't you feel well, Paul?"

"I'm all right."

Lorin didn't look well himself. His fresh complexion had grown perceptibly duller and the strained appearance of his eyes had increased. The whites were yellowish, and Juleson was aware of a sour odor which he was now certain was coming from Lorin. He dismissed his own troubles.

"What's the matter?"

"Nothing. Nothing that hasn't been the matter. I know you don't take it seriously."

"Hold on, now, I take it seriously, if you do. Is Sanitary Slim still bugging you?"

"Yes. He comes to my cell every night and hangs around in front of it. He must think I'm a fool. Last night he told me he had been sent up by the block sergeant to check everyone's shoes to see if their numbers were in them."

"Did you give them to him?"

"Of course not. Do you think I believed him? I told him the sergeant would have to come up himself."

"What'd he say to that?"

"He swore at me. Called me a smart punk."

"Lorin, why don't you let him have the shoes if that will get him off your back. A lot of men have let Slim shine their shoes." Juleson tried for lightness. "He does a good job."

"I can't. I can't involve myself."

"I see. What are you going to do then?"

"I've been considering writing a letter to the psych department. Do you think that's a good idea?"

"It's hard to see how it will help, but it can't do any harm. Probably you're going to have to wear the old bastard out. In time he'll get tired of annoying you."

Lorin rubbed his forehead as if he were trying to erase something written there. "I don't know how much more of it I can take."

"Can you threaten him? He's a coward. Could you threaten to take a club to him and make him believe it?"

"I told you I couldn't involve myself."

"But you are involved."

"Not in that way. I just can't do it, not even if I thought I could force him to take my threats seriously."

"Lorin, I still say you're making too much of this."

"I know that's what you think."

"I don't like to see you upset, but I can't help being aware that most of us would just laugh at the old bastard and forget him and I get the feeling that when you make so much of this you are subtly emphasizing the degree to which you believe yourself to be different from the rest of us."

"Thank you, Paul."

"Now, don't take that attitude."

Lorin smiled faintly. "Don't worry about it. I'll work it out." He turned and walked back to his own desk, and Juleson watched, thinking that the "old breed" had betrayed Lorin once again.

9

Two weeks in enemy hands found Stick's army reduced by half. The youngest General stumbled over the IQ test. His performance was moronic. When this was taken into consideration along with his extreme youth, his passivity, his plump softness, and moist red mouth, the classification committee decided that life in the general population would be impossible for him—he would be used as an engine of dumb flesh, used as the men on the prison ranch were known to use their animals. The committee ordered him transferred to an institution for the feebleminded on the first available transportation.

All Stick knew was that the youngest General was called over the loudspeakers one morning and that was the last they saw of him.

"So what?" Stick challenged the remaining General. "I was going to cut him loose anyway." Stick tapped his forehead. "That punk wasn't keen enough."

"I still wonder what they done with him," the remaining General whined.

"They prob'ly stashed him in some nut house."

"Maybe he asked to go."

"He didn't have that much sense."

Stick didn't have to guess what had happened to the youngest General, he had psychs trying to play with his own head, but he was too keen for them. He cooled them right on out until he had them calling him "son," but the youngest General, that little rumpkin, they probably had him made before he got sat down.

"How you going to get us out of here?" the remaining General asked, as he did almost every day.

"When I'm ready I'll brief you. We're under cover now. This is our submerged period. Every great movement goes through a period like this." Stick looked around contemptuously. "But don't worry. This place ain't nothing."

The following week the remaining General was assigned to school and began to appear on the yard with a fourth grade reader, stuffed with folded exercise papers, under his arm. He came to Stick to ask the meaning of certain words, how to spell others, and Stick began to get angry, but he didn't blow until the remaining General came expecting his approval because he had scored 82 per cent on a spelling test. Stick snatched the paper and wadded it.

"What're you fucking with this shit for?"

"But you said we had to get keen."

"I'll be keen. I'm keen enough for both of us. You get out of that school. You don't see me running around with no book."

Stick snatched the book and sailed it across the yard. It opened in flight, dropping the exercises which were caught by the wind and scattered like propaganda leaflets. The General squeaked with dismay and started after his text.

"You pick that book up, don't come back," Stick threatened.

The General paused, looking apprehensively from Stick to where the book lay open on the asphalt, the pages riffled by the wind. "I'm charged out with it," he pleaded.

"You're charged with it. You're charged with it," Stick repeated, his voice growing shrill. His hands reached up level with his thin shoulders to grapple with something invisible, and his face darkened with blood until it resembled a rusty trowel.

"Fuck that book!" Stick screamed.

But the General, clearly terrified of Stick, had slipped off after his book. He picked it up, stuck it in his belt and began to gather his exercises, watching Stick over his shoulder like a cowed dog. He didn't come back. After that Stick didn't look for his General, and when he saw him he was always moving away.

Stick didn't miss the Generals. The punks had been holding him back. Neither of them had been keen enough. He had come to prison through their weakness. But sometimes at night, among the pressures of his numerous corrective fantasies, he found time to imagine circumstances where they were brought to him for sentencing as arch-traitors. He was always busy—moving armies, razing cities, settling major scores—and he glanced across the mirror-black surface of his desk to say, "Shoot them both." They cried and ran around the desk to fall on their knees and hug his legs. He kicked their faces. This part was particularly vivid. Lying in his bunk, his leg jerked and he sensed a phantom shock running up his toes and felt the sudden yielding as their teeth broke back into their throats.

But at this time his attention was largely occupied by his cell partner and the invention he had discovered this man working on. At first the cell partner, an insignificant forger named Morris Price, had been nothing to Stick except a body to step around when he moved from one part of the cell to another. His slight stature, his pointless eyes, his thin pale hair brushed straight back from a ragged hairline all caused Stick to reject Morris as a potential Vampire. He was through with punks. Morris wouldn't look good in the uniform. His dim dry voice could never issue a convincing order. In the new reality people like Morris did not exist. Stick used his towering height to intimidate Morris into submissiveness. But this was before Stick became aware of the nature of Morris's invention.

During the first weeks they celled together Morris spent most of his cell time reading. He had a ragged stack of paperbacks, many of which he had apparently read at least once before because whenever he started a new one he'd say, "This is a real hotdog—" and give an involved description of the plot. Stick didn't pretend to listen. He wasn't yet aware of the large handicraft box beneath the lower bunk because any sweeping or cleaning done in the cell was done by Morris.

Even when Morris went back to work, convinced that whatever Stick might be he wasn't a rat, Stick still didn't make anything out of Morris's project. He watched Morris sewing together what appeared to be strips of mattress cover, and his quick way with needle and thread only confirmed Stick's impression that Morris was corrupt material.

This went on for a week. Every night after dinner Morris would get out the mattress cover and start to work. He was fussy. He waxed the thread carefully and frequently tore apart an evening's work, only to start it over again the next night. At lights out he folded the large spread of cloth as tightly as he could and hid it in the bottom of the handicraft box. Later Stick discovered Morris had another large section made into his bed, and a third section wrapped around Stick's own mattress.

Finally Stick asked, "What you making?"

"Kitten britches," Morris said coyly.

"I asked you what you making?"

Morris smiled with satisfaction. "I'm making you ask questions, that's what."

Morris had reached the point where the pleasure of telling a secret had begun to seem more attractive than the pleasure of keeping it. He intended to tell. If Stick had sealed his ears like the crew of Odysseus, Morris would have jumped on him and clawed the wax loose. But Stick, not understanding this, had slid off the top bunk and reached in to grab Morris by the shirt.

"You get off me. You get off me," Morris cried.

"You going to tell me what you're making?"

"I was going to tell you." He leaned closer to Stick and whispered, "It's a balloon."

Stick threw Morris back against the wall. "You think I'm a fool?"

"It is. It's a balloon." Morris smiled secretively and sailed one hand up past his face.

"You're nuts."

"Sure, I'm nuts." Morris's sly smile deepened. "I'm so nuts one of these days I'm going to float right over those walls out there."

Stick's face grew quiet. "In a balloon?" he asked softly.

In the next hour he was conducted on a full tour of Morris Price's balloon fantasy, and before the trip was finished Stick was convinced. Morris had sliced the section on balloons from an illustrated encyclopedia and Stick studied a drawing of the first balloon built by the Montgolfier brothers, rising above the fire which had caused its ascent, trailing a sausage-shaped puff of smoke. A few people stood watching and in the corner of the picture a herd of sheep grazed without interest.

"That balloon ain't carrying nobody," Stick objected.

"No, but later they sent up a duck, a rooster, and a sheep and after that they sent up a man."

"What happened to him?"

"Didn't nothing happen to him. He went up about eighty feet and stayed there for four minutes. They had the balloon tied down with a long rope, but they cut the next one loose and it drifted about fifteen miles. You ever notice how the wind's always blowing here?"

"Yeah, but where you going to build a fire? You think they're just going to stand by and let you build a fire?"

Morris looked triumphant. "I knew you'd ask that. Well, I ain't going to build no fire. These hot-air balloons are old stuff. I'm going to use gas."

"All right, where you going to get the gas?"

Morris turned to the sink and punched the button that released the water. "There," he said. "Right there."

Stick shook his head. "You're a real rumpkin, aren't you?"

"You just ain't never heard of electrolysis. All you got to do is run an electric current through water and you got all the gas you need. Hydrogen gas, and that's the best kind."

The hydrogen was going to be liberated in the welding shop by a friend of Morris's and stored in portable tanks. When the balloon was finished the tanks would be smuggled to the gym and hidden on the gym roof. Finally Morris would smuggle the balloon to the gym, make his way to the roof, inflate it, and—

Again he made the flying motion with his hand. "And that's *adiós* mother fuckers. They'll never figure how I made it."

"That's keen. Real keen."

"I worked it all out myself. When they sent me here I told myself there was something they hadn't thought of and I just laid back—"

Stick interrupted to ask, "How many will that balloon carry?"

"Just one."

"You sure it won't carry two?"

"No, I had to make it small, otherwise I wouldn't have been able to get it to the gym."

"That's too bad," Stick said. "You got to leave your friend in the welding shop behind."

"Oh, him. He don't care nothing about going."

10

"HEY, BOY!"

Lorin cringed and looked up from his notebook to see Sanitary Slim smiling at him from outside the bars. He knew the smile was meant to soothe him, but he found it more terrifying than Slim's normal expression of furious disgust.

"I got something for you, Lorin. Heh! You didn't think I knew your name, now did you? I looked you up, boy, that's how much I had you on my mind. And I got to wondering what I could do for you. And I thought, that boy might like these."

Sanitary Slim pulled a pair of civilian shoes from behind his back, and held them up to the bars. He didn't notice that Lorin was trembling. He smoothed the bright toes with his fingers and asked softly, "Ain't they nice?" He turned the shoes back and forth so the light played on their brilliant shine.

"I don't want them," Lorin said.

"Now, don't you say that, boy. These are boneroo free-world shoes. Now you take them and just give old Slim them old shoes of yours and he'll take them down and throw them in the trash. You not going to want them old shoes, when you got fine free-world shoes like these."

Sanitary Slim cocked his head to the side, his eyes glittering with transparent craft.

Lorin began to pound on his notebook with both fists at the same time. "You get away from me. Please, get away from me!"

"Now, boy. Now, boy . . ."

"I'm not going to give you my shoes for any reason. Understand that. It isn't going to do you any good to keep coming around here. Now, please leave me alone."

His notebook had slipped to the cell floor and Lorin bent down to pick it up. He heard Sanitary Slim beginning to hiss above him.

"You're ungrateful, boy."

"Just go away."

"You telling me you don't want these shoes?"

"Please, just go away."

"Punk! Someone's fucking you, boy, and old Slim's going to find out who. Then you won't talk so smart."

Lorin turned to face the rear of his cell and he continued to sit like that until Slim finally gave up and left. Then Lorin wrote a letter to the psych department and put it on his bars where it would be picked up with the evening mail. That night, for the first time in several years, he cried before he fell asleep.

The next afternoon he was paged to the psych department. He was not surprised to be called so quickly. He knew his own psych jacket was coded red. Ordinarily, this was a source of amusement to Lorin, but now it had proved useful. He walked to the hospital, walking spread-legged to ease the rash that had developed at his crotch, and found Dr. Erlenmeyer waiting for him at the main desk.

"Come into my office, Lorin, and we'll talk this over."

"Thank you, Doctor."

They entered the small office and Erlenmeyer sat down behind the desk. On the wall above him a printed sign read: *You don't have to be crazy to work here, but it helps.* Erlenmeyer removed his tinted glasses and rubbed his eyes with his thumb and his forefinger. He held his head thrown back as if he were about to take nose drops.

"Are your eyes still bothering you?"

"Things get no better, Lorin." Erlenmeyer replaced his glasses. "Now, what exactly is troubling you?"

Lorin told him about Sanitary Slim, leaving out only Slim's repeated inferences that he was someone's punk, and he was dismayed to see Erlenmeyer smile.

"A textbook specimen," Erlenmeyer said. "An anal retentive, of course, and a useful type generally speaking. A lot of the world's more disagreeable work is done by people of this type. They're frightened of disorder, dissolution, they equate dirt with sin, and they're under a compulsion to keep things cleaned up."

"Are you trying to tell me he doesn't want my shoes for some dirty reason?"

"No, I'm trying to tell you that isn't the way he sees it. In his strange fashion he's trying to do something for you."

"I don't accept that. Whatever it is he wants it's for himself."

"That doesn't make him much different than most people. How've you been otherwise, Lorin?"

"All right, except for that animal outside my cell."

"Just ignore him," Erlenmeyer suggested. "Or humor him a little if it doesn't bother you too much."

Lorin shuddered, and Erlenmeyer noted this with a faint frown. "How are all your projects?" he asked.

"Progressing satisfactorily."

"Are you still planning to herd all of us old folks into the gas chambers?"

"Don't mock me. I never suggested any such disposition. The matter will be settled by computer, since that is the only method by which we'll arrive at an impartial solution, but, offhand, I would think you will be pensioned off, and resettled in colonies in some temperate and lightly populated country such as Brazil. Until the last of you die out."

"Like the dinosaurs?" Erlenmeyer asked with a faint smile.

"Again you mock. But the simile is an apt one."

"Uh-huh. And how's Rita?"

Lorin blushed. Rita had reigned in his album before Diana, but she had betrayed him when she married one of her leading men. "Doctor," he asked eagerly, "did you ever meet a girl named Diana Dolan?"

"Dolan? Does she make films?"

"Yes."

"Lorin, people such as myself have very little opportunity to socialize with movie stars. They move in a world of their own and it would be good for you to keep this in mind."

"I'll meet her," Lorin said firmly.

"Well, I'm sure she's very nice."

"She's wonderful."

"Uh-huh . . ."

Lorin looked up to catch a pitying look in Erlenmeyer's eyes, and for a moment his self-assurance faltered. "You think that's odd, don't you?" he asked with difficulty.

"I don't know. I only know it's nothing I ever did. When it comes down to it, isn't that how we decide what's odd and what isn't? You're in an odd place and you weren't very old when you came here."

"When will I get out, Doctor? Why do they keep me? I've never heard of a first-termer serving three years for car theft. Eighteen months is the average."

"I hope it won't be too much longer, Lorin, but you did refuse therapy."

"Therapy! You want me to sit around an hour a week and talk about baseball with a bunch of imbeciles. Baseball and bullshit. Where's the therapy?"

"Some men discharge their tensions and concern through the apparently trivial. But didn't Dr. Smith offer you individual therapy?"

"Yes."

"And you refused that too."

"Yes."

"Why?"

"I didn't feel I needed it."

"But surely it would have done no harm, and we could have told the parole board you were cooperating with the program. The token, Lorin, is sometimes very important to people. If they were somewhat naïvely concerned over your potential, at least they would have the satisfaction of knowing whatever could be done had been done before they authorized your release. You have left them in the dark."

"I don't need therapy. I don't want it and I don't need it. It's a waste of time."

"And you're so busy correcting fifth grade arithmetic papers?"

"I have my own work as well."

"But you did ask me why you were still here, and I have tried to give you my understanding of it. I may be wrong."

"It doesn't matter. In two more years my sentence runs out, and then you have no choice."

"That's true. Although occasionally when a number of doctors agree that a subject is a dangerous psychopath, we can assign him what we call a P number and transfer him to the hospital for the criminally insane, where he can be held indefinitely."

"Are you threatening me?"

"No, Lorin, I'm not threatening you. Perhaps you should return to your job assignment."

Lorin stood up. At the door he turned back to ask, "And you're not going to do anything about that degenerate?"

"There isn't anything we can do. Perhaps you can arrange to have him transferred to the Brazilian colonies."

"All right, Dr. Erlenmeyer. Thank you."

Sanitary Slim sulked in front of Lorin's cell for an hour that evening. He pretended to be cleaning, but he was actually accusing Lorin, in a venomous whisper, of dreadful obscenities. Things Lorin could hardly imagine.

"Please, go away," he continued to beg.

"You ain't being nice. You ain't being nice at all. What harm would it do you if I was to shine up your shoes? You tell me that, you being so smart and all. They's plenny a free people what pays old Slim to do up their shoes, and here old Slim's willing to pay you, and you turning him down. The Lord don't love ugly, boy, the Lord don't love ugly. Just let me shine them up one time, and I won't bother you no more. Just one time?"

"No."

"Please, boy."

"No. Absolutely not."

"You stink, boy," Slim said spitefully. "You stink worse'n a he-goat."

Lorin woke up the next morning to find his depression had deepened. He scratched his crotch tenderly, avoiding the places where it was chafed raw. He caught his own smell like decay. He was going to have to find some way to take a bath. He couldn't bear it any longer.

He avoided everyone throughout the day, even Juleson, and didn't even try to work on his Theory of Identity. He finished the class papers as quickly as he could, and went down into the basement where he sat in a darkened room which they used for audiovisual aids. During the third period a class filed in and Lorin sat through a film describing the operation of a turret lathe, and then another on the conservation of watersheds. The films were seldom germane to regular classwork. When a class was scheduled for audiovisual aids they were shown whatever was available. Lorin had already seen most of the films several times.

The night when the shower bell rang he had himself nerved up to ignore Sanitary Slim as if he didn't exist, and it was a shock to discover the tier empty when he stepped out of his cell. He looked both ways, but Slim was gone. Then

Lorin expected he would encounter him in front of the showers, but he wasn't there either. With an overwhelming sense of relief, he stepped out of his shoes, and unknotted the towel from around his waist. He turned to the crowded showers with less than his usual revulsion.

The shouting, the steam, the soapy bodies crowded four and five to a shower head, the obscene jokes and more obscene laughter, all seemed wholesome when compared with Sanitary Slim. Lorin moved forward to stand with the men who were waiting for a chance to squeeze under the water. Lorin had long ago developed a tactic which called for him to wait until just a few minutes before his sense of timing warned him a fresh tier was about to be released, and at that point the press was at its lightest. He stood waiting, imagining the simple pleasure he would find in being clean again, and then some instinct caused him to look around just as Sanitary Slim was bending down to pick up his shoes. He shouted and Slim took off down the side of the cellblock, the shoes hugged to his chest. Lorin looked after him, and began to shudder violently.

When Sanitary Slim returned the shoes, gleaming with polish, later that night, Lorin didn't even complain. He had the feeling he had been raped, and it was several weeks before he could bring himself to open Diana's album, and when he did he found himself staring at an empty-faced girl—a stranger.

11

ONE MORE morning—a few days before Christmas—and as always Chilly Willy stood in the big yard with Nunn and Society Red. The rain was bad, coming down in gray sheets whipped by the wind, and they were under the rain shed at a particular spot they thought of as Chilly's Other Office. Experienced cons avoided this spot on a rainy day and should a fish blunder into it he was invited to move on. It was a small alcove that held the back door to the bakery, but it offered enough shelter to make book.

The three friends were silent. Action was slow, and Chilly was in a grim mood. They had already talked bad about the weather and discussed the opinion, an article of faith to many, that the big yard was probably the only place on earth where the wind blew from all four directions at once. Except naturally in the summer when the asphalt topping was about to boil, and old cons were falling out from the heat, then the wind would come straight and cool from the bay only to pass about twenty feet above their heads. The wind, they decided, confirmed the conspiracy that all nature joined—to screw them around whenever possible. And while Chilly Willy was willing to agree that the big yard was probably the most miserable stretch of real estate in the western hemisphere, he privately couldn't lay it all to the weather.

They had tried to remember what was for chow and then had been sorry they were able to because it was one-eyed hash, a scoop of hash which looked at if it might have already been digested, at least once, half hidden under a chill and rubbery fried egg.

The goon squad had gone by, buttoned to their chins in green foul weather gear, on one of their mysterious errands, and they had told each other what a dog sonofabitch the guard they called the Indian was, and how the Farmer was all right if you didn't try to shuck him, but if you did shuck him and he caught you, you might as well try to climb the wall. And the Spook—no one could hope to understand the Spook, they could only hope to avoid him. Chilly thought of some half-wild thing driven mad by the daily burden of its own pain, but he also considered that the Spook might be playing a part, as all the goon squad might, to make their jobs easier. He tried to picture them at the end of the day sitting in some bar, drinking beer and laughing over how they put the convicts on. Nice guys really, family men—Chilly smiled. The picture wouldn't quite come clear.

And they had talked about who was stuff and who wasn't. Stuff was anything of value and faggots and sissies were of great value to many, and it was a treasure hunt of sorts to search for the signs, the revealing and half-unconscious gestures, that sped the word of fresh stuff on the yard. And they talked about others they thought might be stuff, but who for one reason or another were pretending not to be, and no one was entirely free from these speculations, which even penetrated the circle of their closest buddies.

Chilly had said, "I don't play that game, but if I ever start I'm going to have to try old Red here."

And Society Red had answered, "Tough enough, if you got eyes to swap out. A little tit for tat and you promise to let me go first."

And Nunn, "You're so anxious to go first, Red, makes me wonder if you haven't been cheated before."

"Yeah, your old mother cheated me. You know I don't play that stuff. I've been known to pitch, but I'm no catcher."

"No one cops to playing it, but there's sure a whole lot of suckers going around talking it."

And Chilly Willy had said, "It's something to talk about."

They had talked about everything else and now they were just standing around half hoping something would happen so they could talk about that.

Chilly knew the rain in the big yard was different from that which fell in the free world. Once in a while you might have to run a half a block in the rain, maybe get your topcoat wet, and you might have to stand a few minutes waiting for a bus, or a taxi, but you never had to walk miles in it, or stand for hours watching it come down, imagining every few minutes that it was letting up a little when it was only getting ready to rain harder. Rain served to turn a day which might have just been dull into one that was actively miserable.

The rain shed could have housed a dozen locomotives, but so acute was the overcrowding that even packed in nearly solid only about two-thirds of the inmate population were able to find shelter under the shed. The rest were left to tough out the rain the best way they could. A few walked the yard ignoring the rain. A small cluster sheltered in each of the block doorways. And one isolated man stood on the wooden bench that lined the far side of the yard. He stood hunched, unmoving, letting the rain run down the sides of his face. No one paid any attention because he was a known psych case who most days carried a large bundle of ragged newspapers and had his shirt pocket stuffed to straining with the stubs of lead pencils, all sharpened to needle points. He hadn't dared to risk his precious papers in the rain, but his freshly sharpened pencils saved him from the day's worst terrors. If he stood quite still, dared nothing, avoided any notice, he might be able to survive until lockup and the safety of his cell.

Those who had been quick enough had found seats in one of the chapels and sat there listlessly, listening to one of the inmate organists practicing the selections he would play during the Christmas services. Some in an agony of boredom might even read the Christian literature put out for them.

Others waited out the rain in the library sitting at the reading table leafing through the back issues of the *National Geographic* looking for the occasional photographs of native women posed with uncovered breasts.

Chilly Willy, though he could ease many of the discomforts of the prison, couldn't do anything about the rain. He and his friends bore it with the rest. Except they wore yellow oilcloth raincoats and rainhats, like those the old fisherman wears in the tuna ad, and this rain gear was boneroo, which meant the average mainline inmate could be in water up to his ass seven days a week, and still stand no chance whatsoever of being issued a raincoat. The control of raincoats verged on high politics, and like, say, the baton of the French Academy they were the symbol—more symbol than actual protection against the weather—of power, position, influence, even honor in their society. The yellow raincoats were worn by their proud owners on days when there was even the barest chance of rain, and frequently they blazed to full sunlight standing out against the faded denim of the mainline inmate with the relentless authority of ermine.

Nunn and Society Red owed their raincoats to Chilly Willy. Red had attempted to block his rainhat into a style currently in vogue with pimps and hustlers called the Apple, but the heavy oilcloth, stubborn and style-blind, was reasserting its former shape. One of the woolen earflaps, intended to button under the chin but folded by Red into the crown, had slipped loose to dangle unnoticed. Nunn pulled at it, extracting its full length, fusty as long-handled underwear.

"That's very sharp," Nunn mocked approval. "Makes you look real clean."

Red tucked the earflap back out of sight. "I'm known to be clean, lean and clean, like your old mom."

"That's right," Nunn agreed. "Mom was clean."

"Clean out of her skull. Otherwise she'd have done you up as soon as she dropped you."

Chilly stared out at the space beyond the rain shed where he could see the water striking against the glistening black-top. The only sign that he had been listening at all was that he began to tap one highly polished and expensive shoe against its mate. He watched the men walking in the rain—nuts, ex-ercise freaks, claustrophobes—they dug their chins into their upturned collars, and plunged their hands into their pockets. The wind whipped the bottoms of their pants around their ankles. Chilly noted scornfully that a good third of these ag-gressive outdoorsmen wore sunglasses.

Then he saw Juleson, also walking in the rain, with his li-brary books, wrapped in plastic, dangling from a belt as kids dangled their readers. The books looked thick and dense.

Who's he trying to shuck, Chilly wondered.

Chilly did a lot of reading on his own, but he would have been quicker to parade the yard in lace trick pants than to make a show of himself carrying books. Big thinker, he told himself contemptuously. And deadbeat, he added.

Chilly chose his reading material from the select books that never saw light on the mainline shelves, but were hidden in the back room as a rental library operated by the head in-mate librarian, who charged from a pack to five packs a week depending upon the demand for a specific book. Most of these books were L and L's, derived from Lewd and Lascivious Con-duct, hotdog books heavy with sex, and they were always in demand. But unless they were brand-new, most of the L and L books in the institution had suffered a specific mutilation. An unwary reader would pursue a slow and artfully con-structed fictional seduction, feeling the real and tightening clutch of his own excitement, turn the page and fall into an impossible aberration of context. He would discover several pages missing, sliced out of the book so neatly it was difficult to detect even when the pages numbers clearly indicated they were gone, and almost impossible to detect before actually reading the book.

Most of the big yard thought it was probably some rapist turned hank freak who was cutting the sex scenes from the L and L books, that somewhere in one of the blocks there was a hidden scrapbook filled with the erotic passages removed from the hundreds of novels found mutilated, and nightly the hank freak would read of one coupling after another while he masturbated.

It was a natural theory to evolve since many of them had done the same thing—reading late at night, with their cell partners already asleep, they might come on a vivid cartoon of perfect sexual encounter, no fumblings, no failures, no fizzles, and their hips would unconsciously begin to work in sympathetic rhythm until they seemed to join the glorious phantoms rolling like colored shadows cast on the page below, and labored far above them until they spilled their own strength across the page like a solitary god who, unable to form the conception, might still know loneliness, and even in the rush of final white light sense his purpose pushing unconnected against the emptiness around him.

But Chilly didn't support the hank freak theory—on one count of evidence—the work was too neatly done, it was surgical, and he couldn't picture the hank freak taking the pains. No, Chilly thought, here was the hand of a puritan, a censor, working with the antiseptic precision of righteousness.

Chilly was still watching Juleson, and his restless displeasure had found a focus. Most of the things Chilly hated were safe from his anger, but here was this superior fool walking the yard like he was no part of it. Chilly walked over to the edge of the rain shed, and when Juleson went by again he called him. Then he worked his way back to the bakery door, aware that Juleson was about twenty feet behind him. He turned around to catch Juleson's expression of uneasiness, and he felt, without seeing them, that Nunn and Society Red had automatically moved to back him up.

"I've been meaning to see you, Oberholster—" Juleson began.

"You got my stuff?" Chilly asked, automatically falling into the tone and vocabulary he used for these exchanges.

"Well, no, as a matter of fact I haven't. That's what I wanted to see you about."

"How would it do you any good to see me if you ain't got my stuff? If you can't come up, I'm the last guy you want to see. You didn't draw?"

"No. I'm sorry. I was expecting some money for my birthday, but it . . . it hasn't come yet."

"You know how many times I hear that?"

"This is the first time you've heard it from me."

"All right, when do I get my stuff?"

Juleson shrugged, meeting Chilly's level gaze with difficulty. "To be honest with you, I don't know."

"You be honest. That's a keen virtue. But I can't smoke it, and I can't pay the people I owe with it. How much you figure you'll owe me next month?"

"Why fifteen packs, a box at three-for-two. That's right, isn't it?"

"No, that isn't right," Chilly repeated with satirical patience. "You had *one* month to get up fifteen packs. Now it's twenty-two packs. Another month and it's three cartons. Are you following me?"

Juleson took a half-step back, his face flushing. "Nothing was said—" He paused and then continued in a more reasonable tone, "You're defeating your own purpose. I can probably scrape together fifteen packs."

"What do you know about my purpose?" Chilly asked. "You pick up mind reading out of one of them books of yours?"

"I assume you want your cigarettes back."

"I'm going to get my cigarettes back. If it were a gambling debt, some bet you lost, I might lighten up. I write off a lot of bad paper. But I handed you a box cash, three-for-two, and you're no fish, you know three-for-two figures every month, or did you think you were dealing with the Bank of America? Now I want my stuff, or I'm going to get in your ass."

Juleson started to walk away. He turned after a few steps. "I'll pay you the fifteen packs I agreed to pay you as soon as I can."

"You'll pay what *I* think you owe, not what *you* think you owe, and I'm telling you like it is. You got any weird ideas you can handle me, forget it, I don't bother with collecting. That's Gasolino's speciality."

Juleson was clearly growing angry. "Why do you have to pull this sort of thing?" he asked. "You're not one of these brainless assholes. You surely don't need the cigarettes. What do you get out of it?"

Chilly turned to Nunn. "You notice how this joint is beginning to crawl with amateur psychs?"

Nunn smiled tightly. "As one of the brainless assholes I hope you don't expect an intelligent comment from me."

Society Red started laughing, like water collapsing deep in a drain.

Juleson stared at them white-faced. "Sure, I know. Big joke. Catch some guy short and scare him blue just to be getting a little of your own back. But sometime you're going to pick the wrong man, and you'll be the one who ends up with the shank in him. Then I'll do the laughing, me and everyone else who tries to do his own time and get along without turning this place into a jungle."

Chilly had listened to this, his face quiet and still, but now he stepped forward and began to tap the air an inch from Juleson's chest. "Now, you listen. You're digging a hole with your own fat jaw. You want to pay fifteen packs? All right, you got one week to come up with fifteen packs. That's it. Otherwise I turn the debt over to Gasolino. Now, get in the wind."

They watched Juleson walk away. "There goes a mad sucker," Nunn said.

"What's he going to do?" Chilly wanted to know. "Write a letter to the warden?"

"You really going to put Gasolino on him?"

"I didn't creep up and slip that box in his back pocket. He came and asked for it."

"Yeah, but a lousy box?"

"It's principle." Chilly smiled thinly. "That's something he'd understand."

They finally booked a bet. A man whose hair and jacket looked like animal pelt, so solidly were they matted with the white cotton lint from the textile mill, stopped to bet a single pack on the outcome of the Cotton Bowl game. Then feeling around in his jacket pocket he came out with a cigarette holder that appeared to have been made from a toothbrush handle and some scraps of abalone.

"Three packs and it's yours," he said.

"I'd give three packs to get rid of it," Nunn said.

Society Red took the cigarette holder and waved it with his notion of elegance. "Pretty smooth pimp stick for only three packs."

"Red," Chilly said, "you'd go for fried ice cream." He took the holder from Red and returned it. "We make book. We don't collect handicraft."

The man studied the cigarette holder for a minute, then looked up doubtfully. "Think she's worth three packs? I give two."

"Old buddy," Nunn said, "they saw you coming."

"Yeah, I'm beginning to think so."

The man moved on.

"Where do fools like that come from?" Chilly asked in a tone that didn't suppose an answer.

Nunn answered anyway. "From all over. He figures he's going to work his way out of the textile mill and go into the King business."

"What was wrong with him?" Red wanted to know.

"He was taking up space," Nunn said.

"Your mammy takes up space."

"Knock it off," Chilly ordered. "Give mom a rest."

After this they fell silent again. They would have preferred to pass the time talking, but for a while each of them before saying anything considered that he already knew exactly what the others would find to answer to it, and what he would say to that . . . and it didn't seem worth the effort.

Chilly saw Charlie Wong, the warden's houseboy, coming down the yard in a yellow slicker, probably making a run on the hospital. On impulse, Chilly stepped out and intercepted him.

"Hey, Wong, I want to talk to you."

Wong nodded, smiling, his dark eyes bland as he watched Chilly with a show of polite interest.

"I hear you're getting some pot in," Chilly said.

"Pot?" Wong grinned. "You catch cook. Plenty pot."

"Marijuana," Chilly said.

"Ah, velly bad!" Wong made a swift clawing gesture across his forehead. "Plenty devils."

"You can drop the Oriental Uncle Tom," Chilly said quietly. "I don't buy it."

Wong drew back and studied Chilly alertly. "Uncle Tom?" he asked.

"I've talked to someone who knew you on the streets."

Wong smiled thinly, his eyes suddenly wise. "And you would expose this poor Chinaboy?"

"Did anyone ever tell you I was a cop?"

"Hardly."

"What about the pot? I'd like a piece of it."

"Have you ever heard of a Chinese smoking pot?"

"My information was pretty good."

"I hope you didn't pay for it. I never bring anything through that gate, and I don't intend to start."

"Is that the way you want to play it?" Chilly asked.

"It's the way it is."

"All right," Chilly said mildly. "It was just a notion I had."

Wong's eyes went bland again like a picture going out of focus, and he reached out to tap his finger against the air a half-inch from Chilly's forehead. "Many wheels," he said. "You catch plenty notions."

Chilly smiled. "You're something else, Chinaman."

Wong gave a slight bow and turned to continue down the yard, while Chilly walked thoughtfully towards Nunn and Red.

"What've you got going with that nut?" Nunn asked.

"Nothing. He's in a good spot to hear things."

"Yeah, if you could understand the sucker when he tried to repeat it."

"That's a problem," Chilly said without emphasis.

The crowd under the rain shed began to shift and there was the sudden silence they all knew too well. They turned to watch a pair of hospital attendants pushing a gurney through a corridor forming for them in the crowd. They moved at a quick trot. The inmate stretched out on the gurney trailed his hand, wet with blood, over the side. Red stains like a trail of irregular poker chips marked the path the gurney had taken.

"Another cutting," Nunn said. "That's three just since I came back."

"It's gang action," Chilly said. "They're not looking to kill. They want to make their mark, get blood on their knife. The Chingaderos. The No Names. The Flower Street Gang. Someone was telling me a new bunch was beginning to come in—the Vampires."

"They got their mark all over the joint," Red said. "Must be a hundred of them kids to draw all them bastards with fangs."

"Shit, there's three of them," Nunn said. "Two little punks and a duke, who could probably cause some trouble if he wasn't a stone nut. Big, tall, skinny-assed kid, who thinks he's Genghis Khan, or something. They were in the county with me, came to the joint on the same chain. The nut made the shelf before he even got inside the walls. He didn't want to flash his prune for a skin shake."

"That's what we need here," Chilly said. "More nuts."

Again they fell silent. This time it was almost ten minutes before anyone spoke, then Chilly said, in his educational voice, "The problem for today is—why does shit stink?"

"Who says it does?" Nunn offered in immediate contrary motion.

"That Lola Peterson," Red said, naming a starlet in the last movie they'd seen. "I'll bet hers don't stink."

"I'm serious," Chilly said, "Why does it?"

"It just does."

"Nothing *just* happens," Chilly began to educate. "There's always causation."

"Chilly, you've been reading again."

"It wouldn't hurt you none. Maybe you could figure how to stay out of these joints. How many times have I seen you come back? Three?"

"Two," Nunn said, half angry. "Just two."

"Just two," Chilly repeated mockingly.

"Two times is nothing," Red said. "This is my fourth fall."

"Radio, Red," Chilly ordered. "You're a special case, all heart and no brain, but Nunn here he's supposed to be a schooled hustler, down with all games, so how come he lets a bunch of numb-brained fuzz catch him time after time?"

Nunn was hot. "Because some lousy rat mother fucker always splits on me. That's why. Every other stud you meet on the streets belongs to the bottles. They got four snitches on each block. Every morning the heat knows what you had for dinner the night before, whether or not you took a crap and how many times you made it with your old lady. Studs who used to be solid regulars are out there giving up their own mothers, and that ain't—"

"Hang up," Chilly broke in. "Hang up a minute. Say that's all true, you still knew it when you hit the streets last time. You were down with it. If a snitch gets close enough to turn you that's still your goof. Snitches snitch just like snakes bite and you're still left to do your own dying. The point is, they're whipping you to death out there and you're not even trying to figure out why. If you got your ass torn up every time you shot craps, after a while you'd put craps down and maybe try low ball. Now you tell me why you haven't got sense enough to do at least that much when you're out there on those streets?"

"All right, Chilly," Nunn said, no longer angry. "You made your point. You win, man, as usual. Why does shit stink?"

For a moment Chilly stared at his friend. Then he smiled.

"That's easy. It stinks so you won't eat it."

12

JULESON spent a bad week. The Christmas music disturbed him. Hearing it on the big yard was somehow like watching very old people dressed up for a tea party in the terminal ward. Christmas itself, an institutional holiday, he spent in the cell reading. He had long schooled himself to indifference, but he had been aware that Manning was suffering—the holiday season brought a cruel focus to the sense of loss. Christmas dinner was the best meal of the year and he would have ordinarily enjoyed it if anxiety hadn't taken the edge from his appetite. That evening the Salvation Army had distributed bags of hard candy, nuts, a banana, an orange, and an apple, and in each bag was a wallet-sized calendar.

Juleson had held the calendar and tried to persuade himself that one of the blocks of numbers that made up the new year was the date on which he would leave the prison—"go home" was the universal expression, but this expression seemed as fierce a mockery to Juleson as the carols piped over the institution radio.

Now the week of grace was gone, and nothing had worked out. He had never been able to convince himself that it would. First, he had always been reluctant to discuss his troubles with anyone, a habit he had formed in the county homes where he had spent his youth, and, secondly, it would have to be a very good friend to loan him fifteen packs to pay a debt already gone bad against no better security than he was able to offer. He knew no one that well. He had made it a point to know no one that well. Now, when it was probably

too late, life was instructing him that it was always dangerous to stand outside your community.

He had been able to borrow five packs from a friend in the
library. They had sat on the shelf against the day he could add
ten more. Last night, knowing he would fail, he had impulsively opened one of the packs and shared it with Manning.
Now as he stood the big yard waiting for the gate to open he
was smoking one of the cigarettes and there were two more
loose in his shirt pocket. He stared at the butt in his hand and
wondered grimly at the kind of man he was becoming.

He had passed Oberholster, moments before. Nothing had
been said, but he had felt Oberholster's eyes on him and he
knew that sometime in the hour before the gate was opened
he would have to talk to Oberholster. He had tried to dismiss
Chilly Willy as a shallow poser who was just playing a part, but
he was unable to convince himself. Whatever Chilly was, he
was deeper than that, even though what he did made no sense.

Juleson didn't see Gasolino often. Looking at Gasolino was
like watching a gun or a grenade—he was nothing until he
was used—but like a mortal weapon Gasolino had a deadly
aura, rendered grotesque by his constant smile. A grinning
knife. Juleson shuddered. The thought of a knife unnerved
him. He had faced bullets with nothing of the same terror. A
bullet was somehow impersonal, a knife intimate.

He found himself staring into the rain-pocked water flowing slowly through the concrete gutters that drained the
yard. A wadded candy wrapper turned slowly, and a few
burnt-head paper matches clustered on the dull current like
a small school of blind fish. A number of cigarette butts were
disintegrating—none exceeded an inch in length.

What a mindless indulgence. What had he once paid for
a carton of cigarettes? He discovered it was an effort to
remember—an effort that required a conscious sharpening of
the focus over that whole span of his life preceding his first
night in jail. Though the details of that night were still sharply

etched, the events of even the week before were beginning to fade and blur like an ancient photograph.

Two dollars something—two and a quarter? As he stood trying to remember, still staring into the gutter, he seemed to relive a moment where he saw a fresh carton of Camels slide across the smoothly worn and darkened wood of a grocery counter.

—That be all?

He nodded, holding out the money—two worn dollar bills and a bright new quarter—but Mr. Caporusso waved it aside with a slow thick arm, sleeved with a paper butcher's guard.

—It's you birthday, huh?

The time came back to him. It was four years ago, four years, one month, and a few days. Anna Marie was still alive.

—Yes, Paul said. I'm twenty-six today.

—Then keep you money. And Happy Birthday.

Juleson saw himself offer the money again and again Mr. Caporusso refused it. Imperceptibly memory began to shift into fantasy as the grocer seemed to go on.

—You keep it. Maybe someday those few bucks save you life.

—Thank you, but I hope I never see the day my life's worth only a few bucks.

—Only a few bucks! Listen, my poppa's poppa bought a wife for a few pennies. Prettiest girl in her village. Natch'ly she's in love. Natch'ly she threaten she gonna kill herself—

—The poor girl.

—And, natch'ly, she no really kill herself. But she cry a long time, and then bitch even longer. Then my granpoppa catches her laying for a young man, and kills both of them.

—The boy she loved? Juleson asked.

—What boy?

—The one in her village. The one she loved?

—No, not him. Some other.

Juleson approached Oberholster just as the gate was opening. "I want to talk to you."

"Go ahead," Oberholster said.

"I'd prefer to talk to you in private."

Oberholster looked at his two friends. The old Redhead was smiling, and Juleson noting the quality of the smile felt his anger stir. He wasn't here to eat their shit.

"If you can't pay, say so," Oberholster said. "Don't make a production out of it."

Juleson held his hands out. "I don't have anything."

"All right."

"Listen to me for a minute. I made a mistake. But it was an honest mistake. What I'm saying is that I didn't set out to burn you. And I'm not the kind of guy who would go around talking about it."

"What kind of guy are you then?" Oberholster asked.

"What do you mean?"

"That's what puzzles me. You walk this yard like you were wading through shit, like you were caged with animals. But then you wanted something the animals had, and you held your nose and asked for it, and you got it. Now you don't think it should cost you anything."

"You have it wrong."

"Have I?"

Juleson found himself without an answer. His face seemed hot, and he knew his heavy sense of uncertainty confirmed at least some truth in Oberholster's observation. Unconsciously he straightened his shoulders and said slowly, "I have to tell you I can't pay. I can give you four packs—that's all I have."

"That's not enough, is it?"

"That's up to you. If you want them I'll bring them out tomorrow morning and I'll have to owe you the rest."

Oberholster shook his head. "I'll give you this much of a break, and no more—lock up. Get yourself some protective custody. If you hit this big yard tomorrow morning you're in serious trouble. One way or another I'm going to cure myself of having to look at you."

The old Redhead started laughing.

"Shut up, Red," Oberholster said. He turned back to Juleson. "You got that charted? Lock up, but if you come on the yard tomorrow morning, you better have your stuff."

"My stuff?"

"Your shank, your knife."

"I don't have a knife."

"Borrow one."

"Suppose I do. And suppose I come after you with it."

Oberholster smiled. "Do anything you got balls enough to do—go crazy, sucker—but you better think carefully, and lock up, that's what you better do."

Juleson turned and walked away heading towards the gate, and Chilly, still smiling, watched after him.

Nunn said, "You're not leaving Gasolino much cover."

"He'll lock up."

"What if he doesn't?"

"Then we should see some action. Don't worry about it."

"Why should I worry? I just thought you could have let Gasolino pick his own time and place. He might have wanted to creep on this dude."

"I don't think Gasolino would bother creeping on King Kong." Chilly glanced back towards the gate Juleson was just now passing through, his shoulders held unnaturally square. "Anyway," Chilly continued, "I'd lay long odds he locks up."

Red said, "Chilly's run many and many a stud off the yard."

"What're you?" Nunn asked with humorous contempt. "Chilly's fan club?"

"I work for him—just like you do."

Chilly rocked back on his heels. "Tell him, Red."

Juleson found himself unable to make sense of his job. He was trying to post grades and again and again he found himself, pen poised over a card, staring at the bland yellow wall across from him. He wasn't thinking. His mind was disabled by anxiety.

His supervisor arrived, flushed with enthusiasm. "Paul, come in here, will you?" he said and went into his office. Juleson automatically picked up a pencil and pad and rose to follow.

"Paul, do you know what we're doing here?" Mr. Cleman asked rhetorically, seating himself at his desk. His thinning gray hair was cropped so short it seemed to spot his broad forehead like silver frost. He immediately picked up a freshly sharpened pencil and began to turn it in his hands, hands still marked from the years Mr. Cleman had worked as a plumber.

"We're trying to turn out journeymen trained on obsolete equipment. I was talking to Bob Tribble—you remember him? He's on our printing trade advisory committee. He told me the whole industry's shifting to automation..."

Juleson watched Mr. Cleman's hands shifting in illustration, still anchored by the pencil, two worn red birds struggling over a glossy yellow worm, and he wondered what Mr. Cleman would find to say if he were to interrupt to tell him someone had threatened to have his clerk killed. What could he say?

"... and that isn't all, Paul, much the same sort of thing is happening to our machinist trainees—" He broke off, his face sharpening with concern. "Don't you feel well?"

"I'm all right."

"You don't look well."

"Maybe I'm catching stomach flu—the block's been full of it."

Mr. Cleman shook his head in warning. "You don't want to play around with that stuff. My brother-in-law came down with it last year..." After he had related the course of his brother-in-law's illness, Mr. Cleman asked, "Do you want a pass to the hospital?"

"No, thank you."

"If you don't feel better tomorrow, lay in." He looked at Juleson with a sympathy that was no less genuine for its remoteness. "I often think the ordinary hardships must be doubly difficult to bear here. I didn't know what to say when I went home Christmas Eve—I never do." He looked down at the thick green glass that topped his desk. A line of photographs were pressed beneath the upper edge, two sturdy blond boys caught in a series of poses. "Sometimes I have a feeling of shame that I'm able to go home. Why should I be able to go home? I wonder. But then I can." He tapped the ID badge above his breast pocket. "I have this."

Juleson tried to say something comforting. "You might not know why you're not here, but we do know why we are."

Mr. Cleman smiled vaguely. "You may have something there, Paul." He reached for his telephone and placed a call to the auto mech shop, and began to ask the instructor how grave a disadvantage it was to his program to have to train his students on old model cars.

Juleson passed up lunch as he usually did, but he didn't go to the library, and he was sitting at his desk, still trying to work in the almost empty building, when he saw Oberholster step through the front door. Oberholster paused by the information desk, looking around, and when he saw Juleson, he turned to motion to someone outside. Gasolino came in. Even at the distance of thirty yards Juleson could clearly discern the mad quality of Gasolino's smile. Oberholster pointed, and Gasolino started down the central aisle, moving with a peculiar gliding slouch. Automatically Juleson stood up—his hand reached out and closed over the Scotch tape dispenser on top of his desk. He didn't pick it up, but stood waiting.

Gasolino stopped halfway along the aisle and made an odd little gesture, much as to say, *I see you*. Then he turned back.

The guard came out of the custody office with a sandwich

in his hand. He was still chewing as he asked, "What you guys want?"

"I think maybe I go to school," Gasolino said. He touched his forehead with two fingers, and smiled out at the guard from under his hand. "I want to get keen."

"Open line's at three o'clock," the guard said automatically.

Oberholster walked out without looking back, but Gasolino turned to wave at Juleson.

Juleson sat down slowly. His armpits were wet, and his legs continued to tremble for moments after. By the dull ache in his jaw he realized how hard he had been gritting his teeth. He went on working and wondered why he bothered. However it came out there was little chance he would be sitting at this desk tomorrow. Still he went on with his everyday chores and was still at them when in the middle of the afternoon he was called to the captain's office. He walked across the garden and presented himself at the pass window. He was told to have a seat on the benches. His name was called after a few minutes and he was directed to one of the interview rooms where he found himself facing the warden. It was the first time he had seen this famous man up close, and he wondered if the smooth white hair was not a little too theatrical, the warm blue eyes a little too candid.

"Sit down, Mr. Juleson."

The warden smiled disarmingly and indicated a case file in front of him. "I've been looking over your record. It's impressive, quite impressive. There's good reason to believe that when your case comes up in front of the board in—" He paused to check the date. "In March. They will most likely grant your parole at that time."

"That's encouraging."

"Yes, but—" The warden paused delicately. "We hear things. All sorts of things. Some of them are true, many of them are not, but we feel we have to check up, particularly when it concerns a man whose potential for successful readjustment is as high as yours."

The warden picked up a square of paper and passed it to Juleson, "Do you know this man?"

Juleson recognized Oberholster's mug shot. The photo was dated three years earlier, but Oberholster seemed to have grown no older. Except for his eyes, he looked like a boy. His smooth blond hair was hardly darker than his white face.

"I've seen him," Juleson said.

"We hear you're having trouble with him."

Juleson looked into the warden's eyes and found himself saying, "I don't even know him."

"This is a dangerous man, one of the most dangerous in the institution. It would be very unwise of you to protect him."

"I'm afraid you've been misinformed, sir."

The warden took the mug shot back and studied it briefly himself. Then he stood up and went to a file cabinet. "I want to show you something." He sorted through several folders before he pulled out a glossy eight-by-ten-inch photograph which he handed to Juleson. The subject was the corpse of a Mexican boy. It was photographed from above, and from the throat to the groin there were a great number of small round holes. They appeared black, darker than the primitive tattoo of the Virgin on the boy's chest. His unmarked face would have seemed peaceful except his mouth gaped emptily.

"He was nineteen," the warden said flatly. "He was stabbed thirty-two times. The morning before the fight he wrapped newspapers and magazines around himself, but the man he fought had used two of the trays from the mess hall. We can't prove it, but we believe Oberholster paid to have this done."

Juleson pushed the photograph away. He had had to look at mortuary photographs more distressing to him than any others ever could be, including the thought of his own. The dead boy was an abstraction.

"I'm sorry," he said. "I can't help you."

"And you won't help yourself?"

"But I don't need help, Warden."

The warden closed the file drawer, nodding in close agreement with whatever he was thinking. "You seem to have learned something here," he said, "but it is not what we would like to have had you learn. I didn't come into prison work as a warden—you've probably heard that—I've worked the blocks, the towers, the big yard, and I've learned too. I've developed certain instincts. I think the word's out on you, and I think you know it." He paused studying Juleson closely. "I should order you locked up for your own protection."

"There's no need for that, sir."

"You think you can handle this yourself—no, you think you should handle it yourself, yet if someone had threatened your home when you were still an ordinary citizen, would you have hesitated to call the police?"

"It's beside the point, sir, but there is a difference."

"But why?" The warden leaned forward eagerly. "Your crime was a crime of passion. For a moment you lost control of yourself. That could happen to anyone. It doesn't make you like the majority of these men." The warden waved his hand to indicate the prison beyond the interview room. "It doesn't make you subject to their laws."

"I live with them. I've been living with them for three years."

"Yes." The warden sat down, his eagerness spent. "Yes, you have." Again he turned the fatherly and faintly conning gaze on Juleson. "You won't reconsider? I don't like to order you to protective custody against your will."

"There's nothing to consider, Warden. I don't know how to convince you, but you've picked up some bum scoop."

"Bum scoop." The warden mouthed the expression as if it had an unpleasant taste. "Yes, that happens. All right, Mr. Juleson, I'm going to take your word for this. But should you

171

want to get in touch with me, I'll leave word at the captain's office." He stood up and offered his hand.

They shook hands, Juleson conscious that his palm was damp.

"Good luck with the parole board," the warden said.

That afternoon when he passed into the big yard before lockup he found they were operating the metal detector. This system was built into three-gate, and when it was activated it could be set to detect any concentration of metal greater than the sum of a man's belt buckle and the nails in his shoes. When someone tried to pass carrying more, even a Prince Albert can, a bell rang. Little was ever caught in the Eye, as they called it, but it served its purpose. When men approaching the big yard saw the Eye in operation they immediately dropped their knives, and after lockup the guards would gather the harvest. Knives were manufactured steadily in a dozen shops and custody was satisfied to hold the number down and as much as possible to keep them out of the blocks and off the big yard.

Juleson passed the Eye without incident. He hadn't considered acquiring a knife, not that he had any idea where to get one. He crossed the yard and joined one of the lines forming in front of the south block. When he met Manning in front of the cell he merely nodded at the other man's small talk. After the count had cleared he stretched out on his bunk and closed his eyes. He knew what had hardened him through the interview with the warden, and it wasn't the inverted morality the warden suspected, but simple pride—the sense of his own manhood. He wasn't going to give Oberholster the satisfaction of seeing him take shelter behind the guns of the guardline—even if it cost his life. And that was only one of many alternatives. That was always one of many alternatives. He realized there were things he could not do and remain the man he needed to be. If he locked up—and he had to smile at the irony that this was what both Oberholster and the warden had advised—if he locked up he would be finished in another way just as surely as if Gasolino were to stab him to death in the morning. This lesson lay close to the bone, but Juleson realized that an ordinary man, as he was, might go a lifetime and never have to test it. Yet this was the second time he had found himself facing the question, and he did not intend to fail again. Nor did he intend to make Gasolino's job easy for him.

He turned in his bunk, pressing his face into his pillow, and his quickened senses informed him his blankets were growing dusty again. Blankets were washed once a year—in a week they lost their scent of freshness, in a month the dust puffed when they were sharply slapped. If he had been called upon to symbolize the quality of his imprisonment in a single image he would have thought of himself exposed in a small poorly lit concrete box full of the odor of stale grease. His tongue would be coated with dust.

"Manning?"

Juleson looked up to see the mail officer paused in front of the cell. He heard Manning in the bunk below calling off his number. The officer lifted Manning's letter, automatically glancing at the one below to see if it were designated to the same cell, and in that moment Juleson experienced the swift and irrational hope that his aunt's check, now a month late, would be waiting there, but the officer moved on, his eyes lifted to the cell numbers stenciled above the doors. Juleson dropped back to his pillow. He recognized that his wild surge of hope had exposed to him just how badly he wanted the situation with Oberholster harmlessly dissolved. It would still be honorable to pay.

Manning took his letter from the bars and stared at the envelope. He looked up tentatively. "It's from my wife."

"Is that good?"

"I don't know."

He removed the letter through the slit the censor had

made and unfolded it. Juleson, watching his hands, noted that Manning's nails were still trimmed and shaped. Manning combed his hair in the morning and it stayed as he placed it for the rest of the day. Tidiness was not so much a habit with him as an effortless quality. Somehow he always had the cell clean before Juleson woke in the morning. Juleson would find him on the lower bunk studying circuit diagrams while waiting for the breakfast unlock.

After some consideration Manning had decided to study office machine repair. "Those things are always breaking down," he had told Juleson. "Every time I turned around in the office some fellow had the face plate off the billing machine and was poking at it with a screwdriver for ten dollars an hour." Juleson had been able to persuade Mr. Cleman to assign Manning to the vocational typewriter repair shop over the classification committee's objection that they needed the subject as an inmate accountant.

Now, under the harsh light of the overhead bulb, Juleson noted that Manning was graying, had grayed noticeably just in the month he had shared Juleson's cell. Manning did hard time and the time was hard on him. Juleson wondered how long Manning would have to serve. He realized it was possible Manning could be imprisoned longer for the statutory rape of his stepdaughter than he would serve for the death of his wife. The senselessness of this incredible dislocation shocked Juleson.

Manning lowered his letter and looked up to say, "Debbie's left home."

"Isn't she too young?"

"She ran away with some boy."

"Oh."

Manning was silent a moment, creasing the letter in his hands, then he continued. "I remember the boy. He lived in the same block. He had one of those old cars they fix up and he used to drive back and forth in front of the house gunning the motor. Now I understand why. He couldn't be more than seventeen or eighteen. What are two kids like that going to do out in the world?"

"Your stepdaughter's going on sixteen now, isn't she?"

"Yes, but she's still a child."

"Many marriages have been started at that age."

Manning asked with sudden sharpness, "Did I say anything about marriage?"

"That's probably what they intend."

"Is it? Is it?"

Juleson's remarks had been designed to comfort Manning, but when he saw they were having the opposite effect he decided to keep quiet. What did he know about the complex knot Manning lived within? For that matter, what did Manning know about him?

Manning opened the letter and read it again. Then he replaced it in the envelope and laid it on his side of the shelf next to his toothbrush. "This is the first word I've had from her since the day I was arrested. But she had to let me know. She blames me, of course." He thought a moment. "Now she's alone in the house. My house. I wonder how she likes that?"

The bell rang and they heard the crashing of metal as one of the lower tiers was released for dinner. Manning walked to the front of the cell ready to throw the door open when their own bar was pulled. He looked across at the empty gun rail and said, "It shouldn't mean anything to me. But it does."

They had stew for dinner, stew, hominy, and lemon cake. Juleson made an effort to eat, but the food turned to cardboard in his mouth. He offered his cake to Manning, who wrapped it in his handkerchief to carry back to the cell.

"What's the matter, Paul?"

"I'm just not hungry."

Manning smiled. "That's unusual for you."

"Yes, I guess it is."

Back in the cell the two men took turns brushing their teeth. Manning went first and afterwards took the letter from the shelf and lay down in his bunk to read it again. Juleson brushed his own teeth. He snapped out his partial plate to wash the food particles from the roof, and, as he turned the ragged-looking red denture in his hand, he remembered for the first time in several years how he had lost this plate in a mountain stream.

They had driven up for the weekend and discovered the stream lying below the highway. In great cups of rock it had formed a series of three pools, the water so vivid, so full of the quality of light, it had seemed only a denser extension of the clear mountain air. Impulsively Paul had stopped, piled from the car, and over Anna Marie's objections he had stripped to his shorts and run out on a platform of rock to dive into the largest pool. It was ice cold and when he surfaced, he threw his head sharply to whip the hair out of his eyes. The plate popped out as if it were escaping, flicked the surface and vanished. It reappeared for a moment about a foot down, sinking off on an angle with a fluttering motion. He dove after it, but lost it in the turbulence of his own effort to find it. When he reached the bottom, seven or eight feet down, he found it covered with sand and gravel which would make the plate difficult to distinguish.

Anna Marie had called from the road, "What's wrong?"

"I lost my teeth."

"You what? Oh, Paul . . ."

"I'll find them."

"You'd better. We can't afford any more dental bills."

"Don't worry. I'll find them."

But it had been necessary to drive all the way back to Bakersfield and buy a child's skin-diving outfit—faceplate, flippers and plastic snorkel tube—before he had been able to locate the plate. He remembered that after hours spent in a random and futile search, drifting on the surface of the pool, watching the bottom through the faceplate, he had finally realized that the currents at the bottom of the pool were different from those on the surface. These deeper currents were betrayed by the shifting sand, and following them he discovered his plate where it had been deposited along with several bottle caps, a fishing spinner, and a plastic tube which had once held suntan lotion. He surfaced grinning triumphantly with the plate in place, but Anna Marie hadn't been able to share his feeling that he had met and mastered some challenge on the bottom of the pool. For her the weekend had been ruined.

Now as he brushed the plastic teeth, which were starting to yellow in defiance of their guarantee, he found it difficult to realize that this was the same plate. The continuity of his life had been so implacably broken that it wasn't unreasonable to imagine that the very atoms of this acrylic had been disorganized and recombined in a different pattern. He sometimes had the same feeling when he soaped his genitals in the shower. It was impossible to grasp that this was the same flesh with which he had entered the girls of his life. He had loved these girls, but not with this flesh. This person he had become could never have known such pleasures because if he had, the daily pain of loss would have been unbearable.

He wasn't able to read and he lay on his bunk looking at the ceiling eighteen inches above him. The night slid by. Manning went to the gym for a meeting of the chess club, returned, and settled down for another hour of study before the lights went out at ten. Then Manning was moving quietly putting his papers away in the dark.

"Are you asleep, Paul?"

"No."

"Sorry, I thought you might have fallen asleep with your clothes on."

"I'm just lying here tripping."

"Do you want half of this cake?"

"No, thanks. I'm still not hungry."

When Manning was in bed, Juleson got up to undress. He hung his clothes over the head of the bed, washed his face and hands and climbed under the covers. Already his sheets seemed warm. He didn't expect to sleep.

"Good night," he said.

"Good night," Manning replied, his voice already muffled.

At breakfast Manning asked, "Are you sure you're all right?"

"I may hit the sick line. In case they check me into the hospital, there's something I'd like you to do for me."

"Of course."

"Those four packs of Camels on the shelf, see that Redman in the library gets them, will you? They're his."

"Do you think they'll put you to bed?"

"I don't know."

During the night he had resolved to attack Gasolino as soon as he could find him rather than leave the initiative in the hands of the other man. The chances were that Gasolino had left his shank stashed somewhere in the industrial alley when he heard the Eye was working, and if this were the case he wouldn't be able to pick it up until after the gate was open. Juleson knew this for his best chance. Even without his knife Gasolino wasn't negligible, but neither was he deadly.

Acting on this plan Juleson separated himself from Manning as soon as they left the mess hall and began to comb the yard looking for Gasolino. The men were gathering into social groups, large and small, some stationary, some walking the asphalt. The long wait in the morning was the time to take care of personal business, keep contacts, exchange prison rumors, and tell the lies you had imagined the night before.

The sky was clear for the first time in a week, but it was still cold this early in the morning. A gun bull with his coat collar turned up stood the rail that ran along the top of the east block. He was hugging his rifle to his chest and his breath came in white plumes. Another gun bull paced the top of the north block. Juleson no longer saw these armed guards as anything more than familiar details. He looked for Ober-holster, but he wasn't on the yard yet. He saw Lester Moon waiting at the place where Oberholster always stood. Their eyes met, and Red smiled. Suddenly, as if Red's smile were a match tossed in kerosene, Juleson was angry. All right, all right, he thought, turning on another tack, where was that ape?

Juleson passed along the domino tables, already filling for the day's action, and skirted a group of hobby workers bur-dened with their products like old-fashioned peddlers. Another group of men were reliving the football game they had won Saturday in the lower yard. Ten Negroes with shaven heads performed calisthenics. They called themselves Simbas.

Then he saw Gasolino. He was standing on the bench that ran alongside the north block, leaning back against the con-crete wall. Another man was standing on the bench beside him and a third stood below them. Despite the cold Gasolino wasn't wearing a jacket. His chambray shirt was starched and pressed. His jeans had been bleached to a pale blue. He wore a thin black belt fastened with a silver buckle, inset with aba-lone shell. His pants were rolled up to reveal white gym socks and black loafers. The two men with him were also bone-rooed. Regulars was how they would think of themselves.

Gasolino was telling a joke, acting it out using the bench as a stage, and he was pantomiming abjection, pretending to cower and tremble, when Juleson walked up to ask, "Are you looking for me?"

He hadn't known what he was going to say and his ques-tion surprised him with its blurred ring of cliché. He felt briefly foolish as if he had been discovered in some adoles-cent pretense, and Gasolino, as if he understood this, was par-odying an elaborate amused annoyance, wincing and smiling at the same time as if to say: Is that the best you could do?

"Hey, man," Gasolino said softly. "I was telling my friends a story."

Again Juleson felt a snap of anger as if a faulty connection had for a moment made firm contact. He reached up and, grabbing Gasolino by the belt, pulled him from the bench. In the same motion he slapped him. Gasolino's eyes dilated with amazement.

"What're you going to do about that?" Juleson asked.

Gasolino's smile slowly reformed. He stood lightly in a posture of compact authority and reached for his hip pocket. Juleson felt his breath jerk and catch as instinctively he sucked in his stomach and took a half-step back. Gasolino's eyes glittered with delight. He produced a comb and ran it through his hair.

"You nervous?" he inquired, still softly.

The two men who had been standing with Gasolino had moved off and were watching from ten feet away. Other heads were beginning to turn towards them.

"No, I'm not nervous," Juleson said.

Gasolino's face turned flat and ugly as if the slap were just now registering in some distant center of his awareness. "Then what the fuck you slap me for, punk? You think you start some shit on the yard, the bulls come break it up?"

"Are you afraid of the bulls?"

"I ain't afraid of shit. I'm going to kill your ass. I'm going to cut your guts out."

Gasolino scowled and, moving with incredible swiftness, lunged forward with the comb to make three slashing passes an inch from Juleson's shirt front. Juleson swung at Gasolino, but the other man sidestepped easily.

"Not now, punk."

But Juleson lunged forward and managed to grab Gasolino by the collar, and when Gasolino sidestepped again the buttons were ripped from his shirt. They rattled on the blacktop. Suddenly a crowd had formed around them and now they made a sound as if they had all sighed together. Gasolino's exposed chest was so densely tattooed it appeared blue and the figures pulsed with his breath. His eyes were wild.

"Hey, Gasolino," someone said in the crowd, "you're called out, man."

Gasolino shook his head as if to drive away an irritation. His lips remembered their smile as he began to shuffle lightly towards Juleson, and Juleson took three hard punches before he was able to grab Gasolino and begin to use his weight and strength. Dimly he heard a whistle shrilling. Gasolino was pummeling him around the stomach and chest, but he was steadily forcing the other man towards the north block wall where he intended to batter him unconscious.

A shot sounded. The crowd roared like the ocean and then fell dead silent. Another shot scored this silence. Juleson realized there wasn't an inmate within fifty feet of them now. They had scattered like litter blown from the eye of an explosion only to re-form at a distance, ringing the two men against the north block wall.

Juleson released Gasolino and struck him a hammering blow to the side of the head. Gasolino fell back, his hands held low and outstretched. He looked up along the east block rail where the gun bull was aiming down at them as he jacked another shell into the chamber.

"He can't shoot straight," Juleson taunted, but his voice sounded breathless.

A third shot sounded and the slug tore the blacktop between them, cutting a ragged furrow, and in the same instant Gasolino cried out, whipping around as if he had been stung by a bee. He started running towards the edge of the crowd as an animal caught on the plain runs for the shelter of the surrounding trees. The crowd began to hoot.

"*Run, you sissy cocksucker,*" someone howled with delighted scorn.

"*Run, run,*" others joined in. "*Run, you yellow punk.*"

Juleson stood where he was. He realized he was panting. Two officers broke through the edge of the crowd and made an attempt to head Gasolino off, but he pivoted like a halfback reversing field, and managed to elude them. The crowd opened and closed around him, and Juleson saw someone throw a jacket over Gasolino's shoulders to hide the torn shirt. The gun bull on the north block was running along, blowing his whistle, trying to keep Gasolino in sight, but by the way his head was twisting from side to side it was apparent he had already lost him among the hundreds of nearly identical figures.

The two yard officers, abandoning Gasolino, closed on Juleson. They grabbed his arms, levering them behind his back.

"You don't have to do that," Juleson told them.

"Move!" one of them said.

They marched him directly to the north block rotunda and rang for the elevator to the shelf. He was placed in a holding cell where he remained for two days. No one spoke to him, not even when his meals were served. On the morning of the third day he was taken out and prepared for disciplinary court. They let him wash up, and handed him a new comb, which, after he had used it, they took back and tossed in a wastepaper basket. Then they shook him down thoroughly, and sent him through the door into the committee room.

He was surprised to see the warden in the center seat. His presence measured the gravity of the hearing. Captain Blake sat on the warden's right and he was the only uniformed official present. His hat was on the table before him, but the ridge along the side of his straight black hair still held the square uncompromising line at which he wore it. At the warden's left sat the Reverend Mr. Nugent, the Protestant minister. A young correctional counselor, grade I, acted as recorder. Off to the side of the conference table, as if deliberately emphasizing the ambivalence of his position, sat Dr. A. R. Smith. His small feet were set side by side on the floor, and his two forefingers making "here is the steeple" seemed to support his chin. When his eyes met Juleson's he nodded slightly, and the forefingers communicated the motion to his clasped hands.

"That was a stupid thing to do, Juleson," the warden said severely.

There was no adequate response to such a statement. He stood quietly aware that the captain was staring up at him with what appeared to be anger. The minister too was watching him, but his eyes seemed remote. Dr. Smith was looking out the barred window. The CC-I was writing.

"Sit down," the warden ordered. He waited until Juleson had settled himself, then he asked, "Do you know an inmate named Memo Solozano?"

"No, sir."

"He's known on the yard as Gasolino," the captain added.

"I know him by reputation."

"Do you know he's dying?"

"Dying?" Juleson repeated. His voice sounded fragile.

"Yes, he can't live more than a few days."

"I don't understand. Was he shot?"

"Do you understand that if he had been shot you could have been held responsible under the laws of this state?" This was the captain.

"No, sir, I didn't know that."

The warden continued, "Solozano is dying from the effects of carbon tetrachloride. Apparently he's been sniffing it for some time, but the afternoon of the day you two fought he drank the contents of one of the fire extinguishers located in the gym. This is a deadly and irreversible poison. There's a warning on each unit in English, but he was unable to read English—" The warden paused. There was nothing now of the father in his face. "Did you imagine something like this might happen?"

"How could I?"

"Your intelligence is superior. You have a history of violence."

"I only wanted to force the issue so I had a chance of coming out of it alive."

"And I offered you that chance. And you refused me. You lied to me."

"Do you really think it's that simple?" Juleson asked angrily. "Do you really think you have everything—*everything* —written down here in front of you?"

"Lower your voice," the captain said.

Juleson turned to look at Dr. Smith. He hadn't moved, though his gaze was no longer directed at the window. His face was passive, eyes veiled. The CC-I, pen poised, was watching with interest. His lips were sucked in against one another as if he were tasting salt on them.

"I felt I had to solve my own problem," Juleson continued.

"So again you did something violent," Mr. Nugent said. His voice was fortified with stately intonation as deliberately as breakfast cereal is fortified with vitamin C. "Again you took a life."

"That's not true."

"A man is dying," the warden said. "If you had allowed me to help you the fight on the yard could have been avoided."

"I know that would have seemed best to you," Juleson said, anger again adding an edge to his voice. "Don't make waves. But I will tell you I have been ordered to commit far greater violences for reasons that were much less clear to me, and then if I had *not* obeyed I would have had to face a similar court and they would have been equally sure they were right."

"That's enough of that!" the warden ordered. After a moment of heavy silence, he continued, "There may be something in what you say, but you have lost, at least temporarily, the right to make such distinctions. Fighting is against the regulations of this prison. There is no ambiguity as to that. And we find you guilty of the charge."

"It was Oberholster you owed, wasn't it?" the captain asked.

"No, it was Gasolino—Solozano—as you called him."

Again no one spoke. He felt their eyes on him. Then the warden said with a trace of weariness, "Wait outside."

He waited in the corridor, under the eyes of a young offi-cer. "Pretty rough on you?" the officer asked companionably. They were both small fry under the same distant authority.

"Not too bad."

"It's lucky neither of you guys was killed out there. The Mexican lost the tip of his little finger. Did you know that?"

"No."

"It must have been a fragment, or a nearly spent bullet. Sliced it off neat as a knife. Just the very end." The officer glanced at the committee room door, then continued in a lower tone. "But you won't have any more trouble with that punk. His guts are falling out his ass."

"They told me."

"They should have given you a medal instead of a beef."

A buzzer sounded and a light above the committee room door went on. "They want you back in there," the officer said.

This time the warden didn't invite him to sit down. He stood to receive sentence.

"It's the decision of this committee that you be awarded ten days isolation, and sixty days loss of privileges. Further judgment will be in the hands of the parole board. The report submitted by this committee will acknowledge the extenuat-ing circumstances. That will be all."

Isolation's only hardship was monotony. As is customary in all detention units, a Bible was furnished as part of the cell equipment. Someone had mutilated the title page, and printed "bullshit" in the margins through most of Genesis before his zeal faltered. There was a smoky quality to the word, more suggestive of bitter disappointment than simple condemnation, and Juleson wondered if this same man would have found it necessary to deface the Koran or the Bhagavad Gita had these equally sacred books been provided for his example.

Someone else had made a large drawing of a vampire

on the wall above the toilet. It was crudely rendered, but unlike most comic book and B-picture vampires this one looked as if it might actually drink blood. There was a curious and inhuman strength in the expression of the eyes, not entirely offset by the rude fangs and a pimp's hairline mustache.

His cell was otherwise featureless, and he passed the time pacing back and forth from the door to the toilet, and reading parts of the Bible. It never occurred to him that he might find help or hope of sufferance in this book he had never taken seriously, and it was just at random that he came to I Corinthians 10:13 and found himself intimately addressed: *There has no temptation taken you, but such as is common to man* . . . Still billions of others had resisted their common temptations. He had not.

He began to pace again. There was more he might remember, and he puzzled trying to recall what it was the Biblical verse suggested. Something similar. Pacing, eyes level with the vampire's eyes, he drew a second forgiving quotation from his memory . . . There is nothing human which is alien to me. Recalling now that these were the words of Marcus Aurelius, the last of the Five Good Emperors. It went something like . . . because in my youth I knew all things, there is nothing human which is now alien to me. That was the substance.

Again Juleson met the eyes of the vampire and he smiled, wondering if Aurelius might not concede that here was something alien, and, yet, perhaps no more alien than he must have found his own son, Commodus.

He continued pacing, aware of his persistent conviction of his own . . . evil, he could put no lesser word to his feelings, "evil" was precise, though he knew he didn't believe in the existence of evil, just as he was aware that his conviction he was evil betrayed some inverted and ravenous vanity. Perhaps it was as great a presumption to think oneself evil as it would be to consider that one was good. Weren't both extremes equally attractive when they were needed to escape the conclusion that one was, after all, ordinary? An ordinary man who beat his wife for all the ordinary crummy little reasons.

On the sixth day, Dr. Smith stopped by to see him, telling the shelf officer, "Just lock me in, please . . . I'll call when I'm ready to leave."

"Any way you say, Doc," the guard agreed, turning the key.

Dr. Smith appeared as colorless as always, except for his soft russet eyes, slightly magnified in the lenses of his glasses, searching Juleson's face with warm concern.

"You look none the worse," Smith said.

"After a while, any change, even isolation, is stimulating."

Juleson automatically sat on the toilet, leaving the bunk for Smith, who settled himself somewhat deliberately, lifting his pants from his knees to show his black socks and small black shoes. He glanced around the cell.

"These are Spartan enough," he said.

"That's the whole punishment."

"Are you taking it as punishment?"

"No, but I miss my books." Juleson smiled. "All I have is the Good Book. I've been learning to detect leprosy. Whoever shall develop a sore on his head which does not heal, shall be declared unclean, for the sore is in his mind and the Priest shall come and declare him to be utterly unclean—"

"In his mind?" Dr. Smith asked blandly.

Juleson grinned: "For he is utterly unclean."

Dr. Smith laughed softly, smoothing his hands on his pants. Then he turned soberly to Juleson to ask, "How do you feel about your hearing before the disciplinary committee?"

Juleson shrugged. "It was pointed out to me I had broken a rule."

"Is that how you see it?"

"I see it several different ways, but it comes to this—I did what I thought I had to do. I believe they did the same."

"Yes, perhaps, perhaps," Smith murmured as he crossed

his leg and rubbed his knee. "But I find it disturbing. I'm not going to tell you the choice you had to make was easy. To consult your rule book as the warden suggested. But, as your friend, I'd have much rather seen you accept protective custody."

"You'd want me to hide? Like a child?"

"Why not like a child? Children are eminently sensible in many of the ways they deal with an environment still strange to them and over which they exercise little or no control. So the simile is apt. And I find myself wondering why your healthy instincts didn't demand that you hide from danger, rather than prompting you to measure yourself against some alien code of honor at the risk of your life."

"The code isn't alien," Juleson said. "Any schoolboy would know it. There're boys out on that yard who have refused to grow up. They look forty, but they're still twelve. One of them ordered me off the yard. He said he was going to cure himself of having to look at me. It was like I'd been told not to come out on the school grounds during recess. I wouldn't submit to a bully. No more, no less."

"But, Paul, they're boys, you're a man."

Juleson slapped his leg lightly and turned away though there was nothing in the cell he could pretend an interest in. "I hope I am," he murmured without conviction.

In the silence he heard the slamming of a distant door, then a tuneless humming closer by. Then Smith was saying, "You have a sinister guest there." And Juleson turned to see Smith frowning at the vampire drawing just above his own head.

"He hasn't tapped me," Juleson said lightly. "Apparently the moon isn't full."

"I've had several talks with the boy who drew it, a very strange boy, and curiously passive now. That figure is his . . . totem, his real identity, and he gets something of his own expression into the eyes . . ." Dr. Smith paused, his gaze still fixed on the drawing as if there were something about it he failed to understand. Then he sighed, and added, "But the boy will shortly be Dr. Erlenmeyer's responsibility, not mine—Paul, I've decided to resign."

Juleson felt an immediate shock of loss. "But why? What for?"

"I'm not accomplishing anything, nor am I able to help anyone. A prison is a nearly impossible setting for any therapeutic program."

Juleson was struggling with his hurt and anger, trying to hide his emotions. "Are you going into private practice?" he asked softly.

"No, I have an offer from a school district up north. I'm going to take it."

"And leave your department to Tom Swift."

"Tom Swift? I don't understand."

"That's what they used to call Erlenmeyer—Tom Swift and his electric shock box. And do you remember a patient he diagnosed as psychotic, and treated him personally right up to the day the poor bastard dropped dead, and the autopsy, remember, disclosed a brain tumor as big as a grapefruit."

Smith looked down. "I remember. But it's easier to be mistaken in this kind of diagnosis than you imagine. Frequently brain damage—"

"As big as a goddam grapefruit, it's a wonder he had enough brain left to sneeze with. And, Christ, sorry as he is, Erlenmeyer's still the best of those clowns crawling around the psych department and the counseling center. Sceijec is a twittering idiot who's still trying to figure out how to interpret an MMPI, and Rossmoreland works off his smoldering sense of inferiority by a systematic intimidation of the men he interviews."

Smith was rubbing his knee again. "Unfortunately, those positions aren't very well paid. Only a very rare kind of first-rate man would apply. And it's doubtful—" Smith smiled wryly—"that he would stay long."

"Only the one-eyed kings stay here in the kingdom of the blind."

Dr. Smith leaned forward. "You'll be leaving yourself, Paul, and that's what you should keep in mind. I wrote your progress report early, so I could do it myself before I left, and I have made the strongest recommendation for parole I think wise."

"Thank you, Doctor," Juleson said. "You know, I didn't mean that crap about Erlenmeyer. I was upset."

Smith smiled. "Did they really call him Tom Swift?"

"A few did, yes, and that was one of the nicest things he was called when he was giving shock."

"Yes, I can imagine."

"Is Gasolino really dying?"

"He died yesterday. At that, he lived days longer than we thought he could. Sheer animal vitality. I don't agree with the warden's implication that he might have committed suicide. He'd been shamed, true, but he was only trying to forget it. The fumes of carbon tet didn't get him as numb as he wanted to be, so he drank some. If he knew it was dangerous, this was also a time when he needed to show contempt for danger. An odd twilight creature. I don't think he knew he was dying."

"I hardly knew him," Juleson said.

They talked awhile longer, mostly about what he could hope to do on parole, and Dr. Smith made him promise to write as soon as he was free. When Smith rose to leave the two men shook hands, and again Juleson felt a threatening sense of loss that continued to oppress him for fifteen or twenty minutes until he deliberately turned his thoughts to parole. Born again at thirty. A prospect as exciting in some ways as it was frightening in others. Surely he would never take anything—the firmest security or the cheapest pleasure—for granted. He tried to imagine what he would find to do, what use he would make of the rest of his life, but he discovered he did not yet know the man he had become. He fell asleep and didn't wake up until the food cart was rumbling along the corridor announcing the evening meal. His dinner was handed in. Bread, white beans, greens, and a meat pie. The meat pie was little more than stew served in a metal soup bowl, covered with a thick piece of pie crust, which was baked separately, and put on like a lid. Juleson removed the crust to eat it with his bread, and under it, partially adhered to the stew, he discovered a folded slip of paper. It was onion-skin, soaked through in places with the reddish gravy. He opened it to read a typewritten note: *You had more balls than I gave you credit for, but you only won a round. If you're wise, you'll stay where you are.*

It was unsigned. Angrily Juleson crumpled the note and threw it at the toilet. It bounced off the rim and fell to the floor. He pursued it as if it were a crippled hornet, grinding it beneath his slippered foot. Then he picked it up, smoothed it out, and read it again. A detached part of his mind automatically noted that it had been a long time since Oberholster had cleaned his typewriter keys. The lower case "o" was almost solid. This led him to realize that he had Oberholster right here in his hand. If he were to call the guard and report the note, they would be able to demonstrate that it had been typed on Oberholster's machine. Oberholster had paid him the implied compliment of assuming he wouldn't report the note, and was now warning him as an equal to stay off the yard because he would be embarrassed by Juleson's return to the general population and forced to take some further step. Against his will Juleson was flattered. He sat down, with the note in his hand, wondering at the extent to which his habit of detachment had been eroded. A man had needs, he decided, this was a constant and primary fact of his nature. Drag Lucullus from his banquet table and cage him with swine, and in a matter of days he will be fighting for his share of the swill. Unless he's killed or chooses to die. A rancid truth, if it were a truth—yet look what was happening to him. He had expected demolition, but instead had been subjected to attri-

191

tion, and was finding it harder to bear. He had thought the prison would demand some sacrifice of his identity, but no one had asked for any part of him—still cell by cell he had merged with the uniform he wore.

He finished his dinner, and when he scraped the tray into the toilet, he tossed the note in after the food scraps and pressed the button. He watched the note, skimming the surface like the paper boats he had folded as a child, then it darted, circled into the throat of the commode, and was gone.

On the morning of the tenth day he was released from the shelf and reassigned to his former cell and job program. He was glad to see Manning at the end of the day.

13

Stick lay on his bunk, staring out through the bars. For a while he had imagined he could adjust the atoms of his body to pass at will through the walls, but when he reached out to grab the bars he found them solid. Now he was thinking about Morris Price. Morris had stopped working on the balloon. He said he couldn't get the right kind of thread. Stick had recently been assigned to the laundry in the mornings, and in the loft above the laundry floor he had noticed men working at sewing machines. He should be able to score any kind of thread Morris needed. He leaned over the edge of the bunk. Morris was reading again, curled in the lower bunk as if he were sheltering in a cave. "Hey, Morris," Stick called in a conspirator's whisper, "what kind of thread will fix that thing?"

Morris looked up from his book, seemingly startled. "Strong thread," he said.

"I know that, but what kind of strong thread?"

Morris sucked in his cheeks judiciously. "Nylon would be the best."

"They use nylon on clothes?"

"No, I guess not."

"Well, you tell me what I should ask for, and I'll get you some thread."

"What for?"

"For your bag, what do you think?"

"I mean why should you help me?"

"Why we're cell buddies, ain't we? It don't mean nothing to me, if I can get it easy I will."

"Get the kind of thread they use to sew canvas. Do you think you can get that?"

"I don't know. But if there's any down there in the laundry, I'll get it."

"Hey, that's great."

"It ain't nothing."

The bell sounded for night activities and Stick turned back to watch through the bars as the men passed to the gym. He had spent a lot of time in the gym and he already knew most of the prominent athletes when he saw them. Particularly the boxers. He admired them at the same time that he imagined how he would cut them to shreds if he were able. If he had time to train. Reach and height, he thought, he had reach and height, he could be a marvelous engine of icy punishment. He saw Reuben "Cool Breeze" Moore, the best of the middleweights, walk by, and he wanted to say, *Hey, there, Cool Breeze,* as he heard so many others say, and he was only dimly aware that Cool Breeze was a Negro. The splendid fraternity he belonged to placed him above all other considerations. Still Stick knew one day he would destroy Cool Breeze.

Cool Breeze was unaware of Stick, except as a thin awkward kid who hung around ringside, and if he had been aware of the content of Stick's mind it would only have amused him. The studs loved a classy boxer, a man move nice they don't see nothing more, and if a man's bad with his hands everyone want to whip him. That's nature. But he wasn't studying fighting tonight, he was in another bag altogether.

He ran lightly down the wide metal steps and flashed his ID card at the check-out officer. The officer drew a line through Cool Breeze's name on the daily movement sheet. At relock he would cross another line through the first to indicate that

Moore had returned to the block. A count at ten would confirm that he had entered his cell. A loose net to hold so many dangerous and ingenious fish, but somehow no one ever slipped it. Largely because the gun towers were manned around the clock.

These towers concerned Cool Breeze because tonight he wasn't going to the gym. Banales, another middleweight, was waiting for him, leaning against one of the girders that supported the rain shed.

"Is it on?" Banales asked.

"Yeah. Le's go."

"How're we going to get into the lower yard?"

"I'll show you. You'd never snap."

They moved off, through three-gate, past four-box, past the metal stairs that led up to the gym, and on towards the Protestant chapel. In Cool Breeze's world the Protestant chapel was a whorehouse. It was one of the places you could pay to have yourself ducated to if you were looking for a spot where you could get down, and a number of his friends appeared on the night movement to attend choir practice several times a month. Sometimes they hit on him to go with them.

"Get you dick wet, Cool Breeze."

But he waved it off. He was in training, he said.

"You training to be some kind of monk?" one jibed. And another took it up, "No, Cool Breeze training to be a sissy hisself. Ain't that right, Cool Breeze?"

"Training to knock your dick stiff, you don't keep your mouf off me."

Now Banales asked, "We ain't going in the chapel?"

"No," Cool Breeze smiled. "We going under it."

Just beyond the chapel steps, partially hidden behind them, another set of circular steps descended into a large brick well. Fifty years before, these steps had led down to the legendary Sash and Blind, an early isolation unit, where hard cases had been tempered down in wet straitjackets, but now the same space where men had once lain for days in total darkness was used as a warehouse. The door was never opened and the floor of the well was littered with debris. Cool Breeze tiptoed through it.

"I hope you got your drawings straight," Banales said behind him.

Cool Breeze tried the door. It opened slowly. He could smell the oil recently applied to the old hinges. "They's cool," he said happily. He smiled with guilty excitement like a child who has discovered a secret passage within the walls of his own home, and thus restored his faith in the marvelous and forbidden world just beyond the threshold of his own experience.

"Le's go," he whispered to Banales. "We blasting now."

They moved through the warehouse into the paint shop and climbed through a window to reach the industrial alley. Here they were far out of bounds. A tower commanded the end of the alley, but they were able to slip along the wall keeping to the shadows, and near the far end of the alley they were able to crawl across it on their bellies.

"That's the worst of it," Cool Breeze said.

They passed around the corner of the machine shop and came out on a concrete ramp that led along the edge of the lower yard. Now they could see the wall, bathed in light like a national monument, and posted with a guard tower every hundred yards. To approach the wall at this time of night would be suicide. Cool Breeze noted this.

"Lucky we ain't scheming on that wall," he said.

"Man, man," Banales whispered. "Let's get where we're going."

They crawled across another open stretch and straightened up in the shadow of the boiler room. Cool Breeze rapped shave-and-a-haircut-sixbits on the metal door. The lock sounded immediately after his signal and the door was pulled in to leave a six-inch crack. An inmate he had never seen before looked out at him.

"It costs to come in here," he said.

"Of course, it cost," Cool Breeze whispered. "Get this door open, sucker."

The strange inmate opened the door and closed it quickly behind them. He reset the lock. He was wearing a mechanic's coverall, an older dude with the white face of a night worker. A rag, black with oil, hung from his back pocket. Behind him, three huge boilers were mounted in a row—one and three were firing, but the center unit stood silent.

"Two packs apiece, boys."

They opened their jackets. Cool Breeze had three cartons in his belt; Banales held two. They paid the boiler room attendant and he pocketed their cigarettes without comment. He led them to the center boiler and opened the door while they crawled in one behind the other. The interior was lit with a single bulb, hung from the pipes that ran along the upper curve of the boiler, and the air was heavy with the moist baked smell of rust and steam. Seven men were on their knees around a shallow rectangular box lined with a blanket. One held his fist above his head, his mouth open, as they had all turned to stare at the opening door. Their shadows arched up the round sides behind them like seconds hovering in solicitous attendance.

"Oh, oh, fresh blood," one of them said.

"Hey, there, Cool Breeze, how you get here?"

"Cool Breeze jus' bogart his way in." He worked his way towards the table. "My stuff's good, ain't it?"

"Oh, yeah, your stuff good. Your stuff the best." This was Cadillac Clemmons, running the game. "Get right in here." He gestured at the shooter, a gray boy from the weight-lifting section. "This man got his point. He got a four. Now we seeing what he can do with it. What you think he do with it, Cool Breeze?"

"I think he make it." Cool Breeze put two packs on the table. The shooter came out. He rolled a ten, a six, a nine, and a seven.

"Next man, coming out," Cadillac said. He picked up Cool Breeze's two packs.

Cool Breeze lost his three cartons in a half an hour. He borrowed a carton from Cadillac and lost that too. "It ain't my night," he said.

"Ain't never a fool's night," Cadillac said happily. He offered another carton, but Cool Breeze shook his head.

"No, I freeze now."

He went to sit on his heels near the head of the boiler where he could watch the play. The dice flashed over the gray blanket seeming to gather the light, focus it, and reflect it up into the sweat-streaked faces worshipping over them. The players murmured constantly in hoarse whispers, and Cadillac sweet-talked luck as he would a woman.

"Oh, you fine bitch, you jus' be sweet, you fine bitch."

The adventure had flattened for Cool Breeze. He had raided the big game, gone broke, and now was left with an urgent sense of danger from which all promise of fortune had faded. Losing had made him feel weak and foolish.

The boiler room attendant opened the door to pass around coffee in peanut butter jars wrapped with electrician's tape. The players took a short break to distribute the coffee and Cadillac threw his arm companionably around Cool Breeze's shoulders.

"This my fool," he announced. "When I came to this jail-house they showed me old Cool Breeze here, and they say, This your fool. For all the time you're here. And should you *evah* get broke you jus' come and shoot craps with your fool, and he keep you smoking. Ain't that right, fool?"

Cool Breeze looked up at Cadillac. Cadillac was the ex-heavyweight champ of the joint. Cadillac never could move pretty, but he had fists like leather bags full of ball bearings. Cool Breeze smiled. "You an entertainer, ain't you, Cadillac?"

"Offin's my game, man, and I pimp a taste. Shoot crap, too."

"I be your witness there."

The game resumed. Banales won for a while, lost, then seesawed, and finally went broke just before Cadillac called the end of the game. It was fifteen minutes to nine.

Cadillac held up his hand. "We break, we break together jus' like always. I lead. We do this right we hit the gym line jus' as they coming out." He turned to Cool Breeze. "You pick up?"

Cool Breeze nodded.

"It ain't nothing," Cadillac said.

The winners banked their stuff with the boiler room attendant and one by one, about six feet apart, they slipped out the door.

The alley tower, twelve-tower in the official post orders, was quiet duty. Too quiet. It was understood unofficially that guards assigned here were being either tested or disciplined. Eight hours of staring conscientiously into the darkened alley, a monotony broken only by the regular rounds of the old fire watchman, was harder than working the yard. The alley appeared to stretch away in a sharply narrowing perspective, intensified by the alternating bands of light and shadow caused by the irregular placement of the small night lights.

Shortly before nine o'clock, the officer on duty thought he detected movement in one of these patches of shadow. He had just poured a cup of coffee from his thermos and turned back to his vigilance when the darkness seemed to wrinkle and flex. At first he thought it an illusion, then he considered that it might be one of the cats. He turned his spotlight in that direction, but it showed him only the empty alley floor. He turned the spot off and, as his eyes were readjusting to the darkness, he caught another movement, more definite this time—a large body, too large for a cat, moving quickly.

He stood up, senses tingling. In the weeks he had worked this post, this was the first thing that had ever happened. He lost a moment adjusting to the novelty. Again the spotlight surprised nothing, but now he was certain he had definitely seen *something*, and continuing to work the spot with one hand he reached for the phone with the other. He told the operator to connect him with control. As he waited for the watch lieutenant to come on the line, he was troubled by the impression that the direction of the movement he had observed had seemed to be towards the main part of the prison, not away from it. But that was impossible. Why would anyone be returning to the security area?

He reported a possible escape attempt.

Karpstein, the second watch loot, asked, "Are you sure?" and listened to twelve-tower's guarantees. "All right, all right. Keep your eyes open. And good work." The Karp punched the general alarm and got on the bitch box to all the towers on the perimeter. An unknown number of inmates were seeking to escape somewhere in the lower yard. He alerted the flying squad and phoned the warden, who authorized an emergency count. The night unlocks were already on their way back to the blocks, leaving the school, the gym, the chapels, the library, and the drama workshop. They were hurried into their cells and a quick count was taken. The count was correct. By this time the bachelor officers from the BOQ were standing around the captain's office waiting assignment. The Karp ordered another count. This time a paddle board count. They checked cell by cell, through all the blocks, identifying each inmate by his ID card and checking him off on a master tally. Again the count was clear. The Karp called off the search, notified the towers, sent the bachelor officers back to their rec hall, and phoned the warden at his residence. Then he dictated a "turd" to be placed in the personnel file of the officer on duty in twelve-tower.

The turd was removed several weeks later when they learned, as always through an informer, that a crap game was being held several times a week in the boiler room. They were able to surprise the game and determine the route these men had used to gain access to the industrial alley. The door that had once led to the Sash and Blind was welded shut.

The warden had been viewing television when Lieutenant Karpstein called. He had immediately phoned the sheriff's substation and the San Rafael city police to notify them of a possible alert involving an unknown number of inmates. They would begin to cover the roads around the prison as a routine precaution. Then the warden called the captain of the guards at his residence. After that he returned to the television to watch the end of the program.

He was relieved when he received Karpstein's second call. Though trouble was routine, he still hoped to prevent major trouble, and the publicity that would follow in the wake of a multiple escape would damage not only his personal security but the future of the programs he had dedicated himself to. The press might well raise the question as to whether it was more important to advance the grade level of subliterate prisoners from the second grade to the sixth grade than it was to confine them successfully. They would have a valid point.

A few minutes after Karpstein's second call the doorbell rang and Charlie Wong answered it to let in the captain. To people who knew him in uniform, Jacob Blake never looked quite complete without it. Tonight he wore slacks and sports shirt and in place of a tie he had a strap of rawhide, tasseled at the ends and cinched up with a clasp in the form of a bull's head. The ornament seemed grotesquely frivolous beneath his somber face.

"It was a hummer," the captain said.

"I know, Jake, the duty officer told me."

"Yes—I just thought I'd drop by as long as I was out."

"I'm glad you did. Would you like some coffee?"

"I don't know, it's a little late."

"How about some tea?"

"All right. Thank you."

"Charlie," the warden called.

Charlie appeared at the kitchen door. "Yessir."

"Make the captain a pot of tea." He pointed at the television. "And turn that thing off." When Charlie had withdrawn to the kitchen, the warden smiled. "Sit down and tell me what's on your mind, Jake."

The captain returned the warden's smile. They had worked together for years, and read each other well. "It's Oberholster," he said. "The one the cons call Chilly Willy. I want to break him."

"You don't need my clearance for that."

"I can't nail him. He doesn't seem to have any weaknesses. I can't touch him within the rule book, unless I bust him for gambling. I might be able to make that stick. But it's lightweight. The committee'll give him a little shelf time, then he'll be right back on the yard."

The warden was shaking his head, his expression troubled. "If you're not willing to bust him for gambling, then you'll have to wait until you can prove something stronger."

The captain slapped his leg. "I knew you were going to say that. But I'll tell you something, Mike, I'm full up to here with that white-faced punk—" He pulled the edge of his heavy hand across his throat. "If it were up to me, I'd throw him in seg and bury the key."

"I don't like to do that. I think we have to work within the regulations. That's what we're asking them to do, and when we ignore the regulations, just to make our jobs easier, then we're only confirming what they're already desperate to believe—that we're no better than they are."

"Yes, yes . . ." the captain nodded; he'd heard all this many times before, and remained unconvinced. "But Chilly Willy is a special case—"

He broke off as Wong came from the kitchen with the tea. Wong's eyes were bland as always. "Chilly Willy," Wong said, "he velly bad. Velly bad." When he bent over to serve the tea, Wong's face was hidden and he smiled faintly.

Captain Jacob Blake was restless after he left the warden. He was a man of carefully controlled and balanced tolerances and the strong tea this late in the evening had upset them. He stood for a moment at the foot of the warden's walk—the darkness was mildly scented—and looked out over the modernistic dome of the officer's snack bar where the bay was beating with a faint phosphorescence. An island humped out there, slightly darker than the sky, like the back of a half-submerged animal. He recalled that from the island the prison seemed to be caught in a web of its own lights. He turned and looked up at the dark windows of the armory tower, knowing that most likely the officer stationed there was watching him through his night glasses. He raised his hand and waved it in a gesture close to a salute. Then he started back towards the main gate.

He entered the prison and went to his office where he called for the file on Oberholster. The folder was heavy with the snitch letters the warden had cited, and well worn by official interest. The captain began to study the summaries and chronos again, hoping that as he did some workable plan would come to him.

Two dried lizards, mounted on a plaque, adorned his desk. The head of the smaller lizard was in the mouth of the larger. No one knew what interpretation, if any, the captain made of this symbol.

On the wall facing his desk there was a display of weapons taken in various shakedowns over the years. They ranged in size and shape from an ice-pick knife worked out of tool steel, as carefully finished as a surgical instrument, to a huge ragged sword fitted with a wooden handle wrapped with copper wire. There were a dozen different kinds of saps and bludgeons and as many sets of brass knuckles. There was a metal slingshot, designed to shoot ball bearings, with which some con had amused himself knocking out the electric lights, and a cross-bow built specifically to kill an officer. The quarrel had buried itself in the wall, inches from the officer's head. And a number of zip guns. This display was a part of the captain's antidote for the warden's bleeding heart.

By the time he closed the file, he had not one, but two plans, both of which he intended to try. He called Lieutenant Olson and talked with him at length, and when he hung up he seemed satisfied.

Events played into the captain's hands when two days later a disciplinary report on Lester Moon, AKA Society Red, was brought to his attention. It was assumed that Moon had been fighting with his cell partner. The cell partner, a first-termer named Luther Turnipseed, had left the cell on the morning unlock and reported to the block office. A subsequent examination determined that he had suffered a fracture of the left wrist, a torn scalp and numerous bruises, including an eye which had swollen and turned the glossy purple of an eggplant. When asked for an explanation of his condition, Turnipseed stated that he had fallen from the top bunk. The MTA attending him was overheard to ask, "How many times?"

It was a violation of the rules to allow yourself to be beaten by an unknown assailant, a strategy that sometimes improved the recall of the victim, but since Turnipseed had got his clock cleaned in his own cell it wasn't difficult to determine who deserved the credit. The beef provided the captain with one of the levers he was looking for. He called both men to his office.

He talked briefly to Turnipseed, a short fair-haired old young man with a dull red face and reproachful blue eyes. Turnipseed was still saying he had fallen from the top bunk, but it was clear to the captain that it wouldn't hurt Turnipseed's feelings to be called a liar. There was a righteous whine in Turnipseed's tone that immediately canceled the sympathy due him for his bound wrist and bruised face. The captain could understand how Society Red, penned with this man in a narrow cell, might be goaded beyond his endurance. The captain himself, and his patience was the tenth power of Red's, was prompted to pretend he believed the story Turnipseed was so patently anxious to repudiate. He dismissed Turnipseed and called in Red.

Red and the captain were old sparring partners and over the years a reluctant mutual respect had grown up between them. In the captain's eyes, Red was redeemed by his sense of humor and because he had no viciousness in his makeup. He handled Red with the amused tolerance he might have shown an old but still rebellious mule. Red respected the captain because the captain had always dealt fairly with him. The yard said that Jacob "Stoneface" Blake would rather boot a convict in the ass than off his old lady, but that hadn't been Red's experience with the captain. The captain had let him walk on some beefs where he should have been sloughed and Red was still grateful. This didn't mean he was likely to ever so far forget himself as to tell the captain the truth, nor did the captain expect he would.

"I got a beef in on you, Red."

"I had that figured, Cap."

"What's the story? You two fall out the hard way?"

Red feigned amazement. "Luther Turnipseed and me? We're the tightest of buddies. That tumble he took hurt me as much as it hurt him."

A yellowish flicker of humor stirred in the captain's gray eyes, which for him was the equivalent of a big grin. The other guards claimed he sometimes smiled when he was off duty, but this was something that had to be taken on faith as the existence of the abominable snowman is accepted or rejected depending upon the credence one places in remote and private reports.

The captain continued, "Turnipseed was lacerated and bruised in different ways and in different places than could be easily accounted for by a fall from the top bunk."

"Accidents do happen. And some of them are downright freakish."

"How *did* Turnipseed get so badly banged up?"

"Well, he fell dead into the center of the cap'tol building, right through the grand dome."

The captain picked up a pencil and examined the red rubber eraser. "You'll have to explain that, Red."

"No strain. I was building a model of the state cap'tol. I figured when I got it done, I'd duke it on the gov'nor, maybe make some points, and then that unconscious rumdum bastard falls off his bunk right into the middle of it."

"Were you using balsa wood?"

"No, pine, what they call white pine. You know balsa wood wouldn't of marked old Luther up like that."

The captain leaned sideways, pulled a file drawer and came up with a card which he studied briefly. "No luck, Red," he said. "There's no entry here showing where you bought any wood on handicraft. So either you leaned on Turnipseed, or you're working hobby with contraband wood. Which is it?"

"I hate to say it and maybe put heat on your clerks, but I did for a legal fact buy some wood."

"When was this?"

"About six years ago."

The captain nodded carefully. Again he traced through the entries on the file card, and this time he turned it over. After a moment he looked up, still expressionless, but his large thumb was flicking the corner on the card.

"That wood is the only item you've bought on hobby in all the time you've been here."

"That's right. I'm not too keen for hobby work. I spend most of my time trying to improve my mind, except for the nights I put in on that cap'tol building. That's all wasted now."

"I think we can forget about the capitol building for a moment and get back to your trouble with Turnipseed—"

The captain's phone rang, and he broke off to answer it. "Yes," he said, and frowned as he began to listen.

Red half turned in his chair to look at the weapon display. He had examined it previously, had in fact seen some of the weapons before they had found their way to the captain's wall. In a prominent spot he noted the handmade gun with which Reynolds and Hahner had attempted their break in '48. They had kidnapped a member of the parole board and held him as a hostage. The last break with any class to it. Now when they were scheming on some roadwork, they laid up quiet for a couple of years until they could ease themselves into a minimum security job, and then they slipped off in the night. Still even those who managed to creep were reapprehended with stifling regularity. Small town heat stopped them in stolen cars, their new neighbors saw their wanted flicks on TV, their wives turned them in out of spite, their mothers for their own good. One way or another they came back with a new story to tell.

The captain was still on the phone. Red wasn't worried. He knew he was going to draw a pass. When Stoneface had you he didn't waste time on jawbone. Red allowed himself no alternative but to continue lying—it was the only honorable thing to do—but even should he bust out with the truth, the captain wouldn't believe that either.

Turnipseed, the lousy little Jesus freak, had moved into Red's cell with a Bible, a plastic crucifix, three rolls of Tums, a bottle of Alka Seltzer, a paper cup full of C.C. pills, and a box of Dr. Scholl's foot pads. Red had regarded this plunder with dismal apprehension. It was bad enough trying to cell with someone halfway regular, let alone some knickknacking nut. Turnipseed wasted no time in exposing his principal obsession. The world was coming to an end.

It was going to be worse than Red had thought. "Oh, God," he groaned involuntarily.

"Yes! Yes! Amen!" Turnipseed affirmed what he had mistaken for a prayer.

"How long we got?" Red asked.

"A month, maybe. Maybe more." Turnipseed glanced at the concrete ceiling. "Only the Man up there knows."

"You mean Hogjaw on the fifth tier? He knows?"

"Hogjaw! I mean the Risen Christ."

"Well, let me know if he gives you a hint. I got some stuff owed me and I want to collect it before it's too late."

By then Turnipseed understood he was being mocked and he began to threaten Red with the particulars. Red was going to swell up and burst like a beetle in a bonfire. But before that he was going to be parched with thirst until he strangled on his own swollen tongue. Red assumed since he had already dominoed twice Turnipseed might let him rest, but Turnipseed had an imagination as vivid as it was vigorous and he went on to revive Red for a second time so he could freeze him slowly and see him devoured by savage dogs—

"Look," Red broke in. "If the world ends, the world ends. I didn't buy no round-trip ticket. Now give your north-and-south a rest so I can read this freak book. I got to give it back to Chilly in the morning."

Turnipseed released a series of snuffling sounds, a drumroll of disapproval, and began to make up his bunk. He produced four large safety pins with which he anchored his sheets. After, he stripped to his shorts and sat on the toilet to trim his toenails with a razor blade.

Red was finding the freak book a burn, too wholesome for authentic L and L—the sexual passages were abbreviated and they might as well have concerned the matings of Ken and Barbie dolls for all the resonance they evoked in Red. He liked his bitches funky. After a while he laid the book open on his chest and soon was studying something far more interesting on the outrageous cinemascope of his inner eye.

In his fantasies Red swelled into the role of Cracker hipster and boss stud, a part he played at in life, but missed filling by light years. Now his lashless eyes were cool, insolent, and knowing. His hair, thick and vivid as the brush of a fox, shelved out over his forehead like the bill of a cap. His lean hips were wrapped in Levi's and the muscles of his legs strained against the sun-bleached fibers of his tough and richly symbolic cloth. What he met, he mastered.

When he walked into a beer joint or a honkytonk there was always a moment of respectful and appraising silence as his boot heels struck the floor with total male authority and even the dullest imagination could supply the ghostly jingle of phantom spurs, and there followed a cloud of discreet whispering as those who knew him told those who didn't: *That's Sassiety Red. He's got a pecker longer'n fifty dollars worth of shoestrings, and an understanding so small you could lose it in a gnat's ass. You best walk right careful around him.*

And the bitches—they got soft eyes and weak knees, all except one, always the boss bitch of the lot. She has a mean white face and a sullen mouth; she watches Red with a cool contempt as he walks up to her.

—I'm Society Red.

—That don't tell me nothing. Her teeth are tiny and sharp-looking.

—What's your name, girl?

—Naomi, she might say. Or maybe, Cora Bell. Her white skin is so fine the blue veins are clearly visible at her temples and Red knows her tits will be similarly decorated.

—Let's you and me make it, Cora Bell. I know a hundred ways to pleasure you.

Her china-blue eyes glint scornfully. You don't look like you could pleasure a stump-broke mule.

He slaps her, his fingers tingling with the pleasure, and as she throws her head back he sees her mouth go soft.

Usually at this point a man in a suit runs up. He is the archetypal dude, but Red never sketches him as a ridiculous figure. His pockets are full of ingenious knives, small foreign automatics, and stainless steel knuckle dusters. His muscles are sometimes trained in the various deadly arts—judo, karate, neo-sparta—at times he is a champion boxer. But always he is given away by the glint of polish on his fingernails, the part in his hair, the glow of pomade on his mustache.

—Cora Bell, he says, is this fellow annoying you?

After an exchange of elaborate and soft-voiced insults, they fight, and Red masters the dude without real difficulty. When the dude isn't knocked cold, he becomes vicious in defeat, and when Red walks back to Cora Bell the dude tries to creep on him, usually with a knife or a broken bottle, but Red, warned by the widening of Cora Bell's eyes, always turns in time to meet him with a boot heel in the mouth. Always when he rises from this encounter he catches in Cora Bell's eyes a moment of unguarded admiration before she returns to her former expression of bored disinterest. He knows he has her.

—You fine freak bitch, he tells her, let's you and me go for a long walk.

—I don't care for long walks.

But Red is through playing, he sweeps her up and carries her out. Her arms circle his neck. Without transition they are alone. Sometimes on the edge of a meadow in a grove of pine, the warm night air and a yielding bed of needles. Sometimes in a barn in the dry coarse hay while the cedar shakes ring with rain, and a Coleman lantern hangs hissing from a loop of bailing wire. Sometimes in her bedroom with the large soft goosedown pillows and pale blue comforters, the sweet stew of her different scents, the ruffled film of her underwear, and Red stretched out watching like a panther in a tabbycat's silken basket.

There is always enough light so he can watch her undress, and this takes a long time. Sometimes she parades for him, switching her ass, while she cites him: Tell me what you're going to do to me, daddy. Tell me what you're going to do.

—I'm going to drive you like a truck, baby.

Curiously, beyond this point the details became harder to focus, and Red would hold tight to a small patch of his dream still lit in a luminous corner of his mind. Perhaps only the illusion of her breath, straining and catching beside his ear, or the incredible delicacy of her tits, like globes of light, and sometimes he could feel the pressure of her ankles wrapped over his calves, but never more. He crooned, "Do it, baby, do it good. Do it good! Good! Good!"

"Disgusting!" Turnipseed said.

Red rolled over and found Turnipseed staring at him, his face pinched, his eyes blinking rapidly. Red shook his head. "How long you been in?" he asked.

"Two years."

"You mean you've built two big ones in this jailhouse and you still don't know when to leave your cell partner alone for a few minutes?"

"I don't hold with it," Turnipseed said thinly.

Red was unable to credit what he was hearing. "You don't hold with it?"

"It destroys you."

"Oh, man. If taking your hank could destroy someone, I'd of been boiled down to a grease spot years ago."

"I still don't hold with it." Turnipseed's face was stained a deeper crimson, and he stared fixedly at a point somewhere over Red's shoulder. "You have to control the nature in you."

Red exploded. "I don't have to do nothing you say, punk. Hit your rack."

Turnipseed ducked and disappeared into the lower bunk, and Red, his mood broken, picked up the book again. At lights out he undertook to finish the job he had started, but when he heard Turnipseed muttering in the darkness below him the implied moral condemnation had a disturbing effect, and he couldn't continue. Red decided to wait until Turnipseed went to sleep, but Turnipseed apparently didn't sleep.

This went on for a week. No matter how stealthily Red approached his pleasure Turnipseed seemed to be instantly aware of it. The snorts of disapproval would start. He would get up and stand in front of the toilet for fifteen minutes, or light matches and pretend to look for something on the shelf. Red was ready to credit Turnipseed with second sight because this happened at eleven, it happened at twelve and, if Red could stay awake, it happened at one.

Finally relief came in the form of a wet dream, but the dream frightened Red. The girl, a girl he had once known in real life, turned to an animal beneath him and he woke himself rising out of bed to get away from her.

It was early morning. The block was dead quiet except for the distant sighing, the breath of large lazy demons, from the hot air vents on the bottom floor. Then Red heard a tearing sound as if Turnipseed in the bottom bunk were ripping cloth with sharp, short jerks. Red leaned over to look into the bottom bunk and he discovered Turnipseed asleep and snoring. He was propped up on his pillow, almost in a sitting position, and dangling down in front of him was a handkerchief hanging from Red's springs. Even as Red shifted his weight in his own bunk he saw how the motion was communicated through the springs, to the handkerchief, and, had he been awake, to Turnipseed.

Red climbed down and began to pound on Turnipseed. He had already hit him two or three times before Turnipseed even woke up.

When the captain hung up he obviously had something else on his mind. He looked absently at Red. "I'm going to give you a pass, but don't come in here with a solid beef because you'll wear out that isolation unit."

"Thanks, Cap." Red took his hat from his pocket and fitted it to his head. When he had it square, he stood up.

"One other thing," the captain said. "You run for Chilly Willy—" Red opened his mouth, but the captain held up his hand. "I know, you'll deny it. But I also know most of what comes down on the yard. I *know* you run for Oberholster's book. So. A word to the wise. Back off. Oberholster's due to be busted down to nothing. Drift away in the next week or two—find some new hustle."

The captain stared at Red until he said "Okay" and turned to leave, but he paused with his hand on the door. "Chilly's honest," he said. "He keeps straight books, square to the last butt. The next wheel to come along might be some short-con punk."

"I have reason to believe that Oberholster has caused five men to be beaten in the last year. One of them died. He's through. Tell him I said so."

"I'll do that, Cap."

The captain leaned back in his chair. "Just off the record, Red, what the hell did you buy all that wood for?"

Red smiled. "Six years ago I was still pretty ballsy, I had a little fire left in my shoes, and I figured I might build me some kind of glider and fly right over these walls of yours. I thought about it a lot, but I never got around to starting it. Pine would of most likely been too heavy anyway."

After Red had left the office, the captain permitted himself to smile. He wondered if there were any other place besides a prison where it would be possible to encounter a man like Lester Moon. Possibly in one of the services—he could imagine Red in the Navy, a brig rat of course, an old white hat, shipping over until the sailors' home claimed him. Perhaps in some small Southern town he might manage as everyone's relative and the local wise fool. Possibly in the early days of

the West he could have made his way in some marginal capacity—the captain could picture Red driving a chuck wagon
or a team of mules, but on closer inspection this seemed a
scene from a comedy.

The captain cleared his mind, he had other fish to fry,
but first he made a note to himself to call in Nunn sometime
in the next few days and give him the same word he had
given Red.

Then he left his office, passed through the main gate, and
walked out to the officers' recreation hall where the Fourth
Annual Prison Art Show was in progress. A civilian visitor
had been apprehended trying to slip one of the paintings into
his attaché case. The captain wasn't surprised. The year before the inmate cashiers had taken in four bad checks and a
counterfeit ten-dollar bill.

Chilly just shrugged when Red told him Stoneface had said
he was through. "That don't shake you, Chilly?" Red asked.

Chilly looked up appraisingly at the gray sky as if he were
more interested in determining the chances of rain than anything the captain might have said. He tapped one shoe against
the other in a random pattern.

"It don't exactly knock me out, but it doesn't shake me
either. There's a point you keep sloughing aside, Red—" Chilly
had fallen back on his educational voice, and he paused to
make sure he had Nunn's attention as well. "We're at war.
The bulls are the army of the country we've set ourselves
against. Now you may not like it, but it doesn't shake you to
discover the enemy carries guns. You see?"

"Yeah," Red said.

"You see, but you don't like it."

"They'll shake everything up, Chilly, and it's been going
good."

"If you're going to get hooked on quiet routine, you might

as well grab that lunch bucket because there ain't no good reason for you to be hunching around here in blues with a number on your ass. There's many a place more comfortable than jail if you're willing to pay the price to stay in them. Myself, I never felt like joining them."

"He's got you figured for five tampings this last year," Red said.

"He's giving me a little more credit than I deserve."

"That's what I tried to tell him."

Nunn spoke up to ask, "Why do you think he took the trouble to send you a warning?"

"I think he's trying to play with my head. He's no knight to send a goddam challenge. If he had us by the balls he'd start pulling. No, he's putting a little shit in the game—psychological warfare."

"You think that's it, Chilly?" Red asked.

"That's the way it looks."

"He told me I'd better cut you loose."

Chilly looked severe. "And?"

"I ain't going to do it. Hell, I wouldn't do that if they were going to shoot me in the morning."

Nunn smiled, his eyes satirical and faintly bitter. "That's a little more than Chilly requires of you."

"Radio," Chilly said. He slapped Red lightly on the arm. "You're all heart," he told him. Red smiled awkwardly, feeling a warmth of affection for Chilly he would never be able to express. He listened, for once without jealousy, as Chilly and Nunn decided the practical measures they would take in face of the captain's warning. They decided to cool the trade in nasal inhalers for the time being. There was a stock of approximately eighty tubes stashed in the gym and these would remain frozen except for their own use and the use of important friends. But they would continue to make book. If they didn't someone else would pick up their action and it wouldn't be as easy to get back as it would be to lose. Since with the death of Gasolino they had lost their slack man, it wasn't necessary to make any decision as to further collections. Until a new slack man turned up they were grounded, which was just as well.

These matters decided, they fell into the idle conversation of a thousand other days, and began to argue as to who was the greatest fighter, pound for pound, of all times. Chilly liked Sugar Ray Robinson and Nunn liked Harry Greb. The argument meant nothing. None of them had seen either fighter in action. They loosely quoted what they had read of one authority or another, and Nunn defended for Greb because he denied the present, the time of his own life. Everything good had faded from the world at his birth.

14

WHEN CHILLY made the four o'clock lockup, he found another man in his cell. For a moment he thought he had caught a cell robber—then he saw the upper bunk made up, and the immediate shiver of revulsion he experienced was similar to the sensation he felt when he was touched by someone he disliked. It flickered briefly through his nerves like the cold chemical glow of phosphorescence, and gave way to an equally cold anger. He paid a box a month to the head inmate psych clerk to see that his cell card was stamped: *To Be Housed Alone*. Fat Abbott wasn't taking care of business.

When Chilly looked at his new cell partner it was as he would examine a nuisance that needed to be fixed—a plugged sink, a toilet that wouldn't flush. A brat, Chilly thought, and so firmly fixed was his habit of thinking of himself as older than he was it never occurred to him that this "kid" was, at most, only a year or two younger. The boy was small, slender, good-looking, and his hair and eyes were dark, so dark they made his complexion seem pale. He stood awkwardly, obviously embarrassed to be in another man's home, and reluctant to appear comfortable until some form of permission had been granted.

"Hello," he said as Chilly entered the cell. "I guess I'm going to be your cell buddy." Chilly didn't answer and the boy continued defensively, "They told me to come in here."

"It looks that way," Chilly said.

The boy touched the top bunk. "This bed was empty."

"That's all right, but don't get settled down up there."

They stood the bars for count. To Chilly, with the boy beside him, the cell suddenly seemed smaller. For the first time in several years he sensed the reality of his confinement. He half turned to examine his cell. Everything was superior to mainline. The mattress on his bed was from the hospital, as were the blankets. The toilet was fitted with a seat. The sink had a hot water tap, an incredible luxury installed with connived materials on a forged work order. The walls were freshly painted, the floor covered with throw rugs. The shelves were curtained with an expensive drapery material stolen during the redecoration of the associate warden's residence. Compared to the cells on either side, Chilly's was luxurious, and usually this was how he saw it, but tonight he realized it was a small concrete box into which he was forced at gun point.

When the count was clear, Chilly told the boy, "Go ahead and wash up."

"I already have. Thank you."

There was something mannered in the boy's intonation. Every syllable was separated and precisely stressed. And he moved his hands oddly as if they were tethered by short cords to his belt. Chilly stared at him a moment trying to define the beginning of a suspicion in his own mind, then he shrugged and brushed past the boy to get to the sink. He washed carefully, applied a colorless dressing to his hair, and brushed it straight back. A few years before, his hair had been so blond it seemed white, but now it was beginning to darken, except for a few months in the summer. His own face, looking back at him from the narrow mirror, meant less to him than an illustration in a magazine. He cleaned his brush with his comb and replaced it on the shelf. Then he settled in his bunk to wait for dinner and to plan the moves by which he would get this kid out of his cell.

When the bell rang, the upper tiers were released first. In a few moments he saw Red's legs, and he smiled as he saw them hesitate knowing Red had glanced at the boy in the top bunk and assumed this wasn't Chilly's cell. He started past, hesitated again, and turned back. Red squatted to look in at Chilly.

"What's up?" he asked, rolling his eyes at the top bunk.

"Someone goofed."

"They sure did." Red grinned with a broad slyness Chilly didn't like or understand.

As soon as Chilly was released and they were jostling down the tier towards the center stairs, Red leaned close to whisper, "That kid's stuff."

"Red, you think the warden's stuff."

"No, square business, Chilly, that kid's stuff. When he came in on the fish line this morning I was walking the yard with a guy who knew him in Tracy. That kid was a queen in Tracy. They called her Candy Cane."

"The guy told you?"

"He was there."

"You know, Red, a couple of days ago someone told me you were stuff."

"Chilly, I'm trying to pull your coat. Fuck what the guy from Tracy said, that kid came on the big yard swishing like she had a license to run wild, and if she ain't stuff Marilyn Monroe ain't pussy. I just wish the mothers had put her in my cell."

"We're together there. I wish they had too."

They entered the mess hall and started inching down the long line that led to the steam tables. On the wall above them, an enormous mural depicted the history of the state. The painting had never been developed beyond a brush drawing rendered in various shades of burnt sienna because the inmate artist had been paroled before he was able to finish more than the underpainting. Red's and Chilly's progress towards their dinner was roughly synchronized with the progress of California history. They moved past the early Indian tribes and the Conquistadores, and, as they were beneath Father Junípero Serra, his hands raised in benediction over a group of Indian converts, Red asked, "You going to take advantage of that stuff?"

"You know that's not my game."

"I don't know why not. You might just as well."

"You think so?" Chilly said distantly.

"Well, why not? You're here, and you're going to be here, with every break in the world, at least another ten years. So what difference does it make. You might as well get something out of the miles you're putting down."

"And you think poking some guy in his hairy ass is really living?"

Red shrugged equitably. "It's all hairy, Chilly, the world over. Least those parts of it where I've been."

"Did you ever hear of a guy named Loudermilk?"

"Isn't he the stud that was out at the ranch, and they caught him sticking a pig?"

"Exactly. That was ten years ago. Loudermilk's been out twice since then. He married some bitch and got a couple of kids out of her, and pulled off some sharp capers. He's the kind of stud that if you were his friend and you needed it, he'd duke his last butt on you. But do you think when you mention his name anyone says, Yeah, he's a generous stud, he's good people, or a sharp thief. Or a husband or a father, or all the other things he's been and done in these last ten years? No, they say, Loudermilk, isn't that the stud they caught fucking a pig."

Red started laughing, and Chilly continued, "Loudermilk doesn't think it's so funny."

"Yeah, all right, Chilly, but that sweet freak in your cell ain't no pig."

They moved through the serving line without acknowledging the man who worked there. This was a lower class job —the paper hats, the shapeless white jackets mutilated the personality and fortified the illusion that these inmates were servants rather than just other prisoners doing the jobs assigned them within the rigid commune of the prison. In much the same spirit with which they snubbed the food handlers they pulled their trays away, with a weary and cool scorn, when they were offered string beans, diced carrots, spinach, or salad—kid's food, old man's food, the food of those so prideless they could admit they were hungry and still couldn't supply their own needs.

They reached the table that fell to them in order with only their issue of chicken fried steak, mashed potatoes, thin white gravy, and a square of apple pie, which was baked in a sheet pan and extended with corn starch until the flavor was almost neutral. Red began to unload the bottles of condiments, bought on the inmate canteen, which it was his task and privilege to carry and share. Pico Pico Hot Sauce, Heinz's Chili Sauce, three different flavors of Kraft Cheese Spread (Cheddar with Bacon, Blue Cheese with Clams, Garlic Spread), a jar of Skippy peanut butter, and a jar of Mary Ellen's loganberry jam. He could have carried no more. They doctored the steak with the hot sauce, smeared cheese spread on the pie, and filled out the meal with peanut butter and jam sandwiches. They ate swiftly, in silence, and finishing pushed their trays to the center of the table to sit waiting for the release signal.

It was a violation of the rules to smoke in the mess hall, and this was a rule Chilly obeyed. To disobey was too much trouble for too small a reward, and he wasn't going to give some bull the satisfaction of being able to tell him to put out his cigarette as if he were some high school kid sneaking a smoke. But Red lit up and avoided detection with an elaborate technique he had learned years before in reform school. He cupped the cigarette inside the curl of his half-closed fist, and dispersed the smoke with a constant winnowing, precisely the motion one would use shaving a square stick into round, and each time he finished a drag he slapped the air smartly with his cupped palm to clear the fat puff of white smoke that trailed the cigarette from his mouth. He exhaled into his lap in a tight thin stream.

Chilly watched with idle amusement. "Red," Chilly told him, "you look like a monkey trying to bugger a basketball."

"Your old white-haired granny buggers basketballs."

"My granny, huh?"

"You told me to lay off mom."

"And you think there's a difference?"

"Be a mighty pee-culiar family you come out of if there weren't."

Chilly smiled thinly. "Red, you're too much." At this moment a dependable instinct caused him to look up. His boss, Lieutenant Olson, was coming towards them. "And," Chilly continued, almost without pause, "you just bought yourself a beef."

Red followed Chilly's eyes and immediately stuck his hand, cigarette still cupped, into his pocket.

Lieutenant Olson had been supervising night feeding, leaning, arms folded, against the back wall, watching the last of the main line pass before the steam tables. Unless there was serious trouble, a fight or the beginning of a riot, he had nothing to do except just be there. When the mess hall was secured his shift was finished and he was free to pass through the main sally port and walk up the hill to his house on the reservation where his wife, a big-hipped, thin-legged woman who worked in the inmate trust office, would be starting dinner. A shadow of weariness passed over his normally good-humored face and he rubbed his flushed cheeks with his small pale hand. He made a fractional correction in the rakish set of his uniform cap, and started to patrol the central aisle, automatically looking from side to side. He wasn't looking for anything. It was beneath the dignity of his position and damaging to his reputation as a good head to notice the routine smuggling of chicken fried steak sandwiches, but he took a mild and familiar pleasure in the effect he was causing, not unlike a boy breaking bottles with a BB gun to demonstrate his ability to work a change in the world around him. Olson's glance was an invisible ray that caused convicts to fall silent and stare at the table in front of them.

Then he saw Oberholster, sitting with his clown and messenger boy, and he started through the tables towards them. He missed the implications of the warning Oberholster passed to Red, but since his doctor had forbidden him to smoke in the wake of his second heart attack his sense of smell had grown acute, and he caught the odor of tobacco.

"What's happening, hotshot?" he asked Chilly. He affected the hip idioms of the convicts unaware that their currency was already fading even as he became aware of them.

"I don't feel too keen," Chilly said with a meaningful glance at his tray. "Do you think it might be something I ate?"

The lieutenant eyed the bottles Red hadn't yet returned to his pockets. "If it was," he said in the same dry tone Chilly used, "it was some of that gow you smear all over our good state food."

At first he had thought it was Chilly who was smoking, but now from his look of cramped inwardness, like someone trying not to fart, he realized it was Red, and understood the significance of the hand bunched in Red's jacket pocket.

"You sick too, Red?" he asked fondly, smiling like an uncle.

"Me? No, I feel swell."

Olson looked at their trays, registering concern. "It smells like that chow might have been burnt."

"Burnt?" Red smiled hugely. "Shucks, no. It was dandy. After we denatured it a taste."

"Good. We don't want you getting sick."

Olson rocked back on his heels and folded his arms over his chest. On the edge of the vision he watched Red's pocket writhe as his hand moved spasmodically inside. The smell of tobacco was lost now in the stronger and more acrid odor of burning cloth. Abruptly the clatter of pots and pans increased as the food handlers began to tear down the setup on the steam tables. Olson signaled one of his officers, the gesture of an Air Force major pointing out bandits at three o'clock, and the officer started the release. The first in began to file from the mess hall, each man tossing his silverware into a pail at the feet of a bored guard.

"One more down," Olson said to Chilly. "Time for me to make it out of this nut house." Tantalizing Red he moved to leave, then turned back. "Say, hotshot, I see on the movement sheet where you drew yourself a cell partner."

Chilly shrugged. "I noticed someone in there when I stood count. I thought he'd wandered into the wrong cell."

"No, he's in the right cell. I thought you were immune to cell partners?"

"I did too."

Red was staring past Olson with the look of a man who has just had all his wind knocked out. His lips were white and his arm jerked.

"Well," Olson said, "maybe it will be good for you not to be alone so much." Again he turned to leave, again he turned back, still with the uncle smile. "By the way, Red, if that's a mouse you've got in your pocket, it's against regulations to keep a pet." He grinned and walked away quickly.

"Mo! Ther! Fucker!" Red snarled and began to beat vigorously at his pocket. "Can't you keep that tame cop of yours away from here?"

"Red!" Chilly was laughing, mouth strained open, throat pulsing, completely soundless. "Red!" he said again, the word breaking and shivering with his amusement. "If you could have seen your face. Ha! You looked like—" He broke off again, overcome with laughter.

"Chilly, you dumb cocksucker, this ain't funny. I damn near burnt my ass off."

"Like a pregnant nun."

Red was still beating at the glowing char that rimmed a large hole in his jacket pocket. "Chilly, sometimes you ain't got the brains of a pissant."

Chilly sobered suddenly and picked up the water pitcher. He dashed the contents at Red, wetting his whole side. The cons around them fell silent thinking a fight was starting. Chilly replaced the pitcher precisely. "I've got brains enough to know you put out fires with water, and—" He stared at Red with cool significance. "I'd like to think I'd have sense enough not to shit where I eat."

Red held his arms out from his sides like a buzzard considering taking to the air, but his expression was one of misery. He pulled his wet shirt away from his skin, and squeezed his jacket pocket to make sure the fire was all out. Then he looked at Chilly. "I'm sorry," he said. "I was hot. You know I had a right to be hot. Now what am I going to say if they ask me how I got all wet?"

"Tell them the loot pissed on you. Just to amuse himself. You wouldn't be far wrong."

When he had climbed to his own level, Chilly sought out the tier tender and sent him after one of the block porters. He reached his cell just as the bell for relock rang, and he waited for his new cell partner to enter first before he followed, frowning with distaste as he slammed the metal door. The boy immediately climbed into the top bunk.

"¿Qué quieres, hombre?" the block porter, Rooster, asked, peering into the cell. He was a tiny Mexican with one wall eye.

Chilly took three packs of Pall Malls from an open carton

and passed them through the bars to Rooster. "Deliver a clean set of blues to Society Red. You know where he cells?"

"*Sí.*"

"Do it next."

"*¿Por qué no?*" Rooster cocked his head to stare at the upper bunk. He sucked his breath hissing back through his teeth. "*Está muy bonita chavalla. Ahora tú chingas todo lo que tú quieres, ¿no es verdad?*"

Chilly smiled and said, "*Sí, pero tu madre solamente.*"

"*¡Ai! ¡Ai!*" Rooster laughed and started off, calling back, "*Gracias*, Cheely."

"*Por nada.*"

Chilly settled in his bunk to read, but found himself thinking of the fifty cartons he had invested in this cell, twenty cartons for the hot water line alone, and another ten for a decent crapper, only to have some punk move in for free, and while ordinarily Chilly would have caught the six-thirty unlock to go up to the gym to cut up touches and watch the fighters train he would have to pass now because he didn't want to leave anyone alone in his cell. He exercised as much control as possible, even though he was always aware custody could crash into his cell whenever the notion grabbed them, but he was further aware that custody learned (if you thought of them as a corporate entity like a swarm of ants) only by rote, and their notion of where inmates might hide valuable contraband was limited to those placed where they had stumbled on contraband in the past. The hollow metal bed frame was thought to be a favorite stash and custody had designed a flexible probe with which they conducted regular and secret checks. Also, they had learned to look behind the wire screen in the mouth of the hot air vent, beneath the light fixture, and beyond the first crook in the channel draining the cell toilets.

But custody's shakedown craft was, in reality, as obsolete as the mimeographed lists of underworld slang (where Chilly suspected Lieutenant Olson mined many of the expressions he liked to use) prepared by the prison sociologists, lexicons still defining such almost forgotten usages as "stool pigeon," "snowbird," "copacetic," and "moll buzzer." Since no guard had ever found valuable contraband hidden in the hollow handle of a cell broom, it remained unlikely they ever would. But a new cell partner, feeling uneasy, possibly anxious to please, might decide to sweep the floor, work the pressure fit loose, and discover Chilly's stash of soft money.

Chilly continued reading until he heard the bell ringing to begin the music hour, always close to seven-thirty, and at that time he put his book aside and stood up to make a glass of instant coffee.

The kid appeared to be asleep, still dressed, outside the blankets. One hand, fingers spread, stretched out as if he had been reaching for something in the moment sleep overtook him. His hair, longer than prison regulation, fell across his forehead to cover one eye; his parted lips moved gently, as if, in his dream, he was speaking.

Chilly ran hot water from his private tap until it steamed close to boiling, then he mixed coffee in a large plastic glass, and took a handful of creme-center sandwich cookies from a brightly colored tin which had originally held a fruitcake. He walked to the front of the cell and stood looking through the bars as he ate.

The narrow windows in the block's outer wall, twenty feet away, framed three almost identical views of San Francisco Bay, and the far shore burned with lights, pulsing in some alien display of life. He'd been told this shore was Richmond, and those who had fallen from Richmond claimed it made their nuts ache to watch these lights at night. But Chilly looked at them with the same dreamless detachment with which he viewed his own face in the mirror. A man was a fool to pay dues he didn't owe.

Lonely, cold, phony, and treacherous, a Lesbian whore

simulating orgasm for an army of tricks, that was the world lit by those cold hard lights, the one Chilly saw, with a cold crotch, a numb prick, and a taste for pain, a world ready to turn on the gas and drop an overdose of sleepers.

Yes, a man was a fool to pay dues he didn't owe.

Chilly sipped his coffee and listened to a guitar somewhere nearby, wandering like a gypsy from minor chord to minor chord, growing progressively more plaintive until it suddenly blazed into a brief and furious flamenco.

Farther away, on one of the lower tiers, someone with a deep, slurred voice was singing an almost tuneless and repetitive blues:

> *No more turnips and collard greens*
> *Yes, no more turnips and collard greens*
> *I say, no more turnips and collard greens*
> *Cause that ain't food*
> *What's fittin' for a man . . .*

And on the far side of the block another musician played scale variations on a trumpet, working higher and higher, and Chilly was just as glad the horn was as distant as it was.

He killed his coffee, rinsed the plastic glass, and brushed his teeth. The kid was still asleep. Chilly stripped to his shorts and settled down between his sheets to continue reading. The novel was what Red called a freak book and the opening sections had developed the gradual seduction of a seventeen-year-old boy by a woman ten years his senior. Chilly read impassively, but not entirely unaware of a faint sense of uneasiness which had followed the muffled excitement he felt as he had watched the virgin boy fumbling at the older woman, who was murmuring comfortably and fondly, while she sought him with a practiced hand, pressing him close on her spreading and maternal breasts, until she felt herself captured with a sudden awkward strength.

"I need it, I need it," she had apologized to the boy, all motherliness vanished. "I need it."

And Chilly had formed an image of the woman's body closing around the boy: arms, legs, all wrapped tight, while her hair loosened to cover his head and shoulders. Then he had shaken his head briskly and continued reading. The boy was adding the sixteen-year-old girl next door to his stable when the lights went out, and Chilly closed the novel and slipped it under the bunk. He turned his pillow and settled down, but the slight sandiness of his lids and the faint ringing in his ears warned him it might be hours before he fell asleep.

He began to think his way into the past. Some day the scraps of accidents, the pointless incidents, the chance meetings, and forced partings, the idle whims as well as the careful decisions, his fortunes, his Jonahs—some day it would all be arranged so it made sense, even the ten years he had left to pull would be made to seem significant, some day when he found his personal philosopher's stone ... though he doubted he ever would ... to solve the mystery of who Billy Oberholster really was.

Chilly—Billy then—had encountered police for the first time when he was ten. A small boy, he had dared squeeze through the ventilating system into a neighborhood market to empty the till. Then, rather than leave immediately with the money, he began to explore. But he had no sooner stepped into the doorway leading to the back section when an instinct, which was to grow more dependable as he matured, warned him that someone was standing nearby in the darkness. He started to step back, heard a muffled grunt, saw a flash of white fire, and something warped the air above his head. Later he realized the night watchman had shot to kill a grown man, aiming center and three-quarters up in the frame of the darkened doorway.

He fell to his hands and knees and crawled swiftly along the waxed linoleum into the shelter of the produce aisles. The watchman, uncertain of the number or the size of the burglars he had trapped, prudently covered the front door and called the police. Chilly, cut off from his retreat through the ventilators, realized he was boxed in and he hid the money from the till behind some large cartons on a bottom shelf (he discovered later they were twenty-five-pound boxes of dog food) and then moved as far from the hidden money as he safely could, which brought him to the vegetable section. He crawled into a cabinet beneath the fruit counter. The police found him near the end of a systematic search, and at first were smiling because he was so different from any burglar they'd been imagining. He told them he was only playing, and he looked so young and innocent they seemed inclined to believe him until the night watchman discovered the empty till. Then he told them some older boys had forced him to climb through the ventilator and open the front door for them. When the shot had been fired, they had fled, leaving him behind. At this point he was trying to cry, but he couldn't so he made do by hiding his face in his hands.

Who were the older boys?

He didn't know. Just older boys. They had threatened to beat him up if he didn't obey. They said they knew where he lived and they'd catch him coming home from school.

Why hadn't he told this story in the first place?

He didn't want to tell on anyone.

The police made a careful search around the potato bins, but couldn't find the money. He never knew whether they believed him or not, but they didn't pat him on the head or call him son. They took him downtown and lodged him in the juvenile detention home. His mother came and signed him out the next day, and he was able to reach the store before closing time to recover the money from behind the boxes of dog food. Then, after having managed everything so well, he was careless enough to allow his mother to see him with a five-dollar bill. Her eyes had widened with dismay: "Oh, Billy, you *did* take that money!"

The dominant dream of his youth was directed towards the day he would free his mother of all her burdens, replace his missing father. What he didn't realize at the time, and what she never let him guess, was that he was her gravest burden. During his middle teens he started bringing home comparatively large sums of money and handing them to her without explanation. And she didn't ask because she didn't want to hear a lie, and, even more, she didn't want to hear the truth. She never protested unless the nights when she hugged him to her breast, murmuring, "Billy, Billy, Billy, whatever will become of you?" could be counted as a protest. These episodes caused him intense discomfort; still, when he sensed one coming on, he made no effort to avoid it. In his way, he was as permissive with her as she was with him.

As he considered it years later he might have done all right if he had stayed on the single-o, but though he had many of the characteristics of a loner he wasn't a true solitary. He had a strong urge to gather a gang around himself, with results that were unfailingly disastrous. He went to reform school when he was sixteen and his mother began to write the bleeding letter she had been writing, with brief interludes, ever since.

He was out of reform school but a few months before he staged a string of armed robberies with two other boys. They covered three states, and ended in a running gun battle with the local law, state law, and the FBI. They were sent to prison in the state of their arrest, and upon completion of that sentence they were extradited home in chains to be tried for the robberies they had committed before they left. Again they were sentenced to prison.

Finally Chilly found himself free again at twenty-four, a two-time loser with almost seven straight years of reform school, county jail, and prison behind him. He had never held a job. He had never had a girl friend. But he didn't leave broke. During his second jolt he had started to master the prison techniques he would later perfect and he smuggled out over two hundred dollars in the barrel of a fountain pen, converted to a keister stash. In the lavatory of the Greyhound Bus depot in San Francisco, he voided his bowels and removed the stash. He rented a cheap room. The following day he located a drop who had been recommended to him and arranged to buy a piece. He paid sixty-five dollars for a snub-nosed banker's special, Smith and Wesson, .38 caliber, and remade the purchase price twenty times over before he had had it a week. He moved into a medium-sized hotel on Powell Street and started looking for a woman. There were a large number of single women in downtown San Francisco, but he didn't know how to make a beginning, and confiding his need to some third person who might have arranged to have it serviced was too much like admitting a weakness. The need itself was a weakness, the inability to gratify it an aggravation. To go it alone was to risk rejection, or to expose his ignorance, and he was uncertain of his capacity to weather either of these situations calmly. He was aware of the charge he had accumulated, and he was afraid he might blow it.

Finally, after several weeks a woman had picked him up, and inevitably it was an older woman. Chilly guessed her to be in her middle forties and from the beginning she made him inexplicably uneasy.

He encountered her in the corridor of his own hotel when she stepped out of her room to ask him to help her open a window. He noticed her small plump hand, pale against the dark wood of the door, the fingers armored with miniature pink shields, and he saw how the thin strap of her watch cut into the flesh of her wrist.

"Where is it?" he asked.

"Right here," she said, leading him into the room. The

window was stuck, as Chilly discovered by opening the top half of the sash, because a paper match folder was wedged against the frame.

"Here's your trouble," he said, holding the folder out. He noticed that it wasn't weather-stained, but the woman looked at it with mild amazement as if he had just performed some modest conjuring trick, producing a chain of bright scarves instead of the crumpled folder. She offered him a drink—as a reward, she said. He sipped a tall watery scotch while she volunteered her name—Margaret. She was in town to attend a series of lectures. She didn't give her last name, or mention where she was from.

She sat tidily on the edge of the bed, leaving the chair for Chilly, and rattled on with an uneasy brightness about the unfriendliness of large cities. She was a short, solid woman with thick white calves and thin ankles. Her black hair was smartly set, waved around the sides of her round pale face. Her mouth was tiny and her eyes an alert blue that because of her coloring seemed more vivid than they actually were. The lines of her body were indistinct, blended with the compression of her foundation garments. Her room smelled of bath powder.

"Do you stay here?" she asked.

"Yes, down the hall. Would you like to go to the lounge for another drink?"

"The lounge? Here at the hotel? Oh, I don't think so."

"Maybe some place else? A bar?"

She made a small show of hesitation, then accepted. "All right—I shouldn't, but, yes, I would like that."

In the course of the evening Margaret became sedately but thoroughly drunk, and Chilly, turning most of her questions, managed to learn that she was a high school teacher from Dunsmuir.

"Biology," she said to the bar mirror, then turned to tell Chilly, "Biology One. The things I teach them, they seem so unimportant sometimes. I wonder if any of them remember, and if they do, does it mean anything to them? Other than the charts of the reproductive systems." Chilly was surprised to see her blushing. "If I had married, if I could have married—" She looked away again, this time into her glass, and her small lips were quirked in a mirthless smile.

"I might have had a son your age."

"I'm older than I look."

"You're not very old even if you're older than you look."

"Does it bother you?"

"Bother—no, but it puzzles me."

Chilly smiled faintly, "I've led a sheltered life."

"I don't mean that. I wonder why a nice-looking young man like you hasn't anything better to do than spend an evening with a middle-aged schoolteacher."

"Oh, come off it. Isn't this exactly what you hoped would happen?"

"I'm enjoying myself. This is—" She touched her glass lightly with her fingertips as if indicating a classroom exhibit. "This is recess. But you? I was wondering about you?"

"I don't know what to tell you. I don't even know why we're talking about this." He reached over and took her wrist. "That's a nice-looking watch."

"It's inexpensive."

He slid two fingers up the sleeve of her jacket. Her skin there was warm and smooth. She reached over to cover his hand with her own.

"You don't mind?" she asked.

"No, I don't mind."

When they returned to her room, she went into the bathroom to undress. Chilly stripped swiftly, still taking time to fold his clothes neatly, and got into her bed. The sheets were cool. He stacked the pillows and lay half propped in the center of the bed with his hands clasped behind his head. He felt more curiosity than excitement, and when Margaret came from the bathroom in a robe and crossed quickly but unsteadily to turn out the light, he watched her closely. With her body unbound and without her high heels she seemed almost squat. Her hams pumped solidly and her lowered breasts swayed against the thin material. Chilly swallowed slowly and when the light went out the darkness seemed to slap the air.

Later he was never able to retain any of the smaller details. When they had finished, lying separately again, Chilly was left with the feeling he had been wasting his time. Not only the immediate time just past, but all the time he had spent thinking about this encounter and hoping for it. It wasn't that he hadn't enjoyed it, but he hadn't enjoyed it enough to compensate for the time and money he had spent on this old woman.

He got up after she was asleep and by the light of a match looked through her purse. She had a little money, two fifty-dollar American Express travelers' checks, and a Bank-Americard. Her name was Mildred Allain and she lived at 250 Cochilla Street in Chico, California. She carried a membership card in a teachers' association, and back to back in a plastic envelope were two photos of a younger woman with four children.

Chilly replaced the wallet, and dressed. He turned to take a last look at Margaret-Mildred. She lay solidly where he had left her, and now that the lipstick was worn from her small mouth, her face appeared round and featureless like a white balloon, shadowed only by the foreshortened ellipses of her lashes against her cheeks. He remembered her saying, just as he moved to mount her, "This is awful . . . just awful." Then she had groaned deep in her throat.

He saw her once more, briefly, as he was crossing the lobby the next day. She was looking at the magazines racked on the counter of the cigar stand, and there was something in her posture that suggested to Chilly she had seen him first and turned away to avoid an encounter.

The days that followed never seemed quite real, they had the feel of holiday as if they stood apart in bold red against the working calendar of his life. Everything he attempted with his gun succeeded but the size of the scores he could attempt were sharply limited by the condition that he was working alone. Trying to balance the safety factor between a number of small stings and one large sting was a complex exercise in probability, but he concluded that the greatest danger lay in repeated exposures to the bitch of chance, and he started to look for partners.

Chilly realized that the underworld, as it is imagined by newspapers, didn't exist in San Francisco, but there was a loosely cohesive and always shifting sub-world which included a small manpower pool, fed by a trickle of youngsters outgrowing the teen gangs, and another trickle of older men out on parole. Chilly tended to like and trust men who had solid reputations behind the walls, those who were known as good people, and it was two such men that he approached. They knew Chilly in the same way he knew them and if they had any hesitation it generated from the half formed apprehension that Chilly might find it too easy to kill. Not in heat or panic, but as the most logical way to prevent any future identifications. Robbery, at best, was a desperate measure, attractive only to men who had no significant talent for anything else, whose energies, appetites, and ambition still demanded that life show them some chance, some opening no matter how slender, through which they might enlarge themselves. But murder committed during a robbery was also suicide. They were satisfied Chilly was cool enough; in fact, they were afraid he might be too cool, but he persuaded them that in spite of his youth and lack of major experience he knew what he was doing, that he was capable of leading them, and if he ever played the fool or the nut he did it late at night, locked in his own room under the covers.

The robbery—they hit a high-class night club on the

Peninsula—went off with a dreamlike smoothness, each man handling his job with the resolution and the desperate bravery of a commando team taking an objective deep in enemy territory, and it wasn't until afterwards that the hidden blueprint of failure first suggested itself.

They took in excess of twenty-seven thousand dollars, and Chilly expected they would sit on the money as agreed, but the other two men, now that the money was a splendid reality, couldn't find any way they could trust him or each other not to rob the stash while it was cooling. This was what they said, but their real feeling was that they had won this money by exposing themselves to great danger, had passed the trial of a hero, and they didn't want to postpone the festival. If they hid the money, they tarnished their exploit with sneakiness, or they turned it into a business transaction, and either transformation outraged their hunger for glory. They refused.

It was a tense moment. The large pile of bills spilled on the white bedspread. His two partners were on one side, Chilly on the other. All of them armed. Their tensions still keyed high.

"We agreed to wait," Chilly said formally.

The other two shifted closer together, intensifying the division. Raquel, the oldest and also the smallest, said, "There's no reason to wait now. We got away clean." Clear in his voice was a note of pleading. He was asking Chilly not to make trouble.

"There's still every reason to wait that there was when we decided that's how we'd play it. Nothing's changed."

Caterpillar Collins, a heavy-set young man, a year older than Chilly, thrust his large face forward, a device that had served him well through the years he was earning the nickname Caterpillar—after the tractor in tribute to his abnormal strength. He was fond of saying, "They don't call me Caterpillar cause I'm round and fuzzy."

Now he said, "Fuck waiting." His jaw out. The gesture was childish, but his light blue eyes were not simple.

"We've all spent too much time waiting," Raquel added.

"Yeah," Caterpillar agreed harshly. "Every time I turn around someone's telling me to wait. Now you, Chilly. I say, I'm not waiting. I want my end."

Raquel took a half-step forward, seeming to plane the fist of one hand into the palm of the other—the effect was conciliatory, without menace, his hands busy with each other were not studying his gun.

"That's about it, Chilly," he said. "I know you want to argue, but there's nothing but aggravation in that. We have a right." He reached down and picked up a bundle of bills much as he might take a bone from in front of a dangerous dog. He straightened up slowly, cautiously, then when Chilly didn't move he suddenly smiled and tossed the bundle to Caterpillar. "We'll take nine big ones apiece and leave you the overlay." He picked up another bundle. "For expenses."

Chilly walked to a chair and sat down. He crossed his legs and lit a cigarette. If they had been somewhere reasonably isolated, he would have tried to kill them. As it was he smoked calmly, watching them going ahead with the division of the money. He noted a swollen look of foolishness coming into both their faces. They began to talk too loud, to swagger, their eyes grew bright.

Early the next day Chilly moved from the hotel into an apartment in a quiet section of town. If he had been asked to guess which of his two partners might split on him he would have without hesitation named Caterpillar. He could imagine the spoor of big bills Caterpillar would lay through the bars of the tenderloin. It would only be a matter of time before he attracted the interest of the police through their informers. And while this was precisely what Caterpillar did he somehow managed to elude the percentages.

Raquel fell into a harsher trap. He had been chippying

with heavy even before Chilly contacted him, and when his money grew long he was able to make several large buys and become properly hooked. When the barb was well set, one of his suppliers gave him up to the police as part of a long-term reciprocal agreement, and Raquel, in turn, after three days without his stuff gave up Caterpillar and Chilly in exchange for a fix and a promise of a county jail sentence. The police, pleased to have captured major game on a routine trapline, put out APB's on Caterpillar and Chilly. They had Caterpillar in days, and Chilly a month later.

When Chilly stepped into the city prison, Caterpillar came running up to him as if he had completely forgotten how they had parted. "Raquel put us both in the shitter, man," he said. "He was strung out. Up tight, up tight. They hung him out to dry and he puked us both up." Caterpillar's face twisted like a child on the verge of tears. He spun and hit the metal wall, causing it to boom dully. Then he stood quietly staring at his fist, already beginning to swell. "I thought he was good people."

"So did I," Chilly said.

Though both Chilly and Caterpillar refused to cop out, they were routinely convicted through Raquel's testimony, who had been tantalized into continuing cooperation with irregular trips to the county hospital for what was logged as "sedation." Since this was Chilly's third conviction, and the holding charge was technically a "heinous" crime, the judge, a hanging judge with fixed opinions as to the possibility of re-habilitating multiple robbers, applied the habitual criminal statute in spite of Chilly's age and hit him with the bitch to run consecutive with his term for robbery.

"Jesus," Caterpillar said later in an awed tone, "they killed you."

"That's what they're supposed to do," Chilly said.

Chilly was still awake at the twelve o'clock count, and he was still awake an hour later when the boy slid from the top bunk to use the toilet. Then he began to undress in a half-crouch. He stripped to his shorts and folded his clothes on the foot of his bed. Chilly was aware of him moving inches away, the white shorts muted to blue in the dim light, the darker flesh blending into the shadows leaving only its scent, the acrid scent one carries away from county jails where the infrequent showers are lubricated with harsh brown laundry soap. The taut springs of the upper bunk strained as the boy vaulted into it. The webbing sagged, gathered and sagged again as he turned, like a dog settling phantom grass, seeking comfort and sleep.

Chilly was still awake at the two o'clock count, but by four he was also asleep.

As soon as he arrived at work the next morning, he asked Lieutenant Olson for a pass to the psych department.

"You going to get your cap unsnapped, hotshot?"

"Do you think I need it?"

"I don't know. I'm not paid to think about things like that."

"It would be interesting to determine just what it is you are paid for."

Olson was writing out the pass, his pen paused and he looked up coolly. "You push, Oberholster. Do you know that?" When Chilly didn't answer, he signed his name and held the pass out. "Maybe they'll be able to tell you why in the psych department." There was a quality to his smile that Chilly didn't understand.

Fat Abbott had a private office, set off from the general clerical pool with plywood panels. He was seated sideways at his desk typing ducats when Chilly came through the door. He immediately held up a heavy palm.

"I know, I know . . ."

Chilly sat down in a metal folding chair beside the desk. "What happened then?"

"The captain's office picked up the hold. They picked up ten. Yours was one of them."

"Can you fix it?"

"They say they need the room."

"Shit."

Abbott settled back in his padded swivel chair folding his heavy arms over his wide chest. His eyes were all surface, smooth and bright as tan plastic. "I don't know. They're always crying for cells, and asking for a review of the psych holds, but this is the first time they've just jumped bogart and snatched them. The doc was hot enough to fuck, but three of the ten were my action so he couldn't say too much."

"Can you do anything?"

"You'd do better to hit on Mendoza, the assignment loot's clerk. He might be able to get your cell empty, and with it empty I could ease the hold back on. But I can't move nobody —I don't have that kind of juice."

"That's the kind of juice I pay for."

Fat Abbott opened the bottom desk drawer and removed a carton of cigarettes. He held them towards Chilly.

"What am I supposed to do with that?"

"Rub it in your chest."

"Put it away."

Fat Abbott replaced the carton and swiveled back to face Chilly. He smiled. "That kid in your cell's got a jacket."

"What kind of jacket?"

"A freak jacket. He's a righteous little freak. I wondered what kind of freight they'd loaded you with, so I eased into the record room this morning to take a look. He was picked up in drag and they were booking him into the woman's wing of the county jail before they snapped. Before that he was a broad in Tracy."

"I heard that."

"It's straight. A righteous little drag queen." Fat Abbott smiled again and hugged his chest. "If I were you I wouldn't be in no hurry to get *that* out of my cell."

"That's you, Fat."

Abbott studied Chilly for a moment, then said, "You don't have no way to take up slack, do you?"

"You been reading my jacket too?"

"They call you a psychopathic personality."

"And what does that mean?"

"I don't know, but you've got lots of company. They spread that label around."

"Then I don't feel so bad."

Abbott laughed. "It's hard to picture you feeling anything."

"You're not a psych, are you, Fat? Does it rub off, working around here?"

"Chilly, you begin with the idea everyone's simple. Sometime that could be a mistake."

"Well, Fat, you might say I've made my mistakes. I'm going to sound on Mendoza. If he can move for me, I'll let you know. Meanwhile our deal stands against future favors. We'll both be around awhile."

Fat Abbott, who was doing life himself, nodded. "That's a lock. Okay, let's leave it there for now. There's a chance the classification committee or the doc himself will order the kid into seg to keep those nuts out there on the big yard from killing each other over her. When they learn that ain't your action, there's going to be a lot of suckers hitting and hitting hard. I wouldn't want to be in the middle of it."

"If he's got a jacket that heavy, I wonder why they let him on the big yard at all?"

"I don't know. Maybe they're trying something new. Maybe she just slipped by them. She can't last. With your protection she might get by. That wouldn't stop no talk, but it would cancel a whole lot of action."

Chilly stood up, slapping the desk as he rose. "No thanks.

I have enough trouble trying to keep someone from putting a shank in Society Red. I don't need another pet. I'll see you on the yard."

"Okay, Chilly."

The cell loot's clerk wouldn't touch Chilly's work. Mendoza was a tall elegant Mexican with graying hair and distant black eyes. He carried himself with extreme coolness and the natural remoteness of his handsome face aided the illusion of poise. He communicated almost exclusively in the set phrases of the hipster, and it was a while before one realized Mendoza was a fool, but when the realization came it was with the force of revelation. Seemingly in an instant, like the shift of an optical illusion, his air of elegance deteriorated into dumb farce.

"En gee," Mendoza said, making a cooling out gesture off to his side, like a bishop blessing a midget, "no fucking good. The loot came down on all my action. You dig? If I move I'm dead."

Chilly said, "It's worth ten boxes to me."

"Not for no hundred boxes. You can't smoke on the shelf. I'm sloughed. You dig?"

"What's going on?"

"Who knows?" Mendoza's hand moved at his side again, this time to suggest the deviousness of official mentality. "They get hot on one thing. Next week they're in a new bag."

"When you can move," Chilly said impatiently, "get in touch with me. This is something I want done."

Mendoza blinked solemnly. "Easy over, Chilly. I dig."

Chilly turned and walked away. He passed through the garden on the way to his own office, noting that the fountain in the center was plugged again and the standing water turning stagnant. A man from the landscape gardening crew knelt before a rose bush, wrapping the trunk in burlap, and another pushed a lawn mower as if it weighed five hundred pounds. Lieutenant Olson was still at his desk, going through the monthly requisition from the outside warehouse. He took in Chilly's set face and smiled down at the surface of his desk.

"Get your business taken care of, hotshot?"

"Yeah."

"Good, now maybe you've got time to take care of mine." He threw the requisition over where Chilly could reach it. "How much did you pad it this month?"

Chilly, who never padded the requisition, said, "No more than usual."

"Submit it then." Olson stood up. "I'll be out at the snack bar."

"Okay, Loot."

"And, Chilly—don't take everything so grim. None of us get exactly what we want."

"I'll remember that."

Chilly worked on through lunch, and then, detailing the porter to answer the phone, he went up to the gym. He paused briefly on the last landing to look out over the bay and then down into the big yard where the domino tables formed hubs of activity like booths at a fair. He stepped into the gym and the tone of the area was immediately set by the sound of showers and the staccato rattle of a ping-pong ball, counterpointed by the deeper thump of a handball. Caterpillar wasn't on duty in the supply cage, and Chilly had nothing to say to him to make it worth finding him. He stood for a moment looking into the boxing section. In the raised ring a couple of lackluster welters circled and pecked at each other. Another man worked the heavy bag, slapping at it like a bear.

Chilly heard a distant surge of music and turned to walk through the weight-lifting section. A single iron freak was making dead lifts of what looked close to a thousand pounds. The veins stood out at his temples like blue rubber tubes.

"Hi, Chilly," he said, smiling sweetly.

Chilly nodded and passed on. At the end of the weight-lifting section an iron door led on to a primitive theater where movies were shown as a part of the recreation program. Chilly heaved at the door. It opened to the side in tracks and was difficult for one man to handle. He managed to crack it a foot, slip inside, and close it after him. A group of fifty or sixty men sat in the semi-darkness watching a Standard Oil travelogue. Most of them were seated on metal folding chairs, but a few, the gym regulars, had homemade easy chairs, pieced together out of scrap wood, cotton waste, and old blankets. One of these chairs was understood to belong to Chilly, and as he approached, the man who had been sitting in it stood up quickly and moved to the side.

"Any good?" Chilly asked.

"No, same old crap."

The same films were rotated over and over again, but Chilly didn't tire of them. Repetition couldn't make the exotic landscapes any less strange, because the richness of all their possible realities was only implied and at each reviewing subject to fresh interpretation. The present sequences had been filmed in Equatorial Africa. On the screen tribesmen were dancing beneath huge straw hats—crouching into a deep squat so the great brims trailed in the dust, they whirled and whirled like a cluster of giant lilies broken loose to toss and spin on the current of a stream. Then the scene shifted to another group dance where they pranced in a long line, holding spears, led by a man in a devil mask. Their faces were blank, hypnotized, streaked with dust and sweat.

In the seats just in front of Chilly, one Negro leaned over to whisper to another, "Ever' time they put a brother in a flick they either got him holding a broom or a spear."

And the other whispered back, "Yeah, but them some *fierce*-looking suckers they got there."

A dozen drums boomed on the sound track, and smoke

shifted in silvery folds through the cone of light from the projector. A dim yellow glow filtered through the boarded windows, making the faces in the audience appear almost as alien as those on the screen. Chilly shifted uneasily and rubbed the back of his neck. He lit a cigarette and as he turned back to the screen he noted, with an electric shiver of his nerves, that someone was staring at him. A gunsel, he thought immediately, using the term they applied to any kid on the make for trouble or a reputation as a hard rock.

The gunsel lounged against a twelve-by-twelve, thumbs hooked in his back pockets, and something in his posture, combined with his height, his thinness, his small smooth triangular head reminded Chilly of a praying mantis. Chilly met the gunsel's eyes briefly, without challenge, then turned back to the screen. He was used to the curiosity of others, he knew he was pointed out on the yard by men whose names he would never know, but a part of his awareness detached itself from the travelogue and remained alert for any move. The gunsel didn't stir, but he continued to stare, and after a moment Chilly shifted around to stare back. The gunsel's eyes were lost in shadow, but Chilly sensed the life there as he would sense the presence of an animal in a cave. Their gaze remained locked like children trying to stare each other down until Chilly tired of this exercise, and beckoned with his head.

The gunsel straightened, still taller, and came towards Chilly. As he drew closer, Chilly was able to see that he was bonerooed—pants glazed with starch and pressed to knife creases, and he had decorated his cap with a leather band, anchoring it at the sides with white buttons. His mouth seemed only half formed.

"You got nose trouble?" Chilly asked softly.

"Nose trouble?"

The gunsel didn't lower his voice. The men around them stirred and turned to watch.

"Why are you gunning me?" Chilly asked. He was still relaxed in his chair, but a cold center of tension was forming in his chest. This might be a nut. If something came down and he was made to look bad it would be all over the joint by four o'clock lockup.

The gunsel leaned forward, holding one hand out in a gesture of quiet, and Chilly saw a fresh tattoo, still scabbed over in places, on the inside of his forearm—the tattoo of a vampire.

"You Chilly Willy?"

"You know I'm Chilly Willy."

"I want to talk to you."

Chilly remained silent. The gunsel straightened again and glanced briefly at the men who were still watching in the hope they might witness some violence. Their interest was avid. He turned back to Chilly.

"I want to get on the night gym list."

Chilly smiled and someone else laughed in the darkness. The gunsel jerked around, stung by this mockery. "It's important," he said less to Chilly than to the man who had laughed and his tone was one of high seriousness that was almost convincing.

"What makes you think I can get you on the gym list?"

"You're supposed to be the wheel."

Chilly pointed at the tattoo. "You a Vampire?"

"I'm the duke. They call me Stick."

"Where do you guys come in from?"

"All over."

"There are a lot of you here?"

"More'n you guess. But we're not scheming on you."

"That's good." Chilly studied Stick, and though there was little physical basis for comparison, Stick reminded him of Gasolino—while in the face of even the weariest slob there was some faint resonance, Stick's face was numb and the numbness was like armor.

"We'll talk night gym," Chilly told him. "But on the yard. Right now I'm watching the flick."

"Can you fix it?"

"See me on the yard."

Chilly waited for the duke of the Vampires to contact him as they gathered before the four o'clock lockup, but the gunsel didn't show. Chilly brushed it off—he would hit again or he wouldn't—and went to join Nunn and Society Red who were watching a domino game.

"Big stuff down here," Nunn whispered.

"How much?"

"Ten boxes a corner."

"These suckers are ready for Vegas."

The players had a high-stake sheen to their faces and they played with relative quiet, studying a long time between moves. Chilly checked the diagram of the game trying to determine the outcome.

"There's your cell buddy," Red said, and he followed Red's nicotine-stained forefinger to see the boy walking the yard with another man. The man, a player named O'Brien, leaned over the boy with a patently conning sincerity, and the boy was moving with a studied gracefulness that was somehow too exaggerated to be truly feminine. It was mimicry.

"Tell me that kid ain't pussy," Red continued.

"He's pussy," Chilly said, "but that don't mean I'm interested."

"You going to have her moved?" Nunn asked.

"When I can."

"Listen. Listen, Chilly." Red had his coat sleeve. "You have that sweet bitch put in my cell. Can you do that?"

"I don't know, Red. Right now I can't get him out of my cell."

"Uh-huh," Red said knowingly, "huckily buck."

"What do you want with a freak?" Nunn asked. "I thought you laid up every night and dreamed about movie stars."

Red grinned. "That's right, but they're sometimey bitches. Sometimes they show, sometimes they don't. But that little freak—" Red looked back to where the boy was clearly playing the coquette with O'Brien. "She'd be there."

"Well," Nunn observed, "it looks like O'Brien'll have her wired up before you get the chance."

"Chilly, you going to 'low that?" Red asked.

"Jesus, Red, give it a rest. Isn't it bad enough I've got the sissy sonofabitch in my cell?"

That night after dinner, when the ducat officer passed the cell, he called "Cain," laid a ducat on the bars and passed on. The boy climbed down from the upper bunk to take the slip of paper. He studied it for a moment, then turned to Chilly.

"What's this?"

"It's a ducat. Didn't they use ducats in Tracy?"

The boy's eyes flickered and he colored faintly. "No."

"Let me see it."

Chilly read it at a glance. "You have to go to the psych department for an interview at nine-thirty. You know where that is?"

"Back in the hospital?"

"That's right."

"What do they want with me?"

"If you don't know, how would I know?"

"I don't like psychs."

"That doesn't surprise me," Chilly said dryly. He paused for a moment, then asked, "What'd O'Brien want?"

"O'Brien?"

"O'Brien had you jacked up just before lockup. What'd he want?"

The boy colored again. "He wanted me to move into his cell."

"That's out."

"All right."

"I'm going to move you in with a friend of mine."

"A friend of yours? Maybe I won't like him."

"You'll like him. He's real likable."

The boy studied the floor and Chilly noticed how long his lashes were. He sighed and said, "I have a friend on the streets. Do you think he'll come over here to visit me?"

"What do you think?"

"I hope he does."

Chilly raised his book, tacitly indicating he wanted to read. "Excuse me," the boy said. "I didn't mean to interrupt you."

"That's okay. In a week or so you'll move in with Red."

"If you say so."

The boy jumped back into the upper bunk. Chilly read a page, then lowered the book to ask, "You got cigarettes?"

"No."

"There's plenty on the shelf. Take what you need. If you want coffee, or some scarf—help yourself."

"Thank you."

"It's all right."

Stick approached Chilly for the second time in the morning before work call. Chilly, noting that this kid looked even stranger in full daylight, took him aside to ask, "How bad do you want on that gym list?"

Stick answered as he had the day before, "It's important."

"You Vampires do any collection work?"

"We can."

"All right. I got a guy I want whipped on. You do the job and you're on the night gym list."

"How bad?"

"I want him to know he's been worked on. You don't have to kill him."

"That's worth a little more than a gym assignment."

"You want to bargain?"

"No. Okay, who is it?"

"Come on, I'll point him out."

They walked the yard twice before Chilly spotted Juleson squatting on his heels, leaning against the east block wall. As usual he had a book in his hand, but he wasn't reading—his eyes were watching something in the sky above the mess hall roof while his finger marked his place.

"You see the stud with the book?"

"Yeah."

"That's him."

Chilly started to walk away, but Stick called after him, "When will I be on the list?"

Chilly paused, "You don't have to ask that. When the job's done."

If it gets done, he thought, studying the buttons sewed to the side of Stick's cap.

That evening at dinner, his new cell partner stuck close to Chilly in line and ended up seated at the same table with Chilly and Red. Chilly told him to help himself from the various bottles Red was producing from his pockets. Red watched the boy, his eyes bright.

"Takes the mean edge off that shit, don't it?" Red asked.

"Yes, thank you."

"No reason for you to eat mainline," Red continued. "You never ate mainline in Tracy, did you?"

"No," the boy said. "I had a friend in Tracy."

"You've got a friend right here, Candy."

"Where did you hear that name?"

"It's your name, isn't it?" Red asked.

"I've used it—for a stage name."

"Candy Cane. Yeah, I heard about it, I heard—"

"All right, Red," Chilly said quietly. "Let it wait."

They finished the meal in silence, but as soon as they were locked in the cell, the boy said, "I don't like him."

"You don't like who?"

"Your friend. Red. I don't like him."

"He's all right."

"And you're just going to give me to him? What do you think I am?"

Chilly stared levelly. "All right, what are you?"

"I'm a person. You can't take that away from me. I'm a person."

"I'm not trying to take anything away from you. Listen, you silly little bitch, this is *not* Tracy. If someone doesn't stand in front of you, you'll get your little ass killed, or someone will be ripping you off every time you try to take a shower. Not that I give a damn one way or the other, but Red says he wants you, and that's good enough for me. No one, and I mean *no one*, is going to mess with what's Red's, because that's the same as messing with me. So call yourself lucky and knock off the highsiding. I'm going to catch the night gym line. If you need anything, help yourself."

Chilly left the cell on the six-thirty unlock. It was already coming on evening. The big yard always seemed strange to him at this time of day, empty and still wet from the daily hosing. He crossed quickly, listening to his own footsteps which he could never hear in the daytime. A frail moon, just beginning to show, lay above a scud of cloud, and for a moment Chilly tried to sense how it would feel to be walking down a street in San Francisco, or Cleveland or Paris, France. For the moment that the dream lasted it seemed he could hear the music of a sidewalk speaker and the horn of an approaching car.

In the gym, he went to the inner office to talk to Caterpillar. In Caterpillar's face, already going solid and lightless, Chilly saw the mirror of his own aging, although he knew his was interior. Caterpillar sat with his feet on the assistant coach's desk. The wall behind him was solid with flicks clipped from different tit magazines.

"What's the shit?" Caterpillar asked.

"Nothing much. I want you to put a stud on the night gym list for me."

"Okay. What's his name and number?"

"I'll let you know in a day or two. I just wanted to make sure the list was still cool."

"We keep it cool." Caterpillar smiled. "I hear you latched on to a broadski."

"I got one stuck in my cell if that's what you mean."

Caterpillar laughed. "You stick her, Chilly?"

"You know I don't play."

"I know you say you don't. I thought maybe you were beginning to mellow a taste."

"Mellow? You mean go soft in the head."

"Ah, what the hell, Chilly," Caterpillar said equitably, "what difference does it make? Hips, lips, or armpits—I don't turn nothing down."

"They say, if you pitch, you'll catch. Any truth in that?"

"I ain't been tempted yet." Caterpillar turned his head to the side. "But maybe if you give me a little kiss on the ear."

"No, I hate to hurt your feelings, Cat, but I got better-looking stuff in the cell."

"Chilly, you're supposed to have the best of everything."

"I'll still pass. And I'll check you later."

Chilly found both Nunn and Red in the boxing section watching the elimination bouts to determine who would fight on the next card. He made a few bets and won three boxes before it was time to close the gym. He passed the cigarettes to Caterpillar and walked back across the yard with Nunn and Red. The moon was vivid now, a few days from full.

"Did I catch good with Candy?" Red asked.

"Sure," Chilly said. "You fascinated her."

When he returned to his cell, the boy was in bed and apparently asleep. He found a note on his pillow. It was signed "Candy." He scanned it, getting the gist that Candy "liked him a lot" and wanted "to give him a party." Chilly tore the note up and tossed it in the toilet.

"Don't write me any more notes," he said harshly.

15

STICK HAD read every scrap of material Morris Price had collected on the art of ballooning, and he was able to check Morris's figures on the lifting power of balloons of various sizes. The vessel under construction—it shaped up now as a long thin tube—should raise between one hundred and seventy-five and two hundred and fifty pounds.

Morris, never quite satisfied, was trying a new stitch he had learned from a sailing manual, and Stick watched him complete a seam, paint it with latex glue and test it by determining that it would hold water.

"That's good enough," Stick said.

"How do you know?" Morris had been turning testy, and now he stared resentfully at Stick.

"It won't leak."

"It's got to be right."

"It'll be keen. And if it works for you, maybe I'll try it."

"It'd still be cool," Morris agreed, some enthusiasm coming into his eyes. "They're never going to figure how I made it. I'll just be gone." He snapped his fingers at the ceiling. "Just like that. Into thin air."

"What're you going to do then?"

"What do you mean?"

"I mean, where you going to go?"

"I hadn't thought too much about it. Maybe Mexico. Canada, maybe, and maybe I'll catch a ship somewhere."

"You gotta have a plan," Stick warned severely, but apparently Morris could see no further than the rising balloon, and while he could, and frequently did, picture this vividly, he only had the vaguest impression of its coming down.

Stick watched the progress of the balloon with as much patience as he could generate, and meanwhile he had the job for Chilly Willy to think about. In the next few days he was able to determine that the Hit, for that was how he thought of Juleson, the Hit moved in a limited pattern that never seemed to vary. He went from the yard to the ed building and back again with an occasional side trip to the library. He couldn't be beaten in the ed building because there was always a guard on duty, and there wasn't any point along his daily route where an ambush was practical. This left the library. And it wasn't the safest place to attack a man, but it did have several attractive features—the long semi-tunnels formed by the bookshelves were often deserted, and there was only a civilian librarian in charge and he was frequently gone for long periods. Further, it was possible to predict that the Hit would be in the library at noon whenever he appeared on the yard in the morning with more than one book. It would have to be the library.

Stick was still assigned to the laundry in the morning, but he made a point of spending his afternoons in the library, thumbing through a pictorial history of the Second World War, so he would be considered a familiar figure. He noted that the nonfiction stacks near the rear of the room were lightly used. He removed a heavy metal handle from a piece of laundry equipment and smuggled it into the library, where he hid it behind a set of religious books on one of the lower shelves. The books were coated with dust and hadn't been checked out for five years.

All through this period he continued to caution himself: "Be keen." Involved in an actual plan of some complexity, he spent less time in the grip of fantasy. When he rehearsed what he would do, as he did many times each day, he saw himself working with his own hands, his own muscles, his own mind. True, there was an aura in these enactments, one of mastery, and his own figure was always followed by an individual spotlight, but he sometimes thought of things that might go wrong and considered how he would protect himself against them. He had stopped marking the Vampire design wherever he went.

Still he planned ahead. He spent a major part of his mornings in the laundry adding details to the uniform he would wear. The guards' uniforms were dry-cleaned in the same plant, occasionally the metal buttons were lost. Stick now had four of them. He needed to replace the leather band on his hat with metal, and he had managed to steal another inmate's watch for the expansion band. He needed two more bands. There was a clothing repair shop above the laundry and he had intimidated one of the inmates assigned to a sewing machine and forced him to remodel a denim work coat into an Eisenhower jacket. He had fashioned shoulder patches out of sheeting and rendered them with colored pencils he had stolen from the desk of the inmate clerk. He needed more leather. Leather was important. But more than anything he needed boots.

He allowed the Hit to use the library once while he drifted behind him. Keen, he was getting keener. He saw that the Hit had trouble finding anything he wanted to read. He searched the shelves from end to end, sometimes standing for minutes reading the beginning of a book only to replace it. The Hit never paid any attention to who was around him. People had to ask him to move so they could get by. He's unconscious, Stick decided, and he saw half a dozen opportunities to come down on him before he finally checked out two books and left.

Stick watched through the library window as the Hit walked towards the ed building. Enjoy them books, he thought.

That night in the cell, Morris began to put the last two sections together. He had fashioned a harness from strips of cloth braided into ropes. Two more of these ropes sewn to the middle of the balloon were to act as tethers.

"When it's full," he told Stick, "I'll cut it loose, and—" Again his hand described the magic moment.

"You speak any Mexican?" Stick asked.

"Hell, no."

"How you figure to make it down there with them Pancho Villas?"

"I don't know for sure I'll go there. Like I said, maybe I'll grab a ship."

"Ship to where?"

"I don't know. I ain't got no definite plan. Hell, if I could go where I wanted, I'd go to Fresno. I had a woman in Fresno once."

"You can't be fucking around with no woman," Stick said severely.

"She's gone. I looked for her a half-a-dozen times. Pretty nice old girl. She was real artistic. She used to work in a bakery icing cakes, you know, putting all that fancy stuff on them?"

"You're not keen enough for that balloon," Stick said.

Morris, who had often been told he was not enough of one thing or another, bowed his head over his work. "I was keen enough to think of it and keen enough to do it. I meet a lot of guys who talk about getting out of here—they're hard and sharp as crocodile teeth, they say. Well, they're still walking that big yard and they'll be walking it after I'm gone."

"I didn't say you weren't keen on the balloon side, but you got to scheme ahead."

Morris was tearing out the seam he had been working on, slashing at the stiff black thread with a razor blade.

"What're you doing?" Stick demanded.

"Pick, pick, pick," Morris cried. "You'd think this was *your* balloon. But it ain't, it's mine and it's going to be right when I use it. I ain't building no parachute just in case. It's got to be right."

"What was the matter with what you done?"

But Morris wouldn't answer him.

16

SOMEONE in the cells around Juleson was trying to learn the saxophone. Every night the first awkward and mournful notes began to sound immediately after the music bell rang at seven-thirty, and Juleson pictured the aspiring musician assembling his horn, adjusting his reed, and waiting with the instrument in his mouth so he wouldn't waste a second of the hour allowed to him for practice, correctly assuming he needed every moment of it.

At other times Juleson tried to picture the animal he would imagine if he didn't know these sounds were made by a man, and he saw a small—the big voice was obvious camouflage —sorrowing, cowardly creature the color of sunbaked mud, crouched in the far corner of its cage, its feet soiled with its own filth, but its eyes hopeful in spite of their manifest stupidity. Large, round, dull eyes, stained with hope, while its bell-shaped muzzle throbbed and quivered with a frustrated need to communicate.

For several evenings the saxophonist had been trying to learn "I Only Have Eyes for You." He rushed anxiously through the first bars like a broad jumper gaining momentum for some final leap and invariably tripped over the accidental in the eighth measure, sprawled, fumbled around, and, undaunted, started over.

For Juleson this tune formed a key that held the power to unlock painful memories. The key didn't always insist upon its right to union with the lock, the memories were not always painful—their brighter hues and darker shadows had been scorched and faded by too many repetitions of his remorse. Even if he had felt it as an obligation he could not have maintained the vigor of his original suffering. For months at a time he did not remember at all, and at other times he seemed to be engaged in a ritual. He sensed that his entire inner show of concern was overstructured, that except for rare moments even his grief and shame lacked naturalness.

At seven-thirty he was reading the first of the two books he had checked out—*A Short History of Iceland*—when the bell rang and the horn sounded behind it, the small creature roused by the larger, and Manning said, from the bottom bunk, "There's your friend."

"Where does he get the energy? The hopefulness?"

Manning, busy with his own work, didn't answer, and Juleson allowed himself to see another saxophonist of not much greater skill, standing in solo stance, his posture more practiced than his music, on the small stage at the end of the Italian-American Social Club where the friends and relations of the bride had gathered to acknowledge the union of Anna Marie Patello and Paul Juleson. A function of the tribe, he had thought, but he had been uncomfortable as a stranger. "Who is this boy Anna Marie's marrying?" Several times during the course of the evening he had been asked if he were Italian. His dark hair and deep tan prompted the question, and he would have been glad to answer yes.

The five-piece band, high school musicians, had been an economy. For days before the wedding various amateur groups had been phoning Anna's home to offer their services at the reception. The leader of a western group had been particularly persistent, blandly unable to comprehend that his recitation of the costumes and specialties offered by his group seemed as inappropriate to Mrs. Patello as a chorus of Bantu drummers.

"Get an accordion," Mr. Patello hollered. "That's all you need—an accordion."

"Papa, these kids don't want no accordion."

"What'sa matter with an accordion?"

It was impossible to tell him. The leader of the high school group—"combo" was the word they used—turned up as the son of one of Mrs. Patello's friends. He and the other boys were willing to perform for five dollars apiece and all they could eat. They were not a bargain.

Anna Marie had requested "I Only Have Eyes for You," and presented herself to him, moving through the gathering dancers, tiny, finally, on this night, confident, her luminous complexion, fine eyes, and off-center teeth all held up to him, all she had to give, as they danced.

"I had this played for you," she said.

"I saw you talking to young Stan Kenton."

"His name's Raymond Florio."

"Your mother told me. I was just making a joke."

Her arm tightened around his neck. "Do you know what Mother's Avon lady said? She said we danced beautifully together and if we passed through life as beautifully as we danced everything would always be wonderful for us."

"Is the Avon lady here?"

"Everyone's here."

It was true. For Anna Marie, everyone was there. Close to five hundred people, only a few of them known to Paul. An Army buddy had dropped in to haunt the bar like a stained shadow, and a former teacher, who now lived in San Francisco, had put in an appearance.

"You look tired, Paul," she had observed.

"It's the excitement."

She turned to study the hall. "Somehow I never pictured you having a big wedding like this."

"Anna Marie's family arranged it." He smiled. "I paid the priest myself."

"Well, that after all is traditional. The bride's parents pay for the wedding, and we must assume they have bought what they wanted."

"I'm enjoying it."

"Good." She paused, studying him. "I hope you'll be happy, Paul. You deserve to be."

He remembered that her lipstick had seemed like tinted grease. His brother-in-law, his wife's sister's husband, had drunk himself sick and vomited all over his rented dinner jacket. It was impossible to clean and had to be paid for. This furnished talk for a month.

When he and Anna Marie left the reception they went straight home to the apartment he had rented and undressed in the dark. He wore a new pair of shorts he had bought just for this moment. It never occurred to him that she might be even shyer than he was. Shy and frightened as well.

Her mother and an older aunt had taken her aside during the day for the purpose of sharing a woman's knowledge with her, and they had terrified her with their stories of a man's excesses. The aunt whispered, "Your uncle clawed me all along the sides. He was like a maniac. I carried the marks of his teeth for months." The aunt sighed, her eyes fluttered. Her mother gave her a bottle of petroleum jelly. "This will make it a little easier," she said.

Anna Marie never said a word, lying in the center of the swaying bed. The Vaseline was in her purse. He found her in the dark and pulled her to him. Rubbing her sides. She was so small. He was vaguely surprised to discover that her hidden skin was not as smooth as that of her arms. He put her on her back and tented himself over her on his knees and elbows. He pushed in gently, and even when this was done without difficulty he continued softly. It was all over quickly and he found he was still excited.

"May I . . . again?" he asked.

And she said quietly there in the dark, "If you think you should."

Later, as he was on the verge of sleep, she said, "I thought it was supposed to feel different than that." And sketched one of the lines along which their future battles would be fought.

The next day, the sister and her husband came by, eager to see what they could glean, and the husband asked, "How many bullets did you shoot last night?"

Paul shrugged, declining to answer, but Anna Marie had squared around to challenge him, though at the time he didn't recognize it for what it was. "You were like a baby," she said. "I had to hold you in my arms both times." He nodded, thinking to please her.

And the sister said, "Look, he just nods."

They acted as if he had convicted himself of something. What did it mean? That she took even the small consideration he had shown her for weakness, or only that she was willing to represent it to her family as weakness? Or was she punishing him because the night had been a disappointment to her? He didn't know. He still didn't know . . . and was it worth all his anxious reappraisals? He knew it wasn't. A marriage had gone violently sour. Marriages were going sour all over. Still the first flecks of rot had seemed tragic, and even when the fruit was mush in both their hands, neither of them had been able to let go of it.

The truth, then—they had held nothing else in common.

He tried to see her as he had seen her first, carefully reconstructing her air of freshness and untouched passion, the bright, new, unopened container, and listening carefully to the inflection of her voice, studying the lulls in her expressive face, he was forced to realize he should have known better. He had superimposed a dream over her face. And the dream hadn't even been his own, but one he had borrowed. The fault remained his.

"You going to shave, Paul?" Manning asked.

He felt his cheeks. "No, not tonight."

"I think I will."

Now Juleson heard the heavy metal wheels of the water

truck a few cells away, and watched Manning place their can at the bars. The water man came into sight, pulling his truck like an ox. He filled the can, using a frayed red rubber hose.

Manning shaved with face soap, they had nothing else, but with his light beard he found it less uncomfortable than Juleson did. He worked the soap into a stiff lather and patted it on his face. Through the mirror he saw Juleson's eyes over the edge of his book.

"No good?" Manning asked.

"It's all right. I just can't hold my mind on it. I suppose I should have taken up something like you have. Made some use of my time."

Manning was sharpening a razor blade on the heel of his palm. "You have lots of time." He smiled. "I don't mean to do. I mean in your life. For myself, I can't afford to waste anything."

"You're not that old, Will."

"No, but I don't have any real idea how old I am, because I don't know how long they'll keep me here. But even if they let me out tomorrow, I'd be much older in several ways than I was when I came in." He turned back to the sink, fitting the blade into the razor. "You're young enough to make a fresh start. I'm not."

"Still I could have put this time to better use. I don't know why I didn't. There were so many things I thought I wanted to learn when I didn't have the time, then when I had too much time—" He grinned wryly, indicating his book.

"Anything you learn is valuable."

"No, this is an indulgence. The distant—in time or place —it's a trip. Unless you're a specialist of some kind. I might as well read shoot-'em-ups, for all the value I get from what I do read."

Manning made no answer. He was guiding the razor down his cheek, his mild, temperate eyes following the stroke. A modest man. He had asked too little. And Juleson? He had asked too much.

"Do you think she'll come?"

Manning looked at him through the mirror. "Pat?"

"Yes."

"I don't know what to think."

"Do you want to see her?"

"Yes, I suppose I do, but I'm not sure it's a good idea. I keep asking myself what it is she wants."

"What could it be?"

"There are a lot of legal things—title to the house, the car, insurance policies. She may want my power of attorney."

"Maybe she's sorry she threw you to the police."

"She had a right to do that."

"Even so, she didn't have to exercise it. You weren't making a steady thing of the girl—you probably wouldn't have bothered her again."

"I'm not sure of that."

"Still in terms of all your lives, that might have been better than what has happened."

Manning turned to stare at him. "It was grotesque."

Juleson was embarrassed by the intensity of Manning's gaze. "I shouldn't talk about it. My interest is . . . irresponsible."

His interest was more complicated than it was easy for him to admit. In a sense he envied Manning his crime, and he couldn't help contrasting the other man's impulse to his own. Sexual aggression, even the most brutal, could be seen to stem from some basic hopefulness, and his own sterile violence appeared inhuman by contrast. He was able to concede that his view might be naïve, lacking in sophisticated insight, or more reasonably faltering in the profusion of such insights acquired at second and third hand, but he resisted fiercely any tendency he sensed in himself to slip off the hook through a manipulation of standard values. Those values he had carried out of childhood, and no matter how he might have come to

dilute them with qualifications, he still didn't want them reversed. He didn't want to be told, with the weight of a conviction exceeding the suspect charm of novelty, that violence
might be a mask of love. Such tenets would form the foundation and ridgepole of an existence too baffling to cope with. In
preference he accepted guilt. Almost, he seemed greedy for it.
Still he continued to go back over the ground.

It had been a picture wedding. When the photographs were
delivered they could easily have been assembled for the pages
of *Bride*, a mock ceremony staged with a close eye to classic
detail. Running from the church in a cloud of rice and can-
died almonds. Cutting the cake, their hands enfolded on the
knife. Anna Marie throwing her bouquet. Anna Marie throwing her garter. Anna Marie posed with her parents. Paul with
his ushers, all of them in rented dinner jackets. White jackets
and maroon ties like dusty moths. He did look tired. His mouth
was styled in a vivid smile, but his eyes were exhausted, and
the effect was to make them appear years older than the rest
of his face.

The photographs were full of a marvelous and emblematic
significance as if the wedding had been purified of everything
but its symbolic value, and Paul sought his own image in
print after print, not to compare, but to see it there in per-
manent relation to those others. The orphan had stolen a
family.

But if he had planned in his orphan dreams how he would
use marriage as a beachhead for his assault on some community, Anna Marie had rehearsed for life in movie houses and
in front of the television set. She rendered the episodes of
their life together into the stock situations common to ro-
mantic films and responded according to the models she had
studied. She knew her lines. This was how life was magnified
and salvaged from the commonplace, but Paul could seldom
be sure whether he was dealing with Anna Marie or with
Lana Turner. And most of the time he refused to recognize

that there was a difference. Still something had aged the eyes in those photographs.

The times when she moved beneath him with the heat of her own blood in her face were very rare, and often he saw the shallow glaze of impersonation.

Shortly after they were married she began to devise testing situations—propositions beginning with, "If you loved me . . ." At first he was agonized. She was constantly pretending to throw their life away to see if he would retrieve it, and even when repetition had dulled his anxiety he was still heartsore to discover that she could conduct such exercises. Far more than he didn't want to endure the trauma of their obscure quarrels, he didn't want her to be capable of the devices she employed. He continued to hope for magical solutions, but each mechanical recapitulation of their courtship was shabbier than the preceding. Still there was something between them.

Four years passed. She refused to have a child because she was afraid he wouldn't love her while she was fat. She formed an addiction, at least psychological, to a diet pill that dulled her appetite and prevented her from sleeping. She inhabited the house at night like a hamster, nibbling on Fig Newtons and Snow Balls. Often he would find her in the morning propped up in front of the television, asleep, the screen blank, or already into the morning testing patterns, the room blanketed with the even electronic hum that seemed loud in the quiet house and somehow shameful with its implications of waste and disorder. They made few friends. Instead of a botanist he became a landscape gardener. She was a nut. The lovely girl was a nut.

But it was as just to say the handsome boy was a nut. He beat her periodically, and thus squandered the emotional energy he would have needed to leave her. He knew it was necessary, if either of them were to realize anything from their lives, but he couldn't leave her. He couldn't force himself to make the break.

And that was it, he thought, closing the history of Iceland and laying the book aside. He needed a smoke. Had there been tobacco in the cell he would have broken his resolution without hesitation. He couldn't leave her even after he understood that it was their mismatch—she had recognized it earlier, and understood it better—which was driving Anna Marie wild. The fresh young faces in the wedding pictures had been a terrible fraud.

"What time is it?" he asked Manning.

"I don't know. Close to lights out."

Juleson got up to wash and undress. He brushed his teeth and folded his clothes over the end of the bed. Then he got under the blankets and opened his second book. It was a stock mystery by an author he sometimes enjoyed, but after several chapters he found he could read no more. He leaned half out of bed to drop the second book to the floor.

"Remind me to take that back to the library, will you?"

"All right."

Manning was gathering and folding his circuit diagrams. "You're going to be ready, aren't you, Will?"

Manning paused to consider. "No, I think I'll need additional instruction on the more complex units, but I will have a head start."

"That's what I meant."

"It may not come to anything."

Juleson continued to watch Manning, and from his raised position he noticed, as he had before, that Manning was beginning to go bald through the crown. The course of nature, cruelly accelerated by imprisonment, continued to rob Manning, still he made every preparation he was able to make to continue living profitably. His vital energies didn't seem to be necessarily linked to his hopefulness.

The lights went out, and Juleson turned to his pillow. He envied Manning. When Juleson had first come to prison his most significant act had been to pick up a nail in the lower yard. The nail was old and had probably been lying where he found it for several years, because it had formed a clot of rust which gave it roughly the shape of an arrowhead. He thought nothing of it when he stooped to pry it out of the hard earth—he could have picked up any of a dozen other objects—and he carried it in his hand for the rest of the day. Rubbing it with his thumb, bouncing it on his palm. Then rather than throw it away he had put it in his pocket. Without ever acknowledging to himself that he was keeping the nail he changed it from one pair of pants to another as automatically as he transferred his comb each time he took a shower and changed clothes. Often during the days he would find himself holding the nail, rubbing it with his thumb. He carried it for over two months, and when finally he threw it away, it took great effort not to pick it up again. It was only afterwards that he was willing to admit that the nail had become a charm. Then when he realized it was a charm, he wondered why he had thrown it away.

Now, lying in his narrow bunk, the night around him tense as an open mouth, he wondered why he couldn't forgive himself. Even when he knew the entire world and all its history had acted as his crime partner. Even Anna Marie had forgiven him. Still when he saw her face it was just after he had hit her. He realized she had provoked him, as she had many times in the past, until he had done just what she wanted. Still he felt the shock in his wrist and saw the single tear that flew from her eye as her head snapped to the side. He saw it arc out glittering with pain. She turned to run, her heels flopping clumsily.

"You're just like my father," she had shouted.

"Baby, I'm sorry."

He chased her into the living room and grabbed her as she was trying to open the front door. "Baby, I'm sorry," he said again.

She pulled out of his arms to back away, her eyes furious with tears, her cheek already swelling. "Stay away from me. Just stay away from me. I don't want your apologies. I don't want you. Any man who'd hit a woman is rotten clear through."

"Please, please . . ."

All he wanted, all he needed was to regain the illusion of peace between them, but he knew she wouldn't allow it. It would be days before the blow could be smoothed away, and this was so truly her plan that he felt a fresh stir of anger. She stood watching him, her thin chest heaving, her eyes seeming to glitter.

"Let me go, Paul."

"Where are you going?"

"Just let me go."

"You haven't any place to go at this time of night."

"Are you going to let me go? You think you can just hit me, then say, 'I'm sorry,' and it's all right?" She touched her cheek and her mouth hardened. "Get out of my way." She moved to shove past him, and, suddenly furious again, he smashed her to the floor and kicked her in the ribs.

She curled into a tight ball, her head buried in her arms. "Oh, God," she screamed. "*God!*" Piercing as an animal baffled with pain.

He dropped to his knees beside her, dismayed. He touched her arm.

"*Help!*" She yelled it at the top of her voice. "Help! Please, someone, help me."

"Annie, Annie, Annie, I'm sorry. I'm sorry. Please, baby, I'm sorry."

"Police! Someone get the police!"

He picked her up, holding her tightly to muffle her struggles. Still her legs pumped wildly and she thrust at his face with her hands. "I could have you put in jail. That's where you belong, with all the rotten wife beaters."

He carried her into the bedroom and placed her on the bed.

"Did I hurt you bad?"

But she wouldn't answer now. She turned her face away on the pillow, crying quietly. He stood above her, sick with shame.

"Annie, I love you."

He sat on the bed and pulled her to him, feeling her face hot with tears. "I love you," he repeated brokenly.

"Oh, Paul, I never thought you'd hit me. I never thought you'd hit me. I always told myself I'd never marry a man who'd hit me. Not after listening to my mother all those years."

He rocked her as if she were a child, and after a while she stopped crying. Still he brooded over her, broken in the strength of a young girl's dream of the perfect husband who would never hit her as her father had hit her mother.

For two days, she limped around, her face ashen, and on the third day she began to hemorrhage. She died an hour after she was admitted to the hospital, the same hospital where she had been born, twenty-two years before.

Paul pled guilty to second-degree murder.

The next morning it was raining on the yard, and Juleson walked up and down just under the edge of the rain shed. There were a number of restless men trying to walk in the same narrow way and it was necessary to turn and twist in order to keep moving at all. Several times he stopped to stare out over the rainswept yard. Once he saw two seagulls descending in a perfect double helix only to end in a squabble over a scrap of orange peel. Once he was aware of Chilly Willy on the far side of the rain shed, standing with his two lieutenants in the shelter of the bakery door. Again he urged himself to make an effort to pay Oberholster. He supposed in a sense he no longer owed Oberholster since he had survived the other man's attempt to collect, but should he also pay now it would put a better end to the situation. He would have to make the effort. He shifted his library books to the other arm, and continued walking.

When he went to the library at noon, he still retained from the previous night the half-formed conviction that he should begin to study something of real use, but faced by the massed weight of all the books he found it difficult to concentrate. A language maybe—he had often thought of studying French or Spanish. He walked back to the aisle where the language books were shelved. Perhaps he should start with Latin. It had often seemed to him that this language of law and medicine held powerful secrets in its rounded sentences. He took a first year Latin from the shelf and opened it.

He was vaguely aware of Stick passing behind him—a quarter-glance at the face above and just behind his shoulder —and he thought briefly of a baby bird, a hawk or a falcon, left to starve in the nest. Then he turned to the first verb and read: *porto, portas, portat* . . .

17

THE FIRST blow was solid, directly across the dome of the head. The Hit's knees buckled and the book slipped from his hand and dropped to the floor. He sagged forward and his chin hung up on one of the shelves, causing his head to pull slowly to the side drawn by the weight of his body. Stick hit him twice more, knocking him loose. He fell full length, and, except for the twitching of his legs, lay quiet.

This happened in less than three seconds. Stick was amazed. It was so easy. He stared down for a moment, seeing where the blood was just beginning to leak through the broken wave that had crested in the Hit's hair, then he shoved the bar in his belt, buttoned his coat, and walked unhurriedly out of the library.

It was another five minutes before someone found Juleson and reported it. Two other men who had seen him earlier had quietly left the library without saying anything.

Stick had gone directly to the big yard, where he found Chilly Willy standing on the edge of the crowd just leaving the mess hall after the noon meal. He stood ten feet from Chilly and waited until he could catch his eye. When Chilly left his friends to come over, Stick said, "It's done."

"When?"

"Just now."

"Did you do a good job?"

"Yeah, I did a good job."

"You'll be on the gym list tonight."

Chilly walked back to where Nunn and Society Red were waiting for him.

"What'd that rumpkin want?" Nunn asked.

"He wanted to borrow a box."

"Did you loan it to him?"

"Have I started to look foolish to you?"

"I just wondered," Nunn said.

"He's a weird-looking sucker," Red said.

"I wonder how you look to him?"

Nunn smiled. "Like an old punk looking for revenge."

"I got your revenge—" Red indicated his crotch. "Right here."

"Shit," Nunn said slowly, "you can't do nothing with that thing. That's just a handle to turn you over with."

"You try me," Red challenged.

But Nunn had turned to stare after an empty gurney wheeled at a brisk trot by two hospital orderlies. "There's someone's trouble running to meet him," Nunn said.

Chilly nodded. "It's been too quiet around here. Something was due to come down."

"Let's see where they're heading," Red suggested.

But Chilly shook his head. "They'll be back."

The three friends moved over to the edge of the shed where they would have a good view of the gurney when it returned on its way to the hospital. They stood, talking idly, looking up towards three-gate like people waiting for a parade to start. When the gurney reappeared the orderlies were no longer running. They moved at a walk, one on either side, their faces solemn, but not altogether unaware of the effect they were causing. Someone ran up to ask, "What happened?"

One of the orderlies answered, "A piping."

"How is he?"

"He's cooled it."

Juleson's head was turned to the side, and as the gurney

rolled by Chilly looked into his face. The eyes were half open. Well, sucker, Chilly thought, it happens like that sometimes.

Nunn said, "It seems like I've seen that guy around."

"Yeah," Red added, "I've noticed him once or twice myself."

"You went a little heavy, didn't you, Chilly?" Nunn asked.

"You think so?"

"If you had heat before, what're you going to have now?"

"Nunn, I don't even know what you're talking about. Or why you're talking at all. Do you?"

"No, you're right."

Red was still looking after the gurney. "That's a long ride," he said slowly.

The work whistle blew and Chilly returned to his job. He found the old porter just finishing with the mop. "Hit it for a minute," Chilly told him, and walked across the damp floor to the loot's desk. He picked up the phone and watched until the old man had crossed the room and closed the door behind him, then Chilly dialed the gym.

"Gym office, Inmate Collins—"

"Cat, this is Chilly. Put that clown on the night gym list. But if it goes sour leave me out of it."

"Has he got heat on him?"

"I don't know. I don't think so."

"Okay, call it done."

Chilly hung up and settled back in the loot's chair. He touched his temples with the tips of his fingers and rubbed gently as if he were manipulating something both sensitive and dangerous. He had pictured a gang beating, where everyone got into each other's way and Juleson would have been more humiliated than hurt, but now he was beginning to realize that he had not been dealing with a gang. So the pipe. So the pipe.

Lieutenant Olson came in. "You like that chair?" he asked.

Chilly stood up, moving towards his own desk.

"I think you tore your ass this time," Olson continued.

"And what's that supposed to mean?"

"Don't you ever get tired of that act of yours?"

No more than you get tired of yours, Chilly thought, but he kept silent.

Olson sat down at his desk and tipped his hat to the back of his head. He had styled his face to an expression of moral disapproval, but somehow he looked only gratified. "They want you over in the captain's office. Maybe they can explain it to you."

"Do I need a pass?"

"No, you don't need a pass."

Chilly started through the garden. Halfway across he met Mendoza, the assignment loot's clerk. Mendoza passed him, eyes straight ahead, but he whispered, "Check yourself, Chilly, they think you had that cat taken out."

Chilly paused for a moment in the center of the garden, where the walks crossed each other. The fountain was still plugged, but the winter grass was brighter and cleaner than anything else in the prison. The day was clear and he could feel the faint warmth of the sun through his shirt. As sometimes happened he had a fractional vision of one of the many other lives he might have lived, and he experienced a remote stir of emotion—a distant echo of that other man standing in an open field—then he turned and continued on towards the captain's office.

They softened him up by making him wait. He sat for an hour and a half on the wooden bench in the corridor leading to the captain's private office. Here everything was hushed and informed with an air of high seriousness similar to the atmosphere of hospitals, police stations, courthouses, the unmistakable flavor of responsibility and power, the control of life or death. The captain's confidential clerk, a neat, smooth-featured young officer who held the rank of sergeant, moved

277

back and forth carrying different cards and folders. His walk was faintly mannered and the fit of his uniform pants too snug, and this combined with his fresh face was enough to mark him in the minds of most inmates.

Chilly sat quietly. He had no case to make in his own mind. He knew nothing at all. When he was finally called to face the captain, he was surprised not to find several members of the goon squad present, the hands standing behind the brain, but there was only the confidential clerk, who sat down on a straight chair, crossed his legs, pen poised over a steno pad.

The captain was reading a file—Chilly assumed it was his. He stared for a moment at the part—straight as if it had been ruled in the captain's thick black hair, then he shifted his gaze to the group portraits hung in a line behind the desk. Former wardens and their staffs—the style of the uniforms marked the different eras, but to Chilly the faces didn't seem to change. Further to the left there was a series of ID photos taken in the early days—the prisoners in stripes with shaven heads glared fiercely into the lens. They had heart, Chilly thought. The bald heads looked like misshapen rocks. Now they were an idle curiosity and it was a beef to shave your head. The prison officials were afraid your mother might write the governor to complain of prison brutality. Chilly smiled.

"Something funny, Oberholster?"

The captain was staring up at him. There was nothing theatrical in the harsh white face, the remote eyes—this was the captain, and he could be respected as a known quantity.

"Just a thought," Chilly said.

"It's fortunate you're able to amuse yourself."

Chilly shrugged and raised his eyes to a point three inches above the captain's head.

"You know why you're here," the captain said. It wasn't a question, but that was how Chilly chose to read it.

"No, but you'll get around to telling me."

"I need very little of that, Oberholster. You had a man killed a few hours ago. Don't you feel anything at all? Doesn't anything seep through that shit you have for brains?"

How they wanted you to feel as they did—or as they pretended to feel—for if you didn't join their cause, it was somehow weakened. A single holdout seemed to cast a shadow of doubt far out of proportion to his substance.

"I had no one killed," Chilly said.

"I heard different."

"You hear wrong."

"Who did the pipe work, Oberholster?"

"Still wrong. If those rats of yours can't bring you the straight scam, they'll bring you a straw man. I'm convenient. You already hold me responsible for most of what comes down. What's a piping?"

"A death, Oberholster. A death. You want to walk over to the morgue and take a look?"

"I've seen dead men before."

"I don't doubt that."

"Shouldn't I be talking to the district attorney?"

"Why, are you guilty?"

"If I'm suspected of complicity in a capital crime, isn't that the business of the district attorney?"

"Is that the way you want to play it?"

"How about the warden, why isn't he here?"

"That's enough!" Captain Blake closed the folder. "I knew it was pointless to talk to you. What made me think I might find a shred of decency in you?"

Still the same theme—the captain appealed to the better nature he pretended not to believe in. "You earn your living running this prison," Chilly said. "That's not how I earn my living."

"You don't earn your living."

"So you want me to help you earn yours?"

"Wait outside."

Chilly left the office and resumed his seat on the bench. The confidential clerk followed him out, careful to avoid his eyes, but Chilly saw that the steno pad was still blank. Window dressing. He sat smoking, and when he saw the Spook coming through the door at the far end of the corridor, he dropped his cigarette in a butt can and stood up. The Farmer and the Indian crowded behind the Spook, bears led by a fox.

"Well, well," the Spook murmured, his head tilted and his full lips creased in a bitter and intelligent smile. "The big man." He addressed his partners over his shoulder. "We have the honor of dealing with the legendary Chilly Willy for the first time."

The Farmer said, "How do you suppose a little bastard like that causes so much trouble?"

"Ohhhhh." The Spook drew the sound out, cocking his head again to watch Chilly with a soft knowing alertness. "He works hard at it. Don't you, boy?"

Chilly made no answer. He stood waiting.

"Well, you know we got to do this," the Spook continued. "So you might as well come along."

The Farmer and the Indian moved to either side of Chilly and locked both his arms. They marched him on his toes, at a quick step, through the garden, past four-box, three-gate, and through the big yard into the north block rotunda, where they took the elevator to the shelf. The sergeant in charge of the shelf looked Chilly over and asked, "What've we got here?"

"An important guest of the captain's," the Spook said. "For A-twelve. Just let me have the key. We shouldn't be too long."

Chilly had heard of A-twelve. It wasn't a regular holdover cell, but a padded cell used for the occasional psych case too violent to handle on the psych ward. They were held in A-twelve until they could be transferred to one of the hospitals for the criminally insane. The Spook unlocked the door and sketched the be-my-guest gesture characteristic of his mocking courtesy. Chilly stood in the doorway looking at the canvas walls.

"Is this me?"

"Yes, right in there."

As the Spook was speaking, the Farmer pushed Chilly, sending him sprawling into the cell. He lit on his hands and knees; the canvas floor felt like a wrestling mat. The goon squad moved into the cell to form a rough circle over him.

"Would you like to stand up?" the Spook invited.

He stood up and the Indian shoved him towards the Farmer, who shoved him towards the Spook, who, surprisingly strong for his size, shoved him back at the Indian.

"Hey," the Spook said, "how's this? This move you?"

Chilly, stumbling and half falling between the three men, grasped their object. He was supposed to become enraged and swing on one of them, and as soon as he did they would book him for striking an officer. He smiled slightly. The Spook, ever alert, said, "He likes this. This is his idea of fun."

They began to throw him harder. The Indian was huge, three hundred pounds of hard rubber, and the Farmer seemed made of steel and leather. They slammed him against a wall, his shoulder collapsed and he felt the canvas burn his cheek. When they picked him up again he seized on the tactic of going limp, and each time they shoved him he fell to the floor. They picked him up again and again. He saw that the Indian was beginning to breathe heavily and the Farmer was red in the face. Finally the Indian drew his foot back, and the Spook quickly cautioned him.

"Easy, Fred."

Chilly heard them above him and he could almost sense their congested violence—for the first time in his life he was grateful for the protection of the courts.

"He's a smart little cocksucker," the Indian said.

"Sure he is," the Spook agreed. "He's real smart. That's why he's such a big wheel. He's holding aces. But we're holding big casino, little casino, cards, and spades. He'll find that out."

"It can't be soon enough," the Indian said.

"Oh, we'll get him," the Spook said. Then to Chilly, "I hope you're not so shook you can't make it back to the yard?"

Chilly stood up. They allowed him to walk out of the cell and down to the end of the corridor, where the Spook handed back the key.

"He's not staying?" the sergeant asked.

"Not this time," the Spook said. "We just wanted to talk to him."

They released Chilly outside the north block, and as he watched them walk away, the Spook a step ahead, he took his comb from his pocket and reshaped his hair. A few of the unassigned inmates walking the yard had paused to stare at him. Ignoring them, he loosened his belt to smooth and resettle his shirt.

"Chilly!"

Red was running towards him, grinning with relief. "Jesus, am I glad to see you. I heard they had you gaffled. The goon squad. Someone said they marched you right across the yard."

"You think it'll ruin me socially?"

"Did they cut you loose?"

"No, they got sloughed on the shelf. Now stop running your gibs and do something for me. Go up to the gym and tell Cat to send me a tube. And tell him that business I gave him is still cool, and still on. Then bring the tube back to me. And you better make that two tubes."

"You gonna hit the cotton, Chilly?"

"Jesus, Red—no, I've got a cold. Now, get going. And pick up a tube for yourself."

"How about Nunn?"

"He knows where it's at."

Chilly decided not to return to his job. He didn't want to look at Olson's face. He moved to the nearest domino table and sat on the end of it. The action was slack in the middle of the afternoon, and the table was empty except for another man sitting at the far end. He was whittling a toothbrush handle with a piece of razor blade, whistling over his work. Chilly touched his cheek with the tips of his fingers. The canvas burn still smarted, but it was nothing compared to the burn in his chest. He understood the text of the lesson they had worked on him—any power he had gathered was illusionary, he was existing on the margin. They had pointed out that the only considerations that stopped them from smearing him were the very rules he held in such contempt.

Red returned, making his way across the yard like a worn but still cocky rooster. He took a seat beside Chilly and placed two tubes, held together with Scotch tape, near Chilly's hand.

"Cat says he did the thing."

"Good." Chilly dropped the tubes in his jacket pocket. "I want that lame to get what he's got coming. If he gets bent out of shape there's no way to predict what he might do. That's the trouble with nuts."

"Did they work on you, Chilly?"

"No, they wanted to play with my head some more. Relax, nothing's going to happen."

"Yeah ..." Red rubbed his hands together and looked around at the walls, and Chilly following his gaze wondered if Red too was realizing for the moment that they lived here, as much as they were allowed to live, on the sufferance. In the post above three-gate a gun bull stood, his rifle at port. An old man with a red puffed face who wore round rimless glasses and smoked a pipe. When he worked ground posts he was known to be good-natured and a little simple, but lift him twenty feet and put a rifle in his hands and he became a symbol of the cold and untiring mechanism that held them prisoner.

"How's your cell partner?" Red asked.

"He's in there."

"You haven't forgot me have you?"

"How could I? You remind me every day."

"I guess I do. I'm still on the single-o since that nut Turnipseed moved out, but one of these nights I'm going to lock up and find some hairy-assed old bastard in there with me."

"That's the same thing he's going to be thinking."

"I don't care what he thinks. I wish you could get that brat in there."

"You don't wish it any more than I do."

As soon as the count cleared, Chilly cracked one of the inhalers to remove the cotton cartridge. His face worked into an expression identical to anguish and his throat stiffened with revulsion as he caught the aromatic fumes of oil of lavender—a beautiful name, but the smell alone was enough to make him sick with the memory of the hangovers he had endured behind this wino's drug. It recalled the many sleepless hours lying alone in his dark cell, his skin so sensitive the tiny creases in his sheets were an irritation, when he had tasted the oil of lavender flooding back up his corrupt throat, smelled it in his sweat and woven it into his depression as he drifted out on the far edge of his courage and hopefulness where nothing seemed possible or worthwhile.

He removed the blade from his razor and cut the cotton into four sections. He drew a glass of water, tossed a section of cotton into the back of his throat, gulped at the water, gagged reflexively, and succeeded in swallowing. He clenched his teeth against the taste and threw his head from side to side as a fierce shiver of revulsion went over him. He turned to find the boy watching him from the top bunk.

"You want some of this cotton?" he asked.

"What is it?"

"It's something like bennies—*blancas*—only not as good."

"I've heard of it."

"You want some?"

"All right."

The boy gagged on the cotton and coughed it into the washbasin. He started to reach for it, but Chilly said, "Let it go. Here's another piece. Throw it to the back of your throat—" He illustrated. "Most of your taste buds are in your tongue, and if you can get it past them, it goes down a whole lot easier."

The boy succeeded in swallowing the second piece, but he had to control the impulse to vomit as his face turned red, his eyes sick.

"Thanks," he said weakly.

"Better save your thanks until tomorrow. You might not be so grateful."

"Why does it taste so awful?"

Chilly smiled. "It's not part of their product planning to have anyone eat it, though I don't imagine they really care what you do with it. You could rub it in your armpits as long as someone buys it for some reason. Personally, I think I've been supporting the company single-handed."

"How long does it take?"

"Just lie down and wait."

By the time the bell rang for dinner, Chilly's stomach had tensed, his throat had dried, and his appetite had failed. He went to the chow hall with Red to pick up the meal, but neither of them ate. They sipped at the hot black coffee. Gradually the slack in Chilly's confidence tightened over a ringing uneasiness and his view of the day's events began to undergo a subtle alteration. Once again he had moved beyond them—beyond the range of their control and beyond the power of their imaginations. He smiled into his coffee, and saw his reflection rippling on the dark liquid—the shadows around his eyes banded his face like a mask.

Red was tearing up the five slices of bread allowed him as his issue to decorate his tray with the scraps. The drug prodded him beyond his normal talkativeness into garrulity and extinguished his sense of humor as if a nerve were frozen. His usually amiable eyes grew pointed with a tension indistinguishable from anxiety, and the muscles at the corners of his jaw moved like balls beneath the skin. He was trying to explain to Chilly why the inhalers bum-kicked him.

"It shrinks the walls. It brings jail right down around me. For days, hell, for months I never think about the outside, but all I have to do—" He mimicked dropping cotton. "Domino! I'm strung out. I start thinking about real pussy." He waved his hand over his tray. "Real food."

"When did you ever get any real pussy?" Chilly asked deadpan. "A skunk would have to be deaf, dumb, blind, and not smell none too good either before she'd put out to you."

Red didn't smile. "I wasn't always fucked up like I am now. I used to be a pretty foxy-looking youngster."

"Red, I've seen your mug shots. You had more hair. Otherwise you haven't changed a bit. What would change you? You haven't done anything but lay up in these jails. And don't tell me you don't like it here. You're happy as a sissy in Boy's Town."

"Maybe. But not when I start chewing this cotton."

"I don't remember putting no gun to your head."

"That's right."

"Why do you take it then?"

"I don't know."

"Probably because it's hard to get."

Red shook his head. He was laying a long strip of crust over the cold mound of mashed potatoes, concentrating on the job as if he were inlaying fine wood. "Most of the time it's like I was half dead. You see. I know I'm a clown—I play the fool, but that's not all there is to me. I feel like I've got to force myself to wake up, but then it's painful—"

Chilly had the grace not to smile.

"I look around, and I see the shape I'm really in and don't see no way to scheme on no improvement. That make sense to you?"

Chilly pointed at the bread. "What're you wasting that for? Little kids over in Viet Nam would be glad to have it."

"Fuck little kids over in Viet Nam! What does that mean to me? If I don't tear it up, they'll stick bread pudding to us."

Chilly laughed. "They'll stick bread pudding to us anyway...Lighten up, Red. I hardly know you."

"I hardly know myself. I know one thing." He looked over at Chilly, his expression almost hostile. "I wish I had that sissy in my cell tonight."

"That's what you keep saying."

"You hanging on to him, Chilly?"

"Would it be all right if I was?"

"I guess it would have to be."

"You guess. I haven't got enough juice right now to light up a sick firefly, and on top of that I got to listen to you nit-shitting about that punk. If you haven't got your hand halfway straightened up by tomorrow, stay in the cell because I'm not going to be in no mood to listen to you snivel."

"Yeah . . . all right."

As they filed from the mess hall they passed Lieutenant Olson, standing behind the officer checking silverware. He smiled at Chilly. "Well, hotshot, you still walking?"

"Shouldn't I be?"

"You're the best judge of that."

"I might make it for a while yet."

"Yes, you're known to be lucky."

Olson was still smiling after them as they passed into the black and Chilly said to Red, "I'd like to know what's making him so happy."

"I thought you were tight with him?"

"That's his story. I've never quite believed it."

They climbed the wide metal stairs, and paused on the fourth tier landing. Red managed a faint smile. "I didn't mean to oversport my hand."

Chilly studied him thoughtfully. Then he shrugged. "I'll see you in the yard in the morning."

"Yeah. Ain't neither of us going no place."

18

STICK FOUND it cold on the gym roof. He came over the top of the fire escape and into the wind Morris was counting on. The wind blew steadily from off the water and Stick shivered and turned his collar up. He walked in a crouch over the graveled tarpaper, his steps crunching softly, passing through the black snouts of ventilator exhausts to climb halfway up the metal pylon that held the television antennas. From this vantage he was able to determine that he was above the normal range of vision from the guard towers positioned below him—to see even the edge of the gym roof the tower bulls would have to stick their heads out the windows and deliberately look up. Morris was keen enough in some ways—and in other ways he was a champion fool. Stick smiled to himself as he thought of Morris still in the cell, stitching away fussy as a broad, while he imagined Stick was singing in the choir.

Turning his head slowly, Stick saw the three bridges, brilliant over the black water, and the towns—he thought of electric flowers—scattered along the edge of the bay, and San Francisco itself, glowing as if it were on fire. The richness impressed him—the power of all these lights, the machines, the people—a treasury. He experienced a thick crowded feeling in his chest, which he took for a sense of his destiny, and his ears rang with elation. He could almost reach out to those distant lights, banding the throat of the bay, and crush them one by one.

—Stop, Vampire, they screamed.

Beautiful! He breathed deeply, the wind rushing at his

open mouth, in love with the pure night air here above the world. A sharper gust blew his cap off and whipped his long hair into his eyes, stinging like sleet. He jumped down from the pylon and ran swiftly on tiptoe to recover his cap where it rested against the base of a triangular housing. He replaced his cap and knelt to press his ear against the tarpaper. He could make out the hum of a motor and a murmur of distant shouting. He laid his cheek against the exhaust vent and felt a breath of warm air. Again he smiled to himself. "Keen," he crooned aloud.

He didn't want to leave the roof, where he felt close to an important mystery. He lay on his back and looked up at the stars. He imagined the heavens were a board on which he played a game where he was the only one who knew the rules, and when he saw a dark swiftly moving object with one small red eye and one small green eye enter the playing area, he sensed a moment of genuine shock before he recognized it for an airplane. Then he began to send missiles to track the plane, and noted a brief flare of white light as it blew apart in the air.

He crawled commando style to the edge of the roof. Below he saw the roof of the education building just on the other side of the industrial alley, and across and still lower he saw four-box. Two officers stood talking on the porch, their faces diminishing sharply under the bills of their uniform caps, and as Stick watched, one slapped the other on the shoulder and they both began to laugh. He took an imaginary grenade from his belt, pulled the pin with his teeth, released the spoon and the firing pin bit sharply into the primer. He counted one-steamboat, two-steamboat, three-steamboat before he tossed the grenade down at the feet of the guards where it bounced once and exploded. A sheet of red flame with BA-ROOM! printed across it enveloped the two men.

Stick drew back from the edge and returned to the head of the fire escape. He climbed down one flight and re-entered the gym through a window that led into a room where the sports equipment was stored during off seasons—now it held clusters of bats, buckets of balls, bases like stacks of pillows, and racks of uniforms. He continued through a metal fire door into the weight-lifting section, into the scent of sweat, salt, and liniment and the ring of heavy metal. Several hundred men were working out, their faces stern with the gravity of ritual—acolytes still slender and sore and heavy old priests with twenty-inch arms and fifty-two-inch chests. Iron freaks, Stick dismissed them with contempt. They were as lacking in true manhood as the chess players hunched over their boards in the little room set aside for them. Stick entered the boxing section and went to the back ring where Cool Breeze was working out with one of his sparring partners. The way Cool Breeze moved around a ring was the most beautiful thing Stick had ever seen.

When he returned to the cell at nine o'clock he found Morris reading. "Is it done?" Stick asked.

Morris sighed and closed the book on his finger. "It's not right."

"What's wrong with it?"

"It's not right, that's all."

By now Stick had developed certain techniques for dealing with Morris and he continued with the appearance of patience. "What exactly's wrong with it?"

"I should have nylon thread."

"You talking about resewing that whole bag with nylon thread?"

Morris held his book up to study the cover. A woman sat at her vanity removing her stockings. Through the large mirror a man in a black suit was visible—he held a gun. "It has to be right," Morris said absently.

"There ain't no nylon around this joint. Ain't I told you that? I brought you the strongest thread they got. Now what the hell's the matter with you?"

"I don't do nothing by halves. When I go—" Morris's eyes beat for a moment with febrile energy—"I'm going. They can whistle 'Dixie' for me."

"You can't go nowhere until you finish that goddam bag." Stick managed a thin smile. "Hell, I'm looking forward to seeing you fly."

"Yeah, won't that be something?" Morris sat up, laying the book aside. "Can't you just picture that? Right over their heads—just like a goddamned big-assed bird. Oh, I'll finish it. Don't think I'm not going to finish it. Maybe only a few more nights . . . but then I got to get that gas up on the roof and that ain't going to be easy." Morris lay back down and picked up his book. "No, that's going to take some doing."

"Your friend got that gas in those cans?" Stick asked.

"Sure."

"What's he getting out of this?"

"Satisfaction."

"He must be strong for satisfaction."

"He's a buddy."

"Well, you got good buddies, Morris."

19

Aｆｔｅｒ ｌｏｃｋｕｐ Chilly had settled down with the papers, reading them with closer attention than usual, able to involve his mind in events that were without real significance to him. He could have been reading fiction, and if it were fiction his taste ran to the macabre—PLANE HITS HOUSE, 3 PERSONS DIE. POLICE PROBE PHONY BENEFIT SHOW FOR BLIND. 8 PERISH IN GREEN BAY FIRE. He found these three items on a single page. And while he had been looking for a charm of negative power, he laid these deaths, these corruptions, against the death of Juleson, and against the echo of Red's voice mourning, not that he had no hope of improvement, but only the state of consciousness that forced him, however briefly, to realize his condition. Red was old now. Everything he had said stunk of old man. On some buried level of his mind he knew he was finished and it was his principal fortune that he seldom was forced to review this intimate accounting. Red had been walking the big yard off and on for twenty years, more on than off, and before that he had busted his ass down South chopping cane and picking cotton. What could he hope for? Even if he could have taken himself apart and built a new man with the same pieces, this Red would take one look at the cold deck he had been handed to play with, and cash himself in. But Chilly—he stared in at himself—he felt he could have played their game and won. He had chosen not to. But there was so much he had not known and would now necessarily never know, and sometimes, like tonight, he wondered. Pausing with the paper open to the society page and its daily crop of brides, he wondered. He studied the photos intently as if he could somehow crack the bright smiles and expose the secret lives behind them. It was important he find nothing there.

The boy—Chilly still didn't know his first name—had been shaving, whistling cheerfully. Now he was starting to clean the cell.

"Do you want me to wipe off your books?" he asked.

"If you get anything out of it."

"I just feel like doing something." He ran the back of his hand along his freshly shaven cheek. "That stuff's total."

"It's all right."

"Where do you get it?"

"From a friend."

"He must be a good friend."

The boy was rinsing an old tee shirt in the sink, and Chilly sat up to ask, "You going to wash those books or just wipe them?"

"With a damp rag. That's all."

Chilly stood up and went to the bars. He reached up and seized them with his hands, unconsciously falling into the classic pose associated with all prisoners, but his posture was devoid of despair, or entreaty, or even defiance—he held there as routinely as a commuter holding to a strap on a crowded bus. He had felt a sudden impulse to look out at the narrow strip of lights, and he stood watching the flickering neons, and the cold blue fluorescents that marked the course of a hidden freeway. In his heightened awareness it seemed strange, a freak of his own consciousness, to consider the people in the cars passing along the freeway, aliens in a distant land, only a mile away. The consideration recalled the first time he had passed from one state to another, from Arizona to California, as his mother had driven West in the hope of finding his father. His conception of the essential separateness of these two states had been so distinct he could still recall the shock of surprise he had felt when the earth and the trees did not turn red as the colors had changed on the map.

He allowed his thoughts to drift twenty years in the past recalling the impressions gathered along that southwestern highway—the dullness of the desert, crumpled brown wrapping paper, the clouds of dust moving on the horizons and the distant mountains seeming no more substantial, the listless officials at the border station, their old car faltering along the sun-softened blacktop, the same dusty licorice of the big yard on a warm day, his mother's face struggling to contain her anxiety, but showing it nevertheless in the feverish tenderness she bathed him in—these sensations swept across his mind like the motley tail of a kite, and then rose swiftly and diminished into some high and unenterable part of his mind, but he thought: Even then you were on your way. He remembered how, huddled in the corner of the seat, his resentment and determination had knotted over his feelings of helplessness as he had hung there with an enforced passivity in the grip of events largely set in motion by others. Carried along.

Now he was able to call the tune, and Juleson, poor tight-assed snob, had danced to the end of it, but there was no pleasure in that, not even a dry cold lunar satisfaction. Juleson's props and postures, all the second-hand furniture of his mind, they were all back in stock, waiting for the next man who could come to try the part—to use and be used by them, to act, and be acted upon. But Juleson was out of it—so maybe he should have put the gunsel on Red and done an ultimate favor for an old friend.

Chilly returned to his bunk and began to read the sports page, and by the time he was finished the boy had cleaned the entire cell. He stood by the sink looking at what he had accomplished. The painted concrete floor still bore the thin gloss of water, and the back wall was faintly dusted with scouring powder.

"It looks better, don't you think?" the boy asked.

Chilly folded the paper. "Yes." He smiled faintly, noting that his lips felt brittle. "You're on a work kick."

The boy shifted his shoulders. "I never minded working."

"Then why do you make the joints?"

"Oh, checks. My friend was passing checks. I was helping him."

"And he let you ride the beef?"

"I offered." The boy smiled sweetly, but it seemed the sweetness of an artificial flavoring. "It's easier for me to be here than it would be for him."

"Wasn't he a sissy too?"

"No, not exactly. He was very butch."

"Well, what about Tracy?"

"That was different. You know, when you're a juvenile they can put you in for anything. My parents—my father, he wanted it. I guess he thought they were going to cure me. They cured me all right. I was done more ways than I thought was possible, whether I wanted it or not. They treated me like property, handing me around from one to another. Those big kids, they wanted to show what studs they were."

"And you didn't like that?"

Again the subtle shifting of the shoulders—not a shrug, not a flounce, but an exteriorization of some inner uncertainty, not caused by the present question, but beneath all causes.

"I'm not a thing," the boy said. "At least, I don't think I am. But Tracy could have been pretty wild if it hadn't been for that." He turned and looked up at the shelves. "You have a lot of books."

"I just have them, that's all," Chilly said, feeling an obscure uneasiness. "They're mostly reference works I've picked up here and there."

"Just think if you knew everything in those books."

"Do you think that would help?"

The boy was lighting a cigarette. He shook the match out with a flourish. "Oh, I'm not looking for help."

"Then that makes you different in more ways than one."

"Don't get spiteful." He was holding his cigarette pinned loosely in two fingers, his palm bent back off the stem of his wrist, forming a flat where something small might have perched. "Please, it was nice just talking to you. I won't bother you, if you don't want me."

Chilly smiled with reluctant amusement. "Look, what's your name? Your real name. Not this Candy shit."

"Martin. Isn't that a monstrous name? It means warlike."

"It's a little better than Candy—what's that supposed to mean?"

Again the shifting shoulders. "It's what they call me. Candy Cane. I didn't say I liked it."

"You didn't say you didn't like it either."

"It's all right. A little silly."

"Well, look, Martin, I'm not worried about you bothering me."

"I didn't mean that. I just meant I wouldn't embarrass you."

"I'm not easily embarrassed."

"I know. A lot of the men on the yard are afraid of you."

"That doesn't mean anything."

From somewhere down the tier Chilly heard the sound of a broom hitting against the bars. He rolled the paper and handed it to Candy. "When that tier tender comes by, ask him to take this up to cell fourteen on the fifth tier."

"All right. Who cells there?"

"Old Red. I don't know why he reads the paper. He thinks it's science fiction, long as he's been jailing."

"That's the man you want me to cell with?"

"Yes."

"He doesn't even look clean."

Chilly laughed out loud. If he passed this remark on to Nunn, Nunn would never let Red forget it. "Red's all right," he said. "You're looking for action, and Red's laying to give you all you can handle."

"But I like to pick my own friends. You're trying to use me just like they used me in Tracy. Am I supposed to like it? Maybe you think I bend over for dogs and horses, or anything with a prick?"

"I hadn't thought about it," Chilly said coldly. "But don't panic. So far you're not scheduled to make any move."

"Can I stay here?"

"No, I don't think so. But I'll get you in with someone you like. Now get up to the bars and catch that tier tender."

Martin walked to the bars and looked out at the lights. He was silent for a moment, then, "It's strange," he said, "but I have the feeling something wonderful's going to happen. It doesn't make any sense because I know nothing's going to happen, but I feel just as if I knew it was. Do you ever feel like that?"

"That's the cotton. Tomorrow you'll be convinced it's something terrible that's going to happen."

"I hope not. I like this feeling too well."

"Well, that's easy. More cotton, more feeling—for a while anyway."

The tier tender pushed his broom into sight. He paused staring at Martin. First he stared at his face, then at his feet. It was Sanitary Slim. Martin pushed the rolled newspaper half-way through the bars. "Would you take this up to the fifth tier, cell fourteen, please."

"Please? Now, ain't that nice. But they didn't send me up here to be no errand boy."

"I'd appreciate it."

"You would, huh?" Slim took the paper and stuck it in his belt under his coat. "I'll take it up after I finish my sweeping."

"Thank you."

"Your mouth is just full of pretties. How'd you like your shoes shined?"

Chilly stood up. "Just move out," he said.

"Who you talking to—" Slim stared into the cell, past Martin, and when he recognized Chilly, he continued in a lower, whining tone, "You got no right to order me around. I'm just as good as you. We both wearing blue, ain't we?" Slim appealed to Martin. "Ain't we both wearing blue?"

Martin ducked away from the point of Slim's question, still pushing in his feverish eyes, and moved towards the rear of the cell. Chilly was coming towards the bars, and as they passed, crowded together in the narrow aisle between their beds and the wall, Martin squeezed Chilly's arm—the same grip of reassurance a woman gives a man.

"You better knock off the highsiding, you degenerate old cocksucker," Chilly said.

Slim paled and his mouth began to work furiously. "You'll get yours—you and your pretty punk. Your time's coming. I've been walking these tiers for more years than you've been alive and I've seen a whole lot of you red shirts come and go. Don't none of you last long. You think you're running everything on the yard, but you're just a big target for anyone, bull or convict, who sees you."

"Get away from this cell," Chilly said.

"What you gonna do? Spit at me?"

Slim stared a moment longer, then he shifted his weight and began to sweep. He took four or five strokes, gentle as a lover, then paused to pull the newspaper from his belt and toss it over the tier. He continued out of sight.

"What an animal," Martin said.

"Make some coffee," Chilly told him curtly.

"How do you like yours? Strong?"

"Put a level spoon in my glass. You want some more of this cotton?"

"Yes, I guess I do."

They both took another piece, washing it down with the coffee. Chilly sat frowning even after the coffee had cleared the foul taste from his mouth. After a moment he said, "If a little's good, then more must be better."

"Yes," Martin agreed eagerly.

Chilly looked up at him, his eyes remote. "I meant just the opposite."

"What's a red shirt?"

"That's an old expression for troublemaker. If you fell out of line too many times they issued you a red shirt. Then whenever there was trouble on the yard the gun bulls had orders to shoot the cons in the red shirts first. But that was fifty years ago. The old cons took it as a mark of respect. Maybe it was. Now they assign you to group therapy."

"They're going to assign me to group therapy."

"Then you better go."

"Why?"

"Don't you know how lucky you are to be on the big yard? If you want to stay off queen's row, you better lay low and do exactly what you're told."

"I don't want to be penned up with all those dizzy bitches."

"Why not?"

Martin smiled. "What would we do—bump pussies?"

"You might get more down like that."

"No, thank you. I know what moves me."

"Well, to that extent, you're lucky."

Chilly took a swallow of coffee. It was already lukewarm. The plastic glass seemed to leach the heat from the water without ever growing hot itself. Still he was able to drink the bitter liquid with active enjoyment, and it seemed to start a chain of warmth that spread through his stomach, to his bowels, to his scrotum, and with the sense of warmth came a mindless and purely physical crawl of excitement. His glands, alerted by his unconscious and sharpened by the cotton, were sending him a message. He found his eyes fixed to Martin's face. The drug had purified the boy's features, removing all hints of grossness which had served to remind Chilly of his true sex. There was a tight fixed sparkle in the boy's eyes, and his skin had taken on a similar taut luminescence, which Chilly suddenly understood, without reasoning, is associated with beauty because it appears impervious to corruption. This skin would glow undiminished for a thousand years. As the moment expanded he had a diffuse sense of his own multiple selves, he could be anyone, anywhere, changing identities on each heartbeat. It became clear to him that as a child he had nourished himself at a witch's tit, and the volatile fluid hissing from the hot nipple had turned cold as it entered him, searching through his body to fill the large cavities, where it froze into the permanence of a malignant enchantment. Now he had a vision of how he might be free of it.

As he thought this, he talked to Martin on an entirely different level, telling old jailhouse stories, the myths he had inspected with reverence only a few years ago, and the boy listened with parted lips, pulling his lower lip between his teeth periodically to renew its shine with his saliva.

The lights went out. The evening had collapsed into a single hour and that hour had passed swiftly. Chilly still held the plastic tumbler, a quarter-inch of cold coffee slipping in the bottom like an exhausted acid, and his mouth tasted hot and dry and stale, a volcanic cave, from the dozen cigarettes he had smoked. He handed the tumbler to Martin.

"Get me a glass of water."

He heard the pipes throbbing deep in the building, heard water splashing against the sink, marking how vivid and somehow significant these impressions were, and at the same time he marveled at his own detachment. His mind seemed distant from his body. He was observing everything, even his own most intimate self, from the vantage of one of his other existences, and he had lost the feeling that what was happening to his body was necessarily happening to him. He was prepared to recognize that there were entire continents of his spiritual geography which were still alien to him. Now it seemed he stood on an isthmus scenting the smell of a jungle —a smell compounded from large white flowers, with petals like flesh, the blind rut of animals and the rot of black earth charged with the dead. The odor came to him like an ancient and elementary teacher under whose discipline he must study. Without awareness he had made his preparations, now he was ready to learn, because beyond the jungle he sensed mountains where it was possible to climb and climb into a cold clear light.

"Here."

Martin handed him the water, and sat down on the edge of his bunk, and for Chilly the movement of the springs as they adjusted to the boy's weight quickened with intimacy, his own body floated with a warm elastic buoyancy, and as he drank, the water seemed to go down in solid cold lumps. Martin's cheek was outlined against the light from the single bulb above the gun rail, and the last traces of artificiality had vanished from his face with the overhead light. He seemed to be waiting.

"Did the ten o'clock count go by?" Chilly asked.

"Yes."

He found Martin's hand in the dark, and placed it where he wanted it and where it wanted to be, wondering as he did why he still considered it a form of surrender to take control. But then it was done, and he need do nothing more.

For a while Chilly felt nothing, or almost nothing, only a dull pleasant sensuality like the pressure of his bowels, and he wondered again if he had been wasting his time, if it were possible for him to enter the jungle at all. His eyes had adjusted to the semidarkness. He found he could see the part in the boy's hair and he traced it to its base, a cowlick, a vigorous twist of black locks, that disclosed a small gray island of scalp. He heard the noises the boy was making around him and these sounds grew louder until they seemed the restless powerful rush of the sea, and the cowlick began to spin until it became the black waters of a whirlpool opening to disclose a giant pearl. The pearl became the moon which brightened and swelled into the sun as without warning he was taken over by a sensation, which later in his anxiety to analyze anything so powerful he thought of as a glowing transparency. The opaqueness, the dross of his spirit, and the awareness of his body were briefly burned away in a burst of pure feeling. "*God!*" he said for the first time in his adult life when he meant it for more than idle emphasis.

It was only after this sensation had faded from the peak of its intensity that he was able to recognize it as merely pleasure. He groaned like a slave feeling the fresh bite of new shackles, and simultaneously he discovered his hands gripped to the sides of Martin's head, and that pressure too, the texture of flesh and hair, became informed with the aura of his pleasure. Then he realized the nature of the collaboration his hands were involving him in, and he snatched them away. Martin hadn't released him. He jerked his hips back and at the same time, in a motion so automatic it seemed reciprocal, he cuffed the boy with his open hand. Martin fell to the side, slipping off the bunk to land propped on his spread fingers, his head thrown back, his mouth still loose, and his features, now lit in a narrow fan of light, showed a contrary mingling of distress and hostility.

"I'm sorry," Chilly said automatically.

"It's all right," Martin said wearily. His tone was informed with the patient fatalism of someone who lives by a difficult and dangerous job, but the conformation of his eyes still suggested a painful bitterness.

Chilly stood up and went to the sink where he washed himself thoroughly, dried with an extra towel, and buttoned his pants. He took a fresh pack of cigarettes from the shelf, opened it, and held the pack out to Martin, still sitting on the floor.

"Smoke?"

"Sure, daddy."

Chilly lit up and in the glow from the paper match he saw that Martin was holding his cigarette to his mouth, obviously expecting a light, and his unconscious pose was identical to all the women waiting for the same male attention in a thousand cigarette ads. Chilly smiled and offered the match and as he did Martin reached up and lightly touched his hand with her fingertips.

"You might as well be a skunk," Chilly said.

"What?"

"A skunk. A broad. You might as well be a broad. If they tacked balls on you it was an accident."

"I know that."

"But they did, didn't they? And nothing's going to wish them away."

"You liked it," Martin said calmly. "You liked it a lot. A woman couldn't do it as well."

"I don't know why not. That and a lot more."

"Get yourself a woman then."

Chilly laughed and caught Martin by the hair, holding him lightly. "You're not going to do that again?"

"You want me to?"

"It might be all right."

"Did you like it?"

"Yes."

"You're really a nice person," Martin said.

Chilly smiled to himself in the dark, a peculiar strained smile. "I wouldn't count on that," he said.

20

STICK WAS on the night gym list for ten days before Morris would say the balloon was finished and even then Stick had to goad him into it. Stick had continued to caution himself to be very careful with Morris—Morris was both the most important and most fragile component in a great machine, still if it didn't function the urge to shock it to life was irresistible.

Morris had been saying: Almost ready.

"It's been *almost* ready for days," Stick said scornfully. "I don't think you want to fly at all, I don't think you have the balls for it."

Stick was squatting on the floor by the cell door, his thin face white and fierce between his sharp knees, staring in at Morris, where Morris was again trying to find shelter in the small cave created by Stick's bunk above him. The balloon was folded in his lap. A double loop of stiff black thread stuck up like antennas where he had been strengthening the fittings of the harness.

"I got the balls," Morris said thinly. "I got more balls than a pool hall."

"Mouth," Stick said scornfully. "Mouth's all you got. You're long on mouth."

Morris lifted the folded balloon and shook it. "You call this mouth? Does it look like mouth? If it's any of your fucking business—it's done. Done-dee—done! All I got to do is move the gas."

Stick shifted on his heels, folded his arms over his knees, and rested his chin on them. "Just the gas," he said in a different tone. "Maybe I was wrong. Morris, I got to give you credit. You really got it ready to go?"

"It's ready."

"So I'm going to watch you fly. And here I thought you were just jacking off your jaw."

Morris nodded, gratified. "That's how much you knew." He traced the thread to the needle and continued sewing. "And you ain't alone. There's a whole lot of people thought they could shit on Morris Price, they were crowded in line waiting for the chance."

"But you're going to show them now," Stick said steadily, wondering if there might not after all be a page in the history for Morris, the humble and tireless worker.

Morris looked up—not seeing the webbed springs of Stick's bunk, or the blistered paint of the cell ceiling or even the I-beams and galvanized iron of the block roof, but UP, a magical abstraction. A glaze of light passed over his dull eyes. "Yes, I'll show them." Then the light faded. "As soon as I get the gas on the roof."

The next evening at lockup, Stick had the metal pipe he had already used so effectively once before. He waited until after dinner, then while Morris was washing his face, he slipped the pipe from his belt, tiptoed forward and hit Morris above and behind the ear. But Morris was much harder to kill than Juleson. The first blow knocked him to his knees but didn't put him out and he twisted around to look up at Stick with an eerie blend of shock and ferocity from which was missing any element of surprise. He cried out and lunged forward to seize Stick around the legs in an effort to upset him. Stick went on hammering at Morris's head, but the angle robbed his blows of much of their impact, and then he was tumbled over on his back, falling the length of the narrow aisle. For an instant he was vulnerable, but Morris, rather than pursue the advantage, ducked behind the end of the bunk and began to scream for the guards.

Stick snapped up and threw the pipe between the braces that supported the top bunk. It brushed aside a towel hung there and hit Morris in the pit of the stomach. He doubled over, breathless, no longer able to cry for help, and Stick picked up the pipe to finish the job.

He placed Morris in his bunk, with the covers drawn to his chin, leaving his unmarked face to show for the benefit of the guards making the various counts, and he arranged a towel under his head to soak up the blood so it wouldn't leak out and stain the pillow.

Next he removed the balloon from the hobby box and placed it in a ditty bag he had sewn from denim, the same type of bag, though half again as large, as the boxers and wrestlers and other athletes used to carry their personal gear to and from the gym.

Then he began to assemble the uniform he planned to wear. He had new shoes with six-inch tops, dyed black and polished to a high gloss—each thread of the stitching along the rim of the sole had been covered with rubber cement, rendered impervious to the dye, and now formed an ornamental border. Only the basic shape of the work shoe spoiled the effect of high style. He had had his pants reshaped so the narrow legs emphasized the blunt male power of the heavy shoes, and his Eisenhower jacket formed a wedge of equal maleness. The shoulder patches, the Vampire in a circle of blood, the brass buttons, the bits of ribbon and decorations formed a blaze of personal ornament as dense as that of a savage painted for a feast. His hat, now fitted with three expansion bands and another Vampire patch, he hid in the ditty bag along with the balloon, and he covered the gaudy Eisenhower jacket with a larger and shapeless coat. When the bell rang for unlock he left the cell and passed unnoticed in the crowd heading for the gym.

Over seven hundred men were turning out for gym. Wrestling matches were scheduled, the chess club was hosting a team of students from a local college, and the weekly incentive movie would be shown in the primitive auditorium adjoining the weight-lifting section.

Both Nunn and Society Red left their cells—they had heard that the incentive movie was a tough flick, full of boss broads who didn't mind flashing. Will Manning had decided to take a few hours from his studies, the still empty cell depressed him, and he headed towards the chess club with the mildly pleasurable anticipation of meeting a new opponent. He was a thorough, steady player, and, unless rattled by some brilliant stratagem, usually won.

Chilly and Candy, for that was what he now called her, stayed in the cell. They were both at the ragged end of a cotton trip, exhausted but still unable to sleep. They had spent the better part of the previous night in the same bunk, separating only for the twelve o'clock, two o'clock and four o'clock counts. A line drawn in Chilly's mind, which he had thought he would never cross, had fallen away like a strand of cobweb the first time he had touched it, and he had pitched into an area of awareness that had either been beyond or forbidden to his imagination. He no longer cared when his hands, or even his mouth betrayed him. Still the cotton seemed a necessary preparation to the miracle he had discovered, and he had entered a cycle, controlled by the drug, where he knew brilliant peaks and leaden shallows. Just now it was the latter.

He lay in his bunk, shading his eyes with his forearm. His mouth was foul. At some point in the abandon of the previous evening he had bitten the inside of his lip; now it was infecting. He found it painful to talk.

Candy, still restless, was trying to read. Once she sat up to ask, "Would some hot cocoa help?"

And Chilly, whispering carefully, said, "Just cool it, baby. Let me wear this out."

As soon as he was able to slip unnoticed into the supply room, Stick climbed to the gym roof. He had been up here several times now and he felt secure as he unpacked the balloon and spread it out. It covered the space of two sheets, rounded, seeming to float against the black tarpaper like an enormous jellyfish, the harness stretched out as the tendrils. He took off the larger coat and fitted his hat to his head—his narrow eyes were lost in the shadow of the long bill—and circled where he stood trying to sense the quality of the night. He wet his finger and held it up to determine the direction of the wind. It blew steadily from the bay towards the nearest wall fifty yards away.

Satisfied, Stick began to tether the balloon, using eye screws he had positioned a week before, and when he was finished the slack mouth was draped over one of the larger ventilator shafts. Next he recovered a quart bottle of cleaning fluid he had hidden and started back down the fire escape. For security reasons that had nothing to do with fires, the escape ended level with the second floor windows. The additional thirty feet to the ground would be bridged by a portable extension ladder, should the need ever arise.

Stick opened the second floor window, and stepped into the stale dry air of a small room used for the repair and storage of bedsprings. One wall was stacked with discarded mattresses. The inmate assigned to bedspring maintenance had for months swept his trash into a corner where it was piled up over a foot high, seemingly contained by the worn broom angled over it. Stick ripped apart several of the old mattresses and added the cotton waste to the pile of trash; he broke the broom on his knee and added that, then he laid other mattresses around this mound as if it were a fuse, and, finally, he poured the cleaning fluid over it and lit it. It ignited quickly. When he was satisfied the fire would spread, he climbed back to the roof. Long before the building burned and collapsed, the superheated air rushing through the ventilating system would have filled his balloon, and in the confusion and panic his flight would go unnoticed. Keen! He squatted down to wait.

Manning was playing second board against a sophomore, a small, neat, nice-looking boy, and Manning couldn't help considering that he was, at most, only a few years older than Debbie, around the same age as the boy she had run away with. His opponent, leaning over the board to study a concentration on the right side, impressed Manning as vulnerable. His skin was fresh and soft. His slender white hands didn't look as if they had ever held anything heavier than the rook he was now moving. Still there was nothing soft in his game —he was making a firm and resourceful attack from a strong central position. Manning felt the pressure, but he didn't believe the boy could beat him. At some point his concentration would falter, he would overlook some minor pivot, or he would simply not be able to drive the shaft home.

Between moves Manning looked over the boy's head through the narrow windows that led to the main part of the gym. They were shut off here as if they might dilute the virility of the recreation program, a narrow compartment partitioned off with plywood panels into the shape of a freight car. They were playing twenty boards on a single long table and Manning was aware that the air was already growing stale. He shrugged mentally and reminded himself he was a prisoner and fortunate to have this recreation and, perhaps, fortunate to be alive. He thought briefly of Juleson, but drew away from a subject as painful as it was incomprehensible. If he moved a little to the side, he could see a narrow slice of the boxing section, and he watched a young Negro working out.

Cool Breeze was working on the speed bag. Glossy with sweat he moved around the bag hammering as if he were a machine constructed for the purpose of destroying it. The rhythm was as precise as snare drumming. Several of Cool Breeze's fans along with his inmate manager stood watching.

One of the fans said, "Cool Breeze looking good."

"I bringing him along," the manager said, a black gnome with battered ears and a rocklike density to his features. "I teaching Cool Breeze ever'thing I know."

"You think he rip the title off this time?"

"He rip it off. Cool Breeze got great class, plus big heart. Look how he move so nice."

Cool Breeze's rhythm seemed to sharpen.

The incentive movie was a burn. The scheduled film had failed to arrive, and another had been subsituted. Still both Red and Nunn stayed to watch—they were here and there was nothing else to do. Nunn watched with idle contempt, focusing on the edges and the background of the picture, finding the unintentional more interesting than the intended. The story line followed from the supposed weakness of a man raised to wealth, a John Julian Norton III, and an early scene attempted to establish his breeding by showing him in a drawing room, in a belted silk smoking jacket, deftly manipulating brandy, cigars, and an improbable upper class accent. His bored wife sat, legs crossed, that tent of sweet and treacherous flesh, while the Best Friend, blondly handsome, leaned against the mantel exchanging significant glances with the woman whenever John Julian's back was turned. It was laboriously apparent they had formed some scheme against him. Nunn watched the butler. He wondered about this man dressed in the butler suit, to match his butler face, and watched the actor carefully to see if lost in the background he would relax and betray that he was only an actor, rather than only a butler, but he apparently cared more for the illusion than the principals. His performance was the most convincing detail on the screen, and this seemed proper to Nunn—the illusion of reality would be more important to the props than it was to those who ordered them.

"Chilly's gone into something else," Red whispered beside him, as if they could only discuss it here in the anonymity of an audience, as if they were conspirators in a TV play.

"So?" Nunn asked.

"What should we do?"

Nunn smiled in the dark, not without a flavor of pity. The king is mad and it is the fool who shows concern while everyone else pretends the situation is normal. "Is Chilly doing anything you wouldn't do?" he asked.

"That's different."

"Maybe not so different . . ." For a moment Nunn fell silent with a diffuse vision, as if one of Chilly's educations had lingered in his mind, and he considered how circumstances might draw an identical response from each of a thousand individuals as if the illusion of difference was all in how the matter of their lives had been reflected through the prism of experience. Still it was apparent that Chilly Willy was finally blowing his cool. And, as with any unique event, it was impossible to predict where and how it would end.

"He'll burn out on the little bitch," Nunn said, "and pass her on to you."

"You think so?"

"It's a lock."

On the screen, fortune had played into the hands of the conspirators. They were all three, John Julian, the Wife, and the Best Friend, on the desert, near the Superstition Mountains, and John Julian has broken his leg in a fall. His Wife and her Lover prepare to abandon him, grateful that they will not have to shoot him since this would take a kind of guts they are not sure they have. They provide him with a few days' food and a pistol. When he begins to suffer thirst and hunger he will be able to shoot himself. The Lover makes this suggestion with a ponderous scorn, while the Wife looks on, hip classically canted, her face marred with wantonness.

For a while, after they have left him, John Julian stares up into the metallic sky, tears of weakness watering his eyes. They have schemed on him for his money, his manhood, and, now, his life. Gradually he begins to grow angry, and, predictably, using his rage as a rock to brace himself against, he begins to fight back. He splints his leg and fashions leather pads for his hands so he can crawl across the desert without mutilating them.

Nunn looked away. Would he do that?

The fire incubated for over an hour, making only minor gains. The mattresses smoldered with a faint crawl of blue flame, while the small flames licking timidly over the heavy gray planks of the flooring were yellow. Once the flash fire from the trash and cleaning fluid had died out there was little smoke or brightness.

On the roof, Stick grew impatient. He walked restlessly up and down keeping to the blind center of the roof, fighting the temptation to return to the second floor to check on the fire. Repeatedly he held his hand over the mouth of the ventilator exhaust and each time it seemed the stir of air had grown warmer—still the balloon lay slack.

Stick had made the mistake of closing the window and the fire was starving for oxygen. It might have burnt itself out if Angelo hadn't opened one of the doors leading into the mattress room. He was on his first round of the evening, mechanically padding along, lost in an ancient dream the form of which had worn away until the dream coursed his mind as nearly pure feeling separated from its original stimulants. In the dream he had not killed the wife he loved. She lived. He had grown old with honor.

He shouldered open the heavy door and it seemed to him a sheet of flame rose from nowhere. He stared at it stupefied, unable to connect this demonic presence with the danger he had patrolled against for so many years. Instead he thought of punishment. Finally it had come for him and he was no more ready than he had been fifty-seven years before. He screamed hoarsely and turned to run, with a slow heavy old man's hobble, towards the illusion of safety.

In an instant the whole character of the fire changed. The room roared like a kiln. Where it had licked, the flame now spurted. It wiped the far wall and left it burning. It gushed through the door Angelo had left open. The entire soft dry inner structure of the building lay open to it.

The balloon stirred like something coming to life. Stick sucked in his breath and watched like a fascinated child. It wasn't until this moment that he realized he hadn't expected it to work. The balloon lumped and straightened, shifted, lumped again, and straightened, growing firm. Stick found himself remembering a general science flick where a moth had been shown struggling to free itself from its cocoon. The insect had rested periodically, and the balloon too seemed to pause to regain strength before renewing the struggle.

With the game in its forty-third move, Manning had been able to shift the balance and gain the initiative. Now that he was certain he had him defeated, Manning could begin to feel sympathy for the boy across from him. They had not exchanged a word since they were introduced, but Manning had followed the game in the boy's face—at first he had been tentative, then as the game began to go his way, confident and determined, and, now that he was beginning to realize he might lose, his face was cankered with anxiety. Early frost. Throw the game, Manning told himself. It means nothing to you. But the generous impulse wouldn't solidify. He continued to plan the moves by which he would press a mate. If he lost deliberately he would only be telling another lie—he had most likely already heard too many. Why else would the prospect of defeat in the artificial world beneath them score so heavily into the young face? Vaguely Manning realized they were beginning to shout in the main part of the gym. He assumed a boxing match was in progress, but when he tried to look through the window, he found it difficult to see into the boxing section. He rubbed his eyes.

On the dual anvils formed by the desert and his own lust for revenge, John Julian was forging himself into a man. Nunn didn't believe it. He stared up at the screen, caught now in the story, but unwilling to allow himself to be persuaded. Red, however, wanted the bitch to get hers. He watched her swimming in the cool waters of John Julian's pool and drinking martinis from frosted shakers while her husband lay in the desert sucking cactus pulp, and Red felt a burning resentment, a storehouse from all the broads who had thrown him for a shine. His mind was fully tuned to this form of entertainment, he knew he would see her humbled and struck down, and he needed to see just this.

"You burning?" Nunn asked.

"What?"

"I smell something burning."

Red quickly patted himself down. He was clean. Then he too caught the acrid scent of charred cloth, and even as it came to him it seemed to grow stronger. The odor excited him.

Out in the main part of the gym someone yelled, "*Fire!*" And the word was repeated in a ragged chorus.

Red grabbed Nunn's arm. "Something's going up."

Nunn pulled free. The ring of gladness in Red's voice was

unendurable to him. He stood up, faintly aware of the rattle of his chair as it fell behind him. The quiet concentration invoked by the film broke in an instant. At first the noise of the crowd had a holiday sound. Then someone cracked the door and a thick cloud of black smoke coiled in on them. The man who had opened the door slipped through it as soon as it was wide enough to pass his bulk. Then a surge of men knocked over the projector and the image left the screen, lofted dizzily across the beams of the roof, and collapsed into darkness. Panic came in that instant.

Red still could not comprehend the danger. He knew the building was on fire, but the novelty of it still delighted him. Then in the red glow from outer sections of the gym, he saw the press around the door. It was open no more than a foot, and with a hundred men trying to crowd against it, it could be opened no further. And those who were gaining a vantage from which they could force the door wider used the opportunity only to slip through it and vanish.

Red was having trouble keeping his footing. Turning, he saw Nunn's face below him. Nunn had sat down. "We got to get out of here," Red said. Nunn's expression didn't change. "*We got to get out of here*," Red screamed. Nunn gave no indication he had heard. And he hadn't. His mind, which had always been so busy, was empty. He felt neither bitterness nor fear. When he began to cough as his lungs protested against the smoke, he felt his body swaying and jerking and it was as if he were once again a child, riding one of the mechanical horses that stood in front of penny arcades.

Red started pushing towards the door but he wasn't able to make a foot of progress. The folding chairs, half of them knocked over, formed a treacherous maze beneath the struggling bodies. The glow from beyond the door was beginning to grow ominously bright, and above the shouting came an enormous roar, the voice of the fire sucking breath through the windows of the building.

Red had a moment of great clarity when he knew that if he didn't do something extraordinary in the next few minutes he was going to die.

He glanced at Nunn again, and Nunn's face was frozen in the identical expression he had worn before. Vaguely Red realized that Nunn was in shock. He reached down wildly, trying to grab Nunn to shake him, and one of his fingers slipped into Nunn's open mouth. He wrenched at the side of Nunn's cheek. *"We got to get out of here."*

Nunn began to cry, and the sight of Nunn crying sparked Red's terror because while he could see him he couldn't hear him at all. The roar had grown elemental.

Desperately, Red looked around. It was growing lighter and lighter and he saw that the fire was beginning to come up the walls, and the floor was hot beneath his feet. The press around the door was hopeless, but behind him against the far wall of the room, he saw two windows, long boarded up to shut out the light, and automatically Red started towards them. He left Nunn where he was.

Manning should have been in a better position from which to escape. The chess room was no more than a hundred yards from the single door leading out of the gym, but the fire had worked into this section first, and the large area of floor in front of the exit and the walls around it were all burning. When Manning and the boy he had been playing with had worked their way over the fallen table and rolling chess pieces and gained a clear way to the door, they found a frantic circle of men who were barefoot or wearing tennis shoes. Many of them had rushed from the showers and the locker room where the alarm was first given only to find the burning floor and the locker room was now in flames behind them.

Manning saw the floor, like a Hindu's bed of coals, and he shouted to the boy, *"Run fast. Don't stop."* And was about to take his own advice when he saw the boy crumple beside him. An inmate had hit him over the head with an Indian club, and immediately dropped to his knees to wrest the shoes from the unconscious boy. The attacker was in nothing but his jockstrap, and his frenzy was so extreme he was trying to remove the shoes without untying them. Instinctively, Manning kicked the man in the temple. He rolled over twice in a sprawl of hairy legs, and came to rest staring back at Manning. He shook his head and jumped up with wiry strength. Manning shifted to stand over the fallen boy.

At this moment, a number of men came running in from the wrestling department carrying a large mat which they threw over the area of burning floor. The attacker swerved away from Manning to run across the mat. A rush of men followed. Manning stared after them. Already the edges of the mat were beginning to smoke.

Manning was halfway across when he remembered the boy. He had no feeling except that he couldn't leave him. Turning, he started back, fighting his way through the men pushing behind him. They plunged into Manning, without awareness of him as if he were an obstacle of wood, and their eyes, like the numb eyes of sharks, were more terrifying than the fire.

The balloon had swollen to straining erectness, pulling against the taut ropes. Stick watched in awe. The balloon was marvelous. Almost humbly, as if he were attaching himself to the base of a giant erection to participate in its massive copulation with the air, he tied himself into the harness. When he felt secure, he took a small knife from his pockets and began to cut the ropes. They parted, singing with relieved tension, and when he severed the last tie, the balloon seemed to plunge.

It went straight up for fifty feet. Stick saw the gym roof, outlined in flame, shrinking beneath him, and he experienced a formless and almost orgasmic elation. He was defeating not only the prison, but the entire world. He hung suspended in the twisted sheeting, senseless with glory.

Fifty feet up the balloon was taken by the prevailing wind, and continued its climb on a long diagonal. It passed over the guard towers, over the outer perimeter of the prison, and continued above the small round hills which surrounded it. Below and ahead, Stick could make out the vivid artery of a freeway. He gave no thought to where he might come to earth. Up here he had found air he could breathe—a sense of life as he could live it.

Suddenly the balloon jerked and dropped twenty feet, caught for a moment, and then dropped again. Straining to look up, Stick saw a ragged flapping, like a broken wing, along one side of the bag. His legs tingled, his stomach felt gone. He was dropping much faster than he had risen. The freeway disappeared again, hidden behind the rising flank of a hill.

Then it seemed to him the balloon took the air, and began to ascend firmly. It rose and rose, pulling towards the brightest star in the sky, and Stick understood he would never return from his flight.

Manning was struggling down the iron staircase with the boy over his shoulder. The side of the building seemed alive with fire, but his good sense continued to tell him it could only be reflected from the windows. Below he saw the scarlet bulk of a fire engine, manned by an inmate crew, and they were unlimbering their hoses to pour futile streams of water against the brick walls, where, at the point of impact, they dissipated in searing clouds of steam. One hose was being used to cool the area around the staircase. Manning felt the spray sweep over him, and the cold water shocked him as intensely as the heat. Other men behind were trying to shove past him. The boy pulled at him like a bag of rocks. You fool, he scorned himself.

On the landing below the flames were gushing from the open doorway, and those men just ahead of him were crossing one at a time; some crawling, others rolling, while a few plunged blindly like terrified horses and seemed to be swallowed in the flame before they staggered out to stumble down the next flight, their clothes beginning to burn.

Manning turned to the inmate just behind him and shouted, "Please, help me." But the man's face was stupid with terror, and he instinctively seized this opportunity to shove past Manning and dive headlong across the landing.

Another hose had now joined the first, and they combined to play directly into the blazing doorway, but the water appeared to have small effect on the flames, other than to release hissing clouds of steam. The man who was now waiting behind Manning began to kick him in the small of the back, and Manning staggered up under the weight of the boy, took a deep breath which he remembered he must hold, and began to run awkwardly, weaving from side to side. He felt himself burning and cried out just as one of the high pressure hoses knocked him down. He sprawled, fighting panic. The boy lay across him, but he managed to free himself without standing, and on his hands and knees began to pull the body towards the head of the next flight. He did this mindlessly as an ant burdened with an aphid.

The final flight of stairs angled sharply away from the face of the building, leading down to the bridge that spanned the industrial alley, and except for flaming debris falling from the burning roof, the danger was sharply diminished. Manning pulled the boy down the stairs, gripping him under his armpits, too exhausted to make any effort to stop the boy's legs and feet from banging against the metal steps.

Then he was aware of a broad, powerfully built inmate, in a white sweatshirt, stooping to lift the boy out of his hands, as he said, "Relax, pop, I'll handle this."

Manning watched him run lightly down the stairs, holding

the boy across his arms as easily as if he were a child, but Manning could only think that help hadn't come until he had no longer needed it, and he stumbled to his feet without any sense of gratitude, but only the half-formed conviction that he had been used, though he didn't have any idea by whom, or what.

Then he heard someone shouting below him: "It's another of those college kids."

"Thank Christ," a deeper voice added. "That's the last of them. Good job, Caterpillar, a damn fine job."

"Thanks, Loot."

Manning recognized the voice that had told him to "Relax, pop . . ." He made his way across the bridge and was immediately turned over to the hospital orderlies by a sergeant. He was determined not to faint, and he was aware of the gurney ride through the big yard. He listened to the diminishing roar of the fire, and a sudden eerie rush of gaiety caused him to smile up at the smoke-blackened sky. "Sure, relax, pop," he told himself, and continued to smile at this fine joke.

Society Red lay unconscious on the roof of the education building for almost three hours, and the fire was beginning to burn itself out before he groaned and rolled over to stare up at the gutted brick shell. He pulled his blistered lips apart to whisper, "Jesus."

He found the window he must have jumped from, now only an indentation in the ruined wall, and he couldn't understand how he had done it. He remembered the boards and looked at his hands to find his nails torn and bloody. You old fart, he told himself gently, you still got some fight left in you.

But then he remembered Nunn, and was immediately sickened and distressed. He remembered pleading with Nunn, whose face was stained orange as a pumpkin in the swiftly mounting fire, and his eyes as empty, even while the tears rolled from them, and he had cried like some brokenhearted child, sitting huddled on the floor. Then Red had had to save himself.

Now he crawled stiffly to the edge of the roof and began to shout and wave his hands. A ladder was raised to him, and he climbed down slowly, whistling softly as his feet touched ground.

21

THE INDUSTRIAL building fire became the single most important event in the warden's administration—to his chagrin, since the disaster was not relevant to the prison, but could have happened anywhere, in any public or private facility. Officially, his responsibility was nominal since the building had been condemned for years, and the appropriation for razing and the construction of new units had been passed over many times. Still a young state assembly man on the make was pressing for an investigation, and the newspaper accounts were shadowed with dark hints of negligence. The usual pattern following any public disaster. The warden was conditioned to the popular taste for the dramatic, the violent, the spectacular, and he rode with the tide of feverish interest. Still he could not help considering that the fire would permanently overshadow many developments which would finally be of far greater significance, and there were times when he felt an unaccustomed weariness. In these moments he thought of himself as the custodian of the public dump. Was it reasonable to expect people to grow enthusiastic over new methods for processing and reclaiming their garbage?

Meanwhile his desk was clogged with reports. Of the seven hundred and thirty-two men checked out to the gym that night, eighty-six were presumed to have died in the fire. Nevertheless, on those victims where an identification could not be established, the warden ordered an APB sent out, and he expected in time they would discover that a few of these

men had taken advantage of the confusion to make successful escapes.

Stick, Sheldon Wilson, was discovered the morning after
the fire beside one of the access roads leading to the institution. He was alive, but his back was broken. The warden
could hardly credit the implications of the bizarre equipment
and the equally bizarre uniform, and he ordered the balloon
sent to the criminology lab at the University of California.
The analysts were able to add little that was not apparent
from a superficial examination except that the seams had
been sewn and resewn many times. They suggested an analogy to hesitation marks in a suicide. The repeated stitching
had weakened the cloth, but this alone had not caused the
bag to rupture. Along the section of the seam where it had
blown the stitching had been only tacked in, and the most
reasonable inference to be drawn from this was that the subject had somehow been panicked into using the balloon before it was completed.

By the time the report was delivered, Morris Price had
been found dead in the cell he had shared with Sheldon
Wilson, and a careful examination of his personal property
brought more of the story to light. It was difficult for the
warden to see these men as real—he could envision them in
the cell together, the balloon between them, but the scene
was without life, a tableau in a wax museum, yet here was
the trigger that had resulted in over a hundred deaths and
injuries. He studied Stick's ID photo, noting the pathetic
arrogance of the pose, the lacquered gloss of the shuttered
eyes, the wasted appearance of the face, deeper than any scar
of malnutrition. Despite the absence of any human characteristic, Stick's face still did not invite comparison with the
purely animal, not even the primordial mask of a lizard, because the overwhelming effect of his appearance was a sense
of incompleteness. How was it possible a single such defective could end or alter the lives of so many others—the real-

ization was numbing—yet until he made the fatal move his life had to be considered as valuable as any other.

Now that he could be punished, if only by making him understand what he had done, Sheldon Wilson had slipped around a corner in his own mind. He never did return from his flight. Paralyzed from the waist down, he was confined in the psych ward. He had pieced together a uniform—a Sam Brown belt of twisted sheet, epaulets from Bull Durham bags, medals of washers and bottle tops. From somewhere he had acquired a necklace of toothbrush handles.

The afternoon the warden had found time to observe him through the one-way glass, Stick had been propped up in bed, wearing his uniform, and the warden could almost picture the phantom army he commanded, so powerful was the impression that Stick was shouting real orders to soldiers just out of sight. But when he fell silent, his face relaxed into a baffled and painful smile of terrifying innocence.

The single redemptive feature of the fire was the rescue of a member of the college chess team by an inmate, who had carried the boy from the burning building at obvious risk to himself. The inmate, a Walter Collins, was known to the warden as the notorious Caterpillar Collins, and he could think of very few inmates he would be even less happy to see honored as a hero, but the fact remained that it had been Collins, and probably there was better stuff in him than his past had given any cause to suspect.

He released the story to the papers, and arranged for an interview with Collins, who handled himself creditably, except for suggesting they print his chest and arm measurements, which most of the reporters took for a joke, and the coverage was generally dignified, except for one tabloid that ran a head: CONVICT STRONGMAN SAVES STUDENT.

A local fraternal order voted Collins one of their yearly citations for extraordinary public service, and the VFW conferred on him a medal for Valor in the Face of Great Personal

Danger. These awards were made on the athletic field before the crowd assembled to watch the Lincoln's Birthday boxing card, and since they knew Caterpillar for a regular they were willing to remain quiet, if unenthusiastic. They respected an artful shuck, but the fundamental insincerity had to be clearly apparent, and Caterpillar appeared to believe himself that he was some kind of hero.

A few moments later they were asked to observe a period of silence, while the bell at ringside stroked off a count of ten, in memoriam for Reuben "Cool Breeze" Moore, who had perished in the fire. The coach spoke briefly, ending, "and a sweet, sweet boy has hung up his gloves."

Yes, a number of the silent crowd had much the same thought: if Caterpillar wanted to pack someone out of that fire why the hell wasn't it Cool Breeze?

22

"WHAT GOES around, comes around," Red said, expressing his sense of all that had happened.

Neither Chilly nor Candy made any answer, though Chilly shifted his lips disagreeably, as if Red's observation were either too routine or too foolish to answer. It was noon and they had been in the mess hall for a bowl of split pea soup because Chilly liked it.

Sometime in the days just after the fire, spring had slipped in on them. Its effect on the big yard was muted, filtered through the concrete and the dead air of the cellblocks, but the rain had stopped, and by midmorning the sun had usually burned away the overcast. On the lower yard the landscape gardening crews were working up the earth in the ornamental borders—they planned to plant azaleas and shooting stars —and the grass of the athletic field was beginning to show new growth—irregular islands of green marking some random pattern of water distribution beneath the earth.

Baseball players were throwing in teams to loosen up their arms, as if some of winter had entered the hollows of their bones and needed to be carefully thawed. The previous weekend they had held the first batting practice, but the pitcher, anxious to reaffirm his stuff for the new season, had thrown so erratically that hardly anyone had been able to get a bat on the ball. The baseball equipment was all brand-new, purchased on emergency requisition and stored in a quonset hut formerly used for spray painting. The administration knew it as axiomatic that it was better to have inmates swinging at a ball than at each other's heads, just as long before, in the same spirit, a prison bandmaster had coined the phrase: "The man who blows a horn will never blow a safe." That he might instead blow pot hadn't been considered. Only a few were ever able to play baseball; the selection of a team was closely controlled by a powerful clique of jockstraps. Others, in pursuit of recreation, now that the gym was gone, played handball against the lower yard wall, pitched horseshoes, threw quoits, or walked around and around the athletic field.

Out in the far-flung camp system, staffed with minimum security inmates, spring was known as rabbit season, and four camp men ran off during the first week of good weather. Three were caught and returned to the prison and the fourth was found floating face down in the Sacramento River.

Candy had filled the place left vacant by Nunn. Not that she performed any of his former functions, but she stood where he had stood, and it was Red who had taken on some of Nunn's acid tone as if he were the principal heir.

"We should start getting some of it back," Red persisted, stirring the cooling fire. He was rewarded with a flicker of thin blue flame.

"Is that what *we* should do?" Chilly asked.

"Enough's going out, something ought to be coming in. Why not at least get the book going? Here it is the middle of spring training, and you don't have no idea who's signed and who hasn't, how the rookies are shaping up. Or the Vegas odds, or anything."

"That's what I need to know—the Vegas odds."

"You always had a fair idea what teams were going to end up close to the pennant."

"Not from no Vegas odds, I didn't."

"Well, however you figured it."

Chilly smiled. "However I figured it, I'm not." Chilly didn't want to argue, he was just batting lightly at Red. Some of the acid had drained from his personality.

Candy was admiring the way the sun seemed to set tiny fires on the dial of the watch Chilly had given her. One, two, four, five, seven, eight, ten, and eleven were each marked with a rhinestone chip. Three, six, nine, and twelve were indicated by a small rectangular garnet. It was a man's watch, but Chilly hadn't been able to imagine the man who would wear it, not that he any longer thought of Candy as a man, and in those rare moments when he was reminded—she had her own curious modesty—he thought of her excess organs as a biological accident. Now he watched her with possessive admiration and it seemed to him that the movement of her eyes behind the dark green glass of her shades, another of his gifts, was like muted phosphorescence in dark water. When she caught his smile on her, she smiled and moved closer until the point of her hip touched his. Then she looked back at her watch.

Red, watching the byplay, scowled.

"Take it easy," Chilly told him. "We can coast for months on what we have left."

"Just let it happen?"

"Why not?"

"I don't know. That fucking fire. I still see it every time I close my eyes, and I can't stop trying to count what we lost in it."

"A few hundred boxes of cigarettes?"

"And the cotton."

"That's being replaced. You ever gone without cotton when you wanted it?"

Red ignored the question. "And Nunn?"

"He bothers you?"

"Sometimes."

"If I'd had to guess, I'd have said you didn't dig Nunn."

"Maybe I didn't. But I keep seeing him sitting there with his jaw jacked open and nothing to say and he always had too much to say."

"Maybe he found what he was looking for."

"Chilly, don't go funny-style on me."

Chilly smiled. He was surprised to be feeling so well, both on and off the cotton, his mind working so neatly, but without urgency. He touched Red on the chest and found his educational voice. "There comes a time when a sucker knows he's beaten, whipped to the bone, and after that he's just waiting for the first good chance to die."

"Bullshit."

"Nunn knew it was all over when he came back last time."

"His third fall?" Red asked. "I'm working on my fifth fall and I'm not thinking about giving up."

"But you like jailing, Red. Nunn didn't. He didn't like it here, he didn't like it on the streets, he didn't like it anywhere. There wasn't anything happening for him and he couldn't get it off his mind. Others—" Chilly smiled faintly at Red. "It don't bother them too much."

Candy had tired of her watch and now sought to enter the conversation. "Life's a ball," she contributed.

"A ball of shit," Red said.

"Baby," Chilly told Candy, "now that you've come to, why don't you jump in the canteen line and get us some scarf?"

"What do you want?" Candy asked.

"A Sidewalk Sundae. How about you, Red?"

"Get me one of them Whale bars, or if they ain't got that, get an ice cream sandwich."

"And shoot your best shot," Chilly added.

Both men turned to watch Candy walk away towards the canteen line. The element of caricature in her walk had increased, but Chilly no longer saw it, and Red never had.

"You're getting righteously hooked on that broad, aren't you, Chilly?"

Chilly turned to study Red with mild humor. "I didn't mean to take over your program."

"Not my program. I love to freak off, but get strung out? That's something else."

"Maybe I'm turning into a come freak."

"Turning? You ain't put a foot outside your cell for the last three weekends. Laying up with that sissy and a tube of cotton."

"I've been doing a lot of reading."

Red snorted. "If you've been reading that bitch has got something printed in her ass and you got an eye in the head of your dick."

Chilly started laughing. "Would you feel better if I switched cells with you some night and let you do some reading?"

"They got cows in Texas?"

"You'd like that?"

"Yeah, but you don't mean it."

"I might mean it. Next month, I might mean it."

"Shit, by next month you'll have that bitch driving to the canteen in a red convertible, if that's what she asks for."

"She don't ask for nothing, except what I'm looking to give her anyway."

"You mean it? About switching cells?" Red asked.

"I don't think she'd go for it."

"She'd go for it if you told her that was the way it was going to be."

"No, I don't think she'd go for it."

"You mean you don't want her to go for it."

"Something like that."

"Huckily-buck."

Candy came back with the ice cream. Half-a-dozen prisoners turned to stare after her. She had three Sidewalk Sundaes. "They were out of both Whale bars and ice cream sandwiches," she told Red.

"Whatever I want, that's always what they're out of."

"Sure," Chilly said, "the warden arranges it personally."

"I believe it."

They stood eating the Sidewalk Sundaes. The yard was clearing as the assigned men headed back to work after lunch. "What're you going to do this afternoon?" Chilly asked Candy.

"I don't know."

"Maybe you better lock up."

"Is that what you want me to do?"

"Lock up if you feel like it, otherwise stick close to Red."

"I'll probably lock up."

"Suit yourself. I'm going to make it back to work."

Chilly and Lieutenant Olson no longer had too much to say to each other outside of business. Olson was cordial, Chilly continued to do an efficient job, though he was beginning to question the value of the entire long-range program which had prompted him to take a job in the first place, particularly now since he and Olson had both apparently withdrawn to some more fundamental level of their personalities where it was necessary to see each other as enemies. Chilly didn't care. He had never made that much of Olson's pretense at friendship, but he still occasionally got the intimation that Olson, behind the congestion of his hypertensive eyes, was enjoying some secret relish. The sharpest point Chilly could put to it was that Olson knew what Candy was, but that didn't make much sense since he had done nothing about it unless, buried deep in his fat, Olson was some kind of machinery himself.

Chilly came into the office, took his jacket off, and hung it over the back of his chair. "What's to it, Loot?" he said.

Olson looked up from a memo and nodded. Another point: he had stopped calling him "hotshot." Just about the time of the fire.

"How much tooth powder did you send the north block on their last regular requisition?" Olson asked.

"A drum—fifty pounds."

"They say they're out. I wonder if someone over there's dealing that stuff?"

"State tooth powder? You couldn't give it away. Someone probably spilled water in it and threw it out to cover his goof."

"You hear something?"

Chilly smiled. "That's just one hypothesis. Someone might be bagging it up in balloons and selling it on the yard for dope."

"I don't doubt it. You probably handle it."

"No, I use chalk dust from the ed building—it's got a better texture. I can probably get the south block to send them some over."

"What's that?"

"Tooth powder for the north block."

"Okay. Do that then." Olson stood up. "I'll be out at the snack bar."

Chilly waited until Olson left the office before he said, "Where else?" Then he called the head cell tender in the south block and arranged to have some tooth powder taken to the north block. The cell tender wanted to know was his clean underwear being delivered to his cell every night, and Chilly said he had no complaint. He hung up and went to heat a pot of water. He made a glass of instant coffee and sat smoking while he sipped it. There was nothing else to do.

He had persisted on this job because it was the only way to earn an assignment somewhere outside the walls, but he was beginning to doubt it would work at all. The classification committee wasn't foolish. They trusted no one. But there was a growing breed of career convict, largely alcoholic check writers, whom they distrusted less than most. They trusted them to be harmless, and these were the men, regardless of time served, who were being assigned to minimum security jobs. Sometimes they ran off, but their escapes seldom amounted to more than drunken sprees where they ran wild for a few weeks with someone's checkbook or credit cards before they were caught and returned like runaway boys. A new inmate was emerging, the waste product of a new society.

Chilly recognized that his chances of being assigned outside the walls were growing more remote rather than improving, and now he had to doubt he could gain such an assignment in less than ten served, and by then the balance would have tipped well past halfway and it would no longer be intelligent to risk his investment by escaping into a world where the odds against success were daily tightened by the growing sophistication of police methods. Yes, the slobs knew their business. It would still make sense to run this year, or next year, but he didn't ache for the chance as he had previously. This was as much as he would admit.

He rolled a piece of inmate stationery into his typewriter and tried to think of something to write to his mother. It was slow going and it always was. His mother had lately taken the position that he was being crucified by the authorities. Somehow she had formed the conviction he was innocent, that he had always been innocent, and Chilly didn't understand how she could support such a notion—if she were sane enough to earn a living, she must be sane enough to suspect her own delusion, but the theme was beginning to dominate her letters to him. She had announced sometime back that she was going to see the governor, and apparently she was still waiting for an appointment. Lately she had met some man who claimed to have connections within the legislature, and Chilly had pictured an aging player driving on his dippy old mother through this most obvious soft spot. Nothing he could find to write her seemed to have any effect on her growing conviction and he had given up with the thought that if it made her any happier what difference did it make?

He had trouble writing half a page, double-spaced, and finally called upon the fire to fill the page down to where it seemed decent to type "Love" and sign it "Billy." He addressed an envelope and walked out on the yard to mail the letter. One of the domino games attracted him, he knew the players to be expert, and he stopped to watch. He tried to determine the bones each player held by his style of play. O'Brien, who had been standing on the other side of the table, came around next to Chilly.

"Hendricks and Rooster," he named two of the players, "are my horses."

"You got good horses," Chilly said.

"They got a lock here."

Chilly, watching the pattern form, rock by rock, nodded in agreement.

"I hear you're easing out of everything," O'Brien said. Chilly turned to look up at the other man. O'Brien's face was large and red, his eyes as gray as rain water. He chain-smoked cigars; there were always five or six stuffed in his shirt pocket, along with several leather-bound notebooks, which Chilly guessed to be full of blank pages, and a good pen.

"Where do you hear that?" Chilly asked in a form of idle contradiction.

"Here and there. Is it true?"

"I might lighten up for a while."

"You taking to other interests?"

Chilly looked at O'Brien again. There was something in the too full lines of his face that suggested a taint of foolishness, and for a moment the cigar in his mouth seemed to be made of candy, a boy's token of vice.

"What do you want, O'Brien?"

"Your connection."

"And what connection is that?"

"Your cotton connection."

"Someone's putting you on. I've never had any part of the cotton."

"Don't come on like that, Chilly. You're not talking to some fish now. Everyone knows you're behind the cotton."

"Then everyone's full of shit."

O'Brien nodded thoughtfully like a man deciding to play his ace. "Then I'll have to hit on Caterpillar."

Chilly smiled. "That's a good idea." Over O'Brien's shoulder he saw that the canteen line was down to just a few men. "You do that," he continued and walked away towards the canteen. At the window he bought two bags of cookies, one applesauce, one oatmeal, and a package of rolls, and he had these in his arms when he appeared in front of the cell at lockup. Candy rolled over in her bunk, still half asleep, to see Chilly standing there like a husband coming home from work carrying groceries and to her it didn't seem at all a pathetic farce. "Hello, daddy," she whispered.

She was up brushing her teeth when the bar was thrown and Chilly entered the cell. She turned around and moved to squeeze him intimately. He felt an immediate throb of warmth.

"Don't start that unless you're going to do something about it."

"Now?" she asked, smiling, the word hollowed and blurred through the toothpaste.

"That's what I mean."

They skipped the dinner line, eating the rolls with hot instant chocolate. Chilly spent the evening reading—first the paper, which he handed up to Candy, then a novel. Candy shaved every night and spent a long time inspecting her face in the mirror, looking along the edge of her jaw for blackheads. They had a snack at eight; cookies, this time with coffee. Candy wanted to talk about one of the places where she had hung out in San Francisco, and Chilly listened for a while before he returned to his book.

When the lights went off after the ten o'clock count, Candy immediately slipped from the top bunk. For a moment, feeling some vague disinclination, he almost waved her away. Then the monotony, the essential emptiness of the day, seemed to compel him to some expression of life and he opened the blankets for her, moving far to the side of the narrow bunk so she could get in. If this is it, he thought, then this is it, and then she had him turned on so he didn't have to think about anything.

He was mounted over her in the somewhat awkward posture they had both found they liked best when the first flashbulb went off outside the cell. Instinctively Chilly turned to look towards the bars, while he heard Candy murmur, "Daddy?" with a presentiment of dread.

A familiar voice said, "Hold it right there, Oberholster," and the flash went off again like a blow aimed directly into his eyes.

A second voice said, "That'll do it."

Chilly heard the bar thrown and then the Spook was inside the cell. "All right, kids. Out of the sack. I hate to break in on this tender moment, but I only obey orders."

"You slimy black bastard—" Chilly began, but then broke off as the full weight of the situation hit him.

"Oh, yes," the Spook agreed equitably, "I'm slimy enough, but then I don't have no shit on my dick. Now you better get dressed. You won't be spending the night here."

As he pulled his clothes on, Chilly thought of the money in the broom, but there would be no chance to get it, or even if he could he was sure to be shook down before the night was over.

There were two other guards, ordinary second-watch block guards, waiting on the tier. One of them held a camera and they both looked angry and disgusted. As they were marched down the tier, Chilly was aware of shadowed faces pressed against the bars.

"What is it?" someone whispered.

And someone else answered, "I think they busted some guys with the pot on."

They were taken to the clinic, where they had to wait, sitting on a white bench in front of minor surgery, until the MTA came in off a call. He came in ten minutes later and stopped to make some entries on the 103-K cards. Then he came over to them, rubbing his arms, which extending from the clean smooth whiteness of his medical smock seemed hairy as the legs of a bear. He looked down at them with an amused scorn that carried flickering somewhere in it a quality as far removed from amusement as healing is removed from murder.

"Are these the lovebirds?" he asked the Spook.

"Yes, indeed." He nodded solemnly. "Came on them just whipping up a batch, but there was no way to tell for sure just who was doing what."

"To whom," the MTA added. "Well, we can clear that up."

They were taken into minor surgery, one at a time, bent over the enameled table and subjected to what the MTA would record as a proctological examination. The MTA made no effort to be gentle, and Chilly, when the rubber-gloved finger was rudely in him, was horrified to experience a curious, almost languid sense of weakness as if something were urging him to slip from the table and sink to the floor where he would be freed of a large burden he had only been dimly aware he was carrying at all. He felt his knees loosen, then some darkness plucked at him and the finger was suddenly gone. He straightened to meet the MTA's blunt and speculative eyes, aware he was trembling.

When he had finished both examinations, the MTA pointed to Chilly, and said, "This one was pitching." His finger moved to Candy. "And this one was catching."

The Spook smiled easily at Chilly. "It must have been your night to play daddy. But the disciplinary committee, they don't make fine distinctions."

They were taken up to the shelf and locked in separate holding cells, and it was only after the solid metal door had closed behind him that Chilly realized not once since they had been taken from their cell had Candy so much as looked at him. And as he sat down on the bunk he realized he had something more to remember. Something still clouded in his mind as the source of an even more dreadful apprehension, a deeper shame, and then he began to remember the printed form routinely sent to any female relation. He had once studied a carbon copy in a confidential file he had paid to have smuggled from the records office. He had been trying to determine whether the inmate in question was a snitch. The form letter was a complete surprise. Chilly had read it through several times. Now he remembered his amusement as the text came back to him.

Dear Madam,

Your son/husband [son had been x'ed out, but on Chilly's own it would be husband that would be struck] has been apprehended in the performance of a homosexual act. It is felt that you have a right to this information, since it may someday have a bearing on your welfare and safety. Rest assured, though this constitutes a serious infraction of the institutional rules, subject will also receive the best treatment it is within our power to provide.

> Yours very truly,
> JACOB BLAKE,
> Correctional Captain

The form letter didn't make fine distinctions either. Chilly drew his knees up to hug them. His throat felt hot, and he closed his eyes, beginning to rock back and forth, trying not to think of his mother opening the official envelope that irrevocably condemned her son to a way of life beyond her understanding, and beyond her capacity to forgive, as no sentence of the courts ever had. Her pain and bewilderment, her instinctive disgust, were vivid to him. And his own ancient ambition to replace his father, never entirely repudiated, ended here as it occurred to Chilly he had replaced him only too well—in kind, a source of further misery and even more punishing desertions.

But as he rolled over to push his face against the coarse wool blanket, it was no longer his mother he missed and mourned, but Candy. The idle little tramp. The vain, empty bitch, it had all ended for her in the moment the flashbulb blazed, though the moment before she had been moaning softly in a manner he realized now he had always known, just beyond his willing awareness, if it were genuine at all, was certainly exaggerated. Before he was even out of her, she was gone, projected ahead to whatever sissy she would pick out on queen's row to turn flipflops with. They had to snatch and run on the row. Chilly saw a brief but vivid picture of Candy bent over in the showers, taking her most genuine pleasure from her sense of humiliation, while some butch freak rammed at her like a billy goat . . .

Again Chilly experienced the warm sense of weakness, and for an instant it seemed *he* was there in the shower, and the MTA's finger had swollen cruelly to punish him as deliciously as he had punished Candy, and then the blackness began to pluck at him again, wrenching his awareness wildly, but not before he felt a shuddering crawl of shameful delight.

Take this hammer, take it to the Cap'n
Take this hammer, take it to the Cap'n
Take this hammer, take it to the Cap'n
Tell him I'se gone, boy, tell him I'se gone

SOCIETY RED walked the big yard alone. With summer coming on the cons were wearing tee shirts, and a lot of them spent weekends lying around the lower yard catching a suntan, and for a few months they looked as if they'd been hanging out at the beach. But Red knew the tans would fade in the fall, without ever having been admired, and winter would find the same white-faced cons huddled under the rain shed, telling each other the same lies.

Red had to walk slowly. His hip was giving him trouble, and one of these mornings he'd have to catch the sick line and con the croaker out of a shot of oil or something before he blew a wheel bearing.

He paused beneath the north block wall to roll a smoke. He was back to smoking state issue, but he'd smoked dust often enough in the years before Chilly had befriended him, and now that Chilly was gone he'd smoke it again. For at least one more year. He lit up, and continued limping along the blacktop.

The parole board had given him another year to beat the yard. They had handled him with the cool remoteness of a research team conducting a vivisection on a cancerous monkey, and he had sensed the numb stirring of his almost forgotten resentment as he answered to their empty formula:

—How do you plan to support yourself?

—I figure to go back to my old trade.

—And that is?

—Pimping for your mammy.

But that was only what he wished he could have said, if he had been able to play the dozens with the board instead of trying to suck up to that one outside chance they might cut him loose. He knew this chance, like all life's wonderful luck, never fell to his hand, but he couldn't control his native hopefulness. Hopefulness continued to come to him like some beautiful bitch who had him pussy whipped. He read the promise of further rejection, further torment, read it clearly in her cold and sometimey eyes, but one flash of her long white legs and he was ready and aching. Next year it would be the same.

"Hey, Red, you antique old mother, what're you limping for?"

It was Cat, cutting across the yard towards him. Red smiled. "I fucked my leg up booting young punks like you in the ass."

"Go ahead on, old man. I heard the board dumped you."

"They shot me down a year."

"You didn't carry them enough time."

"I figured it was plenty."

Cat pulled a pack of tailor-mades from his shirt pocket. "They're cold dudes," he said absently as he took a cigarette and offered the pack to Red, who snapped his roll away to accept the tailor-made.

"Thanks, Cat," he said as they lit up off the same match.

Cat nodded, inhaling deeply so his heavy chest swelled to press against his denim shirt, and, then, exhaling said, "What's a butt between old partners?" He matched his stride to Red's and leaned closer to continue. "I've been doing some think-ing since Chilly got busted. You know?"

Red turned his head to find Cat watching him closely. He frowned. "What's there to think about?"

Cat lowered his voice. "I figure Chilly must of had a pretty fair-sized soft money stash. He turned a lot of butts into cash, a lot more than he needed to pay off that gimp-legged free-man he had on the send, and he must have taken in still more cash off the yard. I know Chilly's style, and he was going to the stash with it, putting it aside against some notion he was turning in his mind, but they scratched him—" Cat snapped his fingers. "Quick! He didn't have time for no cleanup, and I figure that stash is still sitting. Just like he left it. You got any idea where it is?"

The question, just slipped in casually, reminded Red of the interrogatory technique of the kind of detective who came on buddy-buddy. Red shook his head amiably, just as he would have for the buddy detective.

"Nope, I don't. But I wish I did."

Cat leaned still closer, crowding Red. His eyes had grown noticeably cooler, and his voice lost the buddy tone as he asked, "*You* didn't swing with that gold, did you, old man?"

"Shit!" Red said angrily, snatching the bag of dust from his shirt pocket to dangle it before Cat's eyes. "Does this look like I swung with anything? And don't come on heavy with me. I don't like it. And if you'd gone a little further with all that thinking you were doing, it might of come to you that Chilly never flashed his hand to nobody. If he had a stash, you can give long, long odds he was the only one who knew where it was. I sure as hell didn't."

Cat walked in silence for a while. When he spoke again it was clear he'd given up. "I don't know," he said dryly. "There at the end he might of had that little freak wiping her ass with hundred-dollar bills."

Red shrugged equitably. "Well, it was his, if that's what he wanted to do with it."

"That bitch spoiled a boss hustler."

"Chilly just found something he dug more than stacking up piles of butts and playing big man in this crummy side show we got to live in."

"Yeah, and now he's psyched, a stone nut. They say he tried to take himself out. Cut his wrists, for Christ's sake!"

"Shithouse rumor," Red said scornfully.

"The captain's office has him listed for transfer to the pie factory, and that's *no* rumor. I saw the list myself."

This news puzzled Red. He wasn't able to imagine Chilly as a real nut. Somehow Chilly had gone on to a deeper and even slicker game, still playing nimbly with the official mind as he moved towards some secret end of his own.

"Chilly'll be running that nut house in a month," Red said confidently.

"Maybe," Cat agreed doubtfully. "And maybe he's all through. One thing, there's no hole here on the yard where he used to stand."

Automatically Red gazed down at their old "office"—three hobby workers stood there examining a length of red silk one of them had bought to fashion the pillows that were a traditional item in the handicraft store. They were spray painted with the legend: *Souvenir of San Quentin*. A few feet away, O'Brien stood making book. His cigar bobbed steadily as he chewed and sucked at it. Red had heard O'Brien was already running scared. Someone had picked a long shot at Hollywood Park and got into him for something like three hundred cartons, which he still hadn't come up with, and now he was so nervous the only bets he wasn't trying to lay off, according to the yard comics, were those placed by a notorious nut who liked to wager on the outcome of the races featured in the newsreels shown at the beginning of the weekend movies. Red smiled fondly. Chilly had once tried to get the same nut to make a bet on the second Dempsey-Tunney fight. But Chilly never did take the crazy bastard's stuff, Chilly had too much class.

Red studied Cat, still plodding beside him, and Cat was just one more lightweight joint wheel, hiding behind a pair of twenty-two-inch arms, beginning to go to fat, and even if they were forty-four-inch arms Cat would never think of trying to rob Chilly's stash, unless stoneface Blake had practically promised him personally to make sure Chilly was shipped to the nut house.

The two men neared the end of the yard, and on the cream stucco of the inmate canteen building, Red noted a drawing of a vampire. One he had looked at without interest many times as he walked, thinking only the first few times that at least he'd never been unlucky enough to meet up with something like that. Now the drawing was beginning to weather and fade, and it had been partially overlapped by a new figure, a four-legged animal of indeterminate kind, though clearly possessed of slanting eyes, and an entire mouthful of teeth, bared in a crude but vigorous display of ferocity. Scrawled beneath this animal was the single word: *Simbas*.

Red and Cat turned together, reversing like soldiers executing to-the-rear-march, and Cat said, "They put the sissy on queen's row."

"I know," Red said. "I seen her in the line when they ran the row down to the laundry. Swishing and giggling, happy as a pig in shit."

"I still can't figure how the bitch ever got on the yard in the first place."

"They didn't make her, that's all."

"Bullshit. How long did it take you to make her?" Cat asked.

"About one hot second."

"You think some of these old-time bulls don't pick up just as quick, if not quicker, than we do?"

"I suppose—"

"And out of three thousand cells, they stick her in Chilly's, and tear up his psych department hold to do it." Cat was silent a moment, shaking his head. "You think they could actually be that keen?"

"What do you mean?"

"That they might have figured what was going to happen?"

"Cat, you talk like a man with a paper asshole."

"I don't say that's the way it came down. I was just thinking."

Red smiled wryly. "You've been doing your fair share of thinking, but far as I can make out you ain't got no particular talent for it. You best stick to rasslin', and" —he backhanded Cat's softening belly—"pushing iron."

"The new gym's going to be double tough."

"Nunn would be glad of that."

Just then a line of fish began to enter through the gate at the head of the yard, and they moved closer to search for familiar faces among the new arrivals, as well as to draw some measure of security from the awkward uncertainty of the fish, their skins bleached dead white in the county jail, their hair mutilated from the amateur barbering they practiced on one another. Red saw one man he thought he might know. An old man, wrinkled as a prune, bald except for a few strands still straggling across his white scalp, who moved with the indefinable air of one who had entered many strange jails and prisons, and found them all much the same. His face was oddly familiar to Red, but for a long moment he couldn't summon a name, or place this old con in either space or time, then he suddenly remembered a kid he had always paired off with to chop cane, or pick cotton, his running mate in the Southern prison farm where he'd pulled his first jolt. Anson Meeker. The name came back over the years, and he saw a cocky kid grinning at him from the other side of the row as they worked furiously through the last hours of the afternoon to just make their task, having spent the morning coasting while they planned in excited whispers the big scores they'd take off once they were free.

But even as he recognized him, Red knew this old man couldn't really be his long forgotten buddy, and he called out, "*Hey, Meeker*," to prove the impossibility, not to see, as he did, the old man turn and cast along their faces trying to determine, almost anxiously, who had hailed him. His eyes met Red's, flickered, and passed on.

"Someone you thought you knew?" Cat asked.

"For a minute. Might be an older brother."

But Red knew it wasn't an older brother. Red realized Anson's identity clearly enough, but he couldn't begin to form any notion of the terrible and mysterious forces that had so swiftly transformed Anson Meeker from a husky, good-looking kid into a creeping old man. It was only—

Red had to stop and figure. Rather than mark his age and so the year, he counted slowly back through his own confinements, marveling at the growing total, until he realized it wasn't "only" at all, but somewhere well over thirty years ago that he and Anson Meeker had squatted together in the fields eating the usual dinner of boiled cabbage, while they swore to each other (always in whispers) the moment they were free they'd light out for California where they'd heard, at the very least, they had decent-feeding jails. Red had jumped good to his word. But it looked like Anson had held off awhile. Red congratulated himself for once having the good sense to avoid the years of Southern jailing that had worked and starved Anson Meeker into just one more of the beaten and hopeless old bastards who drift in and out of prison, staying on the streets only long enough to drink up their gate money, because they find behind the walls the only life which doesn't frighten and overwhelm them.

For a moment Red experienced an unfamiliar sense of depression, a massive aching dullness as if he had been systematically beaten, but had somehow forgotten it and could now offer himself no explanation for his discomfort. Again he sensed Anson Meeker's eyes crossing his own, saw them stir faintly, grow flat, and pass on.

He turned to Cat and said sharply, "You done thinking, or can I score another of your tailor-mades?"

"It won't break me," Cat said, producing the pack. Red took a smoke and lit it quickly, flipping the match, which fell spinning towards the blacktop, like a burning plane seen at a great distance.

"Thanks for the light," Cat said tonelessly.

Red shrugged, smoking hungrily. He found himself listening to two kids, just brats, who were standing a few feet away, whispering together over a score they were going to take off as soon as they made parole. Some third kid had clued them to an old broad who lived alone, and kept a half-million cash in a shoe box under the bed.

Red shook his head in sour wonder, trying to remember how many times he had heard of this same shoe box.

"Well," Cat said finally. "What else is new?"

"Nothing," Red said.

OTHER NEW YORK REVIEW CLASSICS

For a complete list of titles, visit www.nyrb.com or write to:
Catalog Requests, NYRB, 435 Hudson Street, New York, NY 10014

* *Also available as an electronic book.*